HIS BLOOD

CHRISTINE MORGAN

HIS BLOOD

by

Christine Morgan

2nd Edition 2018
1st Edition Trade Paperback 2014

All Rights Reserved

Dark Recesses Press
657 Craigen Road
Newburgh, Ontario
Canada K0K 2S0

Edited by Tracy DeVore
Cover by Bob Freeman

Library & Archives Canada ISBN
978-1-988837-07-9

ALSO BY CHRISTINE MORGAN

ACKNOWLEDGMENTS

This book could not have been written without the blood-drenched inspiration of those great authors before me, especially modern masters McCammon, Laymon and King.

It also could not have been written without the ongoing moral (and immoral and amoral) support of the horror community. Stay thirsty, my friends.

DEDICATION

To those who like their vampires all bite and no sparkle.

TABLE OF CONTENTS

PART FOUR – THE CONCEPTION

PART FIVE – THE CENTURION

ABOUT THE AUTHOR

PROLOGUE

The vampire took too long to die.

At first, its struggles pleased the crowd, satisfied their thirst for revenge. They taunted and jeered as the sun glared burnished fire, searing the hilltop where the vampire hung in its bonds.

Stolen blood baked to a brown crust on its wounds. Its face was a carved mask, stoic in suffering.

Yet still, it lived.

And lived.

Uneasy mutterings replaced the savage glee of the onlookers, as the day spun on and the monster refused to succumb.

Next came the touches of fear, of dread, as the sun lowered toward the horizon and the shadows lengthened.

The hunters felt their triumph slipping away in slow but eroding rills, as sand blown from the crest of a trackless desert dune.

This was to have been their moment of glory. Here was to have been vengeance for those slain. Here was to have been mankind's salvation. The hunters had proved themselves the better of this most fearsome of foes. Had conquered and overcome.

Was this not proof that they were on the side of good? That they were the rightful? Here was the very vampire king itself, helpless in the scathing heat, denied mercy, denied sustenance. Dying. The flesh shrinking tight over bone, the body twisted.

Yet its power still held a strong and terrible sway over the minds and souls of those who had gathered to watch its undoing. Already, their fear was being fanned into a desperate terror by the vampire's will. Its hot, dying gaze moved from one to the next, reminding them of all they had endured.

Slaughtered children. Youths and maidens lured away with foul magic. Blood drained in the night from piercing wounds.

It had spread its soul-poisoning taint among mankind. Its chosen children had been given the bite, given the blood, given the undeath. These, a dozen or more, had gone on to spread their own evil blight across the land.

Now this one, their creator, was dying... but too slowly.

Its flesh did not smoke and wither at the touch of the sun. It did not turn to dust. It did none of the things that the hunters had hoped for.

What if it lived to see the night? What if the coming of darkness restored its powers? Could iron spikes hold a being that might become mist and drift away, or transform itself into a bat, a wolf?

And oh... if it *did* win itself free...

What they had known before would be nothing compared to that which would follow.

As this apprehension welled in every collective heart, the crowd stirred from a motionless hush. Men looked to their neighbors, eyes wide, doubtful whispers on their lips. Women keened and pulled fitfully at their hair, their clothes.

A common murmur arose from them.

Free it now... yes, free it now, release it... and it might spare them.

If they left it there to wait for the night, it would free itself, and bring horrors a thousandfold down upon them.

This promise glittered in its scarlet eyes, in its lethal grin.

The streets would run red with blood. Babies would be savaged in their cradles. Children would be torn shrieking from the arms of their mothers. The dead would rise up, an army of the dead, ever-hungry and unstoppable.

An old man fell wailing to his knees, and lifted his hands in supplication. Others joined him. Their voices became a swelling dirge, a plea.

Release it... release it now and be spared...

The hunters felt it growing—a panic that would send the crowd into a mindless surging action.

Their orders had been to stand by and let the vampire die in slow and burning agony. To show that mankind was strong, and that they were in the right. Now their victory was revealed to be a fragile and fleeting thing that might suddenly be snatched from them.

Urgent looks flashed among the hunters. Who would be the one to act? Their leaders had been among the first to fall in the furious battle that had netted them their prize. These who remained were young, unsure.

One felt a dig in his ribs and turned.

Beside him stood the burnt man, the man who was not a hunter, not a soldier. His face was gaunt and white, his eyes twin black hollows. The wounds on his throat were cauterized to cracked black char. Cleansed. He had done it himself, with his own hand. The pain must have been fierce, and likely still was, but he gave no outward sign of it.

"This spectacle is a luxury you can no longer afford," the burnt man said in a voice both low and intense. "Do it. Do it now. End it."

The young hunter trembled, swept with a chill despite the molten-bronze heat of the day. His sweaty palm gripped, then slipped, on the weapon he held at his side.

He stepped forward. A sighing moan came from the crowd. He saw pleading and hatefulness and despair on their faces. On the faces of his brother hunters, he saw both a furtive thankfulness—each man glad in his secret heart that it was not *himself* to have been given the command–and a sort of envy.

A hooded and veiled woman-form barred his path. The young hunter had a brief glimpse that suggested a dusky beauty, and dark eyes hidden in deep shadow. In those eyes, for the barest of instants, he thought he saw a glint of red.

His heart lurched. She was one of them! The blood-light in her eyes–

No. It could not be. Not by daylight.

The vampire king was strong, more hideously strong than the hunters had guessed. But the lesser ones, its minions, could not go about when the sun was high.

He had seen no glint. Only a dancing reflection of light, perhaps.

The woman moved aside and lowered her head. He wanted to stop and strip away her veil, partly to see whether that suggested promise of beauty was true. To do so might bring a furious father, husband, or band of brothers roaring indignation from the crowd.

And he had, after all, only imagined or mistaken that red glow.

He went on, the people parting around him. Some, mostly bold boys, darted up to touch his cape or his shield or the haft of his weapon for good luck. He was aware of the expectant silence, the watchful faces, the sun sinking in the west.

Ahead of him, atop the hill, the vampire hung limp in its bonds. Its head had fallen now, so that it no longer swept the crowd with its hateful gaze. The bearded chin rested on a sunken chest, and long tangles of lank hair obscured its features. A wrap of coarse cloth covered its loins. Ribs stood out in stark ridges.

Was it dead already? At last? Had it finally perished as he had been looking at the dark woman?

But no… its fingers twitched, curled. Each ended in long nails like claws, the heels of its hands shredded in long marks from where it had tried unsuccessfully to reach the iron spikes driven through its wrists.

The hunter took another step and the vampire's head snapped up, quick as a striking snake. Leathery lips split back, revealing ivory fangs.

Any trace of the creature's once-handsome visage was gone, leaving its true face: wizened, ancient, terrible. Its scarlet-rimmed stare fixed the hunter with evil, eager hunger.

He fancied that the vampire could hear, or somehow sense, the quickened thunder of his coursing blood.

Its parched tongue flicked out. It pulled against its restraints, heedless that each struggling lunge opened the wounds wider and sent rivulets of muddy red fluid oozing thickly over the blistered skin.

The crowd exclaimed and drew back as one, widening the circle around the base of the hill. The young hunter stood alone before the vampire. He barely noticed the two executed men to either side, men whose lungs had long since collapsed under their own weight and suffocated them to death.

He looked at the barren ground at his feet, where the wooden framework cast a stark black shadow... but the writhing, snapping body of the vampire king itself cast none.

It was in its final extremity, of that he was sure. No silver-tongued words now, no promises of eternal life and forgiveness. Only a frenzied, blazing hunger as it fought to get at him.

The weapon in his hands felt right and purposeful. He raised it and aimed its point at the place where the dead heart would be. He could see it in his mind's eye, that black and wrinkled sack, which did not pulse with life but lay slack, filled with a bitter and rotten blood like the dregs of some vile tea.

One strike, there. There, to the heart.

The crowd was with him now. He heard their murmuring voices urging him to do what the sun had not, to finish this nightmare. One thrust, swift and true... he had only to pierce the heart, and it would be over.

The sharp point punched through skin like parchment, through flesh like half-dried clay. A gout of gritty, dark liquid sprayed into the hunter's face. It scalded, it stung.

He blinked it away and pushed harder. The deadly length drove deep until it had transfixed the torso. The vampire shuddered and gnashed the air. No screams could have been worse than the ghastly silence of its throes.

It still did not fall apart into dust, but with a final violent spasm, some vital essence burst. The head fell forward. The body sagged.

A collective ghostly sigh arose from the crowd.

The hunter stepped warily closer to his kill, braced for the vampire's apparent death to have been a trick, ready for some sudden lunge and attack.

But even when he withdrew his bloodstained lance—it came free with a grisly sucking sound—the vampire did not move. Windblown sand crusted around the edges of the hole in its chest, just as it already caked the nail holes at the wrists and feet, and speckled the bloody dots where the thorny circlet had scored the brow.

The king of the vampires hung dead on the cross.

PART ONE – THE COFFER
February

CHAPTER 1

Michael saw himself walking down the sidewalk past the park, arm in arm with Sarah, and tried to call out a warning.

No good. It was as if he floated over the scene like a phantom. Unseen. Unheard. Unheeded.

Pretty Sarah, from a respected family. Raised in the traditions of the Legion. A good catch. A good match for any young Centurion, especially for one who hoped to go far. Her father was an important, influential man. More, she was sweet and lively and full of good humor. Michael loved the way her eyes sparkled, and the lilt of her smile. She captivated him, distracted him.

He should have been alert. Watchful. Should have taken to heart what he had always been told, instead of paying it lip service in public and scoffing at it in the privacy of his own thoughts. Instead, he'd only been wondering whether Sarah might let him kiss her.

And then, the attack.

He saw it all again, now, from this dreamlike vantage point above the city street. The figures slipping from the shadows all around, as if they were not so much hidden in the darkness as a part of it.

An ambush. Here in the open, with cars droning past not half a block away, with lights and televisions illuminating the windows of the houses on the far side of the street. With the sounds of music and horns and voices and sirens filling the air.

They had walked right into it.

Neither of them, deep down, believing that such things existed. Not here, not now, not in this modern age. Such stories might have been true hundreds of years ago, but now all the training and the preparations were so much empty ritual. Nobody, even in the inner circles of the Legion, could *really* think that there were vampires anymore.

Nobody sane, at least. There would always be a few old-timers who swore that they had met, seen, battled, destroyed.

From his lofty, invisible place, Michael watched as the pack slunk up on this other, oblivious version of himself. This Michael so content in his blissful ignorance, and about to pay the price.

White faces and burning, hungry eyes. Long fingers ending in sharp, dirty nails. Closing in. And him, strolling and laughing, so caught up in Sarah's presence that he didn't notice the danger.

Sarah paused first, losing her smile, and asked in a worried way if he'd heard something. And he dismissed it. A cat, a raccoon in someone's garbage can. Strange noises of the city that they weren't used to hearing out in the quiet of the smaller and more distant town where the Cohort made its home.

He'd put his arm around her, and she snuggled close. Her swaying hip bumped against his as they walked toward the intersection.

And then came the eager hiss of the vampires. Swarming in. Fangs glistening.

He both saw this and remembered it, his mind in two places at once. His eyes seeing from above, and seeing from his own height as the pale dead things rushed to the attack.

They had attacked. Vampires.

Then why was he alive?

Was he alive?

One, affecting the black garb and cloak of folklore, had come at him. Snapping. Snarling.

Michael might not have believed, but he had never shirked his training. His father wouldn't have allowed it. Nor would his father have allowed him to go out after dark without being properly armed.

It was, all things considered, a small price to pay in order to use the car for his date. Sarah wanted so much to attend the concert, and he had been glad for the privilege of escorting her. Of spending so much time with her, just the two of them, alone.

He lost precious moments undoing his thick winter coat. The vampire was almost on him before he drew the weapon sheathed at his hip.

A lunge, a thrust, and the point punched through cloth and into solid flesh. The vampire's triumphant cry became a screech of agony.

It reeled back, clawing at the stake embedded in its chest. Before its hands even found the blunt end, its skin and flesh began crumbling away to dust. The stripped bones of its fingers splintered into shards. It fell prone, kicking, body collapsing into sunken, empty clothes.

Another menaced Sarah, but she was not a daughter of the Legion for nothing. She pulled the slim rod from the leather clip that held back her hair and drove the sharpened wooden length into the eye of a bag-lady vampire.

Michael yanked the stake from the disintegrating corpse – it would not come back, not this one, and he was amazed to find that everything he'd learned was still ingrained in him—and whirled to confront the next.

A boy.

No older than twelve. Still wearing the Little League uniform he must have been buried in, holding an autographed Edgar Martinez baseball bat that his grieving parents had no doubt interred with him. In life, he would have been a cheerfully good-looking kid, freckled and sandy-haired and full of mischief.

Michael hesitated, and the boy swung the bat with inhuman strength. At the last instant, Michael blocked the blow, pain slamming up his arm. His stake flew from his hand.

Something cold and agile leaped on his back.

A teenage girl, a runaway of the streets by the look of her, twined her legs around his waist and circled his throat in a chokehold with her thin, needle-tracked arms. Now she craved a drug of a different sort. Her head darted down, fangs jabbing.

The baseball kid stuck the bat in the way and she clamped down on it, making a sound like an infuriated dog. Michael reached up and back, grabbed her by the shirt, and flipped her forward over his head.

She twisted in mid-air, landing in a spiderlike crouch, teeth bared. The torn shirt exposed naked, wasted breasts and a tattoo of a butterfly-winged fairy whose colors had faded pastel after death.

Sarah, on the ground, screamed. Two of the creatures fought over her while a third tried to drag her out from under them. Michael saw fresh blood trickling from several scratches on her arms, but she looked unbitten.

The baseball bat connected with his skull before he could take a single step to help Sarah.

The Michael who had been there remembered nothing after that. Only a hard crack, and blackness.

The Michael now did not know what had happened next.

He seemed to be alive.

If he had died, and been *changed*, wouldn't he know it? Wouldn't he feel it? Feel drained and cold and… and no longer himself?

If he had died, and been *changed*, would his head be a pounding mass of aches?

Michael stirred and found that he could move. A little, anyway.

He wanted to touch his neck and see if the hated wounds were there, the punctures, but he could not move his hands. His arms were stretched above his head and held there at the wrists. His legs were out straight, tied at the ankles.

It occurred to him that he could feel his pulse beating its dull rhythm through his veins. His stomach churned with hunger and his throat was parched with thirst. Not *their* hunger, *their* thirst. A bad, sour taste caked his mouth. His bladder felt full to the point of acute discomfort.

He wasn't dead, then. Not changed. Not one of them.

Not yet.

But captured by them, and that was almost as bad. Possibly worse.

And Sarah? Did he dare to wonder?

Vampires, here in the city. Real vampires. Why had he not believed? Why had he never really accepted the truth?

Lessons recurred to him. His mind dredged up facts and theories he had thought he'd forgotten as soon as he learned them well enough to recite back to his teachers. Not rote memory after all, but still there. Dark knowledge, darker now.

Vampires. Here and real.

And working in groups. He couldn't recall having heard of such a thing before. Weren't they supposed to be loners, solitary and territorial? Sometimes they might hunt as a pair, or even a trio. But there must have been seven or more that had attacked him and Sarah.

Where was he now? How long had he been here? Was it deadly night? Or blessed day, when their powers would be at their weakest?

Did he, in all honesty, have any real hope of survival and escape?

Why had they taken him prisoner? Why not kill him? Why risk that he might get away, and take word back to the Legion that their foes were very real, and gathering in cooperative numbers?

He lay in utter darkness, utter silence. His senses seemed to think that he was in a large and open space. The air was cool, slightly damp. Earthy, musty. He detected the barest hints of other scents, hauntingly familiar but dancing just beyond his ability to identify them.

The surface upon which he was bound was hard and unyielding. Stone. Whatever held his wrists and ankles felt thick and coarse. Rope. Tied very tight. His fingers tingled as he tried to move them.

How long had he been here? Hours, at least. His sense of time was hopelessly skewed.

By now, someone must have noticed his and Sarah's absence. But would anyone guess what had happened? Would they assume the worst? Or would they think that Michael had succeeded in coaxing Sarah into a hotel room somewhere? That they'd eloped?

Michael flushed with shame. All right, perhaps he'd considered it, but never as more than an idle daydream. He'd known Sarah would never go along with it. She would have answered him with a good sound slap.

And what was he doing, worrying about any of that? He would be lucky if the worst thing in his future might be a lecture or a slap.

Light like a hundred blazing suns stabbed suddenly into his eyes. He winced and squeezed them shut. Tears leaked from the edges of his closed lids.

"It was wise of you to keep him," said a voice like someone speaking through a mouthful of gritty mush. "I admit, he will be useful."

"For a while, anyway," a woman replied.

He heard them drawing near. One set of footsteps scuffed on the floor. The other was a light, soft tread. His nose wrinkled. He smelled a bitter, dusty rot. And some sort of spicy perfume… musky, darkly exciting.

The very skin of his body seemed to shrink, quailing in on itself. His flesh contracted in expectation of a touch. He tucked his chin toward his chest and hunched his shoulders.

"Are you going to claim him after all?" the man asked.

"No. I would never be able to trust him, even as one of my own." Before each of the woman's utterances came a pause, and a subtle gasping inhalation.

Michael heard this, and shuddered with a horrible understanding as more stones of memory overturned.

Only vampires, whose lungs required no oxygen, had to draw a purposeful breath to speak, to force air through their vocal cords. The breath of the undead.

This woman, she of the darkly exciting perfume, was a vampire. No ordinary vampire, either. Most lost the power of speech. Some few retained a phrase or two, or fragments of their former selves, but only the Elder Ones were said to be able to speak and think as coherently as any mortal.

He'd been told that the Legion had long ago hunted down and destroyed all of the Elder Ones. There had never been many to begin with, only a dozen or so. Their powers were the strongest. Only their creator, their king, had been more powerful. An Elder One would be able to direct and control a number of lesser vampires, forcing them to work together contrary to their usual nature.

And hadn't he heard her voice before? It was strangely familiar to him. Like the echo of something heard in a dream.

Yes... he remembered now. That voice like smoke, curling into his mind. A caress, a feather-light stroking over every inch of his body... he recalled cringing from that touch and yearning toward it at the same time.

She had been here. She had spoken to him.

What had he told her? What had he done for her?

His heart skipped a beat. Anything... everything... he would have done whatever she wanted if only she would keep up that persuasive caress...

No! He was stronger than that. He was one of the Legion. A sworn and faithful Centurion.

Michael risked peeking through one half-raised eyelid.

The light, that inferno of a hundred suns, proved to be no more than a single candle. It rose pure white from a brass holder in the shape of a winged angel, and shed its light dimly through the chamber.

The woman who stood near his feet was smaller than he had expected her to be. No towering, terrible figure. Petite. Five feet tall at the most. She looked harmless, kind, beautiful. The candlelight loved her olive complexion and struck gold highlights from the rich sable of her hair. Her features were rounded and pleasant, her lips plum-colored and full. Long sooty lashes fringed soulful eyes as black as the pools of night. He could only see enough of her figure, draped in a simple blue robe, to know that it was shapely.

He could have looked at her for hours. But the figure beside her moved and drew Michael's attention. When he saw the man, he wondered in revulsion how he could have first noticed anyone or anything else.

Split, cracked lips parted as the dead man grinned. His face was that of a corpse disinterred after days buried somewhere hot and dry, where a body did not so much rot as desiccate. Teeth showed through holes in his cheeks, and patches of his skull were laid bare of scalp. His body was short, scrawny, wrapped in tattered bits of old linen.

"Your boy is awake," the dead man said. His was the voice that sounded like gravel and dry, crackling leaves.

The woman turned to regard Michael. A faint smile teased at the corners of her mouth.

"I… know who you are," he said, his throat gone dry, his lips numb. It felt as though the warm blood inside him had turned to icy water.

"He knows who you are," the dead man said. "What about me, boy? Do you know who I am?"

"Leave him be," the woman said. "He's been a great help to us tonight. Haven't you, Michael?"

Michael shook his head as vehemently as his bonds would allow. And yet, at the same time, he couldn't stop looking at her. He knew what she was, a walking evil on the earth. But still, he found that he wanted her.

"You do have a hold on him," the dead man remarked, as if this amused him. "So much for the oaths and vaunted mental strength of a Centurion. They've slipped, haven't they? Especially this last half-century."

"What do you want from me?" Michael asked. "What have you done with… "

For a terrible moment, he forgot her name.

The woman laughed. It was a sweet laugh, not mocking, but it stung him all the same. Her fingers trailed up his leg. His bare leg. He was naked, and her whisper of a touch was getting perilously near…

"Sarah!" he cried. "What have you done with Sarah?"

"Sarah," the woman said, almost purred. Savoring the name. "Sarah."

Her fingers grazed his hip and passed, tickling, up his abdomen to his chest. She paused with her palm resting above the now-frantic drumming of his heart. Her eyes... he could sink in them, be lost in them.

Desperate, he twisted his face away.

The room around him was windowless and low-ceilinged. Racks and casks lined two of the walls. It was, or had been, a wine cellar, incongruously clean and lacking cobwebs. To his left, an arched doorway gave onto a long narrow chamber. The candle's light did not penetrate far, just enough to show him the ends of several stone biers and long wooden boxes jutting out from the walls.

Coffins. The ends of coffins. Not huge and ornate, but plain. Serviceable. Their lids all standing open.

It must be night, then, and the lesser vampires out and about. A hive of them. And this, their mother. Their queen.

"That's right," she said.

He felt a crawling sensation seemingly *inside* his head and knew that she was reading his thoughts.

"There is no hope for escape," she added. "Except in death."

He thought belatedly–very belatedly–of the nickel-plated pistol he had been carrying in a holster in the small of his back. An old-fashioned weapon, quaint by today's standards, but serviceable.

Like the stake, he was not supposed to go out at night without it. Any Centurion who feared he might be overcome and taken was to put the pistol to his temple and pull the trigger. It was their last line of defense against a hideous fate, a quick and true death of their own choosing.

But the vampires had come at him and Sarah so fast, and there had been so many of them, that he hadn't had time.

"That would have been a great loss," the woman, still reading his mind, said. "When you have so much to offer us."

"I will give you nothing," he said. It was hollow bravado, and she knew it as well as he did.

"Michael, you already have."

More memories flickered past him. Her voice, so soothing, so comforting. Asking him questions.

And himself, answering. Helpless not to.

Telling her everything.

"No," he choked. "No, please, no, I didn't. I couldn't have."

She stroked his brow and gave him the sort of fond smile a mother might give a child. Her lips parted and her breasts heaved as she pulled air into her otherwise slack lungs. "But you did. And you will do more, won't you, Michael? You'll help us against them. You'll show us the way to the vault."

The vault… yes, he remembered that, too. The heavy iron door, the key that the Reliquist kept. Jeremiah, the Reliquist, was one of the old-timers who still believed. Who claimed he had faced and fought vampires before.

"Where's Sarah?" he asked again. "What have you done with her?"

The woman nodded to the dead man. He shuffled toward a corner, where Michael now saw a hanging chain that ended in an iron ring. When the dead man pulled down on the chain, unseen pulleys caused a section of the wall to shift. Stone grated on itself. The wall swung inward, carrying casks and wine racks with it.

Firelight streamed out, leaping from torches stuck in leering gargoyle-mouth sconces. The inner surface of the wall was three feet thick in soundproof padding. The floor of shiny white tile sloped shallowly toward a central drain. The white tile ran red with streaks and splatters of blood.

A metal cage hung suspended from the high ceiling. Its bottom swung ten feet from the floor. Sarah was locked inside. Naked.

Blood dripped from her lacerated legs and feet. The vampires gathered beneath the cage could not get at her, unless they leaped for it. But when they did leap, they took swipes at her with their long nails. Her breasts bounced and jiggled as she jumped in a frantic dance to keep out of their reach.

One, a wiry young man, held onto the swinging cage like a monkey and thrust his arm through the bars to grab at her thighs. She made a hoarse cry–hours ago, she might have still been able to manage a scream–and smacked his hands away.

Other vampires stood underneath her with their mouths open, catching the shower of Sarah's blood on their tongues the way children might try to catch snowflakes. Michael recognized the runaway girl, and the boy with the baseball uniform, among them.

"Sarah!"

Her head came up. Sweaty hair flipped back from her face and he saw how tired she was. Past the point of exhaustion. On the verge of collapse.

He read his name on her lips, read the terror in her eyes.

"She's quite limber," the woman said. "And strong. For a long while, she held herself up so that they could not get at her. But she couldn't keep that pose forever. Eventually, she had to lower her legs."

No use pleading with them to let her go. No use begging for their lives. He knew that. Knew how pitiless these creatures were.

Would he have shown mercy if everything was reversed? Would he have let them go?

Never.

The vampire clinging to the bottom of the cage contorted his body and somehow wedged his jaws between the bars. His fangs raked Sarah's foot. She stomped on his head. He lost his grip and fell. His elbow struck a female dressed like a nurse, who retaliated by whirling on him in a fury of slaps, kicks, and scratches.

"They are poor creatures, my blood-children," the woman said, watching the scuffle with a rapt fascination. "They care only for the hunt. A rare few retain some of the memories and abilities they had in life, but most are as these you see here. Savage and cunning, like animals."

Michael could not keep from whimpering. This was what waited for him, for Sarah. To be raped of their humanity and turned into night-beasts. To become the very things that they and their families had hated, and fought, for generations.

"You do not want to be like them, do you?" She leaned over him, dark locks falling past her shoulders to brush his bare chest. "Anything but that. You'd rather die. Well, Michael, I can promise you the final death, if you will do something for me."

From the other room, from the cage, Sarah called to him in her hoarse voice. "No, Michael! Don't listen to her. Whatever she wants, don't give in."

"Lower her cage," the woman said, with a glance over her shoulder at the dead man.

"No!" Michael surged anew against his bonds, his shoulders nearly popping from their sockets with the effort. "Sarah!"

The dead man went into the next room, the abattoir of padded walls and white tile. He moved out of Michael's line of site. The vampires crowded in a circle, shoving each other and hissing with hideous anticipation.

Gears ground, and the cage descended. Sarah scaled the bars with renewed strength. She hooked her arms through the top. Michael could see parts of her he had only seen in his most secret imaginings, her breasts heaving with exertion, her legs opening and closing as she tried to find purchase on the bars. He could see these secret parts and places, but he had never been less interested in his life.

Then he lost sight of her altogether as the grasping, clutching swarm surrounded her.

"Sarah! Sarah!"

The sounds, the sounds were unimaginable. Scraping and slavering and sucking. He heard Sarah's voice splintering in a shriek.

"Stop!" Michael cried. "I'll do what you want, but stop them! Leave her alone!"

"Enough," the woman said.

With a grinding rattle, the chain lifted the cage again. Sarah clung feebly to the bars, her body drenched in blood from dozens of vicious bites. She sobbed.

Beneath her, the deprived vampires snarled their frustration. Their queen called to them. Several hissed in protest, but obeyed when she ordered them out of the abattoir. They filed past her in a sullen line, heads down, like chastened schoolchildren.

When they had left the room, vanishing through the archway and into the long chamber filled with their coffins, the woman turned again to Michael. Her smile revealed the twin points of her fangs.

"You promised," he whispered.

"So did you, to do one more task for me, in exchange for your clean death. That was our bargain. Will you keep it?"

"Let Sarah go, first," he said. "She's no part of this."

"No part of it? The daughter of a Centurion, the sister of Centurions, the ladylove of a Centurion? And, if nature were to take its destined course, the mother of future Centurions? Just because she has not wielded the stake and hammer herself does *not* exempt her from this."

"Then give her what you promised me," he begged. "A chance at a clean death!"

"Should I let you kill her? Would you kill her yourself, Michael? To keep me from biting her and taking her as one of my own?"

"Yes," he said, though not without a shudder.

"And if I did drain her, would you sever the pretty head from her bloodless corpse to ensure she could not rise? Or if she did rise, would you pierce her heart in the final death?"

"I will, if I have to."

Sarah, through all of this, stayed huddled at the bottom of the hanging cage. She was wracked with sobs and did not seem to hear them, or care what was said.

"She's a lovely girl," the woman said in dark, thoughtful speculation. "A virgin?"

Michael flushed. "Of course!"

"It's been a long time since I've had a virgin. They are a rare breed in this day and age. But if you do what I ask of you, I will deny myself that pleasure. I will grant her the same death I grant you. *If* you do what I require."

"I will," Michael said.

The woman stood over him and raised a knife. It was small but wicked looking, and Michael's flesh cringed from the anticipation of that blade slicing into him. He tried to tell himself that it would be better the blade than the teeth. But fear clawed in his mind all the same.

"It isn't what you think," the woman told him. She brought the edge of the knife to the tender underside of her own wrist, and cut.

A thick flow of blood, dark as chocolate syrup, welled from the wound. The smell of it was bitter, and familiar in some awful way.

"Take this and drink," she commanded him, and pressed the oozing wound to his lips.

He held his breath and turned his face away, but she was persistent. He felt the slow, gritty course of it over his cheeks and chin. Some of the blood seeped through his tight-pressed lips.

The taste that spread through his mouth was horrible. He tried to spit it out, but more ran in. And then a deep crimson dream of obedience more powerful than the mesmerism of her gaze flooded his senses.

CHAPTER 2

Seth wished his parents would fight like other people. Like normal parents, with a lot of shouting, blame-flinging, slamming of doors. This heavy silence, as oppressive and crackling as the air before a thunderstorm, as cold and hollow as an open grave, was worse than any noisy tantrum could have been.

Over a casserole.

He sat in his room, trying not to listen to that silence, knowing that it wasn't really about a casserole. Not *just* a casserole. The issue was far larger than that.

"Something, then!" his father had said earlier. "A salad, a dessert, a plate of *cookies* would be enough. I'm not asking you for a five-course meal."

"You know how I feel about this," his mother had replied.

"It isn't for me. It's for Seth. Your own son."

"*Your* son. You've taken so much of him away from me, and now you want the last bit of him. And you have the nerve to expect me to cater the affair!"

Then, the silence. Their version of a knockdown, drag-out. Their version of a joust, with speaking the equivalent of being unseated from the horse.

Seth knew better than to get in the middle, but this one was his fault.

It hurt that on the most important night of his life, his own mother wouldn't be there to celebrate with him. His initiation. Less than twenty-four hours, and the secrets would finally be his. The years of lessons and training would pay off once he felt the red robe settle around his shoulders. He would achieve what he had wanted all his life... and his mother would despise him for it.

Would his father's pride outweigh his mother's scorn?

She always called him his father's son, and Seth supposed it was true, but he could have done without the bitterness with which she said it. He *was* his father's son. His calling was in his blood, inherited from his father as surely as his dark hair, and his blue eyes. Why shouldn't he follow in his father's footsteps?

He glanced around the bedroom, which was still in many ways the room of a boy. Schoolbooks and unfinished homework on the desk, posters on the walls, a few comic books and trading cards stored away in the hopes that they'd someday be worth money. Clothing littered the floor, mixed with CD cases and soda cans.

At the foot of his bed was a table where a tangle of cords snaked from video game controllers to the console hooked up to the television. Most of the games were the violent ones, first- and third-person shooters in which armies of undead monsters went down in gory displays of blood, dismemberment, decapitations.

"They say that these games inure you to violence," his father had told Seth while purchasing them for him. "They say you get desensitized to it. That's what you need. To get used to the mess. And if it improves your reflexes, your timing, and your eye-hand coordination at the same time, so much the better."

At this, the electronics-store clerk had given them both a wary look. His gaze had marked Seth's face, as if expecting to see him on the news not long after.

Well, the clerk would be in for a disappointment. Shooting up the school was the last thing Seth had in mind. He didn't particularly *like* school; it was tedious at best, and the revisionist history they taught was enough to churn his stomach. But school, like a regular job, was one of the things a person had to do in order to maintain certain illusions necessary even in a world gone mad.

If his mother had her way, those illusions would become Seth's real and only life. She'd happily see him go on to college, pursue a career, get married, have a family, and eventually drop dead of heart failure or cancer, just like everyone else who lived their lives blind to the dark reality and who went to death actually expecting their Savior to save them.

Downstairs, the phone shrilled and broke the angry silence that suffocated the house. Seth heard his father answer. His voice took on a sudden urgent tone that caused Seth's skin to prickle although he could not make out the words.

Trouble.

Something was wrong.

Seth looked at the window. He hated this time of year, when the days were short and weak. It was not even seven o'clock, and the sky was the bruised purple of dusk. Sometimes night came so early that it could catch Seth before he got home. He hated walking the darkening streets, his gym bag swinging at the end of his arm, as the shadows pooled and grew.

"Seth!" Footsteps on the stairs, stopping halfway up, and his father's voice calling.

"You're taking him with you?" His mother's query was half plea.

"Get your jacket," his father said, ignoring her.

"Jeremiah, please! He's too young!"

"He's old enough."

Snatching his leather jacket from the back of the door, Seth hurried out onto the landing. His mother waited at the bottom of the stairs, not wringing her hands but her posture suggesting that she wanted to wring them, wanted to wring them white. Her eyes were large and dark and haunted.

"Seth, honey... you don't have to go."

"It's all right, Mother."

Excitement kicked up his pulse. She would only be protesting like this if his father meant to take him to the Cohort. For something important, too, it had to be. He was, after all, less than a day shy of his initiation. Old enough, and more than ready, to be included.

His father gave him a curt nod, and started back down the stairs. Seth followed. His mother stepped back, defeat evident in every line of her body and dismay twisting her face. She spared him one hurt-filled look—*I've lost you,* that look said—and turned away toward the kitchen.

He hesitated, thinking that he should go to her. Try to make her understand.

"It's no use," his father said, stopping Seth with a hand on his arm before Seth had made a single move in that direction. "She won't listen."

As they went through the house and out to the driveway, Seth saw his mother watching them through the kitchen window.

"Why?" he asked. "She... she believes, doesn't she?"

"Oh, yes," his father said, aiming his key fob at the car and pressing a button. The doors unlocked. The Cohort was only a few blocks away, but the cold wind carried the scent of rain. Maybe even snow. "She believes. She doesn't want to, and she hates everything about it, but she believes."

"Then why... ?" Seth wasn't even sure what he was trying to ask.

Why wouldn't she be more a part of things? Why had his father married her if she rejected the very thing that was most important to him? She could support him much more than she did. Seth wasn't expecting her to become a full-blown Centurion like his friend Jason's mother, but if she would bend even a little...

His father only shook his head.

The few blocks passed so quickly that the defroster hadn't made much of an inroad on the fogged windshield by the time his father used another remote to trigger the automatic gate. Several cars were already in the small parking lot. Men and women hunched into their coats, breath puffing around their heads. They didn't take time to talk, only hustled toward warmth and shelter.

The Cohort was a large square of a building, faded brick with white trim and a slate roof. Ivy, dead and brown now, clung to its walls. The external light fixtures were cast iron, designed to look like medieval torch sconces. The whole thing looked vaguely medieval, with narrow, shuttered windows and a defensive air. The wall around the property was five feet of mortared stone and another five feet of spear-tipped wrought iron, all of it but the gates also a-crawl with dead ivy. The grounds were overgrown and indifferently tended. A brick path cut through this dense weedy sprawl.

Word must have spread quickly, because more people arrived even as Seth and his father reached the broad stone steps leading up to a set of double doors.

Isaac, so bundled in parka, hat, gloves and scarf that he was barely recognizable, gestured for them to go in. He was seated in a large wooden chair. A quarterstaff, sharpened at both ends, rested across his knees. Isaac looked miserable, and Seth supposed that many long cold nights of sentry duty were in his own future. Such was the lot of the youngest, newest Centurions. Not only did you sit outside and freeze, but you missed out on what took place in the meeting-hall, only hearing about it later.

Although a palpable energy filled the crowded coatroom, nobody spoke. They shed their outer garments, blew and rubbed on their hands to warm up, and went down a long hall, passing under the sweeping curve of polished oak stairs to the second floor. Up there, from the gallery, portraits of past and present officers brooded solemnly.

At the rear of the building was the dining room, where Deborah would already have the coffee brewing. The large space looked even larger with the tables still stacked against the wall, and the racks of metal folding chairs pushed off to one side. The floor was herringbone, the pattern worn thin with age and the passage of many feet.

Seth spotted Jason in the throng a moment before Jason spotted him. His friend's eyes were alight, and it seemed to be all that Jason could do to keep from pumping his fists in the air and shouting, "Yes!" Whatever else, no matter what the trouble or how bad it was, all Jason cared about was that for the first time, they were part of it.

Jason's exhilaration lasted all of five minutes, and then came crashing down in ruins. That was when the Centurions headed upstairs to the meeting-hall, and sent the boys to help Deborah prepare a meal for those who hadn't had time to get their dinner before the emergency.

"I can't believe we're stuck down here," Jason said, in a low voice. "We should be up there, with the rest of them."

Seth didn't reply. There was nothing he could have said, anyway, that Jason didn't already know. Technically, they had no right to be upstairs. Rules were rules. The uninitiated had no place in a closed meeting. It was for Centurions only.

But that didn't mean they had to like it.

After all, they were less than twenty-four hours away. A few *hours*!

"They should have just left us at home, then, like before," Seth said. "What's the point of bringing us here, only to leave us out?"

Setting a pot of water on to boil for the pasta, Deborah smiled. "Give them a chance, boys. They know what they're doing."

"Do *you* know what they're doing?" Jason asked.

She shrugged and opened a cupboard.

Deborah was as much a fixture of the Cohort as was the carved and painted emblem of the Legion hanging on the dining room wall. As far as Seth knew, she had no husband, no family. He didn't know why. Deborah wasn't that old, and was pretty in a dimple-cheeked sort of way. She was content to live in the building, cook and serve as housekeeper. Or as babysitter, when needed. In a strange sort of way, she was more motherly toward Seth than his own mother was.

"Come on, Deborah," Seth said. "What's going on?"

"All I know," she said, taking out a large stainless-steel bowl, "is that Michael and Sarah never came home last night. Would you get the lettuce, Jason? It's in the bottom crisper drawer."

"What happened to them?" Seth asked.

He knew Michael, though not well. Michael was a few years older than him, and had always struck Seth as being one of the ones who liked the ritual and pageantry, liked being a member of a hush-hush ancient secret society, but didn't really care about the deeper truths and meanings.

"We don't know that anything's happened," Deborah said. "They went up to the city for a concert, and should have been back well before dawn. They might've had car trouble but they should have called if that was the case. Are there green onions in there, too, Jason? And there should be some mushrooms."

"Then why the emergency meeting? Why bring us along?" Jason fetched the onions and mushrooms, putting them on the cutting board.

"Their parents are worried." Deborah smiled and winked, the sort of adult confidential wink that she wouldn't have offered them if they weren't on the eve of their initiation. "Personally, I think they jumped to a hasty conclusion. It wouldn't surprise me if Michael and Sarah were off somewhere together."

"Yeah, but what if they were… " Jason made a sheepish face, as if he couldn't bring himself to actually say the words. Instead, he stuck out the index and middle fingers of his right hand and jabbed the tines of this vee at his neck. "You know. Caught."

Seth shuddered. "If they were, there's not much we can do for them now. Except finish it for them, if we can find them."

This grim suggestion didn't faze Deborah at all. She'd probably heard worse in her time with the Legion. "Would you slice the bread, Seth? There's a jar of crushed garlic in the pantry."

Jason stirred a pot of bubbling sauce. He, at least, looked like the idea of hunting down a hideously transfigured Michael and Sarah, staking them, and beheading them, didn't set well with his appetite. Seth had often wondered what Jason would do if he ever came face-to-face with a really dangerous situation. For someone who claimed to be so enthusiastic about becoming a Centurion, the actual prospect of violence always turned him ashen.

"I didn't think there were many left around here," Jason said.

Deborah started chopping lettuce. "All I know is that everyone's taking this seriously. It's been quiet since… " she paused and turned troubled, unreadable eyes toward Seth.

"Since what?" he asked.

"Well, for a long time," she amended. "And we've all gotten to thinking that we're safe. But Michael and Sarah went into the city. Parts of it have a bad reputation. I know the Centurions have discussed going up there and investigating, but our numbers are so few these days."

"If there are any in the city," Jason said, now sounding like he was trying to bolster himself to the idea of vampire-hunting, "a bunch of them, like in the old times, then they'll need every Centurion they can get. Maybe they'll put us through our initiation early."

"I doubt a single day earlier would make much difference," Seth said.

He looked through the wide window connecting the kitchen to the dining hall. There on the wall, above the clock now pointing to the hour of eight, hung the red and white and gold emblem of the Legion. The sight of it had thrilled him since he was a little boy, when he had first understood what it meant.

The crossed stake and hammer were white, on a blood-red circle edged with a ring of smaller white circles. Below the tools, a gold-outlined rectangle surrounded the gilded letters J.I. All of this was set against a golden banner, the wood carved to ripple and flow like cloth waving in a breeze.

Seeing it now, he shivered as if a draft slipped up the back of his neck.

Deborah grumbled. "Seth, would you run down to the storeroom and get me a new thing of dish soap?"

"Sure," he said, hardly hearing what she was saying. He shook himself. "Sure, Deborah. Dish soap."

To get to the storeroom, he had to descend into the basement. As large as the floors above it, the basement was a windowless box that also housed a gymnasium, the meditation chambers, the armory and the vault. The gym was small but well-equipped, lit by fluorescent panels. The meditation rooms were Spartan. The armory was painstakingly organized, full of racks that held the weapons of the Legion. Seth had never seen the inside of the vault, the iron door of which was kept locked, and opened only to the key his father habitually wore around his neck.

The storeroom was a vast, dark, dusty place crammed with old furniture, chests of moth-eaten robes, record books and ledgers, tools, crates of dishes, a broken exercise bicycle, rolled-up carpets, musty curtains, a drum set, and decorations for various occasions. It had ten-foot ceilings crossed by stout rafters, some of which had disintegrating old cardboard boxes wedged atop them. A few flyspecked bulbs lit the room, which did little to banish the cobwebby gloom. When Seth flicked the switch and turned on even this feeble radiance, however, mice and roaches scuttled for cover.

It was only neat and clean nearest the door, where racks of metal shelves held boxes of napkins, paper plates and towels, garbage bags, plastic cups and flatware, cleanser, detergent, sponges, toilet paper, soap, cases of bottled water and stacks of canned goods.

Seth could not quite reach the bottles of dish soap from the doorway, and had to step inside. The door swung shut and latched behind him.

The lights went out.

He stood perfectly still, eyes wide but useless in the dark. Adrenaline jetted into his veins.

Not for a second did he try to delude himself with notions of thunderstorms or power outages. The lines had been cut.

Dimly, very faintly, he thought he heard screams.

Then, closer, a shuffling run of stealthy footsteps coming his way.

A thin white glow filtered through the cracks around the storeroom door. Seconds later, it opened. Deborah and Jason rushed in, Deborah carrying a flashlight. She closed the door and thumbed the lock.

"Seth!" Her whisper cut the air like a rapier.

"I'm here," he said. "What is it? What's happened?"

"We have to get out," Jason said. All of his earlier bravado had vanished. He looked ten years younger than his actual age, a frightened child. Even his voice was high and afraid. "The cellar doors, quick."

"Shh. They'll hear us, find us." Deborah swept the light around, past drop cloth-covered furniture and trunks full of old robes.

On the far wall, set at an angle, was a short flight of concrete steps up to a slanted bulkhead door. But a stack of straight-backed wooden chairs, an old-fashioned blackboard and a wheelbarrow from which the front wheel was missing blocked the steps. It was a precarious jumble that, if disturbed, promised to make a terrific clatter as everything fell over.

"Vampires?" Seth asked, feeling a cool and calm dread settle slowly over him.

"I'm going to turn off the light," Deborah said. "We'll have to go carefully."

She clicked off the flashlight.

Above, more screams. Shouts. War cries.

"What about the others?" Seth resisted when he felt Deborah grasp for his hand. "My father's up there."

"They can handle it," Jason whined. "It's what they do, right? It's what they're trained for. We have to get out."

Seth didn't know how Deborah could navigate without smashing her toes and shins, but she groped her way through the black and led them with her.

"So it is vampires?" Seth held her elbow and stopped her.

He couldn't see her nod, but felt her hair tickle past him as her head moved. "It was Michael. He... he let them in. He brought them. They couldn't have gotten in otherwise."

"Michael? But I thought... "

"He's been taken, Seth," Deborah said. "He's theirs now."

"He wouldn't! He–"

"He killed Isaac," Jason said, still sounding like a boy of seven.

"Seth, there's nothing we can do," she said. "Except hide, and survive. That's what I've always been told. If anything happens, hide, get out, and survive. Take the children to safety."

"I'm not a child!" He wrenched from her grasp. "And my father's up there!"

"He would want you to live."

"He'd want me to fight!"

She put her arms around him. He could smell sweetened coffee on her breath, the aromas of pasta sauce and garlic bread clinging to her. It was half-hug, half-grapple.

"There are too many of them," she said. "If you go out there now, you'll die with the rest, and there will be no one left to avenge them."

"Are you saying they're dead, they're all dead?"

Jason tried to worm his way between them. "I don't want to die, we have to get out of here, they're going to kill us."

Wood clattered as the locked door shuddered in its frame. From the other side of it, they all heard a vindictive snarl.

"Let go of me." Seth could feel Deborah's heart hammering against his own, and Jason's wet, rapid breathing on his neck.

They let go, and he took the flashlight. Its beam came alive with spinning dust motes. Again, mice and roaches scurried out of its glow.

"Seth, don't!" Jason slapped at it. "They'll know we're here!"

"They already do."

The doorknob squealed. Something splintered.

And the armory was out there, down the hall, past the vampires. He swung the beam around in a searching arc.

More snarling. A gnashing sound. Teeth.

Then the dust motes danced in a new pattern. The beam found eddies of smoke.

No. Not smoke. Mist. Mist curling under the door and billowing up into a humanoid shape.

Seth thrust the flashlight back at Deborah and picked up a wooden chair. The rest did indeed go over in a rattling crash, but he barely noticed.

He beat the chair against a tabletop and it came apart in his hands. The slats were flimsy but the legs were stout. He shoved one toward Jason and moved to meet the vampire as it materialized in front of them.

It had the form of the sort of chubby, harmless-looking man who might sell ice cream from the back of a musical truck or make toys to distribute to needy children. A broad, genial smile, twinkling blue eyes set in nests of kindly wrinkles. The man wore slippers and a cardigan over yellow pajamas.

But the effect of his broad, genial smile was ruined by the glitter of fangs. The twinkling blue eyes were rimmed in baleful red. The cardigan was crusted with dried blood.

This was it.

He'd never seen a real one before but he did not doubt his senses.

A second cloud of mist issued under the door. The chubby vampire bared his teeth at the newcomer and lunged for Seth. Pudgy white fingers ending in split, grimy nails grabbed for his throat.

The training.

One hand high. Knocking the vampire's arms up so that they shot overhead.

One hand low. The jagged end of the table leg pierced the cardigan and the pajama shirt and met the strange, gelatinous resistance of the vampire's flesh. It sank in about two inches before striking a rib.

Seth's grip was jarred free. He knew he hadn't done it hard enough and was astonished to find that on some level, though he had grown up getting ready for this moment, he still hadn't really believed. He had seen this thing turn solid before his very eyes and still pulled his blow because he didn't want to hurt a living person.

The vampire screeched and looked down at the table leg dangling out of its chest.

Behind it, the second cloud had solidified into the shape of a red-haired girl of about eleven, wearing shorts and a Mickey Mouse tee shirt. With what seemed to be a genuinely reproachful look at the chubby man, she turned to undo the lock on the storeroom door.

"Jason, stop her!" Seth shouted, and caught the table leg as it fell. The end was stained. Through the holes in the cardigan and pajama shirt, he saw the gored purple wound and part of a rib.

His arm was seized and dragged down. The chubby vampire's head snapped forward like a striking snake. The fangs nipped a pinch of forearm skin as Seth yanked away.

He ran the crude stake at the vampire again. No hesitating this time, no holding back.

The jagged end drove into the vampire's chest. Dark, gritty fluid gushed out. The vampire screamed and fell over.

Seth straddled the chubby body. He wrapped both hands around the table leg and leaned with all of his weight. He twisted it back and forth, screwing it into the vampire's torso. Ribs gave way with a crunching sound. The vampire was in a frenzy, thrashing and scrabbling at the floor. Then, from deep inside came a thick popping sensation.

The vampire went rigid, bucking his body into a bow so severe that Seth was thrown off. Jaws snapped at empty air. In the wild shadows and sporadic light, Seth could not see the final transformation clearly. One instant, the vampire was whole, and the next had crumbled away. The pajamas and cardigan collapsed. Dust coughed from the collar, cuffs, and sleeves.

The table leg clattered onto the storeroom's concrete floor.

Gasping, turning his head aside so that he did not suck in any of the vampire dust, Seth tried to see what else was going on.

The door stood wide open.

Deborah still held the flashlight, but its beam waved crazily as she tried to scale a pile of old desks and filing cabinets to get away from the two shambling things pursuing her.

They weren't vampires. He knew that right away. The smell of them alone would have told him, their meaty, marshy stink of decay. Their grey-green skin was eaten away in patches to expose bone.

Lazarenes. The walking dead.

"Jason?" Seth cried. "Jason!"

He saw his friend flat on the floor. Jason's feet jittered and his fingers drummed.

The vampire girl hunched over him, mouth fastened like a leech to the side of Jason's neck. One of her pigtails obscured most of his face, but what Seth could see of it was wreathed in an ecstatic, dreamy smile.

"Get away from him!" Seth brandished the table leg, not sure when he'd grabbed it up again.

The girl raised her gaze to him without moving her mouth. The sounds were terrible. Bubbling, sucking sounds like a straw slurping around in the bottom of a milkshake cup. The corners of her eyes crinkled in a grin.

A third vampire stepped through the open door and took in the scene with a regal air.

Seth was shocked to recognize him from the television. Chad Forrest, an anchor from one of the local evening news channels... gone missing several weeks ago. Police mystified. Exclusive reports only on Channel 12. Even in pallid undeath, Forrest's hair was perfectly combed.

Deborah had reached the top of her precarious pile. Holding onto a ceiling beam, where she had set the flashlight, she pushed with her legs at the stack of furniture. It came down in a grinding, sliding tumult. One of the grey-green corpses disappeared under a pair of metal filing cabinets. A drawer shot out, spewing yellowed papers in all directions.

The other lazarene attempted a clumsy dive to safety and ended up with its legs trapped, probably crushed, beneath a massive oaken desk. But that left Deborah suspended in the air, feet kicking several feet above the floor. Her skirt had been torn in the chase, and flapped in strips that revealed her smooth creamy thighs.

The thing that had been Chad Forrest focused on Deborah and licked his lips with a wolfish leer that Seth had *never* seen on the eleven o'clock news. He sprang over Jason–the pigtailed girl growled a warning and leaned protectively over her victim–and ran with eerie speed toward the hanging woman.

Seth shifted the table leg and threw it like a spear. But the makeshift weapon was not balanced to fly straight. It went end over end and bounced off the back of the vampire's head.

The anchorman did not even look around. He continued toward Deborah, moving easily through the wreckage of the toppled pile of furniture. He didn't spare a glance for the trapped and mindlessly struggling corpse.

And Deborah, seeing the vampire, underwent a peculiar change of expression. She stopped kicking, but kept hanging onto the beam. The vampire's gaze was riveted on hers. She stared as unblinkingly back. Her eyes became hooded, smoldering. A slow smile curved her lips. He had never imagined that motherly Deborah could look like that. Lustful, sultry, alluring in some terrible way.

"Deborah, don't! It's mesmerizing you!" Seth called, scouting about for another weapon. He spotted the table leg he had given to Jason, which had rolled away from Jason's slack hand.

But Deborah only hung there, and did not resist when the vampire fastidiously plucked away the shreds of her skirt. Her hips were level with his head. He caught her underwear in his teeth and drew them down.

Snatching up the table leg, Seth jumped and scrambled over file cabinets. He yelled as the living corpse pinned beneath them snared his ankle. He tripped. Fell to his knees.

His right knee came down on the corpse's forehead. The sound was like a watermelon dropped off a balcony. The feel was a sudden mushy *give*, and jellied goo squelched up to soak through his pants. The lazarene went limp.

"Oh, yes," said Deborah. "Oh!"

Seth looked up. She was still suspended from the beam, but her knees were hooked over the vampire's shoulders and his face was buried between her thighs. Deborah squirmed and moaned.

"No!" Seth sprang up, the table leg in both hands, meaning to punch it into the vampire's back.

Something leaped on him from behind. The vampire girl.

The impact threw him forward. He yelled in surprise. The end of the table leg tore through the anchorman vampire's expensive suit coat and made a long, raw gouge from the shoulder blade to the waist.

The vampire, like the next domino in the stack, fell forward too. His weight dragged on Deborah and she lost her hold on the beam. The thud of her body hitting the concrete cut her startled cry short. The flashlight, knocked loose, tumbled and turned the room into a flickering kaleidoscope of brightness and shadow.

The four of them pitched into a heap. Seth was conscious of the girl on his back, her slim arms around his neck in a chokehold.

He was conscious of the anchorman under him, face down. He was conscious of the table leg, still in his fist.

The male vampire flipped Seth off his back. Seth landed on the girl, saw the anchorman rear up and then drop toward him, fangs exposed all the way to the gum line.

He twisted the stake around so that its blunt end was braced against the floor. The vampire landed full on it, impaling himself. A cheated howl exploded from him in a fan of dark blood. Unlike the others, he did not turn to dust but lay there, twitching, face down with blood spreading in a dark lake around his mouth and under his chest.

Lips touched Seth's throat. Pinpricks dented his skin.

He jerked his head around in a violent arc and smashed it into the side of the girl's. She recoiled, letting her hold on him slip just long enough for him to reach around and get a handful of her Mickey Mouse tee shirt. She flailed, all clutching arms and waving legs, as he wrested her off him.

Her eyes, velvet-brown and mournful, found his.

The poor little kid. She was hurt. He could see a bloodless white gash on the heel of her left hand.

He felt sorry for her, and guilty. He'd done that. He'd hurt her.

Only eleven, and she'd never wanted to be mean to anyone. All she wanted to do was apologize. And maybe give him a hug. Wouldn't he like that? A nice hug?

Seth weakened. He nodded.

It wasn't her fault. She couldn't help what she was, and really, when you thought about it, was it so bad?

Velvet-brown eyes. Very pretty.

She was a nice little girl. What would be the harm in letting her hug him? Maybe give him a kiss on the cheek, too. That'd be all right. One quick kiss.

His arms bent, bringing her closer. She had such a wonderful smile. How could he say no to someone with such a wonderful smile?

"Seth!" croaked a strange, froggy voice.

He ignored it. The girl was going to be like his sister. His own baby sister, who just wanted a hug and a kiss from her big brother.

"Don't, Seth!"

The girl convulsed in his arms. Her back arched. Her head flew back. She opened her mouth to scream, but instead of a scream, blood spouted up and rained down.

As she slumped against him, he saw a long, thin fragment of wood sticking out of her back. It looked like the slat of a chair that had sheared off into a sharp angle.

Her spell on him shattered. She withered in his grasp like a dry leaf. He was left holding the tee shirt as the rest of her clothes, her shoes, and the rubber bands that had held her pigtails pattered around his feet.

Seth uttered a revolted groan. He dropped the shirt. It felt germy.

Jason wavered unsteadily on his feet. "I... I got her, didn't I?"

"Got her. Here, hold on. Let me help you."

Seth supported him, alarmed at how cold Jason was. Like an ice carving. And so pale. No color in his face, no color at all. The side of his neck had color, though. It was painted scarlet. The holes there were neat and tidy, spaced close together. His lips, too... they were red and moist, as if he'd been eating very ripe cherries.

"I think I better sit down," Jason said.

"Right. Here." He found an intact chair and lowered Jason into it.

The blood. The blood on his lips.

A huge and awful horror yammered in Seth's brain. He pushed it aside.

"You... you should hide, okay?" Jason swallowed and licked at his red lips. His breathing was shallow. "I can't feel my feet. My hands, too. They're all numb. You have to hide. There's more of them."

"I'm going to see if Deborah's okay. You stay put, and then we'll get out of here. All of us. You're going to be okay, Jason."

A slow, deflating sigh came from Jason. He slid from the chair and sprawled on the floor.

"Jason? Jason, don't do this."

He knelt and tried to find a pulse. Nothing in the wrist. Nothing on the undamaged side of the neck. Nothing when he held his ear to Jason's chest and listened into the silence.

Dead. Jason was dead.

And worse, he had died from the bite of a vampire.

Seth knew what that meant, knew what he would have to do. If he could find the courage.

On legs that felt like stilts, Seth went over to Deborah. She hadn't moved, hadn't spoken. It was easy to see why. Her eyes bulged lifeless and glassy. Her head was bent far over against her shoulder. The fall onto the concrete floor had snapped her neck.

He wanted to bellow and rage and pound the wall. He wanted to cry like a baby and run home to his mother.

But he could not do any of those things. Not yet.

Not with more footsteps approaching.

CHAPTER 3

The ones she sent to search the kitchen and cellar had not returned.

Magdalena inhaled, forcing the air through her vocal cords. "They must have found something."

"Ah, they're amusing themselves with the cook," Lazarus said, with a shrug that caused dried flecks of skin to sift down from his peeling scalp and powder his shoulders like dandruff. "What does it matter?"

"It matters because all of them must die," she replied.

"You don't want to take any more of them?"

"No." Her dark gaze swept the basement hall as she reached the bottom of the stairs. It was dank down here, cool and tomblike. "You may, if you wish. Whatever else they may be, these enemies of ours, their bodies are strong and quick. You might get some good use out of them."

Lazarus blew out a breath between his lips, causing the upper one to tear partway loose and flutter. He smoothed it back into place with the air of a man neatening his mustache. "Do we have need of more? Are we planning another attack?"

"We shouldn't need to." She caressed the iron key. "There. The vault."

Behind her, his eyes as empty as the windows of a vacant house, Michael stumbled along on legs that might have been controlled by a puppeteer. His arms were wet to the elbows with the blood of the one called Isaac, the one whose throat he had slashed. She could smell that blood, young and rich, but too strongly flavored with masculinity for her liking. It barely stirred her hunger.

None of the ones upstairs had been to her tastes, either. Women, yes, most of them mannish in their aggression, none of them young, nubile, virginal. It was that sweet purity she craved, that untouched innocence. When this was done, she would reward herself with lovely Sarah. True, she had promised Michael that the girl would meet a clean death... but such a shame, such a waste. And it was not as if this would be the first time in her long existence that she had told a lie.

The only light down here was in the form of a dull, reddish glow from a room at the end of the hall. It was more than enough to let her see clearly. The smell of more blood hung wet in the air. Weaker than it was upstairs, where the bodies were piled three deep, the carpet soaked, the walls splashed. This was only a bare whiff.

There was something else, too, something that made her brows knit.

"Where are they?" Lazarus muttered. "They didn't come back up, and they couldn't have gotten out the back, not with the cellar doors padlocked."

"They ran into trouble," Magdalena said. Her grip tightened on the hard-won iron key. "I smell the dust of their dissolution and the reek of decay."

"You don't think that *my–*" he began.

"Shh." She moved closer to the dull red light, the blood-scent now overpowered by green meat, the putrescence of the lazarenes.

The light came from a single flashlight that lay amid smashed and overturned furniture. Streaks and fingerprints in blood marred the lens, causing the reddish glow.

None of the bodies that she could see were moving. Two of Lazarus' creations were down, one with an imploded head and the other crushed beneath a heavy desk.

Near them lay a mature woman, her clothing torn, dribbles of red down her thighs from an intimate bite mark. Her head tilted against her shoulder in a gesture that might have been coquettish if not for the angle of her neck and the sightless stare of her eyes.

One of hers, one too new yet to have turned to dust, was face-down nearby. The end of a stake jutted up from his back. His flesh had dried as the blood leaked from him, giving him the look of a mummified corpse. Only his bleached-white teeth and the styled on-camera perfection of his hair were unchanged.

The last was the body of a teenage boy. He was unmarked but for the wounds on his throat and the crimson taint on his lips. His out flung hand clutched loosely around a second crude stake, made from the leg of a table or chair.

Seeing the stake, its end clotted with blood, Magdalena's jaw firmed. She gave no other sign of her anger, not even when she saw the empty clothes and spills of yellowish dust marking the spots where two of her vampires had met their end. The smallest set of clothes had a long wooden splinter still caught in the Mickey Mouse tee shirt.

"He must have been tougher than he looked," Lazarus said, studying the blond man-boy. "And I think, my dear, you'd better take care of him."

"They were told not to… " She stopped herself and counted to ten.

"So hard to raise good help these days."

Magdalena approached the body. He had been drained to the very edge of death, then given to drink. The girl's work, by the petite and delicate look of the marks. Clever child-minx, disobedient creature.

Well, Magdalena had meant what she said… she had not been lying then. She had no intention of welcoming a Centurion— or the son of a Centurion—into her fold. It was a gift they didn't deserve, for one thing. She'd never trust one, never. Not even if he displayed centuries of faithful service. She'd always be waiting for the betrayal. That was not a chance she was about to take. Especially now. Especially now that the precious, priceless item in the coffer was finally within her reach.

"Well?" Lazarus prompted.

"What we came for, first," she said, turning her back on the scene.

Michael, having obediently followed, waited with his bloody hands hanging at his sides. He seemed unaware of his surroundings, his stare fixed on Magdalena instead of on the dead woman, or the young man, both of whom he must have known.

She held up the key. "Take me to the vault," she said.

His eyelids blinked several times in rapid succession. He turned, moving with the stiff jerkiness of an automaton, and left the storeroom. Magdalena and Lazarus followed.

Entering the armory, Magdalena skinned her lips back from her teeth. A dull sensation of heat throbbed in her breast, as if the unbeating heart there contracted in self-defense.

Stakes. Spears. Staves. Bows and arrows. Crossbows with wooden silver-tipped bolts. And crosses, everywhere, crosses. Engraved into spear shafts and quivers, hanging on the wall. Rosewood, silver, iron. Mirrors on the walls and shelves, from full-length ones to small hand-held ones with silver frames... a multitude of mirrors showing Michael's stiff-legged progress and Lazarus' desiccated countenance, but not showing her. Guns, too, and ammunition.

And at the rear of it all, the iron door to the vault. It was set so flush in its frame that she could not have penetrated it even as mist.

She gave Michael the key, and told him what he must do. As he moved to open the door, she retreated to the center of the armory, face set in a feral snarl. She hated this place, could not wait to leave it and see it burn.

Lazarus, unimpressed by sharpened wood and crosses, shuffled around the room muttering to himself as he inspected the Centurions' toys. He did avoid the silver, but silver and fire could only cause him temporary pain. Nothing much here would put an end to the likes of him.

Michael opened the vault and disappeared inside.

Just like that. So easy, with him in her thrall. She had worked long and hard to learn where the Reliquary had been brought, but despaired of ever getting inside. Not that *she* needed a mortal invitation to cross their threshold, but many of the old laws bound her children.

With Michael, though, they had met no resistance. He had approached the door, the young one called Isaac both startled and glad to see him, letting down his guard for one fatal instant. Michael had cut his throat, and then, as Magdalena, Lazarus, and the others watched from the shadows of overgrown trees, opened the doors.

The rest had been simplicity.

He emerged now, carrying a heavy, blocky object. It was a coffer, an ornately carved wooden box with a curved lid and four feet that ended in lion's claws. By any standards but her own, the medieval artifact was old. But even its antiquity did not interest her half so much as what she knew lay inside.

Magdalena felt that dull heat around her heart again, a sensation born not of fear but something else, something she had not felt in so long it was equally alien to her. Joy.

Not even the glint of hammered silver on the coffer's clasp could diminish that feeling. She snatched it from Michael and cradled it in her arms.

"Finally," Lazarus said. "We were close once before, but… finally."

Holding it, careful not to let the hated silver touch her flesh, Magdalena returned to the hall. Much as she would have liked to leave now, to get out of here before anything had the chance to go wrong, there was still one final, messy bit of unfinished business.

In the storeroom again, she was loathe to set down the coffer even long enough to take care of this last task.

Lazarus saw her quandary. He held out his withered hands. "Shall I hold it for you?"

"If you're offering to help, why not do the other instead?"

"You told me that I'm responsible for cleaning up after *my* brood. I think it's only fair to expect the same of you."

Magdalena glanced around the shadowy, cluttered chamber. She was no stranger to dark, forbidding places. On the contrary, she liked them. But something about this room… strange, really.

If anywhere in this building should have set her nerves on edge, it should have been the meeting-hall upstairs, or the armory she'd just left. Those rooms with their crosses and weapons and trophies, where the enemy met to plot and armed themselves to carry out the destruction of her kind, had good cause to disturb her. Not this basement full of old junk.

The solid weight and reality of the coffer reassured her. The night was theirs. A success. Years of searching and tracking and planning, failures and false starts, but she finally had what she wanted. What they *needed*, she and Lazarus both.

From upstairs, she heard the violent glee of her blood-children. The killing was done, but they reveled in the aftermath. They'd be up there wallowing in the cooling blood of their foes. Splashing in it. Finger-painting themselves, perhaps.

"Well?" Lazarus asked as she paused. "Afraid to get your hands dirty?"

Giving him a sour look, she set the coffer on the floor and knelt over the blond man-boy's body.

Lazarus was right. He must have been far tougher than he looked. A warrior, indeed, to have dispatched two vampires and two lazarenes and then clung to life long enough to deal the final blow to the third one, who had been sucking his veins dry.

She drew a long-bladed knife, which she carried for just such an eventuality as this, and set to work.

The flesh of the man-boy's throat parted easily. Only a slow seep of blood remained in his depleted veins. As always, the vertebrae resisted the decapitation. When she had sliced the neck all the way around that central column of interlinked bones, she wiped the knife on the dead man's shirt and put it away.

Then, never liking the lukewarm, greasy feel of them at this stage, she took hold of his head and twisted it until the vertebrae let go and the head popped free in her hands. She pinched through the wiry nerve column of the spinal cord, severing it, and stood, holding the head by the hair.

Lazarus, his leathery face split in a sardonic grin, applauded.

She mastered a violent urge with an effort. Had it been a mistake to join forces with him all those years ago? They did have a common goal, but he could be impossible to deal with.

Instead of striking at him, Magdalena set the head far from the body and wiped her palms on her robe. She picked up the coffer again, still careful not to touch the clasp. An excitement she hadn't felt in an ageless age tingled through her.

Finally.

"We did it," Lazarus said, echoing her thought. "At last."

"It isn't done yet," she said. "This is the first step, the vital step without which any others would be impossible, but we still have the ritual to get through. If that works, then and only then can we truly say we did it."

"Fair enough. Let's get out of here. Do you want to set the blaze, or should I do the honors?"

"Feel free," she said.

He snickered. "Still don't care for fire?"

"I think you should know better than that by now. You have your weaknesses and we have ours, but fire has never bothered me."

As she climbed the stairs, a single silent call got the attention of her remaining vampires, though they were disappointed to leave their gory play. She concentrated on the image of fire—snapping, leaping flames—and felt fear impinge on their kill-frenzied minds.

It might not bother her, fire. Or normal silver, or garlic, or roses. But these things still did have a curious, powerful sway on the lesser vampires. Their blood was thin. The sun would burn them to cinders. Crosses filled them with a furious dread and they did not even understand why. They shied from 'holy' ground and the silvery emptiness of mirrors. They did not *need* coffins and a layer of soil, but she had rarely been able to convince them otherwise.

About some things, she had not tried very hard; indeed, she herself did feel most at ease when passing the day in her own narrow casket, with its sandy soil of a far-away and long-ago land.

The very lore that in some ways worked in her favor also worked against her.

But now, she had the coffer and everything would be different. No more of these feeble, second-rate vampires! Her kind would be strong again. The powers they'd had and lost would be restored to them. No more of this silly business of not being able to cross running water.

The vampires came down the main flight of stairs in a jostling, pushing, shoving confusion. Most of them came bloodied from head to toe. Their clothes were sodden. Some still carried body parts torn from their kills.

A few lazarenes stumped along in their midst, their slow, shambling gait making them seem like unconcerned buffalo in the middle of a pack of hyenas.

None of them, vampires or lazarenes, cared that their side had suffered losses. Not many losses, true, but the ones who had met their end in the basement were not the only ones to perish this night. Though they had taken their ancient enemy by complete surprise, the reflexes of the Centurions were like lightning. Weapons had been in easy reach. Within seconds, the meeting-hall had gone from a scene of sober meditation to a raging battlefield.

Magdalena did have to admit that the lazarenes had their uses. The Centurions had not known how to fight them. A stake to the chest had no effect on the living corpses. Lost limbs meant nothing; a lazarene could drag itself along even if it was missing all four.

And their very appearance was, in some ways, worse than that of the vampires. More horrific. There was the smell of them, that ripe gassy stink. The way they could lose bits of themselves and still keep going. Mindless moving rot, slow but unspeakably strong.

She waited at the bottom of the stairs, near the body of the young Centurion who'd been stationed sentry. His ceremonial staff, sharpened at both ends, was still gripped in his stiffened fingers. From chin to collarbones was an open red wound. Michael had begun this wound, but an impulsive vampire had not been able to resist the siren song of the bubbling blood as Isaac had gasped out his last.

The vampires gave the staff a wide berth. They clustered around Magdalena, holding up their dripping prizes as if awaiting praise. Though they might squabble over their prey, and sometimes forgot their instructions, they were her children in the only way she could ever know. And, like children, they possessed a common, almost pitiful, need for her attention and approval. She had brought them all this way from their usual hunting grounds to strike at the Cohort, and they had served her well.

"Good, good," she said, admiring these offerings they held up for her inspection. "But now, it is time to go. Our work here is done."

They did not even notice the coffer in her arms. Poor things. They had no idea what it meant, what it contained.

Just as well. If they were able to understand her plan and its purpose, they might see it as abandonment, as rejection.

Michael stood untouched among her children and those of Lazarus. His brown hair was disheveled, his eyes filmed with stupor. He had performed well, served her as obediently as she could have wished.

The first tendrils of smoke crept through the air. Lazarus appeared from the kitchen, where it would have been an easy enough matter to start a fire. Indeed, given that the stove had been on, pasta boiling over in starchy profusion and garlic bread already blackened to char under the broiler, the blaze might well have started without any help.

But they had to be sure. She wanted the building destroyed, left a hollow soot-filled shell or collapsing in on itself in a smoldering pile of bricks and embers.

He gave Magdalena a brusque nod, and instructed his lazarenes to follow her outside. He kicked the staff out of his way—the nearest vampires hissed and dodged its rolling length—and hurried up the stairs. Unlike his shuffling minions, he was quick and spry. He had a can of charcoal lighter fluid in one hand and a fireplace click-lighter in the other.

"They'll know it was arson," he said as he reached the top.

"Fine," she said. "Other Centurions will know the truth, but who would they tell? The mortal authorities will never believe them, not without blood-drained corpses to support their claims. And if the others think that the Reliquary was burnt to ashes as well, so much the better."

Lazarus vanished into the meeting hall. She heard him cackle at the condition of the bodies.

"Outside," she said, pointing to the front doors.

The Cohort was well hidden from prying eyes on all sides by tall winter-barren trees and bushy hedges. The wrought-iron fence around the property had crosses worked into its design. Crosses and cold iron. But they had been foolish enough to let ivy grow dense and thick over the fence, obscuring the hated symbols from view. Just as well. Otherwise, she would have had a harder time coaxing her blood-children onto the grounds.

The very soundproofing that kept the secret meetings of the Legion free from prying ears had also kept their dying screams from alerting the neighborhood. By the time anyone became aware of the fire and called for help, the building would be engulfed.

She praised her vampires again, then dismissed them. Eager to show off in front of her, the stronger of them turned to mist while others slunk away into the night. Sated, they would be sleepy soon and ready to retire for the day.

The dazed Centurion remained oblivious to it all. Magdalena thought about leaving him to die in the fire with his brethren, but decided he could yet be of some use to her.

The lazarenes stood slouched and waiting for their leader. Lazarus emerged from the Cohort, pausing long enough to squirt one final puddle of lighter fluid and igniting it before tossing can and click-lighter into the inferno. He closed the doors on the dancing orange light.

"That should take care of everything," he said.

"What about them?" She indicated the stolid, silent corpses.

"I don't think they're of much more use to us, do you?"

"Not immediately."

"Well, then." He brought a small ceramic pot with a hinged lid from his pocket. His face screwed up into a look of pained distaste as he took pinches of salt between his forefinger and thumb, and flicked them one by one at the lazarenes.

Where the salt hit, spreading blackened pockmarks grew on the dead skin. This looked, she thought, like holy water was supposed to look if splashed on her kind. Like acid. Strange how the legends grew, how truth became distorted.

"Back to the earth," Lazarus said. He wiped his fingertips, which had eroded down to the bony nubs from contact with the salt, and put the pot away.

The sickening stench made Magdalena glad that she did not have to breathe. She refrained from speaking to avoid having to draw air into her lungs. The lazarenes, their skin drooping and sagging worse than ever as the flesh beneath it seemed to liquefy, staggered away into the yard. Each found a spot and began to dig through the sod. They burrowed into the ground like worms and pulled their new graves closed after them.

Lazarus made a satisfied sound. "And what will the authorities find when they come to investigate? Recently dug graves and decomposed bodies."

"You do not need to gloat."

"Ah, but I so enjoy it. Think of their perplexity. If they can identify any of them, they'll find people reported missing weeks ago, or bodies that were stolen from the morgue. It won't look good for the Legion, now, will it?"

"They've weathered scandals before."

"Yes, they are very good at bending the truth, aren't they?"

She allowed herself a smile that showed just the tips of her fangs. "But then, so are we."

CHAPTER 4

He deserved to die like this.

To burn, trapped and alone.

It was the price he had to pay for hiding. For trying to save his own selfish life instead of fighting.

The roar of it was all around him. Dragon's breath, the infernal flames. Feasting on the dry wood and old papers that filled the storeroom. Feasting the way the vampire girl had feasted on Jason's blood.

Seth coughed through his shirtsleeve. He held it pressed to the lower half of his face but it didn't seem to be doing any good against the smoke, the fumes, the deadly invisible currents of gas. The heat, too... he could feel it baking through the walls of the chest where he'd taken refuge from the footsteps in the hall. Turning good antique cedar wood into a sweetly scented oven.

He had hidden there, terrified but trying to make sense of the conversation he'd overheard. A man and a woman. Not vampires, because vampires didn't normally speak... unless they were Elder Ones. That possibility had further numbed him with horror. He only knew of Elder Ones what he'd picked up around the fringes of the talk of the Legion. Ancient. Powerful. Never numerous, and supposedly all but extinct by now.

Then how could there have been *two* down here? What did they want? What had they taken?

What had they done to poor Jason? By the sounds of it, he wondered if they might have done his work for him, done something to Jason that would make it impossible for him to come back. Which, in a way, meant he ought to be thankful. His friend would not rise, and he had not been put in the position of staking or beheading Jason himself.

Not that any of it would matter, when they all burned.

The rest of them had to be dead, Seth knew. His father and all of the others.

Grief tore at him. He gasped from the sudden pain of it, took in smoke, and went into a wracking fit of coughs that felt like they were ripping the lining from his lungs.

His arms acted as if on their own. They threw the heavy lid open. At once, a seething furnace embroiled him. Flames capered on the furniture, blazed on rolled-up carpets.

Where the vampires had turned to dust, the flames burned blue.

He heaved his body out of the chest and fell flat. At floor level, the smoke was thinner, and he was able to catch his breath. His throat felt parched, crispy. The concrete floor was uncomfortably warm to the touch.

Seth crawled. His eyes stung and watered. The walls were sheets of fire. The ceiling beams groaned. It was all going to come down on him. Tons of crushing, fiery weight. The entire Cohort caving into the basement.

He got to his feet, staggering half-blind and choking toward the short flight of steps to the cellar bulkhead doors.

Then one beam did come down, a fiery timber slamming into the floor and blocking his way. Seth recoiled, tripped, fell heavily.

No way out. No way out, and he was going to die here, like Jason had died, and Deborah. Like everyone upstairs.

His head fell back, and he stared up at the flames racing across the ceiling, glimpsed through roils of coarse black smoke.

Coward or not, deserved or not, he couldn't just lie here and wait for death.

He rolled over and crawled again. Head low. Sucking at what cleaner air was near floor level.

His hand hit something large and round, and sent it spinning away. He groped for it. His fingers sank into hair. Thick, blond hair. He brought the object around and stared into Jason's wide blue eyes. The neck was a ragged flap from which the end of Jason's spine stuck out, red-streaked ivory like a grotesque candy cane.

Seth uttered a helpless, dismayed cry and dropped the head. It landed nose-first and wobbled away to fetch up against a foot. Jason's foot. The upper half of his body was already on fire, cloth charred away and skin scorching black. The smell was like bacon.

Gagging, sobbing, the palms of his hands feeling like they were about to blister from the hot concrete, Seth crawled past Jason's splayed legs. He thought he was aiming for the door, but in the billowing confusion of smoke...

Then he saw a trail of fire, a long sputtering line of it. Leading from the doorway down the hall. Here and there, patches of the wallpaper curled in orange and yellow tongues of flame. He remembered the liquid sounds that had come just before the blaze started. Gasoline or lighter fluid being splashed around the storeroom... and then poured in a line down the hall so that the fire could be triggered from the relative safety of a distance.

He followed the line, hitching along his knees, holding his shirt to his nose and mouth. His head throbbed with sick drumbeats. The world stretched and receded and bent into weird curves. His eyes felt like they were melting in their sockets.

The stairway was an inferno, black with sooty clouds, howling red with flame. He couldn't see to the top, didn't know if the steps would hold him or if they would break under his weight and plunge him into a splintery thicket. He imagined the searing shards of wood driving into his body, spitting him like a chunk of meat.

But it was the only way out.

Hunkering low, he took several deep gasps of the least-toxic air he could find and held his breath. He wrapped his shirt around his hand and got up. With the padded hand on the wall and his feet away from the middle, near the edge of the risers where the wood should be the strongest, he charged wildly up the stairs.

Seth burst through into the back hallway and into the engulfed kitchen. A wall of flames blocked his way.

Dizzy, sick, his mouth tasting like burnt paper, Seth blundered into a wall. His knees buckled. He slumped there, resting his forehead on something for several seconds before realizing with dumb amazement that it was a windowsill.

His eyes were watering so badly that he was effectively blind. He groped up, felt the frame. Narrow, only eighteen or so inches, but wide enough for him to squeeze through.

He fumbled with the catch, couldn't get it. Rammed his elbow at the glass instead. It shattered with a crash that he couldn't hear over the roar of the fire. He felt wooden slats, shutters, and without stopping to think, he hurled his shoulder against them as if trying to break down a door.

The shutters burst open and Seth belatedly realized his mistake.

Fresh, freezing-cold air rushed in, fueling the conflagration. More fire exploded up all around him. He dove through the window, a spurt of fear-driven strength propelling himself in a flying headlong leap. Shards of glass raked at his sides like tiger's claws.

He plowed into the parking lot like a crash-landing plane, his body at first stiff and then loose as it scraped and tumbled. When he slid to a stop, he thought that there wasn't an inch of him that hadn't been abraded down to the quick.

His breath shuddered in and out. He hurt everywhere.

But... it slowly dawned on him... he was alive.

Close on the heels of that revelation came the thought of the vampires. This brought him upright, holding onto a car for balance and trying to look in every direction at once.

The only moving thing he saw was a tabby cat, eyes eerily reflecting the flames from where it perched, back bristling, in the fork of a tree. Nothing else, living or undead, stirred within his view.

"Hello?" he called, and had a coughing fit. He hawked, spat, tried again. "Father? Centurions? Anyone?"

No answer. He ran—lurching as unsteadily as a sailor trying to get his land-legs—around to the front doors. They were closed, hot to the touch, and thin ribbons of smoke jetted through the cracks. If he opened them, the fire would blast out and roast him alive.

They were all dead in there. They had to be. His father and the rest of them. Killed and now being cremated.

His instincts told him to try anyway, but better sense prevailed.

Seth retreated to the parking lot. He flinched when somewhere in the Cohort glass burst with a jingling sound, and the fire surged again with renewed energy.

The better sense that had cautioned him against opening the doors now told him that he had to get out of here. Soon, the police and fire departments would arrive. They might even think that *he* had done it, and arrest him. He knew he was innocent, but what could he tell them? The truth would sound insane to them.

Seth hid himself in the green and black shadows of the grounds, ears keened for the sound of sirens or any indication that he was not alone.

He reached the fence, dead ivy-choked wrought iron rising out of a three-foot-high wall of stone blocks. He swung himself up and over, mindful of the spear-points atop the iron bars.

By the time he came to the end of the block, he did hear sirens. Behind him, the red glow turned into a pillar of fire as the Cohort's roof collapsed and the blaze leaped high.

He did his best to stay where the darkness might hide him, but doing that made his heart skitter... darkness was *their* realm, and he expected to feel cold hands settle around his neck.

Seth turned onto his own street, shaking all over from the night's biting chill as much as what had happened.

Their house was the same.

With everything else that had gone wrong tonight, he'd almost been convinced that it would be destroyed, too.

His mother was in the kitchen making coffee, and his abrupt entrance startled her so that she dropped her cup. Thick crockery pieces and scalding coffee sprayed across the tile.

"Seth!"

Then she *saw* him, really took in the sight of him. He caught a glimpse of his reflection in the window over the sink. Haggard, panting, smudged with soot, hair sticking out in all directions, scraped, bruised, bleeding. Gripping a sharpened length of wood that he couldn't remember picking up.

His mother pressed her back against the counter, a hand over her heart. The color faded from her face until she was almost as white as a vampire herself.

"Mother," he said. "Mother... I... "

"What?" She more mouthed the word than spoke it. The hand over her heart moved up and found the gold cross on a chain around her neck. Her voice returned, but it was shrill and strange. "What's happened, Seth? Where's your father?"

Seth's throat worked. His eyes stung again, not from smoke now but from the tears he still couldn't shed. "They're... they're dead. All of them. Father. The Centurions. Deborah. Jason, too. They're all dead."

He thought she might faint. He thought *he* might, too. He fell into a chair, letting the length of wood lean against the wall at an angle. Its sharp end came to rest beside the calendar, with tomorrow's date circled. His initiation, which could never happen now.

His mother soaked and wrung out a dishtowel, and brought it to him. He covered his face. The cloth was wet, cool, wonderful.

She sat down opposite him, where a romance novel and a plate with a half-eaten chocolate croissant were on the table.

Telling her was like mining for ore. Each word had to be chipped out. He couldn't look at her while he did it. He kept his gaze on his hands, instead. His reddened, abraded, blistered hands. Hands that had killed two vampires... hands that had held Jason's severed head.

"What do we do?" he asked when he had finished.

She was quiet.

"Call the families?" he went on. "Another Cohort? The Legion needs to know." He thought about making those calls, having to tell the same story over and over again to the wives and husbands and parents and children of the murdered Centurions.

Although he was home and really beginning to believe he was alive, his body still wanted to tremble. The shakes worked through him, spreading out from his core until goose bumps erupted all over his skin.

"No," his mother said, and covered his shaking hands with hers. "Someone else will take care of it. Someone else will know what to do."

"But I was there–"

"Maybe some of the other Centurions didn't go tonight," she said, rolling over his feeble protest. "They'll hear about it and take care of things. It's their business now. Not yours, honey. Not yours."

"My father is dead!"

Her eyes squeezed shut. Her nails dug into his sore hands, bringing more pain.

"They killed him," Seth said. "They killed everybody. And they took something. I heard them. Elder Ones. They must have been Elder Ones, because they talked. And they had something that they took from the Cohort."

"Was it… a box?" She opened her eyes again, and they were haunted, fearful. "A wooden coffer?"

"I didn't see what it was."

"That fucking box!" his mother cried, and slapped the table hard enough to make the plate with the croissant on it jump.

Seth gaped. He had never heard her swear, not once in his entire life, nothing worse than 'darn' or 'phooey.'

She sank her head into her hands and clawed at her hair. "I knew something like this would happen. I tried to tell him, but he wouldn't listen. Hadn't it cost us enough, I said? And he said that the more it cost us, the more reason we had to assure its protection! But he always did care more about the Legion than his own family. Now, look! It's gotten him killed! It nearly got *you* killed! Oh, Seth, we have to be done with this. I don't want to lose you, too."

"What box? What are you talking about?"

"We'll get you cleaned up," she said, looking at him with sudden decisiveness. "I'll throw those clothes away. Put some ointment on those burns and scrapes. They're not too bad. Once we've got you all patched up, I bet no one will even be able to tell you were hurt."

"But we have to *do* something!"

"That's exactly what we're doing." She pulled him up. "Listen to me, Seth. When they ask, and they will, here's what we'll tell them. Your father wanted to take you with him, but I wouldn't let him. You've been here all night. You don't know anything about it."

"You want me to lie? I can't do that."

"Yes, you can, honey." Her tone had taken on a fevered desperation as she led him toward the bathroom. "Hop in the shower. Just toss your clothes out here."

He planted his feet. Taller and heavier and stronger than her, he was immovable. She tugged, she pushed.

"Father is dead," he said. "So are my friends. I can't walk away from that and pretend it never happened. What about revenge? What about this thing they took, this box?"

"Forget revenge!" she shrieked. "Forget the damned box!"

"Tell me what it is!"

"Let them think it burned up," she said, hanging imploringly on his arm. "If they think it burned up, they'll let it go. If not, they'll want to go after it and you'll want to go with them and then you'll die, too!"

He would never in a million years have foreseen himself slapping his mother, but as her voice rose toward a hectic raving shriek, he did. The sound was a sharp smack that cut through her babbling like a knife. She hitched in a breath, put a hand to her cheek, and looked amazed at him over the fan of her fingers.

"I'm sorry," he said, staring at his hand as if it had acted on its own. Given the blistered condition of his palm, it probably had hurt him more than it had her, but the pure shock riveted them both.

She threw her arms around him, crying. "Seth, Seth, I don't want to lose you, too. First Leah and then you, I couldn't stand it. Please, honey. Please don't go with them."

"I just want to know what this is all about," he said, feeling a pent-up tear break loose and go rolling down his face. He hugged her. Then what she'd said made its mark on his mind. "Leah? Who's Leah?"

Her fingertips covered her mouth, the way a person did when wishing he or she could call back words.

"Mother?" Seth pressed.

"I've always wanted to tell you about your sister," she murmured. "But your father didn't think I should."

"My sister!" Since when did he have a sister?

"Clean up, and I will. I'll tell you everything. I promise. But you have to promise me that you'll listen."

"I will."

"And that you won't go off and do anything crazy."

He couldn't really say anything to that, knowing in his gut that if it had to do with the Legion, she would classify it as crazy. She'd always had a thing about the Legion. Refusing to be involved and all. It was hard for his father, what with him being the Reliquist and having a wife who wouldn't even attend the family meetings.

Why *had* he married her in the first place, instead of marrying someone inside the Legion? It wasn't a law that Centurions marry within their own ranks and the circle of their families, but it was custom. A lot easier than trying to explain to an outsider what the Legion was all about. Or why had she, feeling the way she did about the Legion, married him? Had she known? She must have known.

"Go clean up," she said, evidently reading his hesitation and distress. "I'll make you something to eat. Come to the kitchen when you're done."

The shower was bliss and misery as the hot water flowed over his various injuries. He scoured away the smoke, the blood, the vampire dust that had gotten onto his skin, the lazarene muck that had soaked through his pants. If it was infectious–

That made him laugh, despite everything. When it came to infection, he had worse things to worry about. The bite, for instance, of the vampire. Except that the vampires hadn't been interested in passing on their evil curse. Not to Jason. Not, apparently, to any of their slaughtered victims. Why not? Didn't they realize that the worst thing they could do to a Centurion would be to turn him or her against the Legion? Turn them into the very abomination they'd dedicated their lives to fighting?

The bathroom was steamy when he stepped out of the shower. He wiped the mirror and studied himself. The scrapes looked redder and angrier than before, and they hurt worse than ever from the soap. Some oozed beadlets of blood.

He patched himself up with antiseptic sprays and ointments and bandages, drawing upon the first-aid training he had received. With a towel around his waist, he went across the hall to his bedroom to dress.

His mother had retrieved the discarded heap of clothes. The washing machine was empty, so he supposed that she had stuffed them into a garbage bag. Just as well. Even if they came clean of the smoke, Jason's blood, and the hideous slime that had spurted from the crushed skull of the lazarene, he could never wear them again.

She was waiting for him in the kitchen, nibbling on her chocolate croissant and sipping at a fresh cup of coffee. A grilled cheese sandwich and a bowl of soup were in front of his chair. Chicken noodle, thankfully not tomato; after all the blood tonight he didn't care if he ever ate tomato soup, tomato sauce, spaghetti, or any other red food ever again.

Actually, he was surprised he could eat at all. But the moment the smell of the food reached him—golden butter-crisp bread, melting cheddar, hearty broth—he was ravenous. He devoured the meal, washing it down with a tall glass of milk. When the plate was clean and the glass drained, he sat back feeling both replete and guilty.

By rights, shouldn't he have been prostrate with grief? Yet he devoured his food like a starved thing.

"Life goes on," his mother said.

He jumped. "What?"

"You're feeling bad for having an appetite, for being clean and comfortable and safe. When your father, and Jason, and the others never will again."

"Yeah." He looked at her with furrowed forehead. "How do you know?"

"That's how I was after… after your sister. I thought that everything should just stop. That I shouldn't be hungry, or sleepy, or care about those kinds of things. I couldn't understand why I didn't curl up and die from it. I wanted to. I told myself that if it wasn't for you, I would have."

"Did I really have a sister? Leah?"

She nodded. Her smile was small and wistful, her gaze far away. "She was so beautiful. So darling. And, oh, did she ever dote on you, her baby brother! There was nothing she liked better than holding you, giving you your bottle, helping me bathe you. I'd thought she might be jealous, but she loved you so much, Seth… so much."

"How… how did she die?"

The smile faded. "I want you to understand that I didn't grow up in the Legion. I met your father when I was in college, and he saved me from a vampire. I thought they were made up. I never thought they were real. But then, after, I didn't feel like I could trust anyone else, or tell anyone else what I'd seen. I thought that I might run into more vampires any time. It was destroying my life. So, I married your father, knowing that as long as I was around people from the Legion, I'd be all right."

"Okay," Seth said, thinking that was one question answered… though not the one about why *he* had married *her*. Then again, a Centurion rescuing a grateful, pretty college girl…

"At first," she went on, "I didn't want to believe what other things they told me. It made me feel like a fool. Like we were all so stupid for having been tricked for so long. But I told myself that it didn't have to matter. I tried to be a good wife to Jeremiah. I went to the meetings and took food to the potlucks and all of that, and most of the time we were happy."

He tried to reconcile this with what he'd grown up seeing, and was frankly boggled.

"Then Leah was born, and your father was named Reliquist," she said. "It was such a big honor, one he couldn't refuse. Not that he wanted to. We were poor then, but as the Reliquist Jeremiah was allowed to live in a special Cohort out on an island in the middle of a river. You know, running water. The Legion provided a car, and food, and everything else we needed. The agreement was that we'd stay there until Leah was old enough for school, and then someone else would take over."

"That box," Seth said. "The box you mentioned when I told you that they took something. A reliquary."

He listened, amazed, as she told him how they'd lived out there, mostly alone except when the rest of the Legion came for meetings. How he'd been born, and they had been the perfectly happy family. Until the night that the Cohort had been attacked.

"Lazarenes," he said when she described the walking corpses that had invaded their home.

"That's what your father said they were. I had never heard of them. Well, except in books and movies, though never by that name. I heard them break in. I was up with you, getting you a warm bottle of milk. You were teething, and weren't sleeping much. Your father told me to get out, to run." She started crying again. "Leah was in bed. I thought he was going for her. But he went for that box, instead."

A vague impression, not even a memory but the echo of a memory, the ghost of a memory, came to Seth. A rocking, floating sensation. A boat?

Wiping her eyes, she continued. "When Jeremiah came down the dock with the box, I screamed at him to go back and get Leah. He'd thought that I had her, because she hadn't been in her bed. So he'd gone for the box. And then I saw them coming. The dead things. The one leading them had Leah. She was so little, Seth, and so scared. Sobbing. Wanting us to save her."

He wasn't sure if it was memory or imagination, the picture that came into his mind. He saw a little girl, who looked as much like a younger version of his mother as Seth himself was a younger version of Jeremiah. A little girl with honey-colored pigtails and pink pajamas, clutched in the festering, bony hands of a lazarene.

"It could speak," his mother went on. "It gave your father a choice. The box, for Leah."

"But he was Reliquist," Seth said. "He couldn't hand it over."

She looked at him with horrified disgust that he should say such a thing, and he realized he had just proven himself to be every bit his father's son in her eyes.

"He let her die," she said. "I begged him, but he let her die. That thing killed her, Seth. Broke her back over its knee and threw her aside like a piece of garbage. I think your father would have let me die, and you, too, if that's what it took. That box was more valuable to him than his own family, his own children. I never forgave him for that."

"Did you ever find out what was in it?"

Her look was so dangerous that Seth quailed.

"You haven't understood a single thing I've been telling you," she said.

"No, I do, I understand."

"Your sister was murdered because your father wouldn't hand over that box. The entire Legion treated it like something more precious than life itself. And now, it's all *you* care about, too!"

"Mother, no. I can see why you felt that way–"

"If it hadn't been for you, I would have left your father," she said. "I almost did anyway. But I had nowhere to go. No family still speaking to me, no friends, no money. I couldn't take you into that kind of life, and I wasn't about to leave you with them."

"So you just stayed, even though you hated them?"

"What choice did I have?" She leaned over and touched his damp hair. "I couldn't lose my little boy. Even though I knew... I knew that one day he'd take you away from me. He'd turn you into one of them. A Centurion. I tried to discourage it but you know how strong your father is. Was."

Seth said nothing. The very idea appalled him deep in the pit of his heart. Not be a Centurion? It was what he'd wanted for as long as he could remember.

"In their way," she mused, "they're as bad as the vampires. They get their teeth into you and change you and give you a taste for the hunt."

"Mother!" If his father heard her talking like that...

But he wouldn't. Not now, and never again. He was gone. Dead. Without ever seeing his son formally initiated.

Was there a chance of that now? The Cohort was destroyed, but there were others. His father had listings of them, addresses and phone numbers in the red book in his desk drawer. Seth had been trained. He was of age, or would be in a scant few hours. He could petition somewhere else and be accepted.

And leave his mother?

He'd have to, if he wanted to pursue that course. Because sure as silver, she wasn't going to stand idly by and watch him join up with some other branch of the Legion.

She might even see the night's fiery tragedy as a release. No more Cohort. No more husband. Plenty of money, because in their dangerous line of work Centurions tended to be great believers in life insurance. A new start. Freedom for herself and for Seth.

Seth didn't want that kind of freedom. She'd make the ordinary world be his whole life. School and a job, dates and movies. College. A career.

"I'm sorry, honey," she said, reading his face. "I shouldn't have called them as bad as vampires."

Her apology rang hollow. He sat and looked at her, trying to wrap his head around the idea of a normal, mundane life.

It wouldn't even be possible! He knew too much of the truth. Even uninitiated, he had killed vampires and seen friends dead by their hands.

Was he supposed to forget all that? What would they do when darkness fell, as it always did?

Was he supposed to sit back and let the vampires win?

They had murdered almost everyone in the world he cared about. The loss of an entire Cohort was a huge victory for their side. And they had gained the Reliquary. Whatever was in it must be of tremendous value. Having it fall into vampire clutches could not be good for anyone.

Now she watched him with a grim, resigned fatality. As if she knew every thought that had been running through his mind.

"It's too late, isn't it?" she asked. "They've got you."

"I... I can't just let them win. I can't walk away."

"Yes, you can!" She clutched his bandaged hand. "Seth, we can go far away from here. We can start over, in a new place."

"There'll still be vampires. They could be anywhere."

"But they have what they want. They won't be after *you*." Tears glimmered like pearls in her eyes. "As far as they know, there were no survivors tonight. We could even let the rest of the Legion think that you died in the fire, too."

The plaintive hope in her voice was awful. He couldn't stand it.

"Mother, I'm a Centurion!"

"You aren't!" She shot to her feet, striking the table and making it rock. The last of the soup sloshed in his bowl. "And you won't be! I'll make sure of *that*!"

She stormed to the telephone, her sudden fury leaving him nonplussed with soup splattered on his arm. She picked up the phone and jabbed numbers.

"What are you–"

"Hush." She listened. "The answering machine. Good."

"Who are you calling?"

She said in a frantic rush, "Ruth, Ruth, it's Emily Justinius, Jeremiah's wife, something terrible has happened. It's Seth, it's Seth, my son, the vampires got to him, they did something to him! They got into Seth's mind and–"

"Mother, don't!" Seth jumped up so fast that he did better than merely rock the table, he sent it over onto its side with a crash that must have been audible even over the telephone.

"No!" she screamed into the receiver, and then yanked the plug out of the wall.

"What did you do?" asked Seth, feeling white with dread.

"They'll never take you back now," she said, raising her chin at him. Behind the tears, genuine madness seemed to shine in her eyes. "They'll think you're tainted, possessed, under a vampire's mind-control."

Chilled, he realized that must have been what happened to Michael.

Advancing on him, almost wild in her triumph, his mother said, "Any Centurion who recognizes you will try to kill you.

Ruth knows everyone. She'll tell. Everyone, Seth. Your only chance now is to stay away from the Legion forever."

CHAPTER 5

"This is it, then," Lazarus said. "It will work?"

"We have his blood," she said. "It must work."

Candlelight guttered over the pages of the open book. The ink was so dark that it seemed to suck the light into its lines. The candles themselves were set out in accordance with a diagram inscribed opposite an incantation.

"And you know this for a certainty?" the dead man persisted.

"Second thoughts, now?"

"I've never been fully sure that this is the right way."

"We cannot be sure. It has never been done before."

"So," he said, "we're going on the writings of men who've been dead for almost two thousand years."

She smiled. "Why not? The Christians do."

The corners of his eyes and mouth pinched into a scowl. The wrinkles caused by the expression split into cracks, which oozed thin yellow pus. "Since we know how wrong *they* are, I fail to see how I'm supposed to be comforted by that logic."

"We have the writings of an expert in our lore," she said, touching the thick, ivory-colored pages. They were old, flaking at the edges, but had weathered the millennia remarkably well. "Not to mention my brothers-in-blood and my own memories. This possibility has been with us for a very long time."

"In theory only."

"Do you want out?" she asked. "Is that what this is about? Cold feet?"

"If I have cold feet, it is because I am *dead* and my circulation isn't what it used to be," Lazarus said. "That has nothing to do with it."

"Then what is it?" She swept her hair out of her face and tucked it behind her ears in a swift, exasperated motion. "We finally have what we need. After all these years, we've dealt the Legion a mortal blow and taken back what they never should have been allowed to keep. An entire Cohort is in ashes tonight. By the time the rest of them recover, they'll find that they are too late to have any hope of ever stopping us."

"All right, all right," he said, stepping back and folding his dry, bony hands into the tattered sleeves of his shroud. "Carry on."

She returned her attention to the book, checking again the position of the candles and other implements arranged around the unopened box. Her gaze followed the curves and lines of the arcane symbols carved into the polished dogwood and stuttered when she saw the dull gleam of the clasp.

Hammered silver. Hated silver.

One of the few survivors of what had once been thirty such pieces.

Lazarus rustled in impatience, shedding more loose skin. Despite his stated misgivings, she knew that he was as eager as she was for the night's work to be complete. But she did not like to rush. A victory two thousand years in the making was one that should be taken slowly.

The clasp, hammered silver. The shape of the coin still recognizable. She brushed it with her fingernails and drew a sharp breath of air in through her teeth.

"Still strong," she murmured. "Even now, the power of this silver especially is still strong."

"Do you want me to open it?"

"I will do this." She touched the clasp.

Flesh sizzled, and when she pulled her hand away, her forefinger and thumb bubbled black where she had touched the metal. She rubbed them on her sleeve. Other wounds might be quick to heal, but silver–this silver above all others–would linger and fade only slowly.

"Does it hurt?" Lazarus asked. He sounded almost envious. Sensation was, for him, a thing of the distant past.

"It stings." She reached for it again, and found that despite the best efforts of her will, she could not close her fingers on the clasp. Whether merely an atavism, or some other force at work, she could not touch it.

"Let me–"

"No."

Magdalena turned her head. Michael sat where she had left him, slumped, head drooping, elbows on knees, hands dangling and still stained with Isaac's dried blood. His mind was utterly gone now, her dark tide having permeated his being.

"Michael," she said.

He looked up. A line of spittle ran from his chin.

"One last service," she said. "And then the clean death you crave will be yours. Come here. Undo this clasp."

Nothing changed in his expression or demeanor. He moved to her side, looked down at the coffer with all the emotion he might have shown a dead dog, and turned the clasp.

"Very good," Magdalena said.

She raised the knife with which she had cut herself, and caused him to taste of her. As Michael stood blank and uncaring, she set the tip of it over his heart.

A short, hard push and the blade ran between his ribs. Michael gasped and went rigid. Now awareness flooded back into his eyes, awareness and pain and terror. But before he could act—not that, at this point, there was anything he could have done to save himself—she slid the blade side to side, shredding his heart. Blood ran down his chest, ran over her hand in a hot gush. As he collapsed over backward, Magdalena licked the scarlet liquid, then made a face and wiped the rest of it away on a rag.

"What shall we do with him?" Lazarus asked.

"Leave him for now," she said. "Unless you want him for one of yours."

Her puppet thus dispensed with, she returned her attention to the coffer. With the heels of her hands, careful to avoid the silver clasp, she raised the lid.

Lazarus leaned close. Their heads nearly touched as they looked inside.

There it was. Resting on folds of cloth that had once been so pure and white it must have seemed the stuff of angels. Now that cloth was brittle, with the yellowed tinge of old parchment.

The item itself was not much to the untrained eye, just a two-foot length of brittle and ancient wood. It was hewn to a murderous point at one end and hacked off as if by the crude blows of an axe at the other.

"Look at it," she whispered.

"Is it real?"

Her head snapped up and around. "What?"

"Is it?" He recoiled from her fierce expression, but did not back down. "I wouldn't put it past them to fashion a fake, just in case something like this ever happened. The real one could be somewhere else."

"This is the real one," she said. "You cannot *feel* it?"

"You know that I feel nothing."

"Well, I feel it." She looked into the box again, at the terrible weapon.

Just the sight of it made her chest want to contract, as if the ribs tried to draw themselves into a solid protective phalanx around the vital core of her heart. To have such a thing driven into her... pounded to the hilt in rending pain... a rape of the worst possible kind.

Nothing she had endured or submitted to at the hands of her various husbands could compare. Those attacks, she had always survived. And, when all was said and done, she'd always gotten her revenge. They might have thought that they could control her, that she needed them to keep herself safe from the pious priests and torch-wielding mobs, but in the end, hers had always been the last laugh. As they died. Often in agony, sometimes incredulous that a mere woman–vampire or not–had been their downfall.

She reached into the box with her uninjured hand and touched the stake. She shuddered in mingled excitement and revulsion. Her fingers slid along it.

"Careful," Lazarus said. "Who knows what a splinter from it might do to you, if it *is* the real thing."

"I told you, it is," she said. "Here. The blood."

The wood was so dark and the blood so old that it was barely visible. Just a rusty, brownish stain that coated the point and left blots and splashes here and there on the shaft. But the slightest contact with it was enough. Power raced and tingled up her arm.

Heart's blood.

His blood.

"Yes," she said in a hushed voice. She brought her hand up. Tiny flecks, maroon against her skin, dusted her first two fingers.

Magdalena inhaled the scent, but it was too faint to do more than tantalize. The tip of her tongue darted out. The taste was also faint, but it still seemed to rush and storm through her the way it had done two thousand years ago when he had come to her, chosen her, uplifted her and made her more than human forever. Compared to this, Michael's blood was low and coarse and terrible.

"Take this and drink," she heard in the voice of memory.

She had been so weak then, weak from the draining, her neck sore in two throbbing wounds, the vitality that she had freely offered up to him slipping away from her at a fearful pace.

But his hands had been on her. Holding her, sheltering her, lifting her, as he had done on their first meeting. Then, he had saved her life. Now, he took it and gave something else, something infinitely more precious, in return.

He'd put her lips to his cut wrist. She drank. A dark eternity of his blood and his passion, and she had accepted it with gratitude.

Here, again, at last, was the taste of him. The power of him.

"Magdalena?"

She became aware of Lazarus observing her with keen interest. Became aware that red tears ran down her cheeks, tears of recycled blood she could not spare if she hoped to get through the ritual without first feeding.

"I take back my earlier doubts," the dead man said when she had shaken away the past and focused on him again. "It must be real."

"It is." She kissed the bloody end of the stake.

Instrument of his death, when the crucifixion and the burning sun had not done their job for them. She should have hated it with the same fury she held for the cross, or the pure silver that had bought the treachery of one of their own.

Instrument now, though, of hope.

Nodding to Lazarus to move the box out of the way, Magdalena set the stake in the center of the table, above the book and in the middle of the pattern formed by the candles. Her nerves hummed, and she knew that if she'd had a pulse, it would have been galloping along at a furious speed.

Though she already had the incantations memorized, and had been preparing herself for this moment ever since the first time she had dreamed up the plan and learned where the Legion held its most prized relic, trepidation overcame her. What if she wasn't ready? What if she needed more time?

"Well?" prompted Lazarus when she had stood in silent deliberation for several minutes. "What are you waiting for? Judgment Day?"

"This is too important to rush," she said. "We must proceed slowly."

"Slowly?" He barked the word, and tendons creaked as his jaw came unhinged. Three corroded teeth fell out and bounced across the book.

Magdalena brushed them off and shot him a sidelong glare. "I understand your desire to hurry, but we have to think this through."

Lazarus grumbled as he worked his jaw back into place, and she was glad that his speech was momentarily unintelligible. When the jawbone popped home, he grimaced and held his chin up with his hands until the sluggish process that kept him from totally rotting away repaired the damage.

"Easy for you to say," he said, his words still mushy from the missing teeth. "You're not falling apart."

"You've been falling apart for two thousand years," she said.

"And I'm sick of it!" He noticed a large flap of skin on the back of his hand and pulled it loose, then flicked it away.

"Just let me—"

"No, Magdalena," he said. "This was your idea. You came to me, and asked for my help and my support. I've done everything you wanted. I got you that book from the Vatican's library, I've raised up more dead to do your dirty work than I can even keep track of anymore, I've helped you against the Legion. I've waited long enough."

"I've waited, too," she said. "Do you think I haven't been counting the nights until everything came together?"

"You don't show it."

"You aren't the only one who's suffered," she said.

"But at least you have the luxury of knowing you're not the only one of your kind," he said. "Maybe your blood-children are little better than wild dogs, but they're loyal to you in their way and they stick around. Mine never last more than a few hours, a day or two at most. And there was a time, Magdalena, when you weren't alone. You had a dozen others just like you. A family."

"One of them betrayed us."

"Oh, boo-hoo," Lazarus said. His eyes bulged from his head with the intensity of his emotion. If he got much more overwrought, they might burst or explode out of their sockets. "We've all had our–ha!–crosses to bear."

"Enough!" she said. "Lazarus, enough. We shouldn't fight now, not when we are so close."

"Then get on with it already."

"Give me a moment." She closed her eyes and tried to calm her racing nerves. The script of the incantation filled the darkness of her mind in lines of fire.

He had promised to return. She remembered it vividly. When they had come for him, and he'd known that in order to save the rest he would have to give himself up, he'd told her that nothing they did would truly kill him. That he would come back. He would rise again, as strong as ever.

So the wait had begun. And gone on. And on. Stretching into years, decades, and then centuries.

At last, she had come to realize that he might not be *able* to return on his own after all.

His enemies had been too thorough with his body. They had done it in secrecy, not wanting to panic the people, and their very sneakiness had eventually contributed to the spreading myth, the great lie. They'd let it be known that he had been entombed in a cave and sealed in with a huge boulder, when in reality they had burned him, and mixed the ashes with salt, and cast them into the river.

That was why, when the curious who had missed the execution came wanting to gaze upon the corpse of the vampire king, they had rolled away the boulder and found the cave to be empty. The people were convinced he had escaped, when he had never even been there.

How that had all gotten twisted over the years! Sometimes, she still could not quite believe it.

She had no body with which to effect this resurrection. Not even so much as the fabled Shroud of Turin. There were at least six Shrouds that she knew of, some of them done in paint, or smoke, or goat's blood. In the chaotic and brutal times of the Middle Ages, those lengths of cloth with their suggestions of a bearded face and a brow pricked by thorns had been second only to slivers of the True Cross as relics peddled by the sly to the gullible.

The cross had, of course, been burned too. The circlet of brambles had gone into the fire with the body. The only objects to have survived were this stake, and the cup. The stake had, over time, been transformed by legend into a spear, and the cup into a shining Holy Grail instead of the humble clay bowl it had really been.

Magdalena did not know what had happened to the cup after Joseph had taken it with him when he fled home. One thing was certain—he had never mentioned its final fate in this book.

Had he still possessed the Grail at the time? Had he tried this ritual? If so, it must have failed. Contrary to popular belief, the cup had never held the true blood of the king. It had been merely the vessel from which he had sipped, amusing himself at the gathering that turned out to be their last meeting before the disaster. Then, the cup had brimmed with the blood of a sweet child.

The stake, though. The lance. The spear. By whatever name, it was a sturdy sharpened length of wood. It had been thrust into the chest of the vampire king, and it was dark with his blood.

Conscious of Lazarus about to open his impatient mouth again, Magdalena held her hands over the open book and began to read the words aloud. She had not spoken Aramaic in ages, and the sound of it was melodic and almost foreign even to her ears.

The candle flames shrank low and turned to a twilight-purple flicker. She scraped a dried sifting of blood from the stake into a shallow wooden saucer that already held crumbs of unleavened bread, then picked up a cloth in each hand. The one on the right had been soaked in clean water. The one on the left, fine wine.

As her recitation reached its climax, she held the wet cloths over the saucer and squeezed. Water and wine dribbled onto the dried blood, turning it from rusty brown to deep crimson as it blossomed over the bread crumbs.

"Water and wine and bread-of-life," she said, "by blood be born again."

She set the cloths aside. Every fiber of her body was taut with expectation. She did not bother to breathe.

Lazarus hovered at her shoulder, and the unpleasant sound of his teeth grinding in anxiety was the only thing aside from the sputter of the violet-flamed wicks to break the silence. She wanted to tell him to quit it, but dared not speak.

The flames burned yellow-orange again.

The contents of the saucer congealed into a soggy mess.

Nothing else happened.

Magdalena felt pressure in her palms and saw that she had clenched her fists so hard that her nails had pierced her skin in erratic, bloodless stigmata.

"Well?" Lazarus finally asked, in a low mutter.

"I don't understand," she said, turning to the book. "I followed the ritual exactly."

"You mean that it didn't work? After all that, and it still didn't work?"

"Be quiet." She traced the lines of text, mouthing them. Yes, she had followed every instruction. She had pronounced the words correctly. She had done everything right.

Why, then, did the saucer just sit there?

"So it was a fake."

"It is not a fake! It *is* his blood, Lazarus. I tasted it. I know."

"Then explain."

"Something in the incantation... or perhaps the ritual is meant to be done at a specific time."

"Easter?" he sneered. "Maybe the entire book is garbage. Maybe your precious Joseph of Arimathea didn't know *what* he was doing, and made it all up. You said yourself that he'd never tried the ritual."

"Not successfully."

"Which means we have no proof it will really work."

"It isn't about proof. It's about faith."

"Oh, spare my decrepit body. Faith!"

"Or perhaps we're missing something. This wasn't the only book."

Lazarus blew air through flapping lips, spitting fragments of them off. "I am *not* breaking into the secret Vatican libraries again. Mine may be a half-life, but I'm not ready to see it end just yet, thank you."

"There are others that never fell into the hands of the Church."

"Now she tells me," he said, rolling his eyes to the ceiling.

"This *is* the best of them," she said. "Your effort was hardly wasted. I'm saying that there are others out there, others that might contain the missing pieces of the puzzle."

"It's so good to be appreciated. I suppose you'll want me to round up these others, too."

"I'll have to find them first," Magdalena said. "Research them, and see if I can figure out what we'll need."

"You mean you're not giving up."

"Absolutely not. This is... a setback, that's all."

He looked at the wet mush in the saucer. "Some setback. Looks like a failure to me."

Magdalena resisted with great effort the urge to sink her fingernails into his scalp and peel his skull like an orange. Her earlier excitement had turned to sour disappointment and she was exhausted, hungry, and sick of his perpetual complaints. Moving with deliberate calm, she snuffed the candles and closed the book and returned the stake to the box. She left the hurtful silver clasp unfastened.

The contents of the saucer were another matter. Clearly, the moistened bread was not going to transform into his actual body. It would be useless for future attempts at the ritual.

But she could not just throw it away in the trash or flush it down the drain. Not bread dampened with the revitalized blood of the vampire king.

She scooped up the soggy wad and held it over her open mouth. Dark liquid trickled onto her tongue. Ambrosia. She crushed the bread, wringing out every drop, then licked out the saucer like a cat with a dish of cream.

Her eyelids drifted most of the way shut and she ignored everything else as the wine-flavored blood suffused her veins. It felt like floating, flying, death and rebirth. It kindled her hunger into a consuming fire.

For a moment, she saw herself forgetting the rest and steeping the stake in water until every last bit of blood had been leeched from it, and then drinking the resulting brew. But that would be an end to it all, and she brought her thirst under control in time.

Barely.

CHAPTER 6

Seth dozed in the back seat, never quite able to sink fully into sleep because he knew that the moment he did, a policeman would tap on the window and shine a flashlight in at him and want to know what he thought he was doing.

And if not a policeman, a member of the Legion might find him.

Would they really kill him on sight? Not even giving him the chance to speak in his own defense and prove that what his mother had told them wasn't true?

He glumly supposed that they would. No Centurion would willingly risk contact with someone suspected of being corrupted.

How could his own mother have done this to him?

That she would rather sign his death warrant this way than see him join the Legion dumbfounded him. He'd been on his own for a week now and still could not come to terms with the enormity of what she had done to him.

She would sooner see him dead than take up the stake and hammer and follow in his father's footsteps. She was willing to let her husband and everyone else in the Cohort go unavenged.

All because she said she didn't want to lose him. Didn't she see that now, by turning against him and driving him away, she *had* lost him? He could never go home. Not after this.

A week of sleeping in the car, of driving aimlessly from one neighborhood to the next in search of places where he might park unnoticed for a few hours, was beginning to wear on him.

He had fled the house that night, shortly after she made her condemning phone call. It wasn't likely that Ruth would have sent other Centurions after him at once, not with an entire

Cohort burned to the ground, but Seth hadn't dared take any chances.

His mother had been crying in her room when he snuck out, taking the keys and the car. He'd had time to grab some clothes and personal belongings, as well as a red leather suitcase that had belonged to his father, the one he'd ingrained in Seth should be taken with them in case of emergencies, before any other familial keepsake.

Not knowing where to turn, he had left town and driven into the city. His reasoning was that the more cars around him and the more people, the better his odds of going unnoticed. He would lose himself in thriving numbers and busy avenues.

As bad as it was thinking that the police or the Centurions might find him, it was worse to try and sleep with night's cold black face pressing against the car's windows. He had never felt so vulnerable. Crosses and other protective devices at every point of entrance had kept the house safe. If a vampire found him here, there would be nothing to keep it at bay.

Seth dreaded that more than anything. Seeing them in action, seeing what they'd done to Jason and Deborah, had left him terrified to the core. Not even his own prowess in destroying the monsters went far toward comforting him.

Now it was finally dawn, and the coming of the light filled him with relief.

By day, he had only the Legion to worry about. He could keep on the move, avoid the police. He could get something to eat.

Money, though, was going to be a problem. He hadn't wanted to spend any on a motel room, if they even would have rented to an eighteen-year-old with no credit card. He had enough to fill up the gas tank a few more times and keep himself fed for another few weeks, provided that he ate cheaply and sparingly, but after that he was broke.

He stretched and rubbed his face, feeling the prickle of whiskers. They grew in a shade darker than his hair and gave him a low, disreputable look. His clothes were rumpled, and he was down to his last clean outfit. He changed in the back seat, always on the lookout for some early riser who might see him through the car windows and be shocked, or report him for indecency.

Socks, underwear, jeans, a white tee shirt, a red-and-black flannel shirt. He used his fingers for a comb. Dry-brushed his teeth.

His stomach informed him that sustenance would be welcome, so he crawled into the front seat and started up the car. The wipers swept slush from the windshield in long arcs. Tepid air blew from the vents, gradually warming.

The radio announcers talked about traffic and weather and politics as he drove. Nothing about the fire. That was old news, and with no leads, there weren't any recent developments. Seth was sure that the rest of the Cohort, grieving though they may be, were not going to go out of their way to press police to find the murderers and arsonists. What would they say? That the vampires had done it? Vampires and walking dead men?

A diner's neon sign, promising breakfast specials starting at $1.99, beckoned him. Moments later, he was in a corner booth with a cup of coffee and a menu. He ordered the ham-and-cheddar scramble, which came with hash browns and orange juice.

If nothing had changed, he would have been in school. Never been of primary importance to him, it had now dropped off his radar completely. School... he didn't care about school; what was he going to do with his *life*?

He couldn't just forget everything he'd grown up knowing, everything he'd been trained to do. It was all he had. All he'd ever wanted. But that avenue was closed to him, thanks to his mother.

Seth looked at the people around him, reading their newspapers and eating pancakes and arguing cheerfully over sports. They lived under the biggest lie in history and most of them were *happy* with that lie. They thought vampires only existed in books and movies. None of them would welcome the truth.

No place for Seth in their world. No refuge for him in the Legion, either.

His thoughts turned to the red leather suitcase, his father's bag, which had been kept atop the hutch in the den. There would be weapons in it—more trouble for him if he *was* noticed by the police, who would surely raise their eyebrows at a teenage kid driving around with a bunch of stakes, hammers, crosses, garlic—and he wondered if his problems might best be answered with a bullet.

Shoot himself? Kill himself?

Seth poked at his food, his appetite waning. As bleak as things appeared right now, he still didn't want to die. That would be giving up.

Though he wasn't hungry anymore, he cleaned his plate. No sense wasting food he'd bought and paid for. The eggs, ham, cheese, and potatoes sat in his middle like a greasy weight. On his way out, he took a newspaper that another patron had left behind, and sat in the car to flip through it.

A sidebar about the fire said that authorities were baffled, and went on to mention that the Cohort had been 'the lodge of a fraternal order' but no one was coming forward with more information. With the added shocking discovery of several bodies buried on the grounds, the police were very interested to learn more.

How much did the rest of the Legion know? Did they know that the Reliquary his mother hated so much had been stolen? About the Elder Ones?

Seth groaned in frustration. He wanted to talk to someone, tell someone what he'd heard. But the police wouldn't believe him, the Legion wouldn't trust him. He was on his own.

If he was going to survive, he couldn't do it sleeping in his car and existing on $1.99 breakfast specials. He had to find a job, a place to stay. Never mind school. He'd only gone to high school because it pleased his mother and didn't raise questions with the neighbors. Pleasing his mother had fallen to last on his list of priorities.

He turned to the want ads and started circling likely prospects.

The next several days saw his money dwindle and his desperation increase. No one was hiring. Or perhaps they saw something in him, read something in him, that made the shopkeepers and managers uneasy.

A thrift store and a coin-operated laundry had helped his clothing situation as well as providing him a couple of ugly but warm blankets and a pillow. He'd purchased toiletries, and located a community center where he could blend in with the high school swim team and use the locker room shower. He ate dry cereal straight from the box, and cold canned beef stew, and other stuff purchased at a discount grocery.

At nights, he tried to park near churches on the idea that the holy ground would help keep the vampires away.

During the day, he went around searching for a job but with no real hope. What good would it do to fill out an application when he didn't have a phone number, address, or references?

Soon, he came to see that on the streets, none of that mattered. Down in the city's dark and scummy underbelly, among the winos and lunatics and drug dealers and hookers, he passed for just another runaway. He started learning the patterns and routines. There were hostels, shelters, and missions. Soup kitchens and food banks.

One night, while tossing in a fitful sleep in which he dreamed over and over of picking up Jason's severed head only to find his own eyes looking back at him, he was jolted awake by the very sound he'd feared.

Tap-tap-tap on the snow-dusted glass, and Seth sat up in a clammy sweat with his tee shirt stuck to his body and the blankets snarled around his legs.

A face peered in at him, but not a cop face. It was pasty white, with wild eyes and hair hanging in matted dirty-blond dreadlocks. A hand clad in fingerless gloves did the tapping, while its mate splayed pale on the window.

Seth stared back. He let his arm fall toward the floor, groping for the handles of his father's bag.

"Hey, dude," the skinny figure with the dreadlocks said, leering and tapping again. "Nice car, huh, nice car, why don't you open up? It's cold out here."

"Get lost," Seth said.

"Ooh, that's not very friendly. Dude's not being very friendly, Hoag."

Another figure stepped up to the car, this one with a shaved head, no neck, and the thick build of a bulldog well-displayed in a Joe Camel sweat shirt with the sleeves cut away. He had to be freezing, but he didn't show it. "Yeah? What do you think of that?"

When they spoke, they revealed teeth that were more or less ordinary in size and shape. No fangs. Not much familiarity with dentists, either, but Seth didn't care about that.

They weren't vampires. What they *were* was trouble, though, vampires or not.

"I think it's pretty rude, that's what I think," the one with the blond dreadlocks said. "And maybe he's got himself a girl in there all hidden under the blankets, maybe she'd like to come out and party instead of wasting her time with this prick."

Seth threw back the blankets. He was in jeans and a thrift store navy blue turtleneck with orange bleach spots spattered down the left arm.

"Aw, no girl," Hoag said. His fist thumped the window, a meaty under point to his buddy's rodent-like tapping. "So why don't *you* come out, huh?"

"I'm only trying to get some sleep," Seth said. "I'm not bothering you."

"But you *are*," Hoag said. "Isn't he, Ratty?"

Ratty nodded, dreadlocks flopping. "Bothers us that you've got a nice car, dude, a shithead like you with a nice car while we've got nothing. So, tell you what. You get out, we'll take the car, and I won't let Hoag here break both your arms."

"I don't think so." Seth curled his legs under him, ready to spring over the seats and get behind the wheel.

This had been a good spot, within sight of a high cross atop a church steeple, illuminated all night by a spotlight, and it was a shame to have to move on. He'd drifted off watching snowflakes spiral down through the spotlight's beam, white and pretty and peaceful. The snow wouldn't be so pretty once he was out in it.

"Now, look, Hoag, he's going to be stupid," Ratty said.

Hoag hefted a crowbar. "Don't," he advised Seth.

"Get on out of there," Ratty said. "Through the back door. Make it snappy and maybe we'll let you keep some of your shit."

They were going to steal his car, rob and probably beat him up into the bargain. Seth seethed as he stuffed his feet into his shoes. He knew he could take them, that was the thing. Hoag was strong and Ratty looked quick, and there was the crowbar to consider and probably other weapons as well. A switchblade, maybe. Ratty seemed like the type who'd like to cut. But none of that would matter against a trained Centurion.

What *did* matter was that they weren't vampires.

He found himself sourly almost wishing that they were. Then, there would be no dilemma, no hesitation. His course would be clear.

"I'm getting impatient," Ratty said, tapping again.

Seth picked up his father's suitcase. It would only make them want to know what he thought was valuable enough to take with him, but he was not about to leave it behind. And be unprotected on the night streets? No way. If they wanted it, they'd have to take it from him by force. If they tried that, he was going to fight.

Hoag raised the crowbar and smacked it meaningfully into the palm of his free hand. Ratty backed away from the car, flicking his fingers in a come-along gesture.

"I'm getting out," Seth said. "Take it easy."

"What's in the suitcase, dude?"

"It's mine."

Ratty's eyes lit up. "You got dope in there?"

"No."

"Give it over."

He shook his head.

"I said give it over, dude!" There was a snick, and a silver fang popped up in Ratty's hand. A switchblade, all right. "Hoag, hold this shithead, will you?"

Hoag moved in, and Seth moved faster. He swung the heavy bag, which was leather reinforced with wood. It struck Hoag in the chest and knocked him back a step. Things inside clattered and clunked. Hoag staggered, but didn't drop the crowbar.

Ratty darted in and poked the switchblade at Seth, snagging the bleach-spotted sleeve of his turtleneck but missing his skin. His next stab came in high, going for the face or neck.

Seth reacted exactly as he'd been trained, blocking the knife with one arm while he dropped the case. Instead of a stake, he clenched his fist and drove it into Ratty's solar plexus. Ratty doubled over. Seth grabbed him by the hair, grimacing at the oily, hairy texture of the dreadlocks, and introduced Ratty's jaw to his knee in a sharp, violent motion.

The crowbar whistled down and hit Seth in the juncture of shoulder and neck. His right arm went numb to the fingertips and he found himself on his knees in the gutter with no memory of falling. Hoag swung again, missed Seth's head, and hit the car with a loud metallic *ka-ponk*.

The impact jarred the crowbar out of Hoag's hand and made him grunt. Seth, on his knees, elbowed Hoag in the groin and the grunt turned into a howl. Hoag backed up. His heels struck the prone and semiconscious Ratty, and the big man sat down hard on the smaller man.

Hunching to the right to favor his arm, Seth got to his feet. He was peripherally aware that the scuffle had drawn an audience of late-night onlookers, but he was more concerned with working the sensation back into his good hand so he could dig his keys out of his pocket.

"You... prick," Hoag wheezed, laboriously hauling himself upright. He picked up the crowbar on his way. His nostrils flared, and no one would have been surprised to see steam jetting from them.

Ratty, his eyes rolled up and his mouth hanging open, curled into a shape like a human pillbug.

Seth flexed his fingers. The stunned, icy-hot feeling in his shoulder had melted into a vicious throb.

"Cut it the hell out down there!" someone shouted from an upstairs window. "I'm calling the cops! Some people sleep at night, you know!"

Instead of coming at Seth, Hoag went after the car with the crowbar. He caved in the windshield with a single mighty downstroke, eliciting an appreciative hoot from somewhere in the cluster of spectators.

"Hey!" Seth cried.

Hoag's next hit connected with the side view mirror, batting it up and over and into the crowd. He was snorting, and damned near pawing the ground. If he lost the crowbar, Seth thought that Hoag might simply lower his head and charge.

With his left hand–the right was still dazed and tingling– Seth caught the crowbar on the backswing and twisted it out of Hoag's grasp. The big man rounded on him, and Seth rammed the iron length at Hoag's chest without thinking about what he was doing. He tried to correct the murderous strike at the last second, pulling to the left.

The crowbar glanced off Hoag's bulging pectoral and skewered his upper arm, just under a tattoo of a naked Betty Boop. Hoag bellowed. He slapped the crowbar aside and punched Seth in the face.

Seth's nose crunched as it canted sideways. Hot blood spilled down his lip and stars rocketed around in his head. He was flat on his back–he'd tripped over Ratty, too–and had smacked the back of his skull on the pavement. There wasn't enough accumulation of snow to cushion the impact.

A sudden alertness swept the crowd, the alertness of a herd of zebras scenting lion at the waterhole. They scattered.

Hoag, the wildebeest among them, swiveled his head in the direction of oncoming flashing blue and red lights. He snorted again, a steamy exhale of disappointment, and dragged Ratty off the ground.

"Later for you, if I see you around here again," he said, leveling a finger at Seth.

"Ugh," was the best Seth could do. He sat up, felt his head spin, and fought to keep from vomiting up his canned supper.

The police car turned the corner, throwing splashes of light across storefronts and turning the white flurries to a colorful storm. Seth looked longingly at his car but knew that if he tried to get in and drive away, they'd pursue. If he stayed, they would question him.

He jumped up, his head giving another sick rolling drumbeat, and grabbed the suitcase. He was briefly pinned in headlights, and then brakes screamed, doors flew open, and cops sprang out.

Seth ran for an alley, hearing the police yelling after him to freeze, hearing the rushing footfalls of them on his heels. The weight of the case slowed him down but if he left it, they'd find it, and its contents would convince them they had a psychopath on their hands.

There was a board fence at the end of the alley, and garbage cans lined up along it. Trash bags were heaped around the cans. Half a dozen cats exploded out of the garbage, screeching like devils. Seth flung the case over the fence and followed it in a half-graceful, half-headlong lunge.

When he thought he'd outdistanced them, he let his pace slow to a trot. He berated himself for letting this happen. Chased away from his car, his refuge. Now he was out here alone on the streets, in the dark and the snow, with nothing to his name except his father's old bag and the clothes on his back.

Shadows pooled and thickened. He heard music, traffic, and other normal night-city sounds, but they all seemed to come from far away.

He left the alley and hurried along the sidewalk from one patch of light to the next. The few people that passed gave him startled looks and wide berths. He stopped long enough to try and scrub away the worst of the blood from his face, but touching anywhere near his nose caused flares of pain. His shoulder was a steady grinding misery, as if someone were drilling for the bone with a blunt auger.

Ahead of him was an old grey stone apartment building, its doors and windows boarded over. The signs on the walls told of renovation plans, but spray-painted graffiti covered the older signs.

Seth went around to the back and found a door from which the boards had been pried away. He made a face at the odors coming from inside—urine, unwashed bodies, stale beer, cigarette smoke—but went in anyway. At least those odors meant the living, not the undead.

He picked his way down a rubble-strewn hallway, avoiding obstacles thanks to the thin threads of light that found their way in through cracks in the boards. It was moderately warmer inside.

The interior doors had been removed, along with every stick of furniture and most of the fixtures. Rats scurried through the litter of food wrappers, beer cans and yellow newspapers.

Snoring, disheveled men, some of whom cradled booze bottles like teddy bears in their arms, occupied most of the first-floor rooms. Seth found the stairwell, which had boards nailed across its entrance and a sign warning that the stairs were unsafe. He ducked under the boards and went up anyway, with cautious steps.

The second floor was where the younger crowd hung out. Seth was brought up short by a haggard kid his own age, sitting cross-legged in the middle of a mess of crack pipes and used condoms. Behind the kid was a girl in a sleeping bag, her mouth agape in sloppy gasping breaths.

"Get out of here, asshole." The kid had long red hair and an acne-spotted face, and eyes that burned with such a glow that Seth could have easily mistaken him for a vampire if he hadn't spoken up.

Seth didn't argue. He'd had enough fights for one night. He retreated to the stairwell and tried the third floor. The stairs sagged and creaked under him.

Up here, the predominant smells were dust and mildew. He entered the nearest apartment, his feet leaving long scuffing tracks in the grime. His eyes had adjusted to the gloom enough for him to make his way to the tiny bathroom.

The door had been removed, as had the toilet and sink. The ends of pipes stuck out of the wall and floor. The bathtub was built-in, the porcelain chipped and festering with rusty growths. Dried silt covered the bottom.

It would do.

He opened the case and felt through it, choosing what he wanted by touch. A large cross, he laid in the bathroom doorway. Four cloves of garlic went on either side of the cross.

Now that he was indoors, without the windows of the car giving anyone who passed by the chance to look in on him, he removed everything from the suitcase. It was still heavier than it should have been. Some minutes of probing around inside helped him find a pair of loops. He curled his fingers through them and pulled, and the false bottom lifted away.

The hidden compartment held a book. When he saw it, Seth's eyes blurred with tears. He recognized the heavy leather-bound volume.

His father must not have fully trusted the security of the Cohort. Something had made him decide to keep his precious journal elsewhere. Whatever the reason, Seth felt an aching joy.

The secrets of the Legion wouldn't be kept from him after all.

PART TWO – THE SHROUD
March

CHAPTER 7

"How was the funeral?" Jill asked.

Fiona Sevrin pulled off her black hat with its little netting of veil and tossed it onto the coffee table. "Dismal."

A headache centered behind her aching eyes. She massaged the bridge of her nose and groaned. It had been necessary to stare unblinkingly at nothing in order to force her protesting eyeballs into manufacturing enough tears to look the proper part.

"I wish I could have gone," Jill said, "but I understand Karen's parents wanting to keep it small and private. Do you even technically call it a funeral when there's no–"

"Body?"

Jill winced. "I didn't mean–"

Fiona waved it off. "I know. The case isn't officially closed, but by now the cops have pretty much given up."

"She could be alive, though, couldn't she? We don't know for sure that she's dead."

Sinking into her favorite chair, the one by the floor-to-ceiling window wall of tinted glass, Fiona tipped her head back and tried to work the kinks from her neck. "Even if she is alive, it's been too long. Nobody would even know what she looked like by now."

She and Karen Melvey and Jill had been best friends since college. Or, rather, she and Karen had been best friends, and Jill the pathetic hanger-on that they'd never managed to shake. Karen had been the golden good girl of the trio, Fiona the sexy party animal, and Jill the dumpy bookworm who seemed to think that writing the occasional term paper for her friends was a fitting trade for living vicariously through Karen and Fiona's more exciting social lives.

Now Karen was as good as dead, and Fiona *still* wasn't able to shake Jill. Even leeches dropped off after damn near twenty years, didn't they? Once they'd bloated their fill, didn't they pop?

She could have afforded the apartment's ever-steepening rent without a roommate. Ralph Lauren and Vera Wang wouldn't be losing any sleep over her competition yet, but Fiona Sevrin designs were selling to many of the city's pricier boutiques and turning up in magazines, draped artfully on models as gaunt and haughty–if perhaps never as beautiful–as she had been during her own days on the catwalk.

But whenever she imagined telling Jill to move out, and seeing Jill's fat face crumple in hangdog mournfulness, Fiona knew that even she couldn't be *that* cruel.

"I know how hard it's been for you."

"Hard?" Fiona twitched a little guiltily; she'd been daydreaming of having the entire apartment to herself, thinking how she could turn Jill's room into a wardrobe and not have to store her spare clothes at her brother's anymore.

"Well, sure," Jill said. "All of it that the police have put you through. The waiting and everything. The close calls and false alarms, when it never did turn out to be her."

"Oh. Yeah," Fiona said.

She thought of the hours and hours spent mailing leaflets, writing letters, appearing with Karen's parents on the news to make public pleas to the kidnapper. It had gone on and on, like it was never going to stop. But, gradually, interest had slackened as the months turned into years and other cases demanded police attention.

And now, the funeral. Or memorial service. Or whatever the heck you wanted to call it. The only ones present besides Karen's parents and Fiona herself had been the director of the hospital–she had some nerve, Karen's mother had huffed, showing her face–and the detective who'd handled the case.

Detective Kyle Jackson was still blond and tan and buff, looking enough like Brad Pitt to more than satisfy Fiona's demanding fantasies. She wouldn't have minded taking him home for a souvenir, but knew that it'd be a mistake to get involved with anyone connected to the investigation.

"Richard's family didn't go?"

"What?" Jill's question cut into her new daydream and brought her irritably back to drab reality.

"Richard's family. Were they there?"

"Why would they have been?"

"Well… " Jill hooked a handful of tissues and blew her nose. It sounded like a bullfrog croaking in a swamp. "I thought they might have. Poor Richard. Poor Karen. It seems like only yesterday that we were at their wedding. They were so happy, ideal for each other."

"If I don't get out of these pantyhose, I'm going to lose my mind," Fiona said, rising from her chair and heading for her bedroom.

But it wasn't the pantyhose; if she had to listen to one more word about how perfect Karen and Richard had been, she thought she might puke.

Come to think of it, Jill had been the one to fix those two up in the first place. It was an old game by then, Jill introducing her prettier friends to various guys, guys she secretly wanted for herself but figured that having them date her roommates was the closest she'd ever come.

As if either of them had needed fixing up. Karen in particular. Everyone had adored her. Even Fiona's own brother, Anthony, who was just as gay as gay Paree, had gone ga-ga over beautiful, idyllic Karen. Karen the angel. Karen the saint. Karen the too-fucking-good-to-be-true.

"Shit," she muttered.

Fiona's room was spare and sparse and neat, with another of the window-walls looking out on the city skyline. The focus of the décor was an antique dressing table with a bulb-ringed vanity mirror. The dealer who'd sold it to her claimed that it had once belonged to one of the Gabor sisters. Whether true or not,

Fiona didn't care. What mattered was that it certainly *looked* like something a silver screen goddess would have owned.

Beside the vanity were a full-length mirror and a walk-in closet. She stripped off her black dress, black slip, black pantyhose, and posed for a minute in her lace-trimmed black push-up bra and panties. She pursed her lips in a come-hither smile and batted her eyelashes at her reflection. Black looked *good* on her. So what if she was close to forty? If only Detective Jackson could see her now…

Shimmying out of her lacy black undies, she put on no-less-sexy peach colored silky ones from Victoria's Secret and then got into slacks and a cashmere sweater.

Jill was still on the couch when Fiona went back into the living room. The television was on, tuned to a nature documentary, and Jill had made serious inroads into a bag of Reese's miniature Peanut Butter Cups.

Fiona picked up her everyday leather purse and began transferring things back into it from the little black clutch bag she'd carried earlier.

"You're going out?" Jill asked, raising her eyebrows. "Again?"

"It's not a date," Fiona said. "I'm going to my brother's. Later!"

She escaped before Jill could offer to tag along. Unlikely; Jill said that Anthony was nice and all, but something about him gave her the creeps. Fiona understood perfectly. There were times when Anthony gave *her* the creeps, too.

The sun had set. Fiona made sure her car doors were locked, throwing a hasty glance at the moody shadows lurking in the entrances to alleyways. She was all right until she drove past the dense pocket of black that was Landover Park. Then, her skin prickled and she shivered in a way that was almost delicious.

Fiona didn't believe that her brother had seen real vampires in the park one long-ago Christmas night. Anthony got some bizarre ideas in his head. He was smart, brilliant, a genius, but he had always been a little on the nutty side.

Still, she couldn't deny that Landover Park had a bad reputation. It wasn't just the brutally murdered victims of what the papers at the time had called the Nativity Massacre. A steady stream of other people had been found dead in the depths of the park over the years. Many more had simply disappeared from the vicinity. Everyone said it was the stomping grounds of some bad local gangs, but no one ever knew which gangs in particular.

She could have detoured around, but Landover Street, past the hospital, was the most direct route. And if she was feeling honest with herself, she admitted that there was a certain daredevil thrill about the place. She regarded it the same way she regarded dangerous men. Attractive, but don't get too close. Don't let down your guard, or you might get hurt.

Once she had passed the park, her goose bumps smoothed out and she drove the rest of the way feeling warmer. Soon she'd parked in Anthony's driveway and let herself in by way of the kitchen door.

The smell of baking cookies washed over her in a warm mélange of butter, brown sugar, and chocolate. Wire racks on the counters held a cooling dozen, each cookie the size of her palm and studded with gooey, melting chocolate chips.

"Why, Fiona," Mrs. Boryenka said. Her apron was dusted with flour and her broad face wreathed in a smile. "Your brother said he thought you might stop by and here you are in the house."

"Here I am," Fiona said. "Hi, Mrs. B."

She gazed at the cookies and debated with herself. The scale hadn't fluctuated recently, and she *had* had grapefruit for breakfast and yogurt for lunch, but with so much going on today she'd skipped her usual hour of aerobics. She had gained eight pounds since she was twenty-one, and knew that the potential was in her to blimp up, the way her mother and aunts had in later life.

The housekeeper's eyes twinkled. "I lead you into the temptation?"

"I really shouldn't."

"I could put some in the bag for you to take home."

It almost sounded more like a threat than an offer. Fiona caved in and selected a cookie, with a firm mental command that she would stop at one.

"When I am a girl," Mrs. Boryenka said, "and my mother wanted me so much to do the gymnastics, she is very strict. I could eat this, I could not eat that, I have to practice every day for many hours. My coach, even more the tyrant. I could not wait until I was too old for the competition, and I could do whatever I want." She looked down at herself and patted her amply-padded frame. "Maybe that is why I never win the gold medals? But I am happy now. And my Stefan, he liked me better with the meat on the bones."

The first bite of the cookie, which had been soft and chewy and wonderful, suddenly had the taste and texture of wet paper.

Fiona had seen pictures of Mrs. B. as a teenager, all eighty-five pounds of her muscular little body packed into a leotard. Fifty years later, she was twice as heavy, a dimpled and ruddy-cheeked gnome lady with bright eyes and a curly cap of pewter hair.

Unbelievable, the way some people let themselves go. And Mrs. B. had been trim to start with. Not like Jill, who'd been a porker all her life.

Swallowing was a chore, but she did it. "Great cookies, Mrs. B."

"Have another if you like."

"Maybe later. Is Anthony around?"

"In the study where he is very busy. He is a good man, your brother. Did you know he got my Stanislav the interview with the science company?"

"I'm not sure how much clout his name still carries in those circles," Fiona said with a wry smile, "but best of luck to Stan. I hope he gets the job."

Carrying the cookie, no longer wanting the rest of it and just hoping to ditch it somehow, she left the kitchen and found her brother in the study. She stood in the doorway for a few minutes, waiting for him to acknowledge her presence.

His face lit by a computer screen and his fingers flying tappety-tappety over the keyboard, he looked, she thought, like some sort of weird hermit or prophet. His eyes were wild in his thin face. All he needed was a long beard, a pair of sandals, and maybe a crooked staff or two slabs of stone with the Ten Commandments engraved on them.

Anthony was a year younger than Fiona. He'd been one of those obnoxious boy geniuses who'd graduated high school at age ten and gotten his first master's degree at fifteen. While Fiona had been busy with boys and clothes and cheerleading, Anthony had been publishing articles on gene sequencing.

And then, out of total left field, he'd up and joined a seminary. Their relatives had given up even trying to understand him by that time. Fiona remembered one of her aunts remarking that Anthony was going to be dead by the time he was twenty, burned out by his own racing brain. Alternately, he might have a breakdown and end up in a nut house, like Great-Uncle George.

Watching him now, hunched over his keyboard and typing in a feverish blur, she thought that while he'd outlived the first prediction, he was well on his way to making good on the other. That stunt he'd pulled fifteen years ago, that stunt with Karen, was not what she would call the workings of a sane mind. Thinking he had seen vampires didn't say reassuring things about his mental health, either.

"Hah," Anthony said, with a note of satisfaction.

He hit one final key, then sat back and craned his neck from side to side. Even from the doorway, Fiona heard the vertebrae crackle. He saw her, and jumped.

"Boo," she said.

"I didn't hear you come in." He blinked at his watch. "How was it? Any problems? Any questions?"

"No and no." Fiona found room for her slim but shapely backside on a chair only half covered with books. She perched there, feet crossed at the ankles. "Here. Eat this."

He obligingly took and finished the cookie. "*C'est tout fini*, then?"

"Say too finny, all right," she said, giving the words a deliberately awful pronunciation just to make him get that sour look. "So there's no more chance of backing out now if you decide you've gotten in over your head."

"I haven't, and I won't, but even if I did, are you telling me that your lusted-after detective wouldn't re-open the case?"

"Oh, I don't know." She shook her head. "I still can't believe we did it this way. We didn't have to."

"This was best," he said. "No well-meaning but bothersome interference from the relatives."

"What about the rest of your plan?"

Anthony beamed. "In motion even as we speak. I'm due to meet with my hired gentlemen tomorrow night to make the exchange. I'm close, Fee. So close. It'll be a complex laboratory process, though. The most complex I've ever attempted."

"Spare me the technical details," Fiona said. "I wouldn't understand anyway."

"I've explained to you it as clearly as I know how," he said. "I've tried to make it simple. What do you need, words of one syllable?"

"No. Forget it."

"This is a great and glorious thing," he said, his lower lip sticking out in a pout the way it had when he was a little boy, miffed that no one appreciated his brilliance.

Fiona sighed. "You know I'm proud of you, even if you'll go to jail if anyone ever finds out."

"Jail," scoffed Anthony. "I don't worry about *jail*. This is all in the name of science and the name of faith. Two of the highest callings. What could be more pure than that?"

Chapter 8

They had no reason to think that their employer might try to double-cross them, but both Philips and Renard were on alert just the same, because that was the kind of men that they were.

And, as Renard kept saying, it had all gone too easily.

"Not a shot fired, not a person killed, not so much as an airport security guard giving us the funny look," he said. He was short and wiry and lean, redheaded, resembling the fox he'd been named for. "That means it'll all go balls-up at the end, right when we think we're home free."

"Or God will get us for it later," Philips said, feeling a pang of guilt.

He'd done some low things in his time, and had a list of felonies as long as his arm. But robbing a church? That was a new one. He tried to fight off childhood memories of rousing gospel music and a much younger Lamont Philips in the outfit of an altar boy.

"I'll burn that bridge when I come to it," Renard said.

"Stealing the Shroud of Turin from a peaceable nunnery? If that doesn't count as a bridge-burning, pal, I don't know what would." Philips rubbed a gloved thumb along the line of scar that split his left cheek. All in dark fatigues, he knew he was invisible in the night except for his teeth and the whites of his eyes.

They were both equipped to the nines with a rogue's assortment of weapons and tools. Never Boy Scouts, either of them, but always prepared.

After all, it *could* be a trick. They could be walking into the hornet's nest. This placid rural setting might be a ruse meant to lull them into letting their guards down, and then armed men would spring out of hiding and the fight would be on.

It'd be strange to see the serene night shattered by gunfire and explosives, but at the same time, it would be kind of cool. Philips was the one who lived for action. He was never happier than when he was cruising the adrenaline wave and blowing shit up. Renard... well, Renard just liked to kill people, the stealthier the better.

"Think he'll try to cheat us on the money?" Renard asked.

Philips snorted. "Would you?"

"No, but I know us too well. He might think he can get away with it."

"We'll have to wait and see."

Time passed as they waited, their car parked on the side of a winding country road. The only man-made lights to be seen were sparkles in the distance, and the greater sprawl of stars overhead would have daunted many a city-dweller.

"You think it's legit?" Renard asked in an oddly hesitant tone unlike his usual brash manner. "The Shroud, I mean."

"The man says the one we went after is the real one," Philips said. "Me, I'm wary treading on this theological ground."

Granny Bea had told him that if he didn't mend his evil ways, he would go straight to hell. And that lecture had come after he'd been caught shoplifting nothing more than a comic book. What would Granny Bea say if she could see him now?

He and Renard didn't usually talk about the specifics of their jobs. Then again, they were usually hired to steal valuable objects, kidnap the children of the wealthy and influential, or arrange 'accidents' for those selfsame wealthy and influential. In all of those instances, their employers' reasons were pretty straightforward and easy to understand.

In this case...

Philips understood that in certain limited circles, the genuine Shroud of Turin would be worth a fortune, but why would a lone man pay such a steep fee and go to such huge risks for something that wouldn't make him any sort of profit or political advancement? Though there were apparently a few decoys floating around, this still counted as a one-of-a-kind item. Not the sort of thing a person could expect to sell.

"So why does he want it?" Renard asked, mirroring Philips' thoughts.

"Search me."

"Can't sell it."

"I know. Blackmail, maybe?"

"Who would he blackmail? The Church?" Renard slouched in his seat, shaking his head. "Could be he's a collector. We've seen enough of them to know that money would be no object if they thought they could glom the *Mona Lisa* for their private collection and gloat over it after midnight."

"I think he's a priest."

"No shit?" Renard said uneasily. He touched the haft of the long knife at his waist as if for luck, the way a religious man might have touched a crucifix. Renard was never without "Roxy," which he treated better than most of the women he met. "What gives you that idea?"

"A feeling, nothing more." Despite his own troubled and troubling thoughts, it bemused Philips to see any sort of superstition in his partner.

Their infiltration of St. Olivia's had been absurdly easy. No armed guards, no dogs, no security system. The small chapel was unlocked. And the glass-topped case had been right where their employer said it had been.

Looking through the glass at the scorched image imprinted on the cloth had given Philips a qualm, but Renard, at the time, hadn't seemed to care. The doubts must have been working on him ever since, building up.

"Why would a priest steal from a church?" Renard said. "Me, I thought he was a doctor or something. Educated guy."

"Priests *are* educated guys," Philips said.

"Yeah, but the way this one talked it was more like he was a scientist."

Before Philips could reply, headlights swung around a curve and dazzled the interior of their car. The other vehicle pulled off to the side of the two-lane blacktop behind them. Philips activated the hazard blinkers and popped the trunk. If anyone else happened by–unlikely; they had been here for an hour already and this was the first car they'd seen–it would look like roadside assistance in action.

He and Renard got out. They didn't draw any weapons, but they were ready to react in a split second should the need arise.

The driver's side door of the other car opened. Its dome light showed that the driver was the sole occupant, unless someone else hunkered down in the back seat out of their line of sight.

The driver got out and swung the door shut. He wore a long London Fog coat and held a case, not a briefcase but a soft-sided duffel that bulged as if stuffed with what it was supposed to be stuffed with–bundles of money.

A lot of money. For that kind of cash, one of them should have at least been shot at, wounded. The only adversary they'd faced was one sleeping teenage novice, whom not even Renard had had the heart to kill. Nary a firefight or ambush to speak of.

"You're here," the man said. Up close, he proved to be younger than Philips remembered him. Maybe mid-thirties, clean-cut. He was fidgety, nearly dancing in anticipation, his eyes glittering and his teeth chewing at his lower lip. "Were you successful?"

"If we weren't, we wouldn't be here," Renard said.

"You got it, then?"

"That's what you hired us to do," Philips said. He nodded toward the trunk.

Despite his dancing anticipation, the other man hesitated. He had the expression of someone who'd waited so long for a moment that, now it was here, could hardly believe it. His gaze darted toward the trunk, but all he saw were a couple of pieces of luggage and a tool kit.

"Don't forget our money," Renard said.

"Yes, of course. Your money." He unzipped the duffel and tilted it toward them so that they could see for themselves that banded stacks of currency filled it.

"Good," Philips said. "The object is in the suitcase on the left."

"You put it in a *suitcase*?" He sounded scandalized and offended.

"Easier to get through customs."

Renard took the duffel bag and pawed through it, doing a fast count. "Looks like it's all here."

"A suitcase," the man muttered. "Did you have any trouble?"

"Nope," Philips said. "Everything was just how you said it was. Nobody even saw us." He hefted the suitcase out of the trunk, closed the trunk, set the suitcase on the back of the car, and thumbed the catches.

The rest of the stuff was window-dressing–folded clothes, a plastic bag of toiletries, a paperback spy novel. At the bottom was a cardboard gift box the right size to hold a sweater. Philips handed the box over.

"Dear God," the man said in barely more than a breath. His hands shook. He retreated to his own car and set the box on the hood, then lifted the lid. A single finger stroked the coarse cloth inside with a trembling reverence.

"Looks like we're done here," Philips said. He looked over at Renard, who was riffling a stack of bills and grinning like a fox in a henhouse, then back to the other man. "If there's anything else, you know how to contact us."

"Yes, yes," he said, brushing them off with hardly a second glance.

It felt wrong, all unfinished somehow. Philips thought about asking why the guy wanted the thing, even started to form the question before stopping himself. Not their business. Their business was the money in the duffel. He made an inner promise to give a hefty donation to the church, in hopes of making up for it.

They went back to their car, still not relaxing quite yet. Philips kept an eye on their erstwhile employer, but the man only stayed where he was, staring down into the box with a mood that fit somewhere between reverence and avarice.

Philips started the engine. Renard sat with the duffel on his lap and his hand on his gun.

The other man didn't move as they drove away. Philips watched him recede in the mirrors until they went around a curve and lost sight of him. A slow and cautious sense of completion began to creep into him.

Mission accomplished.

Best thing to do now was put it out of their minds. Forget about it. Start thinking about the next job, whatever it might prove to be. This one was one for the record books, though. Definitely one of the weirder experiences–

"Hey, Philips." In the glow of the dashboard lights, Renard looked green.

"Yeah?"

"I think your priest passed us funny money. I'm seeing the same ten or twelve serial numbers over and over."

"I knew it!" Philips spat.

Renard made a funny gasping noise and clutched at his throat. Air whistled thinly in and out of his windpipe. He lurched against his seatbelt, dumping the duffel into the passenger side footwell.

The car slued across the road as Philips slammed on the brakes. He brought it to a stop straddling the broken white line and turned toward Renard.

"What? You choking?"

As soon as he said it, he knew it couldn't be right. Renard hadn't had anything to eat, didn't have so much as a stick of gum in his mouth. And it was not technically possible for someone to choke on his tongue, not even in the grips of epilepsy.

A foamy curd formed on Renard's lips, like the froth at the mouth of a rabid dog. His body thrashed side to side. His head rapped the side window. His knees drummed the underside of the dashboard. His stamping feet burst the bands on the money.

Philips' body went into action even while his mind was reeling. He jabbed the release button on Renard's seatbelt, then lunged from the car and raced around to the other side. He yanked the passenger door open and Renard toppled out onto the asphalt in a litter of loose cash. Eddies of wind picked up and swirled the bills down the road. Philips knelt beside his partner.

Renard's agonized eyes rolled up to him. His face had gone dark and his chest heaved as he tried in vain to draw air into his lungs. More foam bubbled from his lips. His clawing fingers gouged at his swelling throat.

"Hold on," Philips said, trying to sound reassuring while inside he was frantic. Renard was strangling before his eyes, and all he could think of to do was to perform an emergency tracheotomy. He knew the principles of the operation, he had a knife… it might kill Renard, but if he didn't do *something*, Renard was as good as dead already.

But before he could do more than get the knife in his hand, Renard shuddered and released his bladder and bowels and sank back on the pavement. Philips felt for a pulse in the wrist and found nothing.

"Shit!" he yelled into the quiet country night.

He crouched there for a while, fists pressed to his temples while possibilities sped through his brain.

Men like Renard didn't up and die of a seizure for no reason. He hadn't choked. Hadn't been stung by a bee and gone into a severe allergic reaction.

Something had done this.

Poison was the most likely bet.

A fast-acting poison… not something in the air because Philips was unaffected. A contact agent, then. Renard wasn't wearing gloves. A contact agent absorbed through the skin of his hands, which had then gone through his system like a supersonic jet and caused the anaphylactic shock. Swelled his throat closed. Killed him.

A contact agent on the money. Renard had handled the cash with his bare hands.

Betrayal after all.

Anger seared a napalm trench through Philips' mind.

They were both supposed to be dead. Their employer must have expected that their mercenary greed would have them both delving into the money, fingering it, dividing it up.

And it might have worked. Philips could have suffered his seizure behind the wheel, and driven them off the road to tumble down a steep hill and crash, where their bodies would have lain unnoticed for days or even weeks.

He looked again at the car, askew across the white line with the doors standing wide open, a corpse spilling out, and money whirling off into the bushes at the edge of the road. The sky was still black, dawn hours away, but someone could come by at any moment.

Working as fast as he could while still being careful, he loaded Renard's body back into the passenger seat and collected every stray bill that he could find. Counterfeit and poisoned, it was worthless to him, but he couldn't leave it scattered along the road for some local kid pedaling along on his bike to find and pick up.

Another reason to be quick–their treacherous employer might take it into his head to drive along after them at a prudent distance. He'd want to make sure that neither of them survived, might have some plan for destroying the evidence.

Philips didn't like getting back in the car. He was too conscious of the cash strewn loose in the passenger footwell. It wasn't like it was alive, like it was going to attack him in a fluttery paper swarm, but he didn't want any of the bills somehow catching a gust and blowing into his face, against his skin.

He drove with more attention paid to the road behind him than the road ahead. The grim reality of Renard slumped and cooling in the seat next to him kept intruding on the knife-edge sharpness of his thoughts. Renard had been the closest thing he had to a friend, damn it. They had been through a lot together. And now Renard was dead.

"I won't let him get away with it," Philips told the corpse. "If he's like the other ones we've dealt with, he probably thinks that even if the poison didn't get us both, the survivor couldn't do anything. Couldn't go to the police, because what would I say? That the guy who hired me to steal a major religious artifact murdered my buddy?"

Renard didn't answer. Only sat there, the tip of his tongue sticking out of his foam-crusted mouth as his head drooped onto his chest. He stank.

The air in the car rapidly became unbreathable, but Philips couldn't roll down a window and let in any breeze that might throw bills around.

"He'll think that because he never gave us his name, we can't find him," Philips said. "But you know what? While he was drooling over his prize, I got his plates. Maybe he was savvy enough to not be driving his own wheels, but they never think that way."

Philips quit talking then, mostly because he was trying to minimize the amount of foul air he took in.

No headlights came up from behind, and by the time he reached the main highway, he had still not seen any other cars.

He stopped worrying about getting away, and started worrying about finding a place where he could torch the car and its grisly contents.

CHAPTER 9

Although the lab was small, once a basement wine cellar accessible by way of a trap door in the floor of the study closet, it was smartly equipped and adequate to his needs in all ways but one.

"What I'd give for a better computer," Anthony Sevrin muttered.

His was struggling to cope. The screen remained stubbornly fixed, the progress bar moving with the painstaking slowness of a clock's hour hand. If the hard drive began to grind and smoke, he wouldn't be surprised.

The ironic part was that this computer was more than the equal of the ones he'd used in his first job out of grad school. At the time, he'd considered himself spoiled by the very generous funding and equipment. Those computers had been huge banks of electronics, all blinking lights and whirring reel-to-reel tape decks.

Personal computers, back then, had still been the stuff of science fiction. Dream machines of the future. Hardly anyone in the 1980s had anticipated a day when a personal computer would become as common to the modern household as the television or the microwave oven. Not to mention the revolution in phones and hand-held gadgets.

Excitement and exhaustion warred within him. He'd been at it for over twenty-four hours now, and had gotten precious little sleep before that while waiting to hear from Philips and Renard.

Their deaths nagged at him a little. Killing was breaking a commandment, even if it was done as part of God's greater scheme. He'd had to do it. Just like with Richard Cross so many years ago. Richard would have ruined everything. Richard and his stubborn pride.

Anthony always regretted the necessity of murder, and was glad that he wasn't called upon to do it often.

The two mercenaries had done nothing to him, but he could not take the chance that they might ever talk. A few words to the wrong ears, and everything Anthony had been striving toward could fall apart all around him.

The other deaths on his conscience weren't really his fault. He had only been doing his job. He was a scientist. How was he to know that the project's security would be so slipshod? All of that was in the past now anyway. Behind him. Best forgotten. He had far greater and more important work ahead.

Would a grateful world ever recognize him for his achievement? Would they even know of his part in it?

Anthony quashed that line of thought. He was not in this for his own personal glory. Ambition had no place here. Neither was he trying to redeem his past failures. His was a higher, purer calling. God had given him this mission, chosen him for this task.

All he had to do was look at the Shroud to be reminded of his purpose.

The sweeping wonder he'd felt when he had first unfolded the ancient, brittle cloth and beheld the visage imprinted on it recurred to him in a tingle of goose bumps.

To think that he held in his very hands the cloth that had been wrapped around the martyred body of the son of God was awe-inspiring, daunting.

The Shroud was laid out on a long table that took up most of the available floor space. The image on the ancient cloth was that of a man who would have been tall and well-built for Biblical times. The face was careworn in repose, bearded, haloed with shoulder-length hair.

Darker spots marked the cloth in key locations–where the crossed hands might have rested on the chest, at the ankles, along the brow, at the side where the spear of a Roman soldier had pierced the body.

It was from these that Anthony had extracted his samples, doing so with the utmost care. He had the deft touch of a skilled surgeon and did not want to disturb the artifact any more than he had to.

The first step had been to irrigate one of the spots with a fine stream of distilled water shot from a syringe, allowing it to soak into the dry cloth. He'd drawn the resulting liquid into a pipette and transferred it to a petri dish, then added a solution of his own invention.

This was the key, this above all else. This special solution.

Conventional wisdom held that only living cells could be cloned. Bringing extinct species or dead people back to life was held to be unattainable, no matter what leaping advances the science of cloning took in the years to come.

Conventional wisdom, Anthony knew, was garbage. Thanks in large part to him.

He had developed the theory of the solution while still in college, and attained it within a few months of beginning his work with the ill-fated Genetic Engineering Research and Laboratories. The purpose of the solution was simple: to revitalize a dead cell's DNA, thereby making it possible to clone something that had already died.

A pity that it had all gone so hideously wrong.

The company, commonly known as GENERAL, had gone out of business in the wake of colossal lawsuits and public outcry. The few surviving scientists, Anthony Sevrin among them, had scattered into other jobs, and counted themselves lucky to be alive.

The truth of it was that his solution did not belong to him. It had been developed while he was in the employ of GENERAL, and the extensive forms and agreements he'd signed stated that the rights remained with the company.

Well, what they—however few and far between they were these days—didn't know couldn't hurt him. It wasn't like he was using their property for his own profit, either. This was for the benefit of the entire world.

Once he'd revitalized the DNA of the blood sample taken from the Shroud, he had run it through the computer for analysis. He wanted to make sure he had the genuine article before he went any further. That was the task currently occupying the computer's circuits.

"One drop," he said. "One viable drop of blood, please, that's all I need."

The computer had already confirmed that the rusty substance was blood, and was now trying to determine what kind.

He did wonder about the marks that formed the image of the face and body. What had caused those? They looked scorched, as if by the divine fire of God.

During his time at the seminary, he'd fallen in with a group of older boys who fancied themselves conspiracy theorists. It had been from them that Anthony had first heard the rumor that the commonly-known-of Shroud of Turin was a hoax and that the real one was hidden away to prevent any thieves from getting their hands on it.

Later, when he had heard the Word of God and knew what his life's destiny was meant to be, Anthony amassed a collection of books on the subject and did research in some of the finest libraries in the world. He visited churches and monasteries and universities, talking to theologians.

Gradually, the pieces came together.

The real Shroud was at St. Olivia's. Hidden in plain sight in an out-of-the-way nunnery that no one would expect to harbor one of the greatest relics of Christendom.

His computer let out a tired beep as it finished analyzing the sample. Anthony leaned close, heart pounding, holding his breath.

The held breath burst out of him. "What?!"

He read the words again, thinking—hoping!—that he had misread them. But they still said the same thing.

"That can't be," he said. "That can't be at all. This *is* the one! It has to be the right one."

The argument failed to change the words on the screen.

"Goat's blood?" Anthony shook his head. "Goat's blood, no, that's wrong, it must be a mistake."

Stepping back, closing his eyes, and breathing in slow, deep breaths, he calmed himself. When he opened his eyes again, the letters were the same.

"A contaminated sample," he said. "I'll take one from another spot, and run the tests again."

No one was there to reply, but he thought that this sounded like a good idea. The rational, scientific approach. Some goat's blood must have gotten spilled on the cloth at some point in history. Yes. A lot could happen in two millennia.

He repeated the process, though his back and eyes and head ached from the strain and the lack of sleep. Irrigate the cloth. Draw the liquid into the pipette. Treat with the revitalizing solution. Run the analysis.

Wait. And wait. And wait.

At first, he paced while the computer hummed and flickered. Then he sat. Finally, with weariness like iron weights on his eyelids, he leaned back and dozed.

With sleep came the faces. Seraphic faces… except for the fangs, and the red-rimmed eyes.

His own personal dark temptation, beckoning to him. Promising an embrace and a kiss unlike anything Anthony had ever known. The faces, the bodies… sweet dark desires that had haunted him since the night of the Nativity, the night of the birth, so many years ago.

Dreaming, he found himself there again, reliving the wonder and the horror of it all.

CHAPTER 10

Landover Park was a place of winter hush and crystal-black night wonder. Snow muffled his steps and absorbed the city noises. Fluffy layers coated the benches, the boughs, the statues, the paths, the grassy lawns and playground equipment. Streetlights cast halos through which snowflakes fluttered like downy white moths.

The beacon of the Star of Bethlehem guided him, solitary Wise Man that he was, east toward the heart of the park.

Anthony smiled at the comparison. It wasn't entirely apt. But there was just something so fitting, so right, about all of this. Today of all days. Tonight of all nights.

And it was so nice when things went according to plan.

He glimpsed the snow-lined, slanted roof of the makeshift plywood stable ahead. A pole rose from the wooden structure, and the star-shaped golden light twinkled and sparkled from its height. At its base, an angel shivered.

The players were dedicated. He liked that. He could respect that. It took a degree of faith and devotion to be out here, in the snow and the dark, with hardly any audience, dressed in costumes that weren't made for warmth.

At the moment, so late on this solitary Christmas night, the living Nativity scene was not presenting its most divine face.

Joseph and the shepherd and two of the Magi clustered together for a smoke break. The third of the Magi was eating a sandwich. The Virgin Mary sat on a bale of hay, reading a Stephen King novel. The shepherd's boy had hitched himself partway up onto the roof to talk to the angel, a teenage girl in a long white wig with a gold wire hoop attached.

Anthony's gaze focused on Mary and he frowned. She was too ordinary. Her hair was more beige than blond, and she had a round face that was chapped from the cold. As he watched, she sniffled and blew her nose.

Disappointing.

But at least they tried.

He had to give them credit for that much. They did try.

His car was on the other side of the park. He usually rode the bus when he was in the guise of "Brother Tony." People expected it. Part of the whole humility thing, the poverty thing. Plus, it kept his comings and goings from being tracked.

The coat he wore was large, voluminous. When he slipped his hands into the pockets, there were slits that allowed him to reach through the lining and touch the bundle secured to his chest.

The baby was sound asleep, the little darling.

It had been ridiculously easy. Only half of the evening shift nurses had shown up, some citing the snow, others highly suspect illness. Christmas Fever, the nursing supervisor had called it.

Of the ones who did come to work, they spent most of their time in the break rooms or at the nurse's station, gorging themselves on cookies and other treats.

He had slipped into the nursery unobserved, unchallenged. And there had been the infant. Radiant and serene. Perfect in every way.

Divine.

His gloved finger traced the curve of the fragile little head, covered in a striped knitted cap.

He hoped he'd got the dosage right. Sedation was so touch-and-go with babies, but a cry at the wrong moment would ruin everything. It was all God's plan, and God surely wouldn't want Anthony to get caught, so the baby was sure to remain quiet. Still, God did help those who helped themselves. No sense demanding too much of His goodwill. Not when insurance in the form of a sedative was so readily available.

Getting past the living Nativity players would be the final hurdle, barring some surprise encounter with a meter maid or other pedestrian on the sidewalk.

As Anthony was about to move on, he heard a low, strange cry that instantly raised all the hairs on the back of his neck and froze him in place.

A shape raced out of the shadows. Pale, naked, its body so slim and smooth that Anthony could not immediately tell if it was male or female. Strings of hair flew around its head. When it passed beneath a streetlight, it cast no shadow on the stark white snow, but the light fell with awful, revealing clarity on an inhuman face where red eyes burned and fangs bristled from a gaping mouth.

He knew what it was immediately, and without question.

The vampire uttered its strange cry again, answered by others that emerged from the shelter of the trees. One was a girl in a rumpled parochial school uniform. The other was a middle-aged man who looked like any of the countless hundreds of businessmen, accountants, bank managers, and other nine-to-five commuters.

The three of them burst onto the Nativity scene. The Wise Man with the sandwich gave a choked cry of alarm, spraying crumbs from his mouth, an instant before the schoolgirl leaped on him and bore him to the ground. The businessman went straight for Mary, his eyes burning with terrible lust. The pale, naked thing launched itself headlong into the group of smokers. One flailing hand raked Joseph's cheek, tearing it, and Anthony vividly saw cigarette smoke puff out through the bleeding hole.

Atop the stable, the girl in the angel outfit clapped her hands to her mouth and screamed.

The businessman tackled Mary and knocked her off the bale where she had supposedly been sitting in adoration of her infant. Her book went flying. The manger itself tipped over, dumping a small pink form into the hay.

A doll. A Cabbage Patch doll with yellow yarn hair and a vapid, smiling face.

Anthony didn't know whether to be disgusted or amused.

Or in fear for his very life and soul.

He *was* afraid, yes. Terror yammered inside him. But he couldn't move, couldn't look away from the carnage.

The schoolgirl, whose skin might have been the color of cocoa when she was alive but was muddy grey now, ripped off the third Wise Man's false beard and thrust her jaws under his chin. His legs jerked and kicked.

The businessman and Mary hit the back wall of the plywood structure. It wobbled. The angel, waist encircled by a harness securing her to a pole like a rider on a parade float, squealed and held on. Her feathery wings were askew. The shepherd's boy fell backward off the roof, careened into one of the plastic sheep, and went head over heels in the snow.

The naked vampire left Joseph clutching at the ragged flaps of his face, and went for another of the Magi. The man flung a flimsy papier-mâché urn—meant to contain myrrh?—at the creature's head, but it did not slow. There was a wet noise, and a fountain of blood.

The last Wise Man demonstrated his wisdom by running, but was hampered by the long heavy robes and the deep snow and the way he kept throwing back panicked looks to see if any of them were after him.

Thanks to this, he almost ran right into the smartly-dressed woman who appeared, as if she'd materialized out of the night. Seeing her at the last minute, this latter-day Balthazar shouted, "Look out, lady, we have to get out of here!" and grabbed for her arm.

She seized his instead, yanked it to her mouth, and plunged her teeth into his wrist.

Anthony knew that it was time to go. God was with him, but he didn't want to put God on the spot of having to arrange his rescue.

He had seen the very face of evil. Smelled its fetid blood-stink. He didn't doubt for a minute that the forces of darkness had sent the creatures specifically after *him*, Anthony Sevrin. To stop him. To prevent him from carrying out God's will.

The thought of the tiny baby, not even six hours old, coming under the teeth and claws of those dreadful things made him feel faint with revulsion and fear.

He backed away into the cover of the trees, unable to wrest his gaze from the bloodbath. He saw Mary sprawled in the hay, her head torn almost entirely off. He saw Joseph staggering in a drunken circle, trying to hold his face together. He saw the shepherd's boy scramble to his feet and pause in agonized indecision as the angel, fighting with her harness, begged him to help her.

Blood, so much blood, scarlet on white.

Torn flesh steaming.

Anthony felt for the heavy silver cross on its chain around his neck. He fished it out of his coat.

A hand caught at him.

He spun and saw another. White and gold. Beautiful. A Greek statue carved from flawless marble. A smile as cherubic as any angel's.

The past, with its churning memories of forbidden arousal, came back to him as he stared spellbound at the vision before him.

The cherubic smile widened, showing sharp fangs.

A turbulent mix of emotions and memories spun through Anthony. Desire and guilt, fear and longing, temptation and revulsion and sick lust.

He knew what this creature was, knew that the dark powers aligned against him not only sought to kill him but to torture and shame him, lure him, lead him astray.

His hand caught on something, some loop around his neck. He pulled it free and an object swung to thump against the front of his coat. It glimmered milky-silver in the frosty snow-light.

The vampire flinched and hissed as if scalded. Anthony clutched the cross. Its satiny wood and mother-of-pearl soothed him, cleared his mind. He shuddered. Felt unclean, so unclean, from his thoughts and urges alone.

"No," he said. "No!"

He held out the cross. His other hand cradled the sleeping weight of the baby under his coat.

Between the two, an amazing and powerful sensation brimmed in him. He was in the *right*, on the side of God, and by the strength of his faith and his holy love for this child, he would drive this evil thing back to the hell from which it had been spawned!

Advancing a step, he drove the cross at the vampire's face. It would quake before him, it would turn to mist in its urge to get away –

The creature, spitting and fuming, struck out and smacked the cross from his hand. If not for the chain, it would have flipped away into the night and been lost in the snow. As it was, the cross swung in a wild arc and hit Anthony high on the cheekbone. Its edge dug into his skin, bringing blood beneath his eye.

The vampire's screech might have been laughter. It made all the others look up from their grisly work.

"In the name of God!" Anthony cried.

He ducked as the vampire snatched at the collar of his coat. The baby squirmed and made a smothered fussing sound. Anthony thought that only he could hear it, but the greedy gleam of the vampire's hunger took on a new fervor. The innocent blood of a newborn, and could this hellish monster sense how special this particular child was?

Forgetting about the cross, Anthony kicked. His solid black shoe met the vampire's bare knee and it felt like stepping on an eggshell. The screeching laugh became a snarl of pain.

Anthony looked back and saw that the others getting up from the strewn bodies of their victims. In the glow of the fake Star of Bethlehem, the blood on their faces was black.

Branches clawed at his coat as he ran. Snow packed into his shoes. His feet, which had been cold, went numb. He cut a diagonal through the park, horribly aware of the fleet running shapes of the vampires coming after him.

Would they dare follow onto a well-lighted street? He thought that, given the darkness and the snow, they might.

The baby was fully awake now, crying and struggling inside his coat. Those few pounds of live weight felt like a boulder, an anchor. If he dropped his burden, the vampires would be distracted by the helpless offering and give him precious seconds to escape –

No! Never!

Beyond the low stone wall that bordered the park, his car waited at the curb. He vaulted the fence and dug for his keys.

"Hsssss!"

The schoolgirl crouched on the wall, plaid pleated skirt hiked to show white underpants. One knee sock was up, the other bunched around her ankle. Little gold studs glinted in her earlobes. The front of her white blouse bore a gory red bib.

The key went into the slot and turned, but when Anthony pulled on the handle, the door stuck, frozen by an icy rime.

He gave a hard yank, and the car door wrenched open with a brittle cracking sound. Anthony threw himself inside, slamming the door after him. Snow on the windshield and windows prevented any light from coming in, prevented him from seeing out. He locked the door.

The car rocked as something jumped on the hood. A miniature avalanche of displaced snow revealed the girl, glaring in through the glass at Anthony.

The businessman and the smartly-dressed woman flung their bodies against the driver's side, causing more snow to fall away. They could have been partners, executives on their way to a meeting, but for the streaks and splatters that covered them.

Anthony jammed the key in the ignition. A punch quivered the windshield, but it held. The engine caught with a hearty roar. The headlights came on, cutting twin beams in the night.

They retreated as his car pulled, slewing and slipping, into the street. He had one last glimpse of their burning eyes as they melted back into the shadows of Landover Park.

It was over. It was done. He had done it.

The baby was safe.

So little, so special. Even if the rest of the world didn't know. Someday, they would. What he held in his arms represented the hope of all mankind.

If, that was, mankind could hold on and keep from destroying itself until the child was old enough to be the key to their salvation.

CHAPTER 11

The beep of the computer woke Anthony into a disoriented state. He started, looking around to be sure that no one had come in.

He had been dreaming, reliving that momentous Christmas night. The night of the baby, and the vampires. When he had escaped evil, succeeded in his plan, and been more sure than ever that God was with him.

Anthony checked his watch and saw that he'd been asleep for over an hour. It was almost six in the morning. He wiped his sweaty brow, grimacing at the oily feel of his hair. He wanted a shower, stinging and hot.

The computer had finished its second analysis. Goat's blood, the computer screen insisted. The second sample, like the first, was nothing more than goat's blood. A sound of frustration escaped him. He stared at the Shroud, knowing that his next step would have to be a third test from a third blood spot.

And a fourth, and a fifth if that was required.

If every single test failed …

That hardly bore contemplating.

Did he have the wrong one? Was *this* one the hoax? Had it all been a clever ruse, so that an intrepid researcher would follow the trail to the fake Shroud while the one that everybody thought was fake was really the genuine article?

Had Philips and Renard tricked him?

His stomach plummeted down a chilly well shaft inside him. He slapped his forehead.

If they had…

Here he'd thought himself so cunning, lacing the counterfeit cash payoff with a little something of his own design. Both men would be dead within minutes of touching the money, and unable to ever talk about what they'd been hired to do. The poison was short-lived; it would evaporate quickly on contact with the open air and become harmless so that nobody else would be affected. A coroner would be baffled as to the exact nature of what had killed the pair of mercenaries.

But if they *had* tricked him, fashioned up a duplicate or something …

"No," Anthony said. "It's too old. The cloth, the blood stains, all too old to have just been made up."

Despair came down on him with the crushing force of a tidal wave. Somehow, somewhere in his research, he'd taken a wrong turn and concluded that the true Shroud was at St. Olivia's, when its real resting place had to be somewhere else.

He could test all he liked, and he *would* test many more times to be sure, but in his heart, he already knew.

All that time and money wasted! He wouldn't have begrudged the loss of the poisoned money and the deaths of Philips and Renard if it had gotten him what he wanted. But to have thrown it away on a mistake like this gnawed at him, made him feel stupid. And if there was one thing Anthony could not abide, it was being made to feel stupid.

The exhaustion dragged him down. An hour's dream-tormented nap hadn't been enough to take the edge off, only making him more tired. He went about the routine of shutting down the lab in something akin to a daze, moving mechanically from one chore to the next.

When he finished, he wondered if he'd be able to haul himself through the house and upstairs to his bedroom.

It was early morning. Mrs. Boryenka would be rattling around in the kitchen. She favored a mess of butter-fried potatoes and sausage for her daily breakfast. Anthony considered himself more of a coffee-and-toast kind of person, since heavy food left him feeling slow and thick. Right now, though, hungry as he was, the idea of starch and grease and protein seemed like just the thing.

He left the lab via the claustrophobic wooden staircase connecting the former wine cellar to the trap door in the study closet. He shuffled through the study, stifling a jaw-cracking yawn.

The study was floor-to-ceiling bookshelves, and not an inch of it wasted on the display of knickknacks, family photographs, potted plants, or other such nonsense. Ancient texts crowded shoulder to shoulder with the latest medical journals, everything arranged in an order that made no sense to anyone but Anthony.

The house smelled of frying sausages and the musty scent of new-falling rain. The thin grey light of a rainy March morning filtered through the curtains and the open front door.

Anthony stopped at the entrance to the living room, frowning.

The front door was open.

Something was in the foyer. A bumpy pile of something in purple terrycloth.

It was Mrs. Boryenka, face down on the floor in her housecoat and slippers. Her hair was up in sponge rollers and the day's newspaper, encased in a plastic bag against the weather, was near her outflung hand.

Adrenaline surged through Anthony's sluggish veins. He went to the housekeeper, his mind already ticking through possibilities.

Heart attack. Stroke.

He was so intent on running through the list of symptoms that he didn't immediately notice the muddy tracks on the foyer's tile floor. Once he did, he felt a nasty coil of apprehension.

Tracks. Muddy boot-prints.

Mrs. Boryenka hadn't suffered anything so ordinary as a heart attack. A dark stain spread on the back of her housecoat, the blood only visible against the purple from up close. A stab wound or a gunshot. Anthony hadn't heard any gunshot, but that didn't mean anything. His lab had thick walls, he'd been dozing, and the intruder could have used a silencer.

The intruder. Anthony's gaze jerked from Mrs. Boryenka to the tracks. Only coming in. None going out.

The possibility that struck him then turned his bowels shivery and loose.

Philips and Renard.

It had to be. The chances of his house falling victim to just any old burglar right now were absurd.

The poison must not have worked. Or not gotten both of them. The lean, red-haired one had handled the money. Renard. What if his partner hadn't? Philips could be here right now, bent on revenge.

He could see it in his mind. Mrs. Boryenka, opening the front door to get the paper as she always did, so that she could read it while she ate her breakfast. Philips bursting in on her like some sort of commando, seizing her, ramming a knife into her back.

Anthony straightened up and eyed the open door. The rain was pouring down and he was in shirtsleeves and socks, but he didn't care. He had his keys in his pants pocket. He could reach his car and –

And suppose Philips *was* out there, waiting for Anthony to rush headlong into the rain? Or that he'd done something to the car? Anthony was no big fan of action movies but he'd seen enough to imagine dynamite wired to his ignition. The fireball. The shower of twisted metal.

There was a cell phone in his bedside drawer. He hated the things, the constant distraction of them, but with the world as it was, he had given in and purchased one. He rushed for the stairs, his socks silent on the carpet. Near the top, he stepped in a wet place and saw a gob of sticky mud that formed part of a footprint.

The intruder was up here.

Anthony looked both ways down the hall. On his left, the door leading to Mrs. Boryenka's bedroom was shut, as were the ones to the linen closet, the nursery, and the guestroom that his sister Fiona sometimes used. The other doors to the right – a bathroom, the sewing room he'd converted to a private chapel, and the master suite at the end of the hall – were open.

Low noises, like a closet door sliding on its tracks, came from the master bedroom.

Philips was in there. Searching for Anthony Sevrin. Meaning to kill him in retaliation for the poison.

No one had ever wanted to *kill* him before. Except for those vampires in Landover Park that time, but that didn't count because they were merely mindless hunting creatures, like sharks. It hadn't been personal. Not the way that Philips' intention was deeply, intensely personal.

He heard the door to the master bathroom, which squeaked, swing open. Then the rattle of shower curtain rings. Philips was as far from the hall as it was physically possible to be, and once he'd satisfied himself that Anthony was not hiding in the bathtub, he'd be coming back.

Anthony hurried on sock feet down the carpeted hallway in the other direction.

With a frantic backward glance – no Philips yet – he slipped into Mrs. Boryenka's room and eased the door most of the way shut. Relief swept him, but close on its heels came a resurgence of the anxiety.

How was he going to get out of here? The locked window would make too much noise if he opened it, and what would he do then, jump from the second story?

He didn't have much of a choice. It was that or stay here and be shot or stabbed to death.

Anthony poked an eye up to the gap between the door's edge and the jamb. He saw a dark man-shape emerge from the master suite and pause like an animal scenting the air. Navy blue coveralls. Ski mask. Mud-splashed boots. Too big to be Renard, so Anthony knew he'd gotten it right. Philips. With a silenced pistol held low against his thigh and a knife sheath strapped to his belt.

The mercenary moved to the guestroom door and pressed his ear to it, his free hand on the knob. He thrust the door open and went through.

As soon as he was out of sight, Anthony closed Mrs. Boryenka's door. It clicked quietly home, but there was no lock. He wedged a chair under the knob instead, knowing that this would prove only a stopgap measure if Philips decided to kick through the flimsy wood.

He unlocked the window and raised it in its frame. The wood squealed. Anthony winced. Footsteps hammered down the hall as Philips gave up all pretense of stealth.

Anthony knocked out the screen. A gust of wind and icy rain came in, dashing him in the face. He stuck his head out. The porch roof was too far to be of any help.

The knob turned and the door fetched up against the chair. The chair's legs dug into the carpet but held. A fist pounded on the door, rattling it with a hollow, thunderous boom. Then came a sharp crack, a gunshot. The bullet smashed through the door and thudded into the wall beside a framed newspaper clipping of a much younger and much slimmer Mrs. Boryenka with a silver medal around her neck and the five-ringed Olympic flag in the background.

It would have to be the bushes. They were juniper hedge, not thorny roses, but Anthony still didn't relish the landing. He stuck his leg over the sill.

The door jerked. The chair jumped and its legs squalled as they tore through the carpet to the wood beneath. A solid thump as of a man's determined shoulder made the door jump again. A long splinter split off.

Anthony scrambled out and landed in the junipers. Stiff twigs jabbed at him. A rich green scent rose up from the crushed foliage. He tumbled head-over-heels onto the wet lawn and almost gelded himself on a sprinkler head. Without pausing to see how badly he was scraped up, he scrambled to his feet and ran for the garage.

Something streaked past his ear and smacked into the garage door, leaving a hole. Anthony didn't look back. Seconds later, he was in the driver's seat and speeding away from his house.

Chapter 12

He only killed the woman because she'd given him trouble.

The tough old battleaxe surprised him with her speedy reflexes and her strength, and had damn near broken his wrist while wrenching the gun out of his hand. If she had screamed, too, she could have become a real problem.

But she hadn't screamed, and he had been able to draw Roxy from his belt, get her in a chokehold and ram Renard's blade into her back.

Philips didn't like that, a cowardly from-behind blow on a short, chunky grey-haired lady with hair in curlers just like the ones Granny Bea used to wear. Made him look bad. Once those killer instincts took over, though, there wasn't much else to do but hold on and go for the ride.

He'd been casing the house, weighing his options as to the best entrances and exits, when the front door had opened and the woman stepped onto the porch to fetch the morning paper. Philips had seen the paperboy pedal past a few minutes before, the reflectors on his bike winking and flashing in the rainy dawn gloom. The kid's head had been down and hooded in a bright yellow slicker, his arm flinging each paper with robotic monotony.

When the door had opened, he'd seized his moment and gone for it, and that was when his luck turned. Up until then, he'd thought he was doing pretty well tracking down his quarry.

The plates on the car belonged to a Dr. Anthony Sevrin at this address. Sevrin. A few hours at the local library had turned up various articles by Sevrin, all in prestigious medical journals where the jargon was thick as peanut butter. Space-age science like genetic manipulation and cloning. Some hush-hush project back in the eighties, up in Montana or Wyoming or someplace. A lot of people died. It made the papers.

There were no more journal articles after that. Clearly, Sevrin's career had taken a downturn. But it was fair to think that his interests might still be along the same lines.

Cloning. That had rocked Philips. Cloning plus the Shroud of Turin? He didn't know whether to be awestruck or offended.

What mattered, though, was more immediate and personal. Sevrin had killed Renard, would have killed both of them. It was simple enough now to see how an egghead scientist could have whipped up a nice little contact poison.

So, meaning to settle the score, Philips had gone to the house. Strike early, strike fast. He'd taken out the old woman—Sevrin's mother? hired help?—and done a quick canvass of the downstairs to see if anyone else was up. Coffee brewing. Sausages frying in a pan. Chopped potato on the cutting board. He turned off the stove, not wanting the smoke alarm to go off at an inconvenient moment.

The master bedroom was obviously Sevrin's, since the same London Fog coat he'd been wearing when he'd met them for the exchange was draped over a chair and plaques from assorted universities covered the walls. The bed didn't look slept in, and the bathroom was empty.

When he'd emerged, he saw right away that a door previously ajar was now closed, and then the chase was on. Sevrin went out the window. The shot that should have taken him in the leg hit the garage instead thanks to Philips' injured wrist.

Sevrin peeled out, fishtailing at the end of the driveway and coming within inches of clipping a frail old man holding an umbrella and the leash of a soggy cocker spaniel.

Philips did a fade back from the window, cursing, and made his own discreet escape.

The only other Sevrin in the phone book turned out to be listed by an initial. F. In Philips' experience, that meant a woman who thought that using her initial instead of a female name would deter the perverts.

Tracking down the address, he found that F. Sevrin lived in an apartment in an expensive tinted-glass building.

Was F. the owner of the stylish clothes in Sevrin's guest room? An ex? Sister? No relation at all? It wasn't a common name; maybe there was some connection.

Getting into F. Sevrin's building turned out to be a piece of cake.

He timed it to intercept a woman at the doors, hefty, juggling grocery bags and fumbling with keys. Philips, who had changed into khakis and a baggy, oversized sweatshirt that hid his weaponry, hurried up as she pulled the door open and held it for her.

She thanked him with a meek little smile and no eye contact. Unflattering hairdo but not ugly. The sort who had no doubt grown up hearing everybody tell her that she had such a pretty face, such a nice personality, if only she'd lose some weight.

Philips followed her in. He checked the labels above the mailboxes. Apartment 411 had two names listed, Sevrin and Nicholson.

Two names. A roommate, or maybe a boyfriend.

Great. Another complication.

He frowned and blew out a breath.

The fat woman took her grocery bags to the elevator, and Philips caught up with her again there. "Thanks," he said. "What floor?"

"Four," she said, low voice, hardly a murmur, staring at the ground. Not used to talking to strangers. Especially male strangers. Especially big black male strangers, every urban white woman's nightmare.

He pushed the button for the fourth floor, and then for the sixth. The elevator rose with a smooth hum. Philips glanced into the grocery bags. He saw Twinkies, a two-liter bottle of diet Coke, a box of frozen fried chicken, a can of Slim-Fast powder.

The fourth-floor corridor had off-white walls and a durable dark green carpet. The doors were stained to look like oak, with brass numbers.

The woman got off the elevator and Philips continued up to the sixth floor. It was the same, except for a couple arguing in the hallway. They both shot him angry glares as if the intrusion was intentional, and he was glad of the excuse to offer an apologetic smile and hit another button.

The elevator stopped again on four. Apartment 411 was at the far end. As he walked past, he heard televisions and radios and voices. All normal. The doors had peepholes.

He knocked on 411. Sensed an eyeball looking at him through the peephole and did his best to appear innocuous.

The fat woman from the elevator opened the door, perplexed.

F. Sevrin? Not likely. The clothes in the spare room closet had been for someone sleek and trim. Nicholson, then. The roomie.

"Excuse me, miss," Philips said, thinking fast. "Did you drop this in the elevator?" He moved his hand as if to hold something out.

She looked down, and he seized her by the hair, kneed her in the stomach, and hustled her back into the apartment before she could do more than gasp. He shut the door without slamming it and manhandled her around so he could push her into a chair. She dropped into it, peering up at him dazedly through tangled brown locks.

Philips showed her the knife, and the dazed look vanished like she'd been dashed with cold water. She hitched in a breath.

"Now, don't go and scream," he said, pitching his voice low and confidential. "I'm not here to hurt you."

A shaky, whimpering exhale was her answer.

"Are you Miss Sevrin?" He knew she wasn't, but had to make sure.

Her head shook in short, rapid arcs. She swallowed. Squeaked. "I – I'm Jill. Jill Nicholson."

"Roommate?"

She nodded with the same short, rapid arcs. Her eyes never left the knife. Roxy, cleaned and polished, glinted with deadly silver light.

"I need some information," Philips said.

Haltingly, but growing more steady as he failed to cut her or terrorize her any more than he'd already done, Jill Nicholson told him that no, Fiona Sevrin had never been married. Yes, she had a brother. He was some sort of a doctor, Jill didn't know what kind.

"Are they close? Her and the brother? Does she see him often?"

"She visits him," Jill said. "He doesn't much come over here."

He rattled off the address of the Tudor, but Jill only shrugged and looked afraid that he'd stab her for not knowing. "I've never been there. It used to be their grandparents' house, that's all I know."

She wasn't aware of any calls or visitors early that morning, either. Fiona had been gone by the time Jill got up. Jill showered, breakfasted, and at eight o'clock had left without checking the answering machine – "It's always for Fiona, anyway," she said with unconscious dolefulness. She'd gone to work. Her plans for the evening had been to have a solo dinner and then head out to her evening pottery class.

"Sorry," Philips said. "Afraid you're going to miss pottery class today."

Jill cringed. Her chin trembled.

"I'm *not* going to hurt you," he said. "We're just going to wait here for your friend Fiona."

"Are you going to hurt *her*?"

"Not unless I have to."

He paced the living room, which was definitely split between two people with disparate interests. He hadn't tied Jill, but she stayed in that chair as if her butt was glued down, and kept her hands folded primly on her knees.

The answering machine light was stuttering. Philips pressed the Play button and listened with a grim smile as Anthony Sevrin's recorded voice babbled to his sister. Fiona had to call him, he was in trouble, he didn't dare come over, he was pretty sure he hadn't been followed but didn't want to put her in danger, Mrs. B. was already dead.

At that, Jill turned the color of oatmeal.

"You recognize the call-back number he left?" Philips asked.

She shook her head.

"Guess we'll have to wait, then."

An hour and a half later, the front door opened and Fiona Sevrin breezed in.

"I am *dying* for a drink," she announced. "That idiot photographer, I swear, what a —"

She broke off as she saw Jill, now tied to the chair with a swatch of tape over her mouth.

Philips, behind the door, nudged it shut and grabbed Fiona.

The model-turned-designer was close to six feet, with a leggy athletic build, and she probably would have fought like a wildcat if he'd given her the chance.

Five minutes later, though, she was in the chair beside Jill, nursing a lump on the head and cussing him ferociously for hitting her in the face. She had, she said, an important meeting with the editors of *Vogue* tomorrow, and how was she supposed to impress them with a goddamn black eye?

He taped her mouth shut, too.

Then he picked up her phone and called the number that her brother had left in his increasingly frantic messages.

It rang eight times and a man's voice, sounding breathless, picked up. "Fee? Hello, Fee, is that you?"

"We have some unfinished business, Dr. Sevrin," he said.

A cold pause at the other end. Philips heard distant traffic, a jackhammer, a car horn, a shouted invective. A pay phone.

"You owe me some money, doctor," he said when Sevrin still didn't speak. "The stuff you gave us was no good."

An irate squawk blatted in his ear. "Neither was the merchandise you brought me! I bargained with you in good faith and you bring me a phony? Goat's blood, Philips? Goat's blood?"

"I don't know what you're talking about." Neither, by the look, did Jill, but Fiona's expression was so studious a poker face that she had to know something. He had Sevrin on speakerphone just for the fun of it. "You killed my partner."

"You killed my housekeeper!"

"What, you think this all makes us even, and I should leave you alone?"

He could feel Sevrin trying to compose himself. "Well, what do *you* propose, then?" Sevrin asked.

"I propose you pay me for the job and we call it quits." He did not intend to let Renard's death go unanswered, but he wasn't about to tell Sevrin that. "I've got your sister and her friend here. I'm sure you wouldn't want anything to happen to them."

Tears like shimmering pearls poured from Jill's eyes. Fiona's, enormous cover-girl-quality emerald green, gleamed bright with hate. Contacts. They had to be contacts.

"All right," Sevrin said. He sounded appropriately defeated, but there was a sly undercurrent to his voice that Philips didn't much care for. "I'll get you the money. Can you meet me in Landover Park at nine?"

"In a situation like this," Philips said, "it's usually the man with the gun who names the place and time."

"Oh, for God's sake!" barked the doctor. "If you want your money, that's where I'll be."

"No tricks, either. No traps, no poisons, no funny business."

"Right, right, right!"

They haggled over a few other arrangements and hung up. Philips looked at his watch. Almost seven. Banks would be closed. An ATM wouldn't do for the quantities they were talking about here.

"Your brother got a lot of cash around?" He should have gone through the house more carefully, but there just hadn't been time. Come to think of it, Sevrin had probably hidden the Shroud around there somewhere, too.

Fiona shrugged. Her eyes flashed at him, telling him where he could go and what he could do to himself on the way.

He thought about taking her along as a hostage, but marching her bound and gagged through the building would not be subtle. Neither did he trust her to accompany him, not even with a gun trained on her.

"I want you to remember something," he said, staring directly into Fiona's hot-emerald gaze. "I know where you live. Your brother screws me over again, and I'm coming back. I'll find you."

If looks could kill, he'd be dead, sliced up by her sharp glare. The other one, Jill, blubbered into her gag. Steady streams ran from her eyes and nostrils.

Philips showed Roxy to Jill, the blade right up close. Liquid pattered from the seat of Jill's chair to the carpet. The sour-yellow smell of urine rose around her. She tried to scoot backward. The chair tipped on two legs. Philips steadied it.

His attention was on Fiona. "Remember. Next time, this could be you."

Roxy's work was over in seconds. The flesh of Jill's throat parted like wet paper. She barely had time to show her awareness of what was happening to her before the life whiffed from her eyes like the flames of a pair of extinguished candles. More liquid, a thicker splashing of it, soaked the carpet and sprayed onto the wall.

Fiona's complexion went waxy, but her eyes still spat those green-fire sparks at him. He grinned and slid the flat of the blade along her come-hither cheekbones, marking them both in broad streaks of red.

Then, knowing that he'd spent too much time on this already, he let himself out of the apartment. He locked the door and deadbolt behind him with Fiona's keys and dropped the keys down the garbage chute at the end of the hall. He heard their grating, jangling slide into darkness.

As he left the building, he regretted killing poor dumpy Jill. But the arrogant aura around Fiona Sevrin had told him that there really would be no other way to get through to her.

Taking a circuitous route, he reached Landover Park twenty minutes later. It was a few blocks from the apartments, near a large metropolitan hospital. The park nestled like a shady green afterthought amid busy high rises and hole-in-the-wall businesses.

It might have been pleasant enough by bright sunlight, but at dusk it was a shadowy, rustling tree-filled strangeness. Posted signs declared the park to be closed from the hours of 8:00 PM to 8:00 AM.

Philips found the place already deserted. Playground equipment, empty in the twilight, struck him as somehow creepy and post-apocalyptic.

He kept on the move, roaming the park ready to slip into concealment at the first hint of a cop car making a routine sweep. He was leery of Sevrin, too. The man was up to something, but Philips didn't plan on giving him time to spring any surprises. Soon as he saw him, he was going to shoot him.

8:30 came, and then 8:45. Darkness had a solid hold on the world now, and in the thickets of Landover Park, it was as lightless as an oceanic trench. A few lampposts followed the concrete pathways, but many of the bulbs didn't work and the few that did only lent a dim, unhealthy light.

It should have been a good place for muggers, winos, and drug deals. But Philips was alone. No vagrants were setting up camp on the benches. No hookers brought their johns in for a quickie in the bushes. Having people around would have bothered him. Having no people around bothered him even more, for no good reason that he could name. He didn't like this still and quiet darkness. He didn't like the fact that, although he could spot no one, he felt watched.

The hour of nine was five minutes old. Sevrin was nowhere to be seen.

"Don't be fucking with me, Doc," Philips whispered through a clenched jaw. "That's such a bad idea, to be fucking with me. First your sister will pay, and then you."

He heard someone approaching and turned, the gun in his hand but held against his thigh where it couldn't readily be seen.

It wasn't Sevrin.

It was a waitress, walking toward him as if she hadn't a care in the world. As if it was perfectly okay and normal for a lone woman to be in this empty, spooky park after sunset.

She grinned at Philips. What little light there was caught her earrings, and her teeth. They were very white, those teeth. Very... very long.

A hissing sound behind him made him spin, Roxy in one hand and his silenced pistol in the other. He saw a pallid face and a snarling mouthful of fangs lunging toward him.

Philips jumped back and opened fire. The silencer muffled the gunshots into polite theater-coughs. The bullets staggered the pale, savage figure but didn't stop it. He slashed out with Roxy instead and ripped the vampire's Hard Rock Café tee shirt wide open, scoring a bloodless line across the belly beneath.

Vampire. His mind accepted it without any debate, compromising that later – if there *was* a later – he would worry about his sanity. Survival first.

More of them appeared, men and women, adults and kids, a pack of them all baring their teeth and hissing as they surrounded him. The smell of the slaughterhouse hung around them in a cloud.

They closed in, gaining confidence as his shots and slashes failed to hurt them. His punches only rocked their heads back. Claws scrabbled at him, tearing his sweatshirt to ribbons, scratching him, drawing blood. He had a moment's glimpse of them licking red smears from their fingers with a look of rapture in their eyes.

The vampires overwhelmed him and bore him to the grass, snapping at each other as they jockeyed for position. Philips jammed the barrel of the silencer under his chin and pulled the trigger.

The gun clicked. His clip was empty.

Panicked now, he raised Roxy toward his neck. He'd do himself before they had a chance.

A vampire in a policeman's uniform caught his wrist and bit it. Needling pain, white-hot, lanced up Philips' arm. He felt a second bite through his khakis, driving deep for the throb of his femoral artery. Fangs split his ear as he whipped his head from side to side.

The waitress elbowed others out of the way and straddled his chest, knees pressing his shoulders to the ground. She bent with a snake's supple ease, mouth agape as it descended toward his face.

Philips instinctively twisted his head away, and realized a heartbeat too late that he had exposed his throat. He felt the quick and loathsome swipe of her tongue slicking him with rank saliva, and then she buried her fangs to the gum line and sucked as his blood pumped into her greedy mouth.

PART THREE – THE VIRGIN
April

CHAPTER 13

Nobody waited to greet her as she got off the bus.

Natalie hitched her purse higher on her shoulder, clutched her suitcase to her chest, and edged out of the flow of pedestrian traffic. People swarmed around her, their voices a deafening cacophony after the secluded hush that was Our Lady of Sorrows.

They rushed by, men and women, kids and elderly folks. Each and every one of them seemed to have a destination in mind. The bathrooms, the taxi stand, the ticket counter, the snack bar.

The bus station was a cavernous dirty-grey confusion of signs and shouts and milling heads. Despite the posted placards depicting cigarettes inside red circles-and-slashes, the smell of smoke mingled with the other odors of sweat, pizza, sour-wine breath, and exhaust. Loudspeakers blared times and destinations in five or six languages. News and sports on wall-mounted television screens competed with music from radios.

Her eyes felt grainy and her skin felt oily. Her hair was both matted to her head, and frizzing with static electricity. The hot dog and chips she'd eaten at the lunch stopover had left her with an upset stomach and a bad aftertaste that not even an entire can of Mountain Dew had been able to get rid of.

Or maybe it was the guilt that caused the indigestion and bad taste in her mouth.

She wasn't looking forward to explaining how she'd bailed out of school two months before the end of term. How could she tell them she'd decided that Our Lady of Sorrows, while a good school, a great school, full of excellent teachers and peace and quiet, was not for her?

Talk about ungrateful. After all they'd done, the strings they'd pulled, to get her admitted. She'd been a student at Sorrows since she was seven years old. More than half her life.

She hoped they wouldn't be too disappointed with her.

Maybe she'd better call them after all. She had thought it would be easier this way. That, by simply showing up, she'd be better able to make them listen to her decision in person. If she'd called from Sorrows, they would have either dissuaded her over the phone, or come out there and convinced her to stay in the familiar surroundings.

Now that she was in the city, though, the wisdom of her choice seemed much more questionable. She hadn't planned as far ahead as this. The bus station, yes, but what would she do after that?

Lugging her suitcase – for containing so little, it got heavier with each step – she went to a bank of chairs with a view of the main entrance. The chairs were molded from hard plastic the color of a whale carcass, supported by dulled and chipped chrome legs all hooked together in a row. Some had graffiti carved into the seats and backs, or scribbled in black indelible ink.

The bus had pulled into the city while the sun was settling scarlet into a fluffy billow of gold-tinted clouds. Against this riotous backdrop, the skyscrapers stood out in sharp purple-black, the windows beginning to spangle with light. The main freeways, in the throes of rush hour, were glowing ribbons of red and white.

A few people gave her idle glances. Natalie was glad she'd worn regular clothes. She could only imagine the stares she'd be getting if she had worn the school uniform.

Then again, compared to the other teenage girls she was seeing here in the bus stop, she might as well have been in full nun's habit. If anyone at Sorrows tried to get away with jeans like that – jeans so low on the hips that they looked like they'd slide off if they hadn't been so tight – and skimpy tops that showed bare midriffs, with navel rings or tattoos or both, or thongs, miniskirts, tramp stamps… why, it'd be tantamount to the end of the world.

Natalie looked down at her white ribbed turtleneck with its long sleeves, and her denim calf-length jumper. White tights. Boring shoes with thin soles and flat heels. Boring hair, too, and no makeup at all. Her only jewelry was a jade cross on a fine gold chain. No earrings. Certainly no tattoos.

She thought with dour amusement that she probably looked like one of those Amish kids she'd read about, who were given a year to try out city life before deciding to stay home and churn butter. No wonder people kept looking at her.

The sky beyond the grimy windows had gone the color of a bruise. She was tired and hungry and wanted a shower. And most of all, she wanted to just get this over with.

To reach the pay phones, she had to lug her suitcase right past a cluster of vending machines. Natalie firmly promised herself to call first, and then get a candy bar or a package of cookies.

Her first call netted nothing but the answering machine. She tried another number. Ditto. Nobody home. Wouldn't it just be her luck if they'd gone on vacation?

She opted for candy and returned to her chair, munching on a Twix bar while she pondered her situation. She knew she didn't have enough cash for a taxi, and knew it was too far to walk.

Local bus lines? She found a kiosk with schedules and a large map with all the routes traced on it. Bus fare, she could afford.

Our Lady of Sorrows was out in the country, in a nestle of soft green hills overlooking a pristine lake. In the height of spring, it was refreshingly cool, and a sweet breeze always sighed through the treetops and rustled the flower-laden bushes.

Spring in the city was another matter, as Natalie found when she stepped out of the indifferently air-conditioned bus station. There was hardly any breeze, few flowers, and though the sun had gone down its warmth still radiated from the metal and concrete, the way desert rocks held the day's heat well into the evening.

The instant she was outside, a host of horror stories rushed into her mind. Stories about young girls on their own, easy prey for pimps and muggers. Already, she was conscious of a new kind of gaze, a predatory one. Natalie slung her purse so that the strap crossed from one shoulder to the opposite hip. She hardly had anything to make it worth a mugger's time, but they wouldn't know that until they tried. Her grip on the handle of the suitcase was an iron claw. She didn't know why. The only items in the suitcase were a Bible, a couple of books, her assortment of toiletries, and more outfits like the one she had on.

She found the bus stop and waited, heart pounding, for what seemed like a hundred years. Twice, narrow-eyed men slid past her and gave her the old once-over so thoroughly that she wouldn't have felt more undressed if she'd been a pole-dancing stripper in the spotlight. Neither of them spoke, and Natalie was quick to look down rather than directly at them.

The city bus arrived in a hiss and a snort. She swung aboard, paid her fare, and asked for a transfer ticket. With the ticket firmly in the breast pocket of her jumper, she took a seat near the front.

Two nerve-wracking transfers later, she had gone from the downtown heart of the city to an older, tree-lined district where the well-maintained homes had variety and character of their own rather than the cookie-cutter floor plans of the suburbs. She got off her final bus, glad to stretch her legs. She was stiff and numb from sitting so long. Carsick, too, and more tired than ever.

But she was almost there. A few blocks, an easy walk. Though the air had grown cooler, it was still a nice night. Not many stars; when she craned her neck to peer up through the leafy trees, she could only see a fraction of the dazzling display she'd become familiar with out in the mild countryside.

Natalie braced herself for a reception that would at the very least be surprised. At the worst, angry, especially once she stated her desire to not return to Sorrows.

They couldn't *make* her go back, could they? If she was unwilling? Did they have that much power over her? She was only fifteen. Legally, she might not have a leg to stand on.

Unless the very act of leaving without telling the Sisters had been enough to get her expelled. She couldn't go back, then. They'd just have to find something else for her. Another school. Another place to live.

It was a strange prospect, though. Sorrows had been her home for a long time. Part boarding school, and part convent, and except for a few brief visits back here, she had lived in the same small room – almost a cell – since she was seven.

She saw a familiar street-sign and quickened her pace. No one else was out. She had the broad sidewalk to herself, passing manicured lawns and driveways. She saw many lighted windows, and once heard the lively strains of big-band music.

The house up ahead, a Tudor, was dark. And there was something odd about it.

The yard, for one thing. The neat green grass was plowed and torn by heavy tire tracks. A flowerbed was mashed flat.

And stripes that looked like the work of a huge and drunken spider crisscrossed the front porch.

Natalie glanced around, saw no one, and moved closer.

The stripes were yellow bands of crime-scene tape. They wrapped around the support posts of the porch roof and effectively barred the way to the front door. The knob, knocker, and bell were dusted with what she guessed might be fingerprint powder.

The Sisters of Our Lady of Sorrows discouraged but did not forbid television viewing, and there'd been a contingent of girls addicted to reruns of *CSI, Law and Order*, and other crime shows.

Thanks to those shows, she was able to deduce that the hole in the garage door had been caused by a bullet and widened by someone's efforts to extract said bullet from the wood.

What had happened here? *Here*, of all places?

She didn't want to disturb any evidence by knocking, and the house looked deserted.

Deserted... but had the inhabitants left under their own power? Or by ambulance? Or morgue wagon?

Her mouth had gone dry. She found a stick of gum in the bottom of her purse and chewed, thankful for the cinnamon-flavored moisture.

Whatever it was, it couldn't have been very long ago. But why hadn't anyone called her? Why hadn't they let her know something was wrong?

On vacation would have been bad. In the hospital was worse. And dead... that didn't even bear thinking about. A lump clogged her throat.

Other questions swirled in her head. Who would do something like this? Why? Was it deliberate, or one of those awful random acts? The neighborhood seemed too old and graceful and quiet and respectable for drive-by shootings. The thought of Uncle Anthony having enemies was... well, was ridiculous.

She had her keys, had touched them while digging for the gum, but wasn't sure if it would be okay to go in. What if she inadvertently messed up a vital clue?

The night no longer felt as refreshing and pleasant as it had a little while ago. An uncomfortable chill had settled into her bones. The shadows, previously soft and magical, were now hard-edged and ominous.

Fingertips touching the jade cross, she offered a brief and silent prayer that no one had been hurt. Or, God forbid, killed.

Someone *should* have contacted her. She had to find out what had happened. If not a neighbor – Uncle Anthony hated letting anybody poke into his life and business – then Aunt Fiona could have called. She should have gone there first, anyway. It would have been a much shorter bus ride.

The trouble was that she'd never been to Fiona's apartment, only knew the address and phone number because they were on the school records in case of emergency.

Was this emergency enough? Or should she go ahead and ask a neighbor? Under the circumstances, Uncle Anthony would have to understand.

Would the neighbors tell her anything? She didn't know them, and vice versa. Even when she'd lived here, she had never spent much time playing with other kids. Older people or career-minded professionals who lived alone or chose to remain childless owned most of the other homes.

It would have to be Aunt Fiona. Natalie didn't let herself think about the possible reasons that Fiona might have had for not getting in touch with her sooner.

The suitcase felt like it weighed eight hundred pounds. She was tempted to leave it in the garage or the back yard but didn't dare. If the police came back to take another look around, she didn't want them finding a mysterious suitcase that had not been there before.

So, trudging now with all the lightness gone from her step, Natalie went back the way she had come. Her transfer ticket was still folded in her breast pocket.

She waited at the corner bus stop, trying to block her mind from gory images that would have been right at home on an episode of *CSI*. Trying to forget how hungry she was, and tired, and heartsick with dread.

The bus appeared forty-five minutes later and she collapsed into a seat. Her head tilted against the window. She found a crumpled tissue in her purse to dab at the hot, fretful tears that sprang to her eyes.

By the time she realized she'd transferred to the wrong bus, the 65 instead of the 62, it was well past eleven and coming up on midnight. Natalie rushed to the front and had a short, desperate argument with the driver.

He thought she was a runaway, and had all the sympathy for her that he might have had for a leper. No, he didn't know where the Glass Ridge Apartments were. The 62 bus? That stop was back on the corner of Landover Street. Six blocks. And she'd better hustle her little butt, because he thought that the 62 stopped running at twelve.

The other passengers regarded her with foggy, uncaring eyes. No one offered a word of advice.

She got off the bus, her suitcase now nearly dragging at her feet. Only an effort of will kept her from screaming, or bursting into furious, frustrated sobs.

Back in the crush and bustle of the city, activity surrounded her, even at this late hour. She knew she'd never make it back to Landover Street in time to catch the last bus. Her only hope would be to find a phone and give Aunt Fiona another call.

Cars droned by as Natalie plodded along. Her head hung lower and lower. She realized with dull amazement that she was practically walking in her sleep. Her back and legs ached. Her stomach was a growling knot and her bladder was in urgent need of relief.

The shining white gates of Paradise could not have been more welcome, therefore, than a sign advertising a 24-hour coffee shop. Natalie stepped inside, her senses taking in warm brick and oak, brown leather, brass trim, heat from a gas fireplace, brewing coffee, the subdued thump of rock music, a woman's merry laugh.

The place was small, cozy. It had a walk-up counter with a menu on the wall behind and a glass-fronted case of bakery treats. There were half a dozen little round tables, each with a few straight-backed wooden chairs. Other chairs, deep and leather, clustered around a coffee table by the fireplace. A fan of newspapers and magazines covered the table, and more were stuffed into a rack by the door.

As the door swung shut behind her, a beautiful brass clock began striking midnight in mellow, ringing tones.

"Be right with you, hon," a woman called. She was the one with the merry laugh, and had a merry face to go with it. Her only nod to a uniform was a green apron with 'Pamela' embroidered on the bib, worn over regular clothes.

Natalie toted her suitcase toward the fire. A dark-haired guy of probably twenty, sound asleep with his feet propped on a battered old red suitcase, occupied the chair in the closest corner. She felt an immediate kinship with him. He looked the way she felt – as if he was on his own and far from home.

At a nearby table, an old man squinted through bifocals at a crossword puzzle while his companion, an equally old lady, fussed over a beige poof with beady black eyeballs and a pink bow atop its head. Natalie was pretty sure it was a dog, though it might have been a particularly ugly cat. The old lady fed it morsels pinched from a scone on a plate.

At one of the other tables, two men in hospital scrubs talked baseball, joked with Pamela, and drank cup after cup of steaming black coffee. A solitary woman with too much makeup and too tight a dress sat by the window sipping a latte and reading *The Weekly World News.*

Leaving the suitcase by a chair, Natalie went up to the counter. She counted her funds, consulted the menu, and determined that she could afford a cup of cocoa and a muffin.

Pamela came over to her, auburn ponytail bouncing on her shoulder. Her hazel eyes brimmed with knowing pity as she studied Natalie, and Natalie was keenly aware of how much worse she must look by now. Every bit a runaway. She might have been crisp and neat when she left Sorrows that morning, but the hours and the walking had worn her down into a bedraggled waif.

"Hot cocoa and an apple-spice muffin, please," she said. "And do you have a restroom, and a pay phone?"

"Restroom's down that way," Pamela said, pointing past the bakery case to a short alcove that ended in two doors. The first had a shiny 'restroom' plaque on it, the other an exit sign. "No pay phone, though. Is it local?"

"My aunt," Natalie said. "She lives in the Glass Ridge Apartments."

"You can give her a call on my phone, how about?"

"Thank you."

While Pamela poured cocoa, Natalie hurried to the restroom. It was a single unisex room with a lock, and a mirror that showed her drawn, puffy face in harsher detail than she would have wished.

She emerged in a much better state, having washed up and wetted and combed her hair into a semblance of order. A generous mug topped with a cumulus cloud of whipped cream sat on the counter, next to an apple-spice muffin the size of a softball, and a triangular cheddar-cheese scone.

"Excuse me," she said, tapping the rim of the plate. "I didn't order the scone."

"Oh, I know, but we've only got the one left," Pamela said. "Maybe you'd do me a favor and eat it up. I'd hate to throw it out. It's nice and hot, too. I heated it in the microwave and put some butter on it."

It smelled utterly wonderful. Hunger beat pride into submission and Natalie murmured another thank-you as she retreated to a chair with her bounty. It was all she could do not to wolf into the scone like a barbarian.

Once she'd devoured the scone and half the cocoa, the snarling emptiness in her belly had quieted enough for her to savor the muffin. She turned through the pages of a two-week-old copy of *Entertainment Weekly* while she did, reading about movies she couldn't wait to see and music she'd never heard.

Soon, she was feeling full and replete, and well enough to face waking Aunt Fiona with a late-night telephone call.

The two men in hospital scrubs got up, exchanging a few last remarks with Pamela, and ordered large to-go cups. As they paid, and the woman in the tight dress headed for the door with her tabloid under her arm, a new customer came in.

And though she knew it was rude, Natalie gawked shamelessly.

He was her age or thereabouts, tall and gangly and dressed in a way that would have made the Sisters at Our Lady of Sorrows cross themselves or faint outright. His hair screamed off his head in red, black and green spikes that made his pasty complexion look chalk-white. He wore jeans that looked to have been run over with a lawn mower, motorcycle boots, and a tank top made out of tiny rings of metal. Like the chain mail that a knight of old might have worn.

Pamela threw the new arrival a suspicious look that was light-years from the welcome she'd afforded Natalie. The old man with the crossword made a disgusted huffing noise, and his wife pulled her poof-dog closer as if she expected the guy to snatch it away from her and bite its little head off.

The woman in the tight dress looked him over, painted lips pursed in speculative scorn. She started to say something derisive that never made it past the first syllable.

The kid seized her, whirled her up against the wall, and squashed his body up against hers. She squealed. One hard yank and her dress split to the waist. The kid thrust her legs wide apart and got between them, pinning her up against the wall as he buried his face against her neck.

"What the hell?" bellowed one of the hospital workers, dropping his coffee. Scalding fluid sprayed over the bricks.

"Let go of her, damn you!" Pamela cried.

The woman let out a short, sharp scream. She had been trying to shove the kid away, but now her arms fell limp and her head rocked back to rest beneath the brass clock. Blood, an unbelievable scarlet flood of it, poured down her bare chest from a terrible hole in the side of her neck.

CHAPTER 14

Seth woke in a flash, on his feet and not sure when he'd stood. He held his empty coffee mug like he meant to throw it.

One of the hospital workers beat him to it. A cup streaked through the air and struck the vampire in the back. Chain mail jingled. Coffee splashed.

The vampire dropped its victim – she slid dazedly down the wall – and spun to meet this threat.

Its white face was drenched with blood that dripped from its chin and coated its cheeks. It ran its tongue in a slow pass over its lips, and then grinned. For a moment, the shop was frozen in time. Seth stood with his mug poised, Pamela was rigid with shock, the old couple and their dog looked like a waxwork diorama. Only the injured woman moved. She touched her fingers to the side of her neck, which was a gouged red crater. She held her bloody fingers before her eyes. Then her eyes rolled up in her head and she pitched over, unconscious.

The vampire hissed through its fangs.

A girl had come in while Seth was sleeping, a pretty blonde whose hand had instinctively closed around a cross on a chain. He saw her eyes, as wide and blue as the morning sky, and her mouth moving in soundless prayer.

The man who'd thrown his coffee yelled and swung a fist. The vampire ducked under the blow, quick as a cat, and sprang. Split, filthy fingernails sank into the man's throat and sectioned the flesh like a juicy orange.

The yell turned into a bubbling moan. The vampire guzzled the fountain of blood like a dog lapping water from a spurting garden hose.

Seth hurled his solid ceramic mug. It cracked against bone, a direct hit to the temple that rocked the vampire's head sideways. The head swiveled back around, a burning gaze searing Seth with the unspoken promise that he'd be next.

The old man jumped up and broke for the door. His wife shrieked for him not to leave her, but he hadn't gone three steps before the vampire snapped an arm out and clotheslined him. The old man's feet flipped up. He landed on his back and howled as bones snapped.

Behind the counter, the woman who ran the shop snatched up the phone and jabbed her finger at the buttons. She was blanched with shock. Seth doubted she'd be able to say anything coherent. But the call itself, and the ruckus in the background, would bring the police on the double.

He had to be quick.

The second hospital worker grabbed for his fallen friend, trying to stanch the violent flow. No hope; the wound was mortal and already the man's eyes were glazing over.

The vampire, dripping with red, tried to catch the old woman by the hair and came away with a handful of loose blue-white wig. This momentarily puzzled the creature. The woman, her real hair a few sparse strings of grey over a liver-spotted scalp, fell from her chair and crashed to the floor.

The tiny dog, yipping in so high a register that Seth could barely hear it, darted in and sank its wicked little points of teeth into the vampire's leg. A hard kick, and the dog spun through the air. The tumbling body narrowly missed the fireplace, hitting the brick hearth and rebounding, falling like a loose furry rag.

Through all this, Seth had not stood staring aghast like the pretty blonde girl beside him. He'd torn open his father's suitcase and brought out a stake in each hand.

The appearance of the two lengths of sharpened ash elicited a hateful screech from the vampire. It came at Seth, stomping squarely on the old woman's ribcage instead of stepping over her.

Seth shoved the coffee table aside to make room, and tucked his chin down to give some protection to his neck. He held the stakes the way a fencer might have held a rapier and *main gauche.*

His stance was ready, his weight balanced easily on the balls of his feet.

The vampire paused. A spasm that might have been fear twisted its face.

The second hospital worker lowered his dead friend and got up, jaw set in angry resolve.

"No!" Seth shouted.

The man leaped anyway, tackling the vampire from the rear. They stumbled over furniture and trampled the old couple. The vampire flailed out and shredded the man's arm from elbow to wrist. They slammed into the counter hard enough to crack the glass front of the bakery case.

With a sickening snap, the man's arm broke. He cried out and tried to pull away. The vampire manhandled him with inhuman strength and drove him headfirst into the case. The cracked glass shattered. Spears of it ran into the man's flesh. His hands beat crazily. Cream puffs and strawberry tarts and miniature cheesecakes rained from the collapsed shelves.

All at once, the man went limp and sagged into the welter of shards and smashed pastries. His feet rattled and were still.

Seth was two steps from the vampire, stakes poised and wondering how well they would penetrate that chain-mail, when the vampire vaulted the counter like a springing leopard and seized the woman with 'Pamela' stitched on her apron. The phone fell from her grasp. A thin, indrawn scream squeaked in her throat.

The vampire whirled her around so that she was between him and Seth, with the ragged nails poised under her chin. The burning red eyes that met Seth's showed a level of craftiness he hadn't expected.

Pamela whimpered. Tears rolled down her face.

The red gaze shifted from Seth to the stakes, then to the floor, and then back to Seth's eyes again. The vampire jerked his head. His nails scraped lightly over Pamela's neck. The message was clear.

"Leave her alone," called a clear voice. The blonde girl stepped up. She was shaking, but her voice was steady as she held up the jade cross on its gold chain. "Get back. Get away from her."

The vampire exploded in a vicious rage. Pamela was thrown into the wall, her forehead smashing into it. Before she had even begun to fall, the vampire launched himself over the counter again. Diving at the girl. Lips skinned back from a shark's bristle of fangs. Claws outstretched.

The girl backpedaled. Her heels hit the green-clad leg of one of the dead men and she went down.

Seth met the vampire in mid-air with a roundhouse swing. The stake jutting from his right fist skidded over chain mail and sank into pasty white flesh just below the vampire's collarbone.

It wasn't a fatal strike, but it deflected the vampire's leap. Instead of landing atop the blonde girl, the creature collided with a table that gave way under its weight. Splinters of wood pierced it, the bloodless wounds smoking.

Faster than a striking snake, the vampire came up out of the debris and chomped its jaws at Seth's leg just above the knee. The heavy denim tore. Razors of ice and steel ripped Seth's skin, a crooked angle of a bite that only halfway sank in one fang.

Raising the second stake high in both hands, Seth thought of his father, of Jason and Deborah and the others. Then he brought it down, point-first, with every ounce of his strength, at the crown of the vampire's head. The sheared tip breached skull bone with a crunch, the blow also driving that one fang deeper into Seth's leg... then the fang snapped off at the root and the vampire toppled to the floor. White smoke rose from the twitching body.

To be sure of the kill, Seth retrieved the first stake, which had been jarred loose when the vampire had fallen onto the table. He yanked the chain mail aside, baring the chest.

Already, the flesh was turning greyish and dissolute. Seth set the point above the heart anyway, and leaned on it until he felt it penetrate all the way through the vampire's body and strike the unyielding barrier of the floor.

An acrid stink gusted up as the vampire withered away to dust. In seconds, the only things left were flattened, empty clothes, and the dyed spikes of its hair.

Breathing hard, Seth pried the brittle fang out of himself before it too disintegrated. He got up and surveyed the shop. Blood ran down his shin. His knee burned and throbbed.

A bitter oath rose to his lips but he choked it back. He hadn't been quick enough. Caught sleeping. Not on sentry duty, true, but he'd been asleep when the trouble started and that was reason enough for self-recrimination.

People had died. Too many people.

The old couple would probably live, though he knew that elderly bones didn't heal well and their recovery would be slow. Pamela might only be unconscious. But both hospital workers and the woman in the tight dress were dead in cooling swamps of their own blood.

He looked at the blonde girl. She was stippled with crimson droplets but unhurt. Her astonished blue eyes turned up to him. He saw that she was still holding the cross.

"I... I thought that it would... drive him away," she said in a faraway voice like someone on the verge of fainting.

"You only made him mad," Seth said.

"He... he was a vampire. Wasn't he? The way he turned to dust when you ... "

Seth nodded. He didn't like it; he'd hoped that she had been too stunned to realize what was going on. None of the others had been in any shape to witness the end. But she had seen, and understood. Shocked though she had to be, somehow it had gotten through to her.

"I have to leave," he said, scooping up the stakes. He wiped them on a handful of paper napkins from a dispenser, and threw the wad into the fire where they flared with sudden brightness.

"What, like... like the Lone Ranger on that old television show?" She laughed, though it was a brittle laugh. "Who was that masked man? What do I tell the police?"

"I... haven't been trained for this," he was surprised to hear himself say. The vampire's clothes followed the napkins into the hearth, except for the chain mail. That wouldn't burn. The clothes, covered in the dust, burned with electric-blue flames. "This part of it, anyway. A Centurion –"

"A what?"

He bit off the words. The phone was still swinging at the end of its cord, in decreasing swoops. A tinny voice queried from it. Any minute, and he'd hear the sirens.

This time would be worse than what had happened with Ratty and Hoag. The police weren't going to let this pass lightly, not with people viciously murdered.

"They won't believe you," he said to the girl. "You tell them it was a vampire, and they'll think you're insane."

"Am I?" she asked. Her eyes were awash with shock and he didn't think she realized half of what she was saying.

"Tell them whatever you want," he said, limping to his suitcase. He put the stakes back inside and stuffed the chain mail in as well, hating the cold, reptilian feel of the links. "It won't matter. They'll know it wasn't you. They'll call your folks and you can be done with this. It's over for you."

A strange, pensive look crossed her face. "Wait. Can't you explain–"

"No." He stirred the dust with his foot and threw the scraps of red, green and black hair into the fireplace after the wad of napkins and the clothes. The flames snapped and spat.

It wasn't very good, but it was the best he could do. It'd have to be.

The short hallway leading to the restroom also led to a back door, with a sign on it that declared it was for emergency use only. Seth reasoned that this qualified. He hurried for the exit, more lurching now than limping, blood soaking the knee of his jeans and trickling down his shin. He'd have to clean that wound. Disinfect it. Pour peroxide into it until it foamed up bubbling white. He paused to tie a dishcloth from the counter around it as a kind of bandage.

"Aren't you going to help them?" the girl asked.

"I've done all I can."

"Hey!"

"Sorry."

He turned the thumb-lock and let himself out, not into the trash-strewn alley that he'd expected but into a peculiar little nook formed by the angled walls of several buildings. The people who lived and worked here had taken some pains to make the most of the space by installing planters and benches. The plants were not exactly thriving, given that not much sunlight could reach down here, but it was still a surprisingly nice little refuge.

The only way out, not counting the other doors that doubtless led into other shops and apartments, was a skinny passageway between two buildings. A metal gate with a combination lock blocked the passageway's opening. He tossed his suitcase over and prepared to climb.

"Wait, okay? Wait."

The girl emerged from the coffee shop, carrying a purse and a suitcase of her own.

Seth's eyebrows shot up. "What do you think you're doing?"

"Coming with you."

"Says who?"

"I want some answers. I want to know what happened in there."

"You saw what happened in there."

"Yes." She swiped a strand of hair out of her face. "I saw a vampire. A *vampire*, for real and honest-to-God. And *you* knew about it. Or do you go around carrying stakes just for the heck of it?"

"I don't have time for this."

"That's why I'm coming with you."

He clenched his fists, but even in the midst of his exasperation he felt a flicker of something else. A wistful thought of how nice it would be not to be alone in this solitary nightmare anymore. "This is dumb. I don't have time to argue with you, either."

"So, don't." She struggled to heave her suitcase over the gate and couldn't manage it. "Argue later. Tell me later. And help me with this, please?"

"Can you climb this gate?" he asked, taking the suitcase and throwing it over. It landed beside his.

"Sure," she said, sticking her chin out in defiance.

"Here." He bent and made a stirrup with his hands, the fingers laced together.

The girl hiked the skirt of her jumper. "No peeking." The prim remark sounded mechanical, and she still had the dazed look of someone who could hardly believe where she was.

"I'm not peeking! Who are you, anyway?"

"My name's Natalie." She stepped into his hands and he lifted as she pulled herself over the gate. In seconds, she was on the other side and straightening her clothes. "What's yours?"

"Seth." He scaled the gate, hampered some by his hurt leg. "Look, you can't come with me. I... I don't have much of anyplace to go."

"That makes two of us, kind of," she said. "I was trying to get to my uncle's house, but it was all closed off with crime tape. So I thought I'd go to my aunt's, but I got on the wrong bus. I meant to call her once I was done with my cocoa. And now... vampires, I mean, I don't want to take the Lord's name in vain, but... Jesus!"

He flinched. "Don't say that."

"I'm sorry." She lightly hit her forehead with the heel of her hand. "Of course, you'd have to be religious to be a vampire hunter, right?"

"No! I mean ... " He took a deep breath. "You don't understand, that's all."

"I want to." Natalie glanced around uneasily as they left the narrow alley. They had come out on the far side of the block from the coffee shop, where the late-night city life continued undisturbed. "Are there... are there a lot of them? Vampires?"

"Not a lot."

"But you hunt them?"

"Sort of."

"What's a Centurion?"

"Forget I said that."

She grinned at him then, and he was amazed to see that the grin was lively and twinkling. "You'd only want me to forget it if it was important."

It occurred to Seth that, ever since he'd learned of how his father had met his mother while rescuing her from a vampire, he'd been having idle fantasies along those lines himself. Meet some pretty girl, save her life, fall in love. Except that in his fantasies, everything worked out better than it had for his parents in reality.

Now, here he was, having rescued a pretty girl from a vampire, and he was already trying to figure out how to get rid of her.

"Where does your aunt live? I'll take you there."

"She has an apartment," Natalie said. "But it's so late. I can't show up at her door at this hour. I really should call her first. Do you have a phone?"

"No. I know where there's a pay phone, though."

"Okay." She cast another nervous glance at the darker pools of shadow. "Is it safe to be out here?"

"Depends on your definition of 'safe.' That one was the first vampire I've seen in a couple of weeks, for whatever that's worth."

They mingled for a while with crowds of people coming out of bars and a movie theater. Nobody seemed to pay them much attention, though Natalie's top was speckled with blood and they were both burdened with luggage.

"How old are you?" he asked.

"Sixteen in December. You?"

"Eighteen. Did you run away from home, or what?"

"It's complicated," she said. "I was at school. A boarding school. Our Lady of Sorrows. It's kind of a convent, too. I think my uncle hoped I'd discover a vocation, you know, and become a nun."

"You ran away from a nunnery? Like… Ophelia in reverse?"

She looked at him. "Wow, a Shakespeare reference?"

"Hey, I went to school, too," he said, feeling nettled.

"I'm teasing," she said. "How often do I get to tease a guy? Or even talk to one? If the girls back at Sorrows could see me, they'd be jealous."

"Jealous?"

"Teasing," she said again, and twitched a smile at him. He realized she was still mostly in shock.

"I can see why you got thrown out of the convent."

"I did not get thrown out!" she said. "I left on my own. I was tired of being shut away from the world." Her smile faded and he saw the past hour's events darken her eyes with remembered horror. Now she knew where she was, and what she had seen. Now she understood. Her voice took on a tremulous note. "Though now that I know there are vampires out here and people getting killed… "

"You could go back," he said. But of course there *was* no going back. Never any going back. Only forward, for better or worse.

At a gas station, he waited on the tarmac while she slipped into the ladies' room to wash her face and hands and change into a clean outfit from her suitcase.

While she was in there, he thought about ditching her, but knew almost as soon as the idea came into his head that he couldn't. Like it or not, he'd saved her life and was stuck with her. Responsible for her. As in that old Chinese curse.

Maybe she'd fall apart later, when it all sank in, but he didn't think she would. She had guts. Guts, and too much will. He would probably find himself *unable* to ditch her. She'd keep showing up again, like the cat in the old nursery rhyme.

Natalie came out in an outfit similar to the first, except that the jumper this time was brown corduroy and the tights and turtleneck were a buttercream color. "All set."

"Pay phone's right over there."

She found some change in her purse and plugged the coins into the slot. He waited while she made her call, and heard her exhale in disappointment.

"Aunt Fiona, it's me again. Natalie. If you're there, pick up. I don't want to wake you, but I'm… well, kind of in a pinch. I'm at the gas station on… where are we?"

Seth told her, and she relayed it into the phone.

"Well, so much for that," she said, hanging up. "Do you know the best way to get to Landover Street?"

He went cold. "You don't want to go down Landover Street at this hour. Better wait until morning."

"Why?"

"You'd have to pass the park," Seth said. "Landover Park is a bad place. People disappear there, and die there."

"Is it vampires?"

"I don't know. I haven't gone there at night. But it gave me a chill, being there. It had their feel. Their stink. Stay away from that place. If there were Centurions here --" He stopped, closing his eyes in a wince.

"How many of you are there?" Natalie asked.

"Not as many as there used to be," he said grimly. "Not nearly as many as there used to be."

Chapter 15

Natalie had never been happier in her life to see the sky lighten toward dawn.

She hadn't thought she would be able to get a wink of sleep. The bus rides, hiking for blocks and blocks, the terrible things that had happened at the coffee shop, and then what she had persuaded Seth to tell her once they'd arrived here at his grubby hideaway? It all should have conspired to keep her in an unrelenting state of gritty-eyed wakefulness for the next five or six days.

Instead, once he'd insisted that they try to get some sleep and switched off his flashlight, she got drowsy almost at once. Her suitcase made a poor pillow, but the night was warm enough that she could do without a blanket. A spare flannel shirt of Seth's, draped over her upper body, served well enough.

The thin trickle of light through the boarded-over window roused her. She was used to getting up early. The day at Our Lady of Sorrows began with bells before sunrise, and when her eyes opened but her ears heard no bells, she suffered a momentary disorientation.

Everything came back to her once she sat up and saw Seth. He was stretched out on the floor, one hand curled around a stake.

His story had been downright unbelievable, or would have been if she hadn't seen the proof of some of it for herself. The pale kid *had* been a vampire. She was sure of it. She'd seen the fangs. Even acknowledging that the fangs could have been clever enamel fakes, the way he had disintegrated was no movie-magic special effect.

Vampires. All right. Vampires were real. And people called the Legion, or Centurions, knew about them. Acted, in fact, against them. The way Seth described them, they seemed to be some sort of a fraternal order.

"Like the Masons?" she had asked. "Or the Elks?"

Seth semi-agreed to this with a shrug and a nod. "Sort of, but it's more secret. Most people have never heard of us, and hardly anybody knows what we really do or where we really come from. Some even within the Legion probably don't really believe."

"And your job is to hunt vampires."

"Destroy them, if we can."

He'd told her how he was the sole survivor of the attack and fire that had wiped out the rest of his Cohort, and how his mother had then betrayed him to keep him from going to any of the other groups.

"She thought she was doing the right thing, I guess," he said, but his eyes were stormy and his lips compressed into a line. "Trying to protect me. But I didn't want to be protected, or left out. I wanted to do what I was born to do. I had to avenge my father, and my friends. I had to carry on the fight."

Asleep, he looked closer to his real age, or even younger. His dark hair fell down over his brow, and his mouth was relaxed. She knew it was absurd of her to notice such things, but he *was* good-looking. Strong, too, and quick, and smart.

He just happened to also be a crazed vampire hunter and member of a secret society.

But he had saved her, and let her tag along when he could have turned her away. He hadn't let her go wandering off down Landover Street in the wee small hours, there to get stalked and savaged by whatever lurked in the blackness of its parks, doorways, and alleys.

It was the rest of what he'd said that bothered her.

Bothered? That was too mild. Rocked her to the very core. Tore apart the sanity of the world as she knew it.

"Everything they taught you is a lie," he had said. "The biggest lie in human history. The one they call Jesus Christ was not the son of God. He was the king of the vampires."

"What? That's —"

"It's true. I don't know where he came from, or how, but he was a vampire. That's why they hate crosses. It has nothing to do with the cross having holy power. To them, it's a reminder, a taunt, of how their king was killed."

She protested, more offended than she ever would have believed. What he was saying not only went against everything she'd been told at school, but everything her inner heart had believed for as long as she could remember.

"But the Bible —"

"All a trick, all a lie. The New Testament part of it, anyway. Twisting and perverting the truth. Think about the Communion rite. The wine. The blood. That's what he did, don't you see? He had his chosen ones, his vampires, and he gave them of his blood to drink. To control them, and make them powerful."

"You can't really expect me to believe that Jesus was a vampire!" she had cried, louder than she meant. He'd hushed her. "It's impossible, Seth," she added in a whisper.

"Do you believe in the rest of it? The walking on water? The body disappearing from the tomb? The miracles?"

"Well, of course," she said, but warily, feeling like she was walking into a trap. "It's all in the Gospels."

"Which were handed down by the Apostles."

"Oh, no." She wagged a finger at him. "You are *not* going to tell me that the Apostles were in on it."

"They were vampires, too. The ones he created. The Elder Ones. Only the ones that he bit, and drained, and gave to drink of his blood, were ever really strong. They could pass on the curse of vampirism, but only in a weaker, lesser way. Like the one we saw tonight. He was an animal, Natalie. That's the way they are. Cunning, brutal animals. They lose their humanity, their souls."

"You're talking about two thousand years of history, of the Bible, of… of… well, everything that millions of people have accepted and believed. You're saying it's all a… a big con? A spin job?"

"That's just what I'm saying. The vampires started it, and ever since, others have carried it on. All of those churches, all of those preachers, everything… it's based on a lie. He *wasn't* the savior of mankind, but its doom. The ones who saw the truth and tried to stop it, those people, the Jews and the Romans, have been made to look like the bad guys. The one man who successfully fought off the blood-taint and told the Centurions how to find and catch the vampire king, that man has been vilified like no one else in history."

At that, she'd only been able to gape at him, and blink. She finally stammered, "You… you can't mean who… who I think you mean."

"Judas," Seth said evenly. "Judas Iscariot. He burned the taint of the vampire from his body, purified himself, and helped the Romans bring the reign of evil to an end."

It had all been too much, and after that Natalie only bobbed her head in acquiescence when he suggested that they try to get some sleep. She'd sat in silence as he laid out the defenses at the door, the cross and the garlic.

Now it was daybreak, the increasing light showing the room in its dismal splendor. The walls were chipped paint and graffiti, the floor a split and bumpy sheet of linoleum, the fixture in the ceiling a corroded socket absent of any bulb. Seth's belongings, what few there were, he kept neatly arranged. Besides the suitcase, he had a couple of cardboard boxes filled with thrift-store clothes and canned goods.

He'd been on his own for weeks, living here since losing his car. She felt bad for him. To have lost his father and friends that way, and then to have been driven out by his mother the very same night, had to be harsh.

Maybe it had sent him over the edge. She liked him, but it was preferable to believe he was insane than to believe he was right.

Either way, she couldn't stay here with him. She hadn't abandoned the school that had been her home for half her life in order to live like a refugee in a ramshackle old apartment building.

Seth woke the moment Natalie stood up.

"It's me, it's only me," she said, raising both hands with the palms out toward him.

He relaxed, loosening his white-knuckled grip on the stake. "Sorry."

"I have to go to the bathroom."

"The plumbing doesn't work. I've got a bucket in there."

"Oh, goody." Natalie made a face, but the need was too great. The tiny bathroom was all chipped tile and rust-stained porcelain. No mirror, which was just as well. She didn't expect that her looks had improved any after a night spent sleeping on the floor.

When she emerged, Seth had put on clean blue jeans and was buttoning his shirt over a nicely muscular chest. She remembered her manners and turned away, though not before sneaking one good long peek and wondering what the older girls back at Sorrows would make of him.

"I have to find my aunt's apartment today," Natalie said, accepting a plastic bottle of water and using it to wash her face. "If she did get my messages, by now she's got to be worried."

"I'll get you there."

"You don't have to, really."

"I don't mind." He wetted his hair and raked it back with his fingers. By daylight, his eyes were cobalt blue and his chin and cheeks bore a vague, dusky shadow.

"Well, okay," she said, inwardly glad. She wasn't ready to say goodbye to Seth yet. Crazy or not, she liked him.

Breakfast consisted of boxed juice and energy bars. Seth went through his suitcase, nose wrinkling in distaste as he pulled out the jingling silver heap of chain mail. He tossed it into a corner.

"Does the garlic help?" she asked as he retrieved the cloves and cross he'd set by the door.

"I don't know for sure. There's some truth in the old traditions, but not all. Folklore says that they can't resist counting seeds, for instance, but my father never heard of one being distracted from a kill that way. Not that he wrote about in his journal."

"Like on *Sesame Street?*" She affected a bad pseudo-Transylvanian accent. "Vun sunflower seed... two sunflower seeds... ah-ha-ha."

"Don't do that," he said, all seriousness. "Whenever there's a book, or a movie, or even a cartoon character, it makes people more familiar with them and then less likely to believe that they're real. Who's going to believe in real vampires when there's Count Chocula, or that one in the old Bugs Bunny cartoons who turns into a bat whenever anyone says 'abracadabra'?"

"*Can* they turn into bats? Wolves? Clouds of mist?"

"The mist, yes. I've seen it. I don't know about the bats, or wolves. The Elder Ones have the most power. They can hypnotize people, make them do their bidding. That's ... " His voice buckled under a sudden strain. "That's what my mother told the Legion had happened to me. She told them I'd been mesmerized, taken over. So no Centurion will ever trust me again."

"How could she be so mean to her own son? It's just awful. Can't you find them and convince them that she was lying?"

"There wouldn't be any way to prove it."

He snapped the latches closed, and Natalie knew that he'd just snapped the topic closed as well. She picked up her suitcase and her purse and they made their way down through the nasty-smelling staircase to the street. On the way, she had a better glimpse of the shabby conditions and the pitiful residents of the building.

"Isn't there anyplace else these people can go?" she asked as they came out into strengthening sunlight.

"Shelters, loony bins, or jail," Seth said. "Any of those is as bad as the other. At least here, they've got a roof over their heads. I've seen people sleeping in alleys, in cardboard boxes. Or camping out in the weeds under overpasses."

They walked side by side. Even though it was day, Seth stayed on his guard, always watchful. Natalie tried to follow his example but found that the more she tried to be alert, the more nervous it made her. She figured she'd end up a raving paranoid if this kept up. So, she left guard duty to him and looked at the people going by. A lot of them did appear to be homeless, and were either ignored or treated with scorn by the more prosperous ones.

Yesterday's endless trudging, and then a night's uncomfortable rest, had left her legs both stiff and achy. The brisk walk helped, but she was getting tired of carrying the suitcase.

Seth led her to a bus stop. "You said the 62, right?"

"I hope I have enough change," she said, digging in her purse.

"Natalie." He touched her hand. "Be careful, okay? Don't go near that park. Not even in the daytime, but never, *never* at night."

"I'm not going anywhere near that park," she said. "Cross my heart and hope to die."

"Okay," he said, but he didn't look convinced.

"The next bus isn't for fifteen minutes," she said. "Will you tell me more about the vampires?"

"Those are the secrets of the Legion. I haven't been properly initiated yet. I'm not a real Centurion. I'm not even supposed to know this much. I only do because my father left his journal behind."

"Come on, Seth. I think I have a right to know. If you hadn't been there last night, I might *be* a vampire by now." She paled. "Oh, God... is that what's going to happen to those poor people, the ones that got killed? Shouldn't we have done something? They're going to rise up, and –"

"Settle down," he said. "It's not that easy. They have to kill you a certain way in order to make you into another vampire. Drain you to the point of death, and then make you partake of their blood. It doesn't always work. I think most of them don't even know how, praise Judas. Otherwise, if everyone they killed became one, we'd be overrun in no time."

"Are you sure?" Then she did a mental backtrack. Had he really said 'praise *Judas*'? She wasn't sure if she would ever be able to get used to that.

"As sure as I can be." He hung his head. "One of them got my friend Jason that way. If the Elder One hadn't come along and finished him, I would have had to do it. Couldn't take the chance. Or else Jason might have come back."

"So you're saying that none of the people in the coffee shop were killed that way?"

"Right. It was... too messy."

The meager breakfast gave a lurch in Natalie's stomach as she recalled the bloodbath in vivid detail. She'd been trying not to think of it. Of Pamela, who'd been kind to her – but Pamela, at least, had probably survived mostly unscathed. The others hadn't been so lucky.

Her treacherous imagination decided to show her a vision of the coffee shop as it could have been, with her body sprawled there amid the others and a horrible hole in her neck.

"Is there any way," she said, her voice weak, "to know them? I mean, before they start biting?"

"They don't cast shadows or reflections," he said. "They don't show up on film or video."

"How's that possible? They're still... well, bodies, aren't they? I always thought that they didn't reflect because they didn't have souls, but that doesn't make sense. An ordinary dead body, which shouldn't have a soul anymore, it casts a reflection. Right?"

"My father said it has something to do with an aura they give off," Seth said. "An energy of some sort. It... bends light around them, or something. He didn't really know. It's not like we ever had a chance to study them under scientific conditions."

"Running water? Holy ground?"

"Vampires are creatures of the earth. They don't like fire or water. Fire can hurt them, and a lot of them are afraid of it. Water's another story. If it's natural running water, a stream or a river or an ocean, they can't cross on their own. If someone tries to take them across, say, on a boat, the vampire loses its powers and falls into a torpor."

"A what?"

"A state like a coma, or a deep sleep. Man-made running water, though, doesn't have the same effect."

"You mean a stream from a garden hose, or a swimming pool?"

"Yeah."

"So, holy water from a tap wouldn't count, no matter how much it was blessed by a priest?"

Seth frowned. "Holy water's no good."

"Oh, of course," Natalie said, amazed at how rational their discussion sounded. "Because religion's a sham, so there's no such thing as real holy water. Or holy ground, either, I bet."

"They do tend to stay away from churches," Seth admitted. "More because they hate seeing crosses. I doubt it'd really stop one if it was determined. A lot of the rest is folklore, tradition, stuff nobody's ever been able to test well enough. Roses, for instance. Vampires are supposed to have an aversion to roses as well as garlic."

Far down the street, the blue-and-white bulk of a city bus appeared. Natalie glanced at it with a mix of relief and regret.

Seth, meanwhile, went on. "Though they don't *have* to sleep in coffins on their native earth, they prefer it. The lesser ones, at least. I don't know about the Elder Ones. Sunlight destroys some of them, not others. There's so much that we still haven't figured out, even after two thousand years."

"Here comes my bus," she said.

He started, as if he'd almost forgotten why they were here.

"Remember, you promised to be careful and stay away from the park," he said, picking up her suitcase from the bus stop bench.

"I will. But you be careful, too, Seth."

"Yeah."

The bus heaved to a stop, snorting exhaust. A thin-faced man in a uniform squinted out at them.

"Thank you," Natalie said. "For everything."

She wanted to hug him good-bye, but here at a city bus stop with the driver and other passengers looking on indifferently was hardly the time and place. She squeezed his hand instead, as she took her suitcase.

Seth smiled. "Goodbye, Natalie."

"Goodbye."

The doors wheezed shut. She found a seat and watched him out the window, as the bus pulled away from the curb and headed down Landover Street, toward the green and sunlit park.

Chapter 16

The Glass Ridge Apartments didn't live up to their name in terms of the ridge; they were situated on a perfectly flat stretch of land where the streets had been laid out in a grid of right angles. They did, however, live up to the glass part, rising high into the sunny spring morning. The windows were tinted to mirrors on the outside, turning the structures into pillars of golden flame.

From the inside, Natalie supposed, there would be crystal-clear spectacular views of the city. She hadn't been here before, but she had no trouble picturing glamorous Aunt Fiona in a place like this.

The bus ride had been short, only a matter of blocks. Natalie had experienced a single bad moment when the bus stopped directly across from Landover Park. She told herself that even if she hadn't heard about it from Seth, it would have unsettled her nerves, but that was not true.

It didn't look like a lair of unspeakable evil. The trees swayed in the breeze, turning light and dappled shadow into an ever-moving game of tag over the grass. A few people strolled the curving paths or sat reading the daily paper on the benches. Toddlers squealed in the playground while their mothers or fathers looked on.

All the same, she felt like someone had trickled melting ice down her back. She was glad when the new passengers got on and the bus continued moving.

Natalie turned her gaze to a metropolitan hospital and found herself curiously spellbound by its clean white angles. She tried – once more and still with no notable breakthroughs – to think of what she would say to Aunt Fiona and Uncle Anthony when the three of them were reunited.

After what she'd been through in the last twenty-four hours, leaving Our Lady of Sorrows felt like comparatively small change. A vampire had almost murdered her, and it would be hard for even something as extreme as expulsion to have stacked up against a brush with death. Or Undeath.

Of course, she was not about to tell her aunt and uncle any of that. If she breathed a single word of Seth's take on religion to Uncle Anthony, he would fall down in a foaming fit on the spot. She remembered all too well the guest room converted to a family chapel, and the artwork that had adorned her bedroom. And presumably, still did.

She got off the bus at the corner by a small shopping center and walked back up the block. Only when she reached the doors did she realize that it was a secure entrance, and she did not have a key.

A row of intercom buttons was set into the wall beside the door. No names, just numbers. Aunt Fiona's was 411.

Taking a deep breath, she pushed the button.

"Yes? Hello?"

It was a stranger's voice, a woman. Natalie remembered Aunt Fiona's answering machine tape saying that if a caller wanted to leave a message for Fiona Sevrin, to press 1, and for Jill Nicholson, to press 2.

"Is this Jill Nicholson?" Natalie asked.

A pause stretched out. In the background, she heard other voices in low conversation, and the whirring, gurgling noise of something that sounded like a vacuum cleaner held underwater.

"No," the woman said. "She's... not here. Who's this, please?"

"My name's Natalie. I'm looking for my aunt, Fiona Sevrin. Is she there? Do I have the right apartment?"

Another pause.

"Hello?" Natalie said.

"Miss Sevrin isn't here either," the woman finally said. "I'm with the cleaning service."

"Oh." Of course, Aunt Fiona would have maids come in. Menial tasks like vacuuming and washing windows were beneath her. "Well, could you buzz me in? I'd like to wait for her."

A third, and longest, pause.

"I'm not sure that would be a good idea," the cleaning woman said. "It's a mess up here. Your aunt wouldn't want you to see it."

"How much a mess could it be?" laughed Natalie. "Did she have a party?"

"How can I put this? We're not a regular service. Our company specializes in… um… hazardous material clean-up."

Her initial image of liquor bottles and overflowing ashtrays faded. "You mean like chemicals and nuclear waste?" Or was Aunt Fiona running a drug lab?

"Blood."

The single word tolled in her ear like a death knell. The woman continued to speak, saying something about 'work in cooperation with police and criminal investigations,' but Natalie was too stunned to make sense of it.

"Whose blood?" she broke in. Now she was seeing again the yellow crime scene tape across the front door to Uncle Anthony's house, and the bullet hole in the garage. "Is Aunt Fiona all right?"

"She's fine," this stranger said. "She's the one who arranged for us to come in and do the job now that the police are finished up. I think she's been staying at a hotel, though I don't know which one."

"But what happened?" Natalie asked, leaning so close to the intercom that the little black holes in the speaker looked like deep wells. "Who was hurt? How badly?"

"I can't give out that information. I've probably said too much already. Maybe you should try back tomorrow. We'll be done and out of here by then, and she'll be able to move back in. I can leave her a note that you dropped by."

Natalie wanted to argue, but she recognized the tone of finality in the woman's voice. "Okay. Thank you."

There was a click, and she stood looking silently at the numbers 411 over the button. The day was still bright and growing warmer all the time, but inside, Natalie was chilled. The theory that Uncle Anthony's house had been caught up in a drive-by or other accident was not holding up. It'd be too much of a coincidence for disaster to strike brother and sister in the same short span of time.

A dazzle of sunlight bathed her as the outer door opened and a young man in a charcoal-grey suit and burgundy tie came out. He had a briefcase in one hand and a cell phone in the other, his expression harried.

"… there by eleven, and we'll… " he said, striding on his way without a look back. He didn't notice when Natalie caught the edge of the closing door and slipped into the building.

She saw the mailboxes. The one for 411 was crammed full, with a few magazines and catalogs that hadn't fit bundled into a rubber-banded roll on top. Nobody had bothered to collect the mail in a few days. Aunt Fiona must have arranged for the cleaning crew by phone, perhaps getting in touch with the superintendent.

When the elevator doors opened on the fourth floor, the smells of harsh, astringent cleansers abused her nose. The apartment door was open. Yellow plastic sawhorses with 'caution' written on them in English and Spanish blocked the entrance. A large sturdy trash bin was in the hall, the legs of a chair sticking out of it. An industrial wet-vac squatted nearby, looking like a cousin of R2D2.

Moving closer, Natalie saw people in brown coveralls and rubber gloves. They also wore disposable white masks, and the women had hairnets. A company logo was stitched in gold on the backs and breast pockets of the coveralls.

The source of the bubbly vacuum noise turned out to be a carpet shampooer, being trundled back and forth in foamy paths over a section of the living room floor. Other workers used spray bottles and sponges on the nearest wall. In spots they hadn't reached yet, Natalie saw rusty brown stains on the off-white paint.

She could see little else of the interior. Nor did she particularly want to. But there didn't seem to be anything else for her to do except stand here and wait.

A stocky brunette with a hairnet looked out at her, lips pursed in a frown. "Are you the girl I was just talking to?"

"Yes," Natalie said. "Please, can't you tell me what happened?"

There was none of Pamela-from-the-coffee-shop's kindly manner about her. Hard-faced, hard-eyed, she regarded Natalie with a flinty disapproval. "You shouldn't even be up here."

Chastened, and knowing glumly that she wasn't going to get anything more out of this woman, Natalie picked up her suitcase again. It was beginning to feel like a permanent weight attached to the end of her arm.

With no better ideas for the moment, she returned to the lobby. In one corner was a nook with upholstered chairs, large fake plants in brass pots, and a glass-topped square table with an untidy stack of newspapers. She flipped through and, on the second page of the local-news section, found the article.

NO LEADS IN HOME-INVASION ROBBERY, DEATH.

Natalie read it from start to finish, though there wasn't much information. Jill Nicholson, age 39. Murdered. Her roommate – the paper didn't use Fiona's name – had evidently walked in on the scene and sustained minor injuries in a struggle. The perpetrator escaped with a few items of jewelry. Neighbors reported seeing a tall, unfamiliar black male in the building around the time of the crime. Police were investigating. Anyone who knew anything about the crime was asked to come forward.

She went through the rest of the paper, looking for anything about the trouble at Uncle Anthony's, and found nothing. But she did run across a brief blurb about Landover Park, officers responding to shouts and gunfire. A quantity of bullets, spent casings and blood had been found, but no bodies.

Half-hidden by the fronds of an immense plastic fern, Natalie heard Fiona's voice before she saw her.

"I don't like this, Anthony. We can't be sure he's gone. What if he comes back?"

"If he was going to, he would have by now. They took care of him, Fee. We have nothing further to worry about."

"Except the police, poking into my life again." She came into Natalie's view, long legs scissoring briskly beneath the flaring hem of a seafoam-green dress. Her auburn hair was swept up and pinned. But no amount of make-up, no matter how skillfully applied, could hide the puffed bruise discoloring her cheekbone. "I thought I was finally done with that."

Natalie had never heard anything about police poking into Fiona's life before. Then again, she and her aunt weren't all that close. Fiona and Anthony had taken her in as a favor to a family friend, seen to it that she was fed and clothed and raised and educated, but that was about it.

She'd been dumped on them, an obligation, and here she was snubbing what they had given her. Our Lady of Sorrows was neither inexpensive, nor easy to get into. She should have been thankful for such an opportunity. Instead, she'd run away.

Uncle Anthony bore only the slightest resemblance to his older sister. His hair was a darker reddish-brown, his eyes hazel where Fiona's were as green as the jade cross around Natalie's neck. He was of average height and build, not handsome, not homely.

"This has nothing to do with you, Fee," he said, pushing the elevator button. "It will blow over."

"Aunt Fiona? Uncle Anthony?" Natalie stood up from concealment, a nervous tremor in her voice.

They both whirled with the stark, startled expressions of people who thought a berserk maniac was about to rush at them with a chainsaw. In that instant, they *did* look alike.

"Natalie?" Anthony found his wits first. "Good Lord, girl, what on earth … ?"

"What are you doing here?" Fiona asked, a hand fluttering at the base of her throat. "You're supposed to be at Sorrows."

"I've… I've left," Natalie said. "It wasn't for me."

"Not for you? Don't be silly!" Anthony came toward her, his gaze skimming her from the top of her disheveled blonde hair to the toes of her sensible shoes. "You're a fright, too. What *have* you been doing?"

"I tried to call, but no one was ever home. I left messages… and then I took a bus. I went to the house. It was… please, what's going on?"

"You were at the house? When?"

"Last night."

"This is unreal," Fiona said. "Natalie, you can't be here right now. It's a bad time. We've had some trouble. I think that the best thing is for us to get you back out to Sorrows. Let us handle things here."

"I don't want to go back."

"Our Lady of Sorrows is a splendid school," Anthony said, sounding hurt. "I thought you liked it there."

"I did," she said. "But it's been eight years. Most of the other girls my age have transferred to regular high schools or declared a vocation by now, and taken their initial vows."

"Which is what you were going to do," he said.

"I don't want to become a nun, though."

Anthony sucked in a breath. He did not quite clutch his chest and stagger, but Natalie felt it had been a close thing. She flinched in expectation of his sudden outrage and anger.

"Do we have to do this here?" Fiona asked before he could speak. "Now? Like I said, this is a very bad time."

"I know about Jill," Natalie said. "I'm so sorry. Was she a good friend?"

Fiona glanced at the newspaper strewn over the table, and clicked her tongue. "Oh. I see."

"Are you all right? It said you were hurt, and … " Natalie gestured toward Fiona's bruised cheekbone.

"It's nothing." Fiona turned to Anthony, her tone becoming urgent. "Anthony, we can't stand around here like this. Maybe you'd better take Natalie to the car. I'll go up alone and get my things."

"Minutes ago, you didn't want to go up there alone," he said.

"Detective Jackson said he might be stopping by this morning." Her words were pointed, sharp as spears, though Natalie didn't know why they should be. "You remember Detective *Jackson*, don't you, Anthony?"

"Ah," Anthony said. "Yes, right. Come along, Natalie. The car's just out front. We'll clear this up, but not here and now."

"Ten minutes," Fiona said. "I'll grab a couple of bags, check my messages, and we can go. Here, take the mail." She thrust the sheaf of envelopes, catalogs, and magazines at Anthony.

Natalie followed him out front to the car and loaded her suitcase into the trunk, then got into the back seat. She slouched low, dejected and confused. The past twenty-four hours seemed more and more like some disturbing dream. A sick feeling churned in her stomach and her eyes felt hot and feverish.

Uncle Anthony sat behind the wheel, fingers drumming it in a rapid rhythm. Natalie noticed that he kept checking the rear view mirrors, and peering intently at every pedestrian and vehicle that went past. He looked as though he hadn't shaved in a few days, which was a radical turn for him.

"Oh, Natalie," he sighed. "Natalie, Natalie, Natalie, what *are* we going to do with you?"

"I know you're disappointed –"

"I had such plans. Such hopes."

"I'm sorry." She sank even lower on the seat, until she could have rested her chin on her knees.

"You're special, you know. You're not like other girls. Unique. One of a kind. You were to have had a great and glorious destiny. Now, though … " His hands lifted from the wheel long enough to flap in a hopeless gesture.

Her breath caught in her chest and she dashed a furtive tear from the corner of her eye. Not trusting herself to talk without crying, she said nothing.

"It's my fault," he said, low, as if speaking more to himself than to her. "I should have been more thorough, more careful. I jumped when I should not have jumped. If I'd checked, made sure it was the real one… goat's blood. How could I have been so stupid?"

She didn't know what he meant. Goat's blood?

"And now here you are," he said. "What am I to do with you, Natalie?"

"Please," she said. "All I want is to go to a regular school and be like other girls."

"Other girls?" he echoed. "Girls who smoke, drink, listen to awful music, get tattoos, go around with boys?"

"No!" Not all of it, she inwardly amended. She did like music. As for going around with boys, she had already spent the night with Seth; if her uncle heard that, he would have a stroke on the spot.

"You're better than that," he said. "Special."

"I'm not so special. I'm just me."

"Natalie, you don't even know who you are. Your mother was so perfect. A saint. An angel."

Her tears forgotten, she sat up straighter. "My mother?"

"You look just like her, you know. Her very image. As it should be, of course. Her hair, her eyes, her lovely, flawless features. And I know that you must have her sweet, gentle spirit."

"Tell me about her," she urged.

Always before, when she'd asked about her parents, all Aunt Fiona would say was that they'd been friends of hers from college, and they'd died in a terrible accident, leaving Natalie orphaned and alone. And that it was better not to dwell on the unpleasant past.

The Sevrins weren't even her real relatives. She had called them that for as long as she could remember, an honorific with no blood ties to back it up. She knew nothing about her true family.

"I knew from the first time I saw her that Karen was special," he said with a wistful sigh. "What happened was an omen from God, telling me that she was the one."

"Karen," said Natalie. "My mother's name was Karen?"

Anthony cleared his throat. A guilty flush mounted in his face. "Forgive me, Natalie. I shouldn't go on about that."

A bizarre possibility made her squint at him. The way he'd sounded when talking about her mother… had he been in love with her?

Fiona hurried out of the apartment building, loaded down with a make-up case and three bags. Anthony helped her stow them alongside Natalie's one suitcase in the trunk, and she folded herself gracefully into the front seat.

"Any sign of your detective?" Anthony asked.

"None." She looked over her shoulder at Natalie. "Your messages, though. What were you doing at a gas station at midnight?"

"Finding a pay phone," Natalie said. She told them an edited version of the previous day, beginning with leaving Our Lady of Sorrows. She left out Seth and any mention of vampires.

"You were out all night?" Anthony had gone pale. "I'm surprised at you, Natalie. The city can be a dangerous place. You never know what you might run into out there, and you're much too important to put yourself at that kind of risk."

"But what happened?" Natalie pressed. "I was at the house. Where's Mrs. Boryenka?"

"Dead, I'm afraid," Anthony said. "Someone broke in. Home invasion robbery. One of those random, senseless things."

Natalie had fonder memories of Mrs. Boryenka than she had of either Sevrin, but pushed her grief aside for now. "Just like Jill Nicholson?"

"No," Fiona said quickly. "Not connected. Not at all."

As she said this, Natalie saw Anthony give her a brief look, as if about to disagree. Then he caught himself, but the lapse was enough.

"Isn't it horrible?" Anthony shook his head. "What the world's coming to. We need a miracle, we truly do."

CHAPTER 17

"I'm Madeline Margos. I contacted you about the books."

Magdalena hated this, mingling with the living. Being about by day, when she felt weak and vulnerable. The sunlight alone would not harm her. It might burn the weaker of her blood-children, but all it did to Magdalena was to temporarily rob her of most of her powers.

The woman in the doorway almost made it worthwhile. Slim, lovely, with a graceful swan's neck, she wore a simple floral sundress and strappy high-heeled sandals that added another four inches to her height. If she'd been half her age, a nubile eighteen instead of close to forty, she would have been much more to Magdalena's personal tastes…

Reminding herself that she was here on business, not on the hunt, and that she had feasted long and well on sweet Sarah not so long since, she extended a hand. Fiona Sevrin took it. Her touch was hot and sweetly pulsing with life. A fleeting frown crossed her face. Her subconscious, at least, noticed the dead and deathless chill beneath Magdalena's sun-warmed skin.

"Miss Margos, please come in."

Thus invited, Magdalena stepped inside. To her, it was only a formality, not a necessity. She could enter this home unbidden if she wished, any home. But to have the door opened to her, to be made welcome, was always easiest.

Her foot came down on a patch of carpet that looked perfectly ordinary, but a thrill ran through her.

Blood had been spilled there, and not all that long ago. Spilled, and the carpet steam-cleaned until all visible traces were gone, but *she* could sense it. Only a fleeting sense, it was not enough to tell her anything about the victim, but it was enough to intrigue her.

"We're selling the house," Fiona said as she ushered Magdalena through a living room filled with cardboard boxes, bubble wrap, and newspapers. "The books are my brother's, and he wants to find a home for them before we moved. Easier than packing and transporting so many volumes. It's quite a collection."

Magdalena reminded herself to fill and empty her slack lungs with regular breaths. She could hardly take her gaze from Fiona's delicate throat. So much older than she liked her usual victims, and undoubtedly no virgin, but... "I'm eager to see them," she said, though she was not quite as eager as she had been before seeing this lovely woman.

She imagined Fiona Sevrin suspended in a medieval device, all hooks and blades and cruel metal barbs. Naked there, trapped, helpless. Poised above the deep tub where Magdalena would sit waiting, naked herself, one hand on the lever. A pull, and the hooks and blades and barbs would rend Fiona's flesh. The blood, a thick scarlet shower... lavishing Magdalena with its heat... running in rivulets over her body.

That was the way it used to be when she'd gone by another name and been countess of the castle. Dozens of servant girls had met their end in that infernal machine, first hired and then stolen from the surrounding countryside.

"— the study," Fiona said, shaking Magdalena from her reverie.

Floor to ceiling shelves, filled with books, lined the walls. At the sight of them, her eagerness did return in full force. Magdalena hardly knew where to start. So many of them... titles in old languages, bindings worn away by the centuries, but shelved cheek and jowl with modern scientific texts.

"Most impressive," she said, making an effort to keep her inhalations as subtle and even as possible, to mimic the breath of the living. "Why is your brother selling such a collection?"

Fiona shrugged and swept at a curl of hair that tickled ever so enticingly at the side of her neck. "Anthony hasn't been feeling well lately. We've been through some hard times. He says he's lost interest."

"In what?" She ran a finger along a shelf of disparate titles.

"All of it," said a man's voice.

Magdalena turned to look at him. She judged him to be a year or two younger than his sister.

"Anthony, this is Miss Margos," Fiona said. "She's here about the books."

"Yes." He glanced at the shelves with a pained expression. "They did mean a lot to me. Was there something in particular you were hoping to find?"

"Biblical histories," she said. "Grail lore. Any writings of Joseph of Arimathea."

His lips twitched. "I think I can help you, then."

"I'll leave you two to sort this out," Fiona said. "I've got things to pack."

Magdalena made sure not to watch as the other woman walked away. She concentrated on the books instead. The chances of her finding what she sought were slim, but the sight of so many ancient volumes sent a tingle of anticipation through her. Then she spied a section of titles that made her have to hide a wry smile.

"You certainly have quite a selection on the Shroud of Turin," she said, keeping her tone neutral.

"It… fascinated me as a boy." He rummaged through the books. "Did you know there were several Shrouds? Most of them fakes?"

"*All* of them fakes."

He glanced over his shoulder at her. "*All* of them?"

"So I'd heard."

"Are you a scholar?"

"You might say that." She touched some of the scientific journals. "And you're a scientist as well?"

"I try to be."

"A strange combination. One doesn't often see a man of science who also pursues ancient knowledge."

His sigh was full of the weariness of a lifetime. "I have two doctorates and studied to become a priest. I'd hoped to blend those two sides of me and do something so grand, so wonderful, that the world would never be the same."

"What sort of thing?" Her gaze went again to the journals. Genetic engineering. Essays on the principles and ethics of cloning. A book about Dolly, the sheep.

"Never mind," Anthony said. He forced a chuckle as barren and dry as the sandy earth beneath the lining of her coffin. "You'd think I was insane."

"I don't even know you."

"Wouldn't matter. You'd think it, and you might be right." He sighed again. "And I was close, too. So close. If I just could have gotten the *real* one... you're sure that they were all fakes? There must have been a real one. What happened to it? How do you know?"

"Do you mean the Shroud?"

"No, no, forget it."

The pieces came together, and Magdalena had to hurriedly cover her mouth to hide her fangs as she laughed aloud. "You meant to clone the blood from the Shroud of Turin?"

"Don't be ridiculous," he said, too fast, flushing crimson. "It isn't possible. Everyone knows you need a live cell to make a clone. And besides, think of the ethical implications."

"Wait," Magdalena said. She sat down at his desk and steepled her fingers in front of her face. "Let me think about this."

"There's nothing to think about," he said. "I told you, it can't be done. Besides, you're the one telling me that there is no real Shroud of Turin. So what's the use? Without a source of viable DNA, it's just not possible."

"Suppose, doctor, that you had another source of DNA? A legitimate one?"

"Like what?" he scoffed. "The Grail? The Holy Lance?"

"It is not exactly a lance," she said, permitting herself a knowing smile.

His face flushed darker, and she could hear his quickened pulse rushing in his veins, throbbing at his wrists and temples. "You've... you've seen it?"

"I *have* it."

"This is preposterous –"

"For weeks now," she cut in, "I have been seeking, with every ancient spell and ritual at my disposal, to bring about the Resurrection. Every one of them failed. That is why I'm here. I had been hoping that one of your books might hold the information I need."

"You have the true Lance? The blood? *His* blood? You're sure of it?"

"Oh, without a doubt. Tell me your plan."

He sat down in a wingback chair and ran his hands through his hair. "I developed a solution to revitalize dead cells," he said. "The purpose was to enable scientists to clone dead or extinct animals from samples of their DNA. Mammoths and the like, but naturally it would apply to any cells. Not just animals."

"And did it work?"

Anthony nodded slowly. "Too well. I realized the error of my ways after that. I saw that it was wrong to be using this development for profit, when it really should be used to benefit the world. It was what God wanted of me."

"God told you this?"

"Is that so hard to believe?" He shot her a defensive look.

As a two thousand year old vampire, she wasn't about to argue with him over what was and wasn't hard to believe. "Go on."

"At first, I did think it was incredible," he admitted. "Why would God need *me* to do this? Hadn't He managed fine the first time around? Wasn't it arrogant of me to presume to be a modern-day version of the Holy Ghost? But the more I thought, the clearer it became. God works His wonders through us, too. So why shouldn't He choose a scientist this time, instead of a miracle?"

"Certainly," Magdalena said, trying to keep her lips from twitching with irony.

"I was doing this to serve Him," Anthony said. "Not just because I could. I wanted to make the world a better place. It's time, Miss Margos. Two millennia, we've been waiting for the Second Coming. But maybe waiting isn't enough. Maybe, to bring it about, we have to *do* something."

She gestured encouragingly. He was a madman, to be sure. It shined through in the hectic light in his eyes, the pressured speech. But he just might be the sort of madman she could use.

"I've been careful and deliberate every step of the way," he said. "I did my research. I knew that it had to be done just right. Like it was before."

Magdalena raised her eyebrows. "What are you saying?"

"Some foolish people actually think that the Immaculate Conception refers to the Virgin Mary giving birth to the Christ Child," he said.

"I understand." She wasn't about to correct him, though of course she knew that the truth of her long-lost king's origins was far more bizarre even than that.

"Which meant that the first step had to be meeting *that* condition. Finding a surrogate mother untouched by Original Sin."

"Not just any virgin would do?"

"No, of course not!"

"I can see how that might have posed a challenge."

Anthony grinned, and it made him look demented. "Ah, but not for me. I'd already taken care of it."

"How?"

"By –" His face went shuttered, his eyes narrow. "I don't know if I should even be telling you this. I hardly know you."

How she wished it were night, when her powers would be at their peak! She could persuade him then, mesmerize him, make him think and feel and believe whatever she wanted.

"I think we can be of great help to each other, doctor," she said. "We have the same goal, but we're both missing what we need to make it work. You have a technique, but no sample. I've failed in my attempts at rituals, but I have the blood."

"You're suggesting a partnership?"

"Yes." And let him find out in due course how wrong he had been, when instead of the Son of God, he brought back the king of the vampires.

"We know nothing about each other," he said.

"But we do have a common purpose."

She was not above using her corporeal charms to lull men even by day, though she found the touch of any mortal man abhorrent. She'd tolerated it now and then over the long millennia, finding it a useful tool. She had even married a few times. The legends lingered on, surrounding her very-mortal husbands with evil clouds of their own. Tepes. Borgia. Others.

With Anthony Sevrin, she realized that her dark beauty had little effect. He did not linger over her figure, or fall captivated by the dusky spell of her eyes.

No seducing him, then. Just as well.

He had been making thoughtful sounds to himself while Magdalena waited. He turned to her, head high, chin resolute.

"I'd need access to a study and a private lab," he said. "We've had some trouble here lately and, as you can see, are on the verge of packing up to move and sell the house. Fiona's already found a new place, but Natalie and I --"

"Natalie? Your daughter?" Aha, and that would explain the faint signs that suggested the nearby presence of a youthful girl ...

He pointed out the window, into a sunny backyard where a slender blonde teenager sat reading in a white wicker chair. Anthony said something about her being the orphaned child of some very dear friends, but Magdalena was barely listening.

Such freshness, such sweetness, such innocence, such a lovely and succulent temptation!

"Come and stay with me, then," Magdalena said, interrupting his talk of some woman named Karen who had been too perfect and precious for this earth. "Bring your work, your research. Bring your Natalie. Together, we have everything we need. Together, we can do this."

PART FOUR – THE CONCEPTION
May

CHAPTER 18

A light stuttered on the answering machine. Natalie poured a glass of root beer and played back the messages.

One from the real estate agent, saying she'd like to show the house on Tuesday at 1:00, would that be convenient for them?

Another from the manager of the storage facility they'd rented, asking Anthony to call him back.

A hang-up.

A recording reminding any registered Republicans to vote in the upcoming election… which was still months away.

A woman's voice said, "This call is for Fiona Sevrin. Miss Sevrin, I've been unable to reach you at your other number and we had this one as a back-up contact in our files. This is Dr. Archer, from Parkview Hospital. Please call me back. It's about Karen Cross." She left a number and an extension, said thank you, and hung up.

Karen Cross?

Natalie rewound the tape and listened to that one again. Dr. Archer, whoever she was, *did* say Karen Cross.

That couldn't be right. Natalie's own last name was Cross, and her mother's name, as she had only recently found out from Uncle Anthony, had been Karen.

But her mother was dead. Had died when Natalie was only a baby.

Another vote-for-me message, this time aimed at Democrats.

A sales pitch for vinyl siding.

Lastly ...

"Hello? Hello, this is Elise Melvey." The speaker had a flat Midwestern accent. "I'm trying to reach Fiona. Fiona, the hospital called us. They say Karen's taken a turn for the worse. Pete and I will be out there as soon as we can, but I wanted you to know. I'll call you later."

There was a click on the line, and the answering machine turned itself off.

Goose bumps hunched up on Natalie's arms. She set down the glass of root beer before her shaking fingers could drop it.

Another call about Karen? About her mother?

It wasn't possible. How could you be dead and take a turn for the worse?

And if she *wasn't* dead, if she really was in Parkview Hospital under the care of Dr. Archer, why had nobody told Natalie? Who was this Elise Melvey person? Elise and Pete... could those be Karen's mom and dad? Natalie's grandparents?

Except, Aunt Fiona had always maintained that Natalie had no living relatives. That was why custody of the orphaned baby went to her.

She got out the directory and found the address for Parkview Hospital, on Landover Street, near Aunt Fiona's old apartment. Natalie would just bet the hospital was the same clean white building she'd ridden past on the bus.

Before she was fully sure she intended to leave, she was out the door with her purse and her bus pass. The bus routes were more familiar to her now, and soon, she was disembarking in front of the hospital, across the street from the park.

The hospital was large, with frequent maps announcing 'You Are Here,' but that wasn't the problem. She knew where she *was*, just didn't know where she was trying to *go*.

For a while, Natalie roamed the halls and waiting rooms. She looked in the gift shop, bought a brownie in the cafeteria and a daisy bouquet from a sweet old lady selling them in the lobby, watched tropical fish swimming lazily in saltwater aquariums.

Then a light bulb seemed to flick on over her head, and she returned to the elevators, where she found a large board listing all of the departments and doctors.

Archer, Janet. Chief Resident, Long-Term Care. 5th Floor.

She rode up, glad that a hospital was one of those places, like an airport, where someone could wander around alone without being questioned. Glad, too, that a lot of the volunteer candy-stripers were about her age, some of them wearing school uniforms similar to her own under their peppermint smocks.

The 5th floor had that hospital hush, a quiet really made up of numerous low noises. The muted beep of medical equipment, the soft conversations of nurses, televisions with the volume turned down, the squeak of white shoes, and barely identifiable piped-in classical music combined to create the hush.

With her daisies held in front of her, walking like she knew what she was doing, Natalie went along the corridor reading the names on the charts stuck in plastic holders beside each door. In the rooms she passed, the patients were indistinct humps beneath blankets. Few of them were sitting up to read, hardly any of them had visitors.

There was no sense of urgency in the air on this floor. There was little in the way of hope, either. Only patience and long-suffering resignation. This was where people lingered, beyond immediate help but not well, waiting to see whether they would get better, or worse.

She saw a chart with *Cross, Karen M.* typed on the tab. The door was ajar, the room beyond cloaked in cool purple shadows thanks to a lowered blind the color of violets.

No one was nearby. Natalie ducked into the room and tiptoed toward the bed. It was a standard hospital bed, but a shelf over it held a row of stuffed and ceramic dogs. Pug dogs one and all, whitish-brown with black pushed-in faces and curly tails. Some of them wore bows on their heads or around their necks. On the wall was a framed poster of a basket full of pug puppies.

The woman in the bed was motionless, eyes closed, face framed by recently-brushed hair. No one would have mistaken her stillness for natural sleep, even without the constant but subdued beeping and blipping of the machines.

One arm, strapped to a board atop the bedspread to allow the placement of the IV, was thin and lacked muscle definition. The other was drawn up against her chest. Her legs were drawn up, too, bent at the knees with the heels tucked back, putting her almost into a fetal position.

Natalie inched closer, trying to make out details. The woman's hair was a light color, maybe blonde like her own or maybe grey or totally white. Her cheeks were sunken, her lips slack.

Could this poor husk be her mother? This body, as thin and wasted as a stick figure's, a face that looked more ancient and dead than something unearthed from an Egyptian tomb?

Uncle Anthony had said Natalie was the very image of her mother. That might have been true years and years ago, but she saw nothing of herself in the woman on the bed.

And yet... a strong, if undefined, sensation of familiarity held her in thrall.

"Karen?" she asked in a whisper. She touched the back of a curled hand. "Karen Cross? Mother? Mom?"

Nothing happened, no eyes opening in a moment of sudden awareness, and Natalie felt hopes dashed that she hadn't even known she'd been harboring.

She saw a photograph in a silver frame, sitting amid the pug dogs. It showed a trio of young women, two of them in lilac chiffon gowns with big puffy sleeves, the third in a frothy white lace wedding dress. The taller and thinner of the bridesmaids was unquestionably Aunt Fiona. The other bridesmaid was overweight and sadly pretty. The woman in the center, the bride, was a smiling blonde who could have been Natalie's own older sister.

Taking the photograph from the shelf, she studied it more closely. Yes, this was the bedridden patient, radiant and happy in this moment of time so many years ago, a pearl choker around her neck and white roses in her hands.

Natalie brushed a fingertip over the image, and then her own face. The resemblance was eerie. Uncle Anthony had been right.

In a few more years – very few; the bridal Karen looked achingly young – Natalie might look exactly like this.

Hearing someone coming, she put the photo back and picked up the daisies. A shadow bulked in the doorway. The room's light flicked on, and in the onslaught of stark light, Natalie froze, feeling like a deer on the highway.

"Oh, sorry, didn't mean to give you a fright," the nurse said. She was a tall and wide woman who could have done credit to a football team. Instead of the traditional white, the nurses here wore salmon-pink scrubs.

"I… I was just … " Natalie gestured with the flowers.

"Isn't that nice of you?" For all her squared-off, mannish features, the nurse's smile was benign. "I think there's a carafe in the bathroom. Not a Lalique crystal vase, but we do what we can."

"Um, thanks." She found the carafe, added water, and arranged the daisies.

"Don't mind me," the nurse said. "I'm checking the IV. Are you a candy striper?"

"Thinking of it," Natalie said, surprising herself by lying like she did it all the time. "I know some girls who do, and they said I could come down and look around, check it out, you know."

"You probably shouldn't be roaming around on your own, but no harm done." The nurse adjusted the hanging metal rack that held the IV bag, then stood gazing down at Karen Cross.

"Is she all right?"

"In a coma, the poor thing. She's been deteriorating for a while now. The doctors think it's only a matter of time."

"What happened to her?"

"Everyone asks that. Mrs. Cross, here, is like our own Sleeping Beauty. It's so tragic. All that bad luck heaped on one person."

"How long has she been in a coma?"

"Almost eighteen years now."

"That can't be right," Natalie blurted. "Eighteen years? Are you sure?"

"See that picture up there? That was taken the day it happened. Such a terrible thing. She and her husband had just left their wedding reception and were on the way to the airport, going on their honeymoon, when a drunk driver hit their limousine. If you look on the back, it's got the date."

Natalie took the photo down again. Sure enough, someone had pasted a round sticker on the frame's cardboard backing. It read 'Karen, Fiona and Jill,' and a date. September twenty-first, almost eighteen years ago.

"She's been in a coma for that long?"

The nurse nodded. "For a while, they thought she'd come out of it, but she never has."

"What about family? Her husband, her parents? Does she have any children?"

A funny sort of frown puckered the nurse's mouth. "The husband died a couple of years later. The parents live out in Nebraska or Iowa or one of those corn states."

"But no children?"

The only thing Natalie could think of was that her mother must have been pregnant at the time of the wedding, had maybe even hurried the wedding along. The trouble was, it didn't add up. None of it added up. Not the months, because she'd been born on December 25, and there was no way the slim woman in that picture had been six months along. And not the years, either.

Again, the nurse got that funny frown, and didn't answer.

"I'm sorry if I'm being too nosy," Natalie said, politely, when her every instinct wanted to clutch at the nurse and shake the truth out of her.

"Here," the nurse said. "Why don't I show you around the ward? It'll give you a better idea of what you can expect if you sign on as a candy striper."

She couldn't very well refuse, so Natalie spent the next forty-five minutes touring the Long-Term Care Ward and meeting other nurses. They were all cheerful in a mild, low-key kind of way. As the dinner hour neared, the hall livened up a bit with visitors and orderlies pushing wheeled carts containing the meals for those patients who could eat under their own power, or with help.

Her guide, who introduced herself as Kay, let Natalie help spoon-feed orange Jell-O to a toothless old man who drooled amiably and bobbed his head at her. After that, she invited Natalie into the nursing station and offered her a donut from a Krispy Kreme box.

"So, what do you think?" Kay asked.

"It's so sad," Natalie said. She had lost her appetite, and held the donut without biting into it.

A candy striper, a trim young woman with curly blonde hair, darted in and signaled to all the others. "That cute detective is here again," she said, blue eyes all but glowing with eagerness.

"He's old enough to be your father, Cindy," Kay said.

"So's George Clooney, but I wouldn't let that stop me."

"You know," said a male nurse around a mouthful of donut, "this could constitute sexual harassment. You're making my workplace all uncomfortable, talking about men like they're objects."

"Pff," Kay blew at him, and got up to lean over the desk for a look, alongside Cindy and a couple of other nurses.

Finally, even Natalie joined them, looking down the hall to a spot where a tall man in a dark brown suit stood talking with a grey-haired woman wearing a lab coat over a maroon skirt and striped blouse. They were right outside of Karen Cross' room.

"Who's that?" Natalie hissed.

"Detective Jackson," a brunette nurse said. "He's like Harrison Ford, isn't he? Just keeps getting handsomer and handsomer."

"And the lady with him?"

"That's Dr. Archer," Kay said.

"What do they want with m—with Mrs. Cross?" She had almost said 'with my mother,' but caught herself in the nick of time.

"I heard they finally had a funeral for that poor baby," the brunette said to the male nurse. "They must have given up hope after all this time."

"I would have given up a lot sooner," he said. "Sixteen years is a hell of a long wait, never hearing anything. Wish they'd caught the person, though."

Natalie didn't think Kay would elaborate, so she nudged Cindy the candy striper. "What are they talking about?" she murmured.

"You know the lady in that room? I guess she had a baby once, and somebody stole it from the hospital."

"A baby? When?"

Cindy shot a conspiratorial glance around, saw that no one was paying much attention to them, and leaned close. "They sued the hospital, too. Not only because the baby was kidnapped, but because–get this!–the lady wasn't pregnant when she got here. It was like two years later or something. They figure some weirdo must have done it to her while she was in the coma. Isn't that gross?"

"You're kidding!" Natalie gasped.

"Nope! It's what I heard, anyway."

"Who stole the baby?"

"They never found out." Cindy shrugged and went back to a covert admiration of Detective Jackson.

CHAPTER 19

"Let's go over it again," Detective Kyle Jackson said. "The whole thing, start to finish."

Janet Archer pinched the bridge of her nose, edging her glasses higher on her forehead to do it. "Detective, it's been sixteen years. I doubt that I'm suddenly going to recall anything that will crack this case. Believe me, I've been over every detail in my mind a million times."

He consulted a very old and worn leather-bound notebook. "The condition of Karen Cross, her pregnancy, came to your attention when she had already been a patient here on the coma ward for twenty months."

"Yes, that's right."

"What was your course of action?"

"After confirming by means of repeated lab tests, I contacted Mrs. Cross' husband."

Jackson turned a page. "Richard Cross. Severely injured in the accident that resulted in his wife's coma. Lost his right leg from the knee down. Hospitalized for ten weeks, fitted with a prosthetic leg. And what was Mr. Cross' reaction?"

"He was shocked to say the least," she said. "Angry. Furious would be a better word. Understandably so. His bride, who'd been in a coma for almost two years, suddenly turns up pregnant."

"And there was never any indication how it had happened."

"Mrs. Cross underwent a complete examination, which turned up no actual physical evidence of rape. Or indeed of any sexual activity whatsoever."

"Which means?" Jackson asked.

"Which means very little, Detective. Penetration is not always necessary for conception to take place. Genital-to-genital contact can, rarely, result in impregnation."

Dr. Archer hoped she wasn't turning red. She and Sam had been hurried into marriage themselves because of just such an incident, thirty-five years before. Heavy petting gone too far. But she had been a conscious, active participant. Poor Karen Cross, inert in her hospital bed, had not even been aware.

Averting her face from the detective's piercing gaze, she noticed a young girl in white blouse and pleated plaid skirt, arranging a rack of magazines. She made a mental note to talk to that girl or her supervisor later. Candy stripers were required to wear their smocks at all times, and name badges as well.

"The responsible party was never located," Jackson said, more a statement of fact than a question.

"That's correct."

Every male employee and volunteer had been interviewed, both by Janet Archer and the chief of Parkview's security, but there had been no way to determine the guilt of any one man.

"Could it have been Mr. Cross?"

"It's possible," she said. "He was a faithful, frequent visitor to his wife's room before we discovered her condition. But why, if he was the father, would he have denied it? Aside from the dubious and disturbing circumstances, that is."

"There was a substantial lawsuit, as I recall."

"Yes. Both Richard Cross and Mr. and Mrs. Melvey, Karen's parents, sued the hospital for negligence."

"And a second lawsuit, filed later by the Melveys, when the baby disappeared."

"Richard Cross had nothing to do with that one," Janet said, one corner of her mouth a wry tuck.

"He had petitioned to have the baby aborted, isn't that right?"

"But the Melveys contested it. They said that if Richard denied paternity of the baby, which he was steadfastly doing, he had no right to authorize an abortion. Even if he was, by virtue of those few hours of marriage, Karen's legal next-of-kin. The legal wrangling dragged on so long that it was almost a moot point.

Another couple of weeks and the fetus would have been too close to term."

Jackson tapped his pen against his lower lip. "Which way was the wind blowing? Were the Melveys likely to win, or was Cross?"

"I'm no lawyer or judge," she said, raising her hands. "From what I heard, it seemed like Mr. Cross's wishes were going to prevail."

"Then he died," Jackson said. "Timely."

She looked at him, momentarily speechless at what he might be implying.

"With Cross out of the way," he went on, "the rest of his family had no legal recourse, and so the Melveys got their way."

"You can't think that the Melveys had anything to do with his death," she said when she recovered the power of speech. "They're a nice couple, a little befuddled, maybe, but decent and honest people all the same."

"I didn't say that they did," Jackson said. "It nags at me, that's all. All these years, this has nagged at me. That's why, though the case may be officially closed, it's still open as far as I'm concerned. We've got a woman who is mysteriously impregnated, a husband who threatens to abort the baby but ends up dead himself, and then, to top it all off, the baby is swiped out of the hospital when only a few hours old. Add in the fact that a lot of people made a pile of money, and I can't help but be suspicious."

"Believe me, I'd like to know what happened as much as you would," Janet said. "Karen Cross has been my patient since she was admitted here. I was there when her baby was born. But I just don't know what to make of any of it."

"Let's go back to the birth. What do you remember?"

"Everything. It was Christmas morning. I'd gotten up early to put the turkey in the oven, and the kids were waiting to open presents, when I got called in because Karen Cross was in labor." She gave a little headshake of amazement. "It was, I must say, one of the eeriest things I've ever witnessed. That poor woman, comatose, her mind gone, but her body straining with contractions."

"No C-section?"

"We'd discussed it, Dr. Lange and I, but we'd only had a guess of the due date and thought that there were a few weeks yet to go. When labor began, we decided to see how it progressed, and if necessary would have stepped in with an emergency Caesarian. As it turned out, we didn't need to. The baby was delivered normally at six o'clock that evening."

"A Christmas baby," Jackson said. "Healthy?"

"Perfectly healthy, though a little small. She had a full head of blond hair."

"What was done next?"

"A nurse cleaned, weighed, and measured her, then took footprints, and a blood sample. The baby was then fed and taken to the nursery."

"What about the mother?"

"Once she'd expelled the placenta, her body lapsed into its previous state. I think we'd all hoped that the rigors of birth would be the very thing to waken her from the coma, but of course that didn't happen. She was lactating, so a pump was utilized to draw off the milk. Breast milk, especially in the first few days, contains important nutrients that help babies develop their natural immunities."

Jackson waved his pen in a circular motion, as if saying that this was more information than he really needed or wanted to know, and would she please hurry through it to get to the rest.

"With both of them in capable hands, I returned to my office and placed some phone calls. One was to the Melveys, who'd been planning to fly out closer to the due date. Another was to Dr. Willick, the hospital's chief administrator. I also called and left a message for Fiona Sevrin, Karen Cross's best friend. She and the Melveys had made private adoption arrangements. After that, I went home."

"And then?"

"Had a belated turkey dinner and was in the middle of opening presents when the phone rang again. It was the duty nurse, Angela Dombrowski, informing me that the Cross baby had vanished."

"What did you do?"

"I rushed back here and organized a top-to-bottom search of the hospital."

"Do you lose patients often? Babies?"

"Never, Detective Jackson," she said. "Nothing like this had happened in my tenure here, and I had not heard of it happening before my time."

"Who had access to the hospital nursery?"

She pinched the bridge of her nose again. "I've told you. Any member of the staff could have gotten access to the keys."

"Visitors?"

"More than usual. It was Christmas Day, after all."

"Do you recall seeing any members of Richard Cross's family around the hospital that day?"

"No," she said slowly. "No, I never saw or heard from any of them after his death."

"What about Fiona Sevrin?"

"I got a call from her three days later. She'd been out of town on a ski trip. One last fling, she said, before the baby was born and she had to settle down to the responsibilities of motherhood. She was devastated to hear about the kidnapping. I remember how tirelessly she worked with the Melveys. They sent out fliers, went on the news and pleaded for the baby's safe return ... "

"I know," Jackson said.

"Of course you do, I'm sorry. You were right there in the thick of it with them."

"What more can you tell me about Karen Cross?"

"Very little, I'm afraid. She's begun having trouble breathing, and it might soon become necessary to put her on a ventilator. Eighteen years is a long time to be in a coma. She's been living on IV solutions for almost half her entire life."

"You don't think she'll ever come out of it."

"Her chances of coming out of it were never very good. Each year, those chances have dwindled. You've seen how she's pulling into a fetal position, and how her muscles have atrophied despite the best efforts of our physical therapists."

Jackson snapped his notebook closed and returned it and his pen to his inside jacket pocket. He let out a long sigh. "It's like everyone is giving up," he said.

"Sorry?"

"That funeral service a few weeks ago, the one the Melveys held for the baby. A clear sign that they've given up hope. Now, you tell me that Karen is dying. It's as if she knew, or sensed, and she's giving up too."

Janet tipped her head. "Have *you* given up?"

"Maybe." He sighed again. "Every time we'd get a report about an unidentified orphan or runaway, or some kid's body being found, I'd think that maybe this was it, that we'd found Karen's baby. It never was. My head tells me that she's been dead for years. The kind of people who kidnap newborns often do so because they can't have children of their own and desperately want something to nurture, but at the same time they often have terrible parenting skills and tempers, and end up killing the babies. My head says that must be what happened to Karen's little girl."

"But, obviously, something else is telling you different."

"My gut," he said. "My instinct. I don't want to go the rest of my life wondering who got Karen pregnant, and if he was the same person who stole her baby, and where that baby is. She'd be grown up now, as old as that candy striper right over there, if she's alive. Probably having no idea who she really is. If I did find her, I'd hate to shatter her world like that. Imagine suddenly finding out that the person you think of as a parent is really a criminal."

"It haunts me, too," Janet said, stricken by the evident anguish she saw in his eyes. "I go home to my own family every night so thankful that they're with me. And I feel so bad for Karen. I often wonder what I'd do if she did wake up, and I had to be the one to tell her that she'd had a baby, and that the baby was lost. I never met her when she was herself, before the accident, but I believe everyone who said what a genuinely special woman she was."

"You can tell that just by looking at her," Jackson said. "I think every cop who saw her when they worked on the case fell in love with her a little."

"Here, too," she said. "Everyone who works with her feels that way. Our Sleeping Beauty."

Jackson's pager went off. He clapped a quick hand to it, looking abashed the way some people do when their electronic devices commence beeping in a public and quiet space. "I should get back. You'll let me know if anything changes?"

"Certainly."

He left, and as Janet turned toward the nursing station, she saw the same blonde teenager at the magazine rack. Her hands were full of outdated issues of *The Reader's Digest* and *Newsweek*. Janet saw that the girl's face was ashen, and the blue eyes that stared blankly at the magazine covers sparkled with incipient tears.

"Excuse me," she said, in a gentle tone. "Are you all right?"

The girl twitched and hastily stuffed the magazines into the rack all helter-skelter with their pages bent up at the corners. She straightened them. Her chin was quivering.

Janet realized that she must have overheard some of the conversation with Detective Jackson and been deeply affected by it. That happened a lot on the Long-Term Care ward. These young, innocent kids weren't used to the slow misery of chronic illness.

"Fine," the girl said. "I'm sorry. It's just… it's all so sad."

"Yes, it is," Janet said, giving her shoulder a reassuring squeeze. "But we get used to it, and we do the best we can. Isn't that right?"

"Yes, Doctor."

"We should see about getting you a proper smock and nametag," Janet said. "Is it your first day?"

"I'm… trying it out." She sounded for all the world as if she was struggling to hold back tears.

"Do you want to go into the lounge and take a break?"

"No, thank you." The girl smiled a brave, shaky little smile that made Janet want to give her in a motherly hug.

"All right, then. I'm Dr. Archer. If you decide to volunteer here, come and find me. I'd be happy to help you get the hang of the place."

She headed for the nursing station, thinking ahead to a good strong cup of coffee. As she stirred in sugar, and sipped the brew, her mind returned to the blonde girl. That, she thought, was exactly what Karen's baby would have looked like if she'd lived. About the right age, too. Wouldn't it be funny if –

Janet shot from her seat. A nurse, Peggy Daniels, cried out in surprise at the sudden movement, and cried out again a split-second later as her own cup of steaming coffee splashed into the lap of her salmon-pink scrubs.

Paying no attention to this, Janet dashed to the door of the nursing station and stuck her head out into the hall. She threw searching looks in all directions. The girl, where was she, where was the girl?

"What's the matter, Dr. Archer?" Kay asked.

"The candy-striper, the blonde one without a smock," she said. "Where is she?"

"Who, Natalie?" Kay pointed to the elevators. "Said she had to go. The poor kid was all shaken up. I think she'll be back, though. First day's always the --"

"Natalie?" asked Janet in a hoarse croak.

"That's what she said her name was. I didn't get the last name. Why?"

She couldn't answer. Kay had been working at Parkview for close to twenty years, but for the first half of those she'd been an emergency room nurse. Kay hadn't been on the 5th floor when Karen went into labor.

But Janet had been there, and Janet still remembered Dr. Lange saying to all of them that Natalie would be the perfect name for a baby born on Christmas Day.

Chapter 20

Natalie went through the next several days like a sleepwalker. She got up, ate her meals, did her chores and went to bed all in the same murky, troubling fog.

Anthony Sevrin did not comment on her uncommunicative, rote habits. He had never been one attuned to the moods of people around him before, and there was no reason for him to be different now. Instead, occupied as he was with the final stages of packing and moving and selling the house, he hardly seemed aware of her presence at all.

She could no longer think of him as Uncle Anthony. The honorary title had never been very heartfelt anyway. There was no family warmth or closeness. She was... a ward, like in a novel by Dickens or one of the Bronte sisters.

As she shuffled through her routines, and helped box up the last few attic items for their trip to a rented storage unit, all Natalie could think of was what she'd learned at the hospital.

What puzzled her most was *why*. It sounded like Fiona had been set up to adopt Karen's baby anyway. Why a kidnapping? Why never tell Natalie the truth? That her mother was alive? That she had grandparents? Why let those grandparents go on believing that their daughter's only child had been stolen, and probably killed?

And... who was her real father? Who had been so sick and insane as to do something like that to a helpless, comatose woman? Why?

As a child, she'd never lived with Fiona. Always here, in this house. In this room. But it had never felt like her own room. The house had never felt like home.

Now she knew the reason. Her entire life had been a lie. No wonder she'd always felt off-kilter, slightly out of place. She *didn't* belong here. She wasn't here honestly, legitimately.

Where, then, did she belong?

Nowhere.

She was lucky to be anywhere at all.

Her mother's husband wanted to kill her before she was even born. That revelation had hit her like a slap. The man who should have been her father, but wasn't, wanted her dead. He'd profited from her conception, and then tried to take her life. If not for his own sudden demise, he would have gotten his way and Natalie never would have drawn her first breath.

And her mother... not dead, but not alive either. Existing in some living death every bit as horrible as the undeath of the vampires.

Whenever Natalie had felt low and alone, she used to try and seek comfort in the idea that her loving parents were looking down on her from Heaven.

But it was all a lie.

Her mother had never even known she was going to have a baby. There had not been any joy and anticipation in the pregnancy and birth. Natalie had never been held in her mother's arms, or felt her mother's kiss.

Everything she had imagined was smashed to pieces.

The father that she had dreamed of, tall and handsome, so proud and devoted to his wife, was as false as a cardboard cutout of a man. Her real father, whoever he was, had been a rotten, slinking, miserable wretch who would rape a comatose woman.

And Natalie herself, instead of being the product of a true and sacred union, was the illegitimate result of his perverse actions.

On her fifth night since visiting the hospital, the last night before the move, Natalie ended up in the bathroom with a razor blade in one hand and the other turned over to expose the blue embroidery of veins beneath the white skin.

Suicide was wrong, she knew that. One of the worst and most unforgivable sins. She'd go to Hell for sure.

One of the girls at Sorrows had hanged herself from a closet rod, and the Sisters had told the rest of them that they could pray for Allison if they wanted, but it wouldn't do her soul any good.

The razor blade glimmered lethal silver between her fingers. To get it, she'd had to break apart a safety razor, and the shards of pink and white plastic littered the bathroom counter.

One quick swipe? It'd all be over.

"No!"

Angry denial made her fling the blade into the sink. The bathroom was empty except for a single set of towels, a mostly used up roll of tissue, and her toiletries bag. The click of metal on porcelain was startlingly loud.

She'd cut the pads of her fingers. She stuck them in her mouth and slumped against the wall.

"I'm not giving up," she mumbled. Her own eyes stared back at her, wide, as if astounded by what she had just nearly done.

Not until she had some answers.

Natalie pawed through her toiletries bag but found no bandages. She wrapped her fingertips in swatches of bathroom tissue instead, tucking the ends under to hold them in place. Blossoms of red grew on the white.

She returned to the bedroom, now an empty shell of bare walls, a mattress with blanket and pillow on the floor. Her suitcase sat at the foot of the mattress. She changed into a flannel nightgown and slippers, putting her dirty clothes in a drawstring laundry bag that filled half the suitcase.

With most of the house's furniture stowed either in the storage unit or in the moving truck parked outside, every noise seemed magnified. Every creak and groan and footstep. She could hear Anthony moving around downstairs, more of his endless pacing circuits.

He hadn't slept in days, so keyed up that his entire body seemed charged with electricity. He'd developed a short, snappish temper.

It was the project, she knew. Whatever project he'd be working on with that Margos woman had him so frantic that he could not stand all this tedious business of relocating and setting up housekeeping.

If Natalie went to him and started flinging questions about her parents, he might lose control altogether. Not that she feared him in any physical way; he had never raised a hand to her in her life. But he could and would pack her off in a flash, if not back to Our Lady of Sorrows, to someplace even more somber and restrictive.

The thought came to her again... what if *he* was her father? He had idolized Karen; that much was obvious...

To think of him doing something like that was just so repellent that Natalie gagged. She didn't want to think of him doing *anything* sexual, whether with a woman or a man or by himself. It was too disturbingly wrong.

She turned off the overhead light and stretched out on the mattress, with the blanket pulled up to her chin. Anthony hadn't slept due to nervous energy; Natalie's own sleep was slow to arrive, thin, and bothered by dreams she was glad to be unable to remember when she woke.

The door to the chapel opened and closed, catching her on the edge of sleep. She heard the audible but indistinct sound of Anthony's voice in the cadence of prayer. The chapel had not yet been packed up, at Anthony's insistence. It would be last.

As she was on the verge of drifting off again, she was for no reason abruptly wide-eyed and fully awake. The fine hairs on her arms and the nape of her neck rose up and her breath snagged in her chest like silk on a thorn.

Something was wrong in the house.

It was too quiet. She could no longer make out the sounds of prayer. Of course, that didn't mean anything; Anthony was as wont to lapse into silent prayer, as he was to mutter scientific jargon to himself.

No, this was a stealthy, sneaky quiet that set her nerves to clamoring.

Natalie rose from the mattress and put her slippers back on. She crept to the door. The knob was so cold she thought her hand might stick to it, the way it would stick to a chunk of ice. But the knob wasn't cold… she was cold, frozen from within by some fear she couldn't put a name to.

A night light in the bathroom was the only source of illumination in the upstairs hall. It showed Natalie the shape of a man standing outside the chapel door.

She knew at once that he wasn't Anthony. He was too tall, much too broad in the shoulders and chest. Beyond that, she could make out few details. He seemed made all of darkness.

His head turned. She shrank back, afraid that she had made some noise. Or that maybe the breath of a draft caused by her opening door had alerted him.

He faced the chapel again, paused for a moment, and then dissolved to smoky wisps that flowed through the keyhole as if drawn by a wind.

Her heart, which had been skittering, seemed to jerk to a halt.

Vampire? Seth had said… mist …

"Philips! No! Dear holy God, no!" Anthony shouted. "You cannot be here, you cannot be in here!"

It was followed by a low but deadly snarl.

Natalie's fingers clamped so hard on the doorknob that they ached. Her eyes wanted to leap from her head, though there was nothing to see but empty hall and closed doors.

Anthony shrieked. A thudding crash made the house shake and the chapel door rattle in its frame.

"In the name of God!" Anthony called, the words muffled and hysterical. "Begone from this place in the name of God!"

The snarl again, the vampire's spitting, toothy growl. And a cold, mocking laugh.

Seth was right.

Another crash sounded. This time, the chapel door did not rattle, but exploded as Anthony Sevrin flew through it in a hailstorm of splintered wood. He hit the far wall, where only days before there had been a sepia-toned wedding photograph of his grandparents, and rebounded to the floor in a groaning heap.

The light spilling from the chapel was a flickering ruby radiance from the tinted-red glasses of the votive candles. It made the blood coursing down Anthony's face look dark and thick as syrup. From cheek to chin, his face hung in ragged flaps. The arm that gripped a gleaming mother-of-pearl cross in one trembling hand was raked with slashes as if he'd raised it in self-defense.

The vampire stepped into the hall. Blood ran from the knife he held at his side. He cast no shadow. The ruby light seemed to shift and dance around him, through him.

He wore a baggy black jumpsuit that was torn, dirty, and stained. One of his feet was bare, the other encased in a combat boot. His skin was the color of ashes mixed with mud. When he parted his lips, his fangs stood out in stark contrast.

"No," Anthony said, his free hand trying to hold his face together. "You're dead, Philips, damn you, you're supposed to be dead, they killed you, you can't be here. You weren't invited. That chapel is holy ground, and by this cross, so help me—"

"Hsssss!" Philips stepped toward Anthony. His boot came down on a slat of broken wood that rested across another, so that the end tilted up. His bare foot scraped along it and his hiss turned into a wordless bellow of pain.

Anthony lurched to his knees and thrust the cross at Philips. "Back, I say!"

Enraged, the vampire struck out. Knife met cross with a screech of metal that made Natalie flinch. Both items jarred from the hands of their respective owners and lay on the carpet, entangled, looking like some strange piece of modern art.

Philips grabbed Anthony, fists curled in his sweater, and dragged him upright. Blood from Anthony's shredded face rained down on Philips' arms. Anthony kicked and thrashed, but for all the good it did he might have been a toddler in the hands of a large, angry parent.

The red-rimmed eyes of the vampire locked onto the bulging, staring ones of his prey. Anthony sucked in an uneven breath. His struggles slackened. His head fell back limply against the wallpaper, exposing his throat.

Natalie's slippers made scuffing noises as she ran, and she was sure that her quick panting must be loud as the chugging of a steam engine, but Philips, intent on his next meal, did not turn.

She seized the biggest chunk of the broken door. Slivers pierced her palms but she barely felt the brief stings. Holding it overhead in both hands, her jaw set and her lips peeled back in a determined grimace, she drove the point of the board into the vampire's back.

Her weight fell against Philips, who in turn fell against Anthony, pressing him into the wall. The fangs that had been inches from sinking into Anthony's throat missed and gashed his earlobe instead.

Beneath her, the vampire was cold as death but alive with hideous spasms of life. Maroon fluid bubbled from the wound in its back.

It hurled her away with a surge of strength. She stumbled backward over the wreckage of the door and sat down hard in the open chapel doorway.

Most of the furnishings had finally been packed, leaving only the three-foot-high gilded crucifix that Anthony said his grandmother had brought from Italy, and a small bureau whose drawers held matches and a Bible, and whose top was covered with the shimmering rubies of the candles in their red votive glasses.

Philips turned to her. The piece of jagged board still stuck out of his back, too low to have even come close to the heart. It joggled with every step but did not fall free. Behind him she could see Anthony against the wall, blank with shock. He could not help her. There would be no timely intervention by Seth, either.

She would not look into Philips' face. As he leaned down toward her, she snatched up another long splinter and, eyes shut, rammed it upward with all her might. In rapid succession she felt resistance, puncture, and a dribble of liquid like the dregs of a tepid cup of tea.

The vampire uttered a strangled howl and recoiled. Natalie risked a look. The splinter had gone up through the underside of his chin, nailing his tongue to the roof of his mouth and sticking into his head.

Scrambling away, she barely felt the damage she was doing to her hands and knees.

Philips clawed her nightgown, scored her shoulder, and then she was past him and on her feet again with yet another piece of broken door. This one was stout, blunt on one end, pointed on the other. A nearly perfect stake.

He twisted toward her, ripping the splinter out of his chin as he did so. His jaw fell open. A gush of stale blood ran out.

Natalie drove the point of her stake at the breast pocket of his jumpsuit. It skewered an old, flattened half-pack of cigarettes and sank into Philips' chest. He hissed and struck her a glancing blow on the side of the head.

The stake hadn't gone in far enough. She beat at it with the heel of her hand.

He yanked her into an embrace. The blunt end of the stake collided with her collarbone, sending a bolt of pain through her but driving the wooden length another half-inch deeper into him. He snapped at her face. She wrenched her head aside, leaving him with a mouthful of hair.

Then the hallway took a crazy revolution, and the next thing Natalie knew, she and Philips slammed to the floor.

She saw a silvery shine and grabbed for it, cutting her hand on the knife but getting hold of the heavy cross. Rearing up so that she crouched over Philips, she brought the mother-of-pearl cross down on the end of the stake and used it like a hammer, blow after blow, driving it home.

The stinking arctic wind of the vampire's dying scream blasted into her face. He arched convulsively, flinging Natalie to the side. His hands scrabbled at his chest, where the stout piece of wood was only visible as a half-inch stub poking out of a welling puddle of purple-black blood.

In his final moment, Natalie saw Philips' brow furrow in confusion. His eyes found hers but there was no vampiric power in them, only a vague questioning. Then they dimmed, and his head lolled, and he lay still.

She sprang away, shuddering, watching him. But Philips did not sift away into dust. His flesh and skin sagged a little, that was all.

Anthony got slowly to his feet. He and Natalie stood looking at each other over the body, both of them bleeding, neither of them sure what there was to say.

Chapter 21

In their preparations for the move, the kitchen had been all but emptied. The only foodstuffs that remained were intended for an easy breakfast before the final loading. Still, there was tea, and Natalie brewed them each a cup once they had finished patching up their various injuries.

She insisted on doing this chore herself, tweezing wooden slivers from her skin and applying antiseptic ointment and bandages from the first aid kit that Anthony kept in his bathroom.

Anthony himself was in far worse shape, and probably could have done with a trip to the hospital. His violent trip through the chapel door might have cracked some ribs. The gouges on his face and forearm could have used stitches. As it was, he settled for folding thick pads of gauze and taping them into place. His split earlobe looked like it had suffered the painful removal of an earring.

By unspoken agreement, they avoided mentioning the stiffening body in the upstairs hall until they were both as mended as they were going to be, in fresh clothes, and with cups of strong, sugar-laced tea in front of them.

The mother-of-pearl cross, dented from its debut as a mallet, rested on the table between them. Its mellow shine did little to soothe Natalie's nerves. How could it be a comforting symbol to her anymore? That grieved her on some deep inner level where she could hardly bear to look.

She could only imagine how Anthony must be taking all of it.

"His name was Philips," he said, stirring his tea. "He used to work for me."

"Is he the one who killed Mrs. Boryenka?" Natalie asked.

Anthony heaved a sigh. "And Fiona's roommate when he couldn't get at me. I'm afraid that, although for only the best of reasons, I... may have done something that he perceived as... dishonest."

"What did you do?"

"That isn't important. Suffice to say it angered him. He came to the house looking for me, killing Mrs. Boryenka in the process – I regret that most bitterly, Natalie, I do – and when I escaped him, he somehow tracked down Fiona and Jill. He took them as hostages against my cooperation. I agreed to meet with him, but to make sure that we understood his message, he murdered Jill and promised Fiona that he'd return and do the same to her if I tricked him again."

"Which you must have done," she said. "But... how? Why? He was a vampire!"

For a moment, they were silent, listening keenly toward the upstairs in case they might hear the stealthy noises of Philips getting up again.

"Not at that time, he wasn't," Anthony finally said.

"You don't seem... surprised."

"Nor do you," he said, regarding her from under speculative eyebrows. "I have known for quite some time that vampires exist, yes. Obviously, for fear of being branded a lunatic, I've kept that knowledge to myself, confessing only to Fiona."

"Are you a Centurion?" she asked.

He frowned at her. "I beg your pardon?"

"Never mind," she said. "How long have you known?"

"Several years," he said, and his gaze slid away from her in a shifty manner that was as good as a neon sign of deception. "I encountered them in a park one night. I... witnessed them in action."

"But you got away."

"Yes," he said, touching the cross on the table. He, it seemed, still did take comfort from it. "I had this with me. It... did not do what I expected, did not repel them. It seemed to infuriate them, but their very fury gave me a chance to escape. But you, Natalie, how do you know?"

"I saw one the night I came to the city," she said. "After I left Sorrows. It... he?... it came into a coffee shop and started slaughtering people." On the spur of the moment, she decided that she would not tell the whole truth about Seth. "Some of us got away out the back door. I... I guess that as soon as I saw the vampire, I had to believe it was really real."

"Precisely," he said. "That was my very reaction. Although my mind rejected it as superstition and nonsense, my soul knew. And, as a man of faith as I've always been, I soon came to terms with it in a rational sense as well."

"Philips, though," Natalie said, bringing them back to the dead man upstairs. What did they used to put on the old gravestones? *God Grant He Lie Still.* She shivered.

Anthony rubbed the white expanse of bandage. "I could not tell the police about my connections to Philips. I said that I hadn't recognized the man who broke into the house that morning, that he must have been some criminal, some burglar. I claimed that certain items of my grandmother's jewelry had been stolen, but that I must have interrupted him before he could take anything else. There were no such items, of course, but how were the police to have known?"

"Fiona said the same thing?"

"Yes. We hoped that it would be passed off as a gruesome coincidence, both of our homes being robbed, both of our housemates being killed."

They both froze and held their breath as something creaked. The sound was not repeated. It might have been the normal noise of the house settling, amplified by the echo-chamber emptiness of the rooms. Or it might not.

Natalie went to a still-unsealed cardboard box of kitchen implements and scanned the contents with a frown. Not much to choose from. She took a long-handled wooden spoon and a paring knife and sat down again. Hardly able to believe what she was doing, she commenced whittling the end of the spoon's handle into a point.

Anthony sipped more tea. "I agreed to meet him, as I said, though I had no intention of being there. I sent him to that selfsame park, trusting that for once, the evil of the vampires might be turned to good use."

"You set him up to be attacked by vampires?"

"I never thought that they would bring him back as one of their own!" he said, his vehemence taking her aback. "Not after what I saw them do to those other people. They were butchered like cattle, and when the bodies were found the next morning, it was deemed one of the worst mass-murders in the city's history. I followed the case most closely, believe me. They were, given the savagery of the attacks, hastily cremated."

His story was ringing a faint bell. Natalie closed her eyes, concentrated, and clicked in her mind. A vicious mass-murder, a park... Landover Park...

"You're talking about the Nativity Massacre," she said. "I saw a show about it, one of those unsolved-crimes programs."

The girls at Sorrows, the same ones who were as devout about *CSI* as they were about their studies and other duties, sometimes got together to watch true-crime and forensics documentaries. Natalie had been especially affected by the story of the Nativity Massacre, because it happened on her birthday.

Now, with a new shiver, she realized that she had been born in the hospital right across the street only a few hours before those people had been killed.

"I expected," he went on, "that the same fate would befall Philips. I had no reason to believe it wouldn't. Over the years, I've paid attention to the news, to the number of people who turn up dead in that park. I thought he'd be just another statistic. I never dreamed that it could come to this."

Natalie barely paid attention, thinking of her visit to the hospital. She'd seen a priest sitting with a family, no doubt consoling and advising them in their time of need. On Christmas, there'd probably be quite a few clergymen come to visit parishioners and generally spread comfort and good will. One more or less would hardly stand out.

And hadn't Anthony just said he'd had the cross with him that night? Anthony, who'd gone to seminary school and could probably have passed for a young priest with effortless ease?

"—do with him," he said.

"What?"

"I'm wondering what to do with him. Philips. His body. Calling the police is out of the question. Yes, we – you, rather – killed him in self-defense. No one would argue that. The man was armed, and I have no doubt that his reputation would prove to be most unsavory. But he's dead with a length of wood through his heart. More, by the look of the body, he's been dead for weeks. We would be hard pressed to come up with a convincing explanation. I cannot afford any closer police scrutiny."

She didn't doubt that.

"We'll have to take care of it ourselves," he concluded. "I must say, Natalie, your fearlessness, steadfast faith and quick-thinking action were most impressive. More Joan of Arc than… well, than anyone else."

"Joan of Arc was burned at the stake."

A different kind of stake, she thought as she examined the crude point of the spoon handle. Unless Seth just hadn't gotten around to telling her *that* part of the Centurion version of religious history.

"But she changed the world. As you will. And I swear to you, yours will be a much more glorious fate."

"What are you talking about?"

He patted her hand, and she needed conscious willpower not to pull away from his touch. "There'll be time enough for that later. First we must deal with Philips. Will you help me?"

Natalie wanted nothing more right now than to talk to Seth, and ask his advice. If anyone would know how to dispose of the body of a vampire that had not properly turned to dust, it'd be Seth. But she had no way of contacting him.

"I think… we'd better bury the body," she said. "We can't be sure sunlight would destroy it, and it's still hours until dawn. As long as we leave the stake in, it should be okay."

Anthony looked into his tea cup, not as if trying to read his fortune but more like he was wishing the tea was fortified with something stronger than sugar. He downed the rest of it at a gulp.

Between the two of them, they were able to lug Philips' corpse downstairs and out into the large backyard. At two o'clock in the morning, there was no one to observe their clandestine digging.

She'd heard somewhere that people who went through stressful situations often formed a bond. It had been true enough with Seth, but Natalie didn't want that kind of bond with Anthony. Not when she was half convinced he'd been the one, not Fiona but him, to steal her from the hospital.

The dead vampire had not changed. Drying blood glued the end of the stake in place. Anthony picked up the mercenary's knife with a gloved hand – he kept latex gloves in the first aid kit – and set it aside.

"We'll dispose of this later, and elsewhere," he said. "If the body's ever found, it would only add to our problems to have a murder weapon found with it."

"According to the stories," Natalie said, remembering what Seth had told her about the death of his friend Jason, "we should cut his head off, too."

Anthony looked nauseous. "With what, pray tell? My gardening shovel?"

His expression knotted with revulsion as he contemplated the gory job, but there wasn't a lot else to do. At last, after a lot of clumsy chopping and hacking, the vampire's head rolled loose from the stump. A dark and runny ooze spilled from the neck. Anthony turned away and threw up on the lawn.

When the hole was filled in, the shovel hosed off and put away, and the raw patch of earth covered over with a fresh layer of white rock chips from a bag in the garage, they returned to the house to do what they could about the ruined chapel door and the hallway.

"Fiona was right," Anthony said when they were sitting again at the kitchen table with fresh cups of tea. "She didn't believe me about the vampires, but she thought that one way or another Philips would find a way to come back. And she was right. I'm glad, now, that I agreed to her wishes. I wouldn't want to go on living here knowing that he's buried in the back yard."

Natalie let him ramble as she tried to decide on the best way to ask what she had to ask. In the end, though, she knew there was no good way to go about it.

"Tell me about my mother," she said. "The truth."

Anthony stopped mid-ramble and carefully set down his cup. "Your mother?"

"I want to know why you've lied to me all this time."

"Natalie... what... what are you saying?"

Her cup met the table with a tea-splashing bang. "I know she's alive. I saw her at the hospital!"

"What were you doing there?" he asked, his gaze sharp as a needle. "How did you –"

"That doesn't matter," Natalie said. Her pulse fluttered at a hummingbird's pace and despite the tea, her mouth and throat were bone-dry. "I know a lot. I want to hear the rest from you. Are you my father?"

He blanched. "Natalie!"

"Are you?" Her voice rose; she was helpless to prevent it. "Tell me!"

"Not... not in the way you... are thinking," he said.

"You don't know the way I'm thinking," she shot back. "I heard the doctor. I know how she was in a coma for two years before I was even born and that someone--"

"It wasn't like that!" The words fell from him like a rockslide, fragmented and broken. "Not... not like that, Natalie. Never. You must... must believe me."

"Then explain!" She was surprised to find herself near tears, clenching her fists like she expected to have to beat the information out of him. "Are you or are you not my father? I have to know!"

"Only... only in spirit," he said. "I never touched Karen in a... a husbandly way. I wouldn't."

"Okay."

"Even so, I loved her." Anthony stared down at his hands. "Not as a man loves a woman, you must understand that. Never that sort of love. She... she was like an angel. So beautiful, so sweet, so perfect and kind. Never a harsh word for anyone.

Generous of spirit. She was so special, Natalie, so very special. The kind of person that is simply too good for this sorry, shameful earth."

Natalie bit her lip to keep from yelling. She nodded again, her neck creaking because she was so tight with tension.

"I never said anything to her," he said. "I feared she would mistake my intentions. My feelings were only of the deepest, purest admiration. Although I... I must admit I was dismayed when I learned that she was going to marry. I thought that it was wrong for Karen, angelic Karen, to give herself to any man."

A constriction in her chest made it hard for Natalie to breathe. Anthony seemed almost to have forgotten she was there. He spoke as if to himself, or as if in the hush of the confessional.

"I avoided the wedding," he said. "Later, when Fiona told me what had happened... the car crash... I knew it had to be God's will. I'd been right about Karen. She was too good for a husband. God had stepped in and seen to it."

"They said it was a drunk driver." In that moment, she was half-expecting him to say that *he'd* been the one behind the wheel of the other car, that he had deliberately caused the accident that had left Karen Cross in a coma.

"God's will," Anthony repeated, which neither confirmed nor denied her suspicion. "A year later, when she still had not wakened, I knew it was a sign. I knew what I was supposed to do. So I volunteered at the hospital. Brother Tony, they called me. No one suspected. I had the run of the hospital, the freedom to visit any of the patients. Who distrusts a young seminary student?" A scowl darkened his face. "Back then, at least, that was how it was."

All at once Natalie didn't want to hear what she dreaded must be next.

"I was easily able to get the tissue samples I needed," he said. "I brought them here to my own private lab and undertook the process, then returned to the hospital with the embryo. The most difficult part was surgically introducing it to Karen's womb. The instrument is similar to that which they use for performing amniocentisis-"

"Wait, wait, what?" Natalie interrupted.

He smiled at her, the sort of patient smile a teacher wore when explaining to a slow pupil. "I cloned her, of course. I cloned Karen."

"You ... " the rest of the words trailed off into an exhalation. "You mean it was... what do they call it? Artificial insemination. A test-tube baby? Right?"

But other things he'd said came back to her with a vengeance. How much she looked like her mother... Karen's very image...

"Now, do you see?" he asked, almost gently. "I am not your father. No man is. You have no father except God Almighty. You are perfect, Natalie. Perfect and untainted, born untouched by sin."

"I'm... a clone?" She shook her head at the craziness of what he was saying.

"You understand now why you were never told. Why no one was ever told. The cloning of humans was not even considered possible at the time. Even today it is a thorny legal and ethical issue. Had it become known, you would have suffered the consequences. Poor, misguided people thinking that you're a monster instead of the wonderful, special, angelic girl that you are. We couldn't let that happen."

"We? Who else knows?"

"Only Fiona and myself."

Natalie felt a tingling numbness spreading through her body. She didn't want to believe him. What he was saying couldn't be true. "But why kidnap me from the hospital when I wasn't even a day old?"

"You know about that, too, then."

"Was it you?"

"Yes," Anthony said. "It had to be. They would have looked too closely at Fiona, since she'd been involved with Karen's parents."

"Why not just let the adoption go through?" she asked. The larger issue—she was a clone!?!—was still too enormous to deal with. "Wouldn't it have all worked out the same?"

"Ah, but you see, it wouldn't have," he said. "Karen's parents were in no condition to raise you themselves. Mr. Melvey was a housebound invalid as a result of several strokes and his wife had all she could do to care for him. With no other relatives, they turned to their daughter's best friend, but it was clear the Melveys would have insisted on being a part of your life. I couldn't afford that sort of interference."

"But they're my grandparents," Natalie said. Her chin tried to tremble.

"Then, too, there was the matter of paternity," he went on as if he hadn't heard, or didn't think it was worth discussion. "In the public sector in those days, genetic testing was still – pardon the pun – in its infancy, but I was thinking ahead."

"Because I only had my mother's DNA," she said, readily grasping that concept courtesy of all those crime shows.

"It would have astounded them," Anthony said. "To keep you safe from prying eyes and probing minds, it was best to quote-unquote *lose* what few blood samples they'd taken, and then have the mystery miracle baby vanish."

"So you smuggled me away," Natalie said. "A few hours old, and you took me from my mother."

He nodded, with a strange glint in his eye as if expecting to be congratulated for his genius. "I induced Karen's labor prematurely. Some small element of risk involved in that, yes, but every indication suggested that the baby was developing normally. This ensured an easier birth and also saw to it that the blessed event took place at a time when the Melveys would not be present."

She drank tea that, despite heaping spoons of sugar, tasted bitter. Karen Cross, her mother... or her twin? She'd gone from not knowing who she really was to not even knowing *what* she was!

"How could you?" she asked in a near sob.

"What is it that you want from me, Natalie? An apology? Do you fail to grasp that it was the best and only way to guarantee your safety? Why, it was all I could do to make sure that you were born at all."

She wasn't sure what to make of that. She was relieved to know that he was not her biological father, but this was almost as bad.

"Did Fiona know all of it?"

"Not from the start," he said. "When it became clear that the implantation of the cloned embryo was successful, I told her everything. I needed her to stay close to the family, so as to keep me apprised of what was happening."

"What about Richard Cross?" Natalie asked.

Anthony scowled. "The fool. The selfish, vain, cold-hearted fool."

"I heard that once he found out, he tried to... to have the baby ... " Natalie couldn't bring herself to say it.

"He was not about to take on the responsibility of a child not his own," Anthony said. "Not even if it was Karen's child. Precious, perfect Karen, whom he'd claimed to have loved so dearly. He showed his true colors, oh, yes, he did."

"And then he died?"

Wariness replaced the scowl. "For the best, as it turned out. Perhaps it was also God's will."

And perhaps, a dark voice deep in Natalie's heart whispered, the will of Anthony Sevrin. Who hired people like that man Philips.

"You must be exhausted," Anthony said. "I know that I am, and we've still much to do tomorrow."

"That's it?" She gave a little bark of incredulous laughter. "That's all? You drop this on me and expect me to sleep?"

"You wanted the truth, and I've told you. I saw tonight that you have Karen's strength as well as her beauty. I'm pleased, Natalie. No ordinary girl would have shown the will and fearlessness and determination to do what you did."

"I'm not her, though. You know that, don't you? I'm not Karen."

"Of course," he said.

"I don't *feel* special."

"You have her modesty, as well."

"I'm no saint," Natalie said. "I ran away from school, remember?"

"I've been thinking about that," he said. "I originally sent you to Our Lady of Sorrows because I felt it would provide a calm and spiritual environment in which you prepare for your purpose in life. But perhaps I misjudged. Perhaps you never needed that kind of environment to become the woman I know you will become."

"What woman is that? I just told you, I'm not Karen!"

He patted her hand again. "It'll all come clear in time. One day, one day soon, you'll know. All the world will know. You will do great things, Natalie. Great things for this pitiful, miserable planet. I promise you."

CHAPTER 22

"It's right," the crone said. She was tearless, her pinched mouth set in a thin, resolute line.

"What, Elise?" Fiona asked.

God, how she hated hospitals! Awful places. Full of sick people, old people, ugly people. Pasty, drooping, wrinkled husks. Shuffling zombies in paper gowns and cheap cloth robes, going up and down the halls, all of them with that same look in their eyes, the look that fish got after someone threw dynamite into a lake.

And the smell! Always the same. The smell of illness, despair, age, and death. Sour attic smell, moldy grave smell. All the Lysol and flowers in the world couldn't mask it, only mixed with it to make a new and nauseating perfume.

"It's right that she goes now," Elise Melvey said. "It's time. It's her time."

Her time, in Fiona's opinion, had come and gone years ago. But who was she to argue with Karen's mother?

"It's like she was just waiting for the service to be over," Elise added. "For us to say our final goodbye to her dear little baby. Now we can all move on."

Because it seemed called for, Fiona embraced the older woman. Elise did not crumple against her and sob for her lost daughter, lost grandchild. She stood rigid and forbidding, stony as one of those heads on Easter Island. Fiona let go quickly, and was able to refrain from wiping her hands on her skirt.

On the other side of Karen's bed, Pete Melvey sat canted sideways in his wheelchair. He could have more readily passed for a patient than a visitor, except that he wore ratty old corduroy pants and a plaid shirt instead of a paper gown. One side of his face turned down in a Greek tragedy mask. The other was about as lively as that of a department store mannequin. He was all skin folds, stubble, jaundice, and drool.

Fiona made a mental note to talk to Anthony about a living will. She wanted to be put out of her misery long before she got anywhere near as bad off as Pete Melvey.

If her looks started to go, if her body no longer responded to diet and exercise, if her tits succumbed to gravity and her legs to varicose veins, she'd be ready to call it quits. Anthony could whip up some spiffy little cocktail that would be a nice, quick, painless and undetectable poison.

If, that is, he'd do it. God frowned on suicide, blah-de-blah. And, judging by the people in Parkview Hospital, God smiled on the decrepit, homely, and wretched.

"Thank you, Fiona," Elise said. "This hasn't been easy for any of us, and with me and Pete being so far away, we've always been grateful that you've been nearby. I never wanted to think of Karen being alone, with no family. You were like a sister to her."

"I only wish I could have done more," Fiona said.

"We could have arranged to move her to another hospital, one closer to us, but she did love this city. She was so happy, so excited to come here to college. And then she met Richard. They could have had a nice life, don't you think?"

"I'm sure that they would have."

This deathwatch was enough to spoil anybody's mood, and Fiona's mood had been on shaky enough ground lately anyway. At least the painters and carpet installers were finally finished, so she could move into her new, exquisitely decorated place. Maybe this final business with the Melveys would mark the end of her having to spend most of her life dealing with other peoples' messes. Karen's, Jill's, Anthony's, Natalie's, and Mrs. B.'s... she was sick and tired of it.

In a detective show or mystery novel, Detective Jackson would have proved to be one of those brilliant, hyper-intuitive sleuths who'd be unwilling to let the connections between the events go as coincidence. It might have led to the unraveling of the entire sordid story. Conspiracy, theft, illicit cloning, murder, religious mania... it had it all.

Except sex, more was the pity.

Even Fiona's attempts to 'comfort' Richard Cross hadn't panned out. The son of a bitch had rejected her.

Rejected *her*! Fiona Sevrin! She'd been on the covers of *Glamour* and *Femme* that year, but he'd pushed her away because he thought he had to stay faithful to his comatose virgin bride.

That had been before Karen turned up preggers and became, in Richard's eyes, damaged goods.

Well, even if she had been jealous of Karen, which she hadn't, she certainly didn't have any cause to be now.

Her one-time best friend was a stranger. The beautiful blonde coed had become a shrunken hag, whiling away the best years of her life in this room, in this bed, hooked up to machines to fan the fading spark within her.

Pete Melvey burbled something, and Elise bent close to hear him.

"Yes, dear," she said. "That's Karen. That's our girl. Our poor, lost baby."

He burbled louder. His lolling head jerked on his neck. Filmy eyes swiveled to focus in the direction of the room's half-open door.

Fiona turned and saw a girl in a candy-striper's smock. The first thing she noticed was that the smock was too big, and worn clumsily over street clothes. The second thing was that the girl, blue eyes flying wide open in alarm at the sight of the three of them, was Natalie.

Why, that little ... !

"What is it, Pete?" Elise asked, stroking his balding head. She looked around to follow his gaze, but by then the girl had ducked out of sight.

"Excuse me for a minute," Fiona murmured through a clenched jaw, and walked out as calmly as she could.

There... at the end of the hall, jabbing the elevator button as if she could hurry its arrival and make good her escape. She saw

Fiona coming, and flushed a darker pink than the smock. The doors opened and she scurried in.

A quick thrust of Fiona's arm prevented the elevator from closing. She stepped inside herself, let them shut, and hit the Hold button.

"What do you think you're doing here?" she asked, each word clipped and cold.

Pale now rather than blushing, pale but defiant, her brother's little science project glared up at her. "I think you know," Natalie said. "I wanted to see my mother."

"So. You found out. Anthony finally blabbed, did he?"

"I was here a few days ago. I saw her then. Last night, I asked him, and he told me everything."

"Everything?" Fiona arched her brows.

"Yes."

"He told you everything?"

"About what I really am? Yes. Yes, he told me."

"He did, hmm?" She crossed her arms and regarded Natalie. "I'm surprised. What is it that you're planning to do with that information?"

"I don't know yet."

"Because, if you were planning to tell anyone, I hope you realize that it would ruin your life as well as ours. Anthony would go to jail. I might, too, for abetting him. And you, Natalie, what would happen to you?"

The defiant glare fled. The girl hung her head, looking small and childlike in the too-big smock.

"A lot of unsavory people would be very interested in you," Fiona said. "If you were lucky, they'd want to study you, and you'd spend the rest of your life in a government lab someplace. If you weren't so lucky, they'd kill you to make sure that word of this never got out. But if you're thinking that you'd go on to have some happy ending with your long-lost grandparents, you're wrong."

"I'm not stupid," Natalie said. "I figured that out."

"But you're here," Fiona said. "Here of all places. If there's anyone in the world liable to see you and get suspicious, it's the people in that room, on that floor, in this hospital. Pete Melvey *did* see you. Thank God he's too much of a vegetable to say anything coherent. If it had been Elise … "

"I wanted to see them. I deserved it."

"Deserved," scoffed Fiona.

"They're my family."

"If that's what you want to call it."

"Well, it isn't like I ever had a real family," Natalie said.

Fiona laughed. "Is that supposed to make me feel guilty? I never wanted to be a mother. No room for kids in *my* plan for the future, thank you very much. When Anthony came to me and told me what he'd done, and that he wanted *me* to step in and offer to adopt the baby, I was ready to kill him."

"Why did you do it, then?"

"Because he told me the rest of his oh-so-brilliant plan and promised that I wouldn't actually have to be the one changing diapers and dealing with spit-up and crying all through the night. Because I didn't want him to get caught. You go on about the Melveys being your family? Well, Anthony's mine, the only family I have anymore. For whatever that's worth, he is my brother and I didn't want to see him in prison."

"Did he murder Richard Cross?"

She rocked back as if slapped. "What?"

"I think that he did," Natalie said, with an eerie calm. "Or hired it done by that Philips guy, or someone else like him."

"What do you know about Philips?"

"He came to the house last night." The girl looked her square in the eye. "He was a vampire."

"Oh, for God's sake!" cried Fiona. "Don't tell me you believe that shit too!"

"I saw one the first night I was here. In a coffee shop. And last night, I saw Philips. As a vampire. I ran a stake in his heart and Anthony chopped his head off with a shovel. He's buried in the back yard."

"You're as crazy as he is," Fiona said, shaking her head. "All these years, I'd ask him if you really were growing up normally, not showing any bizarre traits. He kept assuring me that you were fine. Now, this."

"I am fine!"

"I never should have trusted Anthony to make any good judgments of someone's mental and emotional state."

"I'm not crazy," Natalie said fiercely.

"No?" Fiona laughed. "You will be by the time he's done with you."

"What do you know about that?"

"I thought you said he told you everything."

"I… he said something about destiny, but … "

"My advice? Forget it. As for Philips, another of Anthony's ingenious plans in action… did he honestly believe that 'vampires' were going to kill the man for him?" She made quote marks in the air as she spoke.

"But they did —"

"Stop!"

"But it's true!"

"This maniac stabs Mrs. Boryenka, breaks into my apartment, blacks my eye, ties me up, stabs Jill, and Anthony thinks that by sending him for a walk in the park at night, it'll solve all his problems?" She rolled her eyes and added in a mutter, "When he told me how he'd poisoned the other one, I suspected he was headed around the bend, but this really confirms it."

"Poisoned? What other one?"

"Left that part out, too, did he? Philips had a partner. Not only did our dear Anthony cheat them out of the money he owed them by giving them a bunch of counterfeit bills, he coated the bills with a fast-acting poison of some kind."

Natalie, stunned, leaned against the wall. Her rear end bumped the control panel, and the car started down.

"Some behavior for a man who thinks he's saving the world, isn't it?" Fiona asked. "But, well, you can't make an omelet without breaking eggs. A few murdered mercenaries here and there doesn't add up to much in the greater scheme of things."

"All I want," Natalie said, after a few steadying breaths and a flurry of blinking back tears, "is my own life. You're not my parents, not my aunt and uncle, not even my legal guardians, are you? No, you couldn't have been, after he stole me!"

"If this is leading up to you wanting to strike off on your own," Fiona said, ignoring her questions, "you have *my* blessing."

"You… never liked me very much, did you?" Natalie said. "What did I ever do? None of this was my idea, my fault."

"Never liked you? Why, Natalie, what's not to like? Because of you, I've spent the past sixteen years having to watch my step and dodge nosy questions from the Melveys, Jill, and the police. Just for you. Precious, perfect, special Natalie. Just like Karen. Everyone always loved Karen. Karen the saint, Karen the angel. And now here you are, Karen reborn. Almost literally."

The elevator halted and the doors opened. Neither Natalie nor Fiona budged. A man with a white lab coat and a hectic expression got in, seemed to sense the crackle of hostile energy in the air, looked from woman to girl to woman again, and backed out with a muttered apology. The doors slid shut and the descent continued.

"It isn't me," Natalie said. "It's her you hate."

"Oh, it's you, too," Fiona assured her. "Even when you were a baby, I could see it coming. You got more like her every day. Prettier, sweeter. And so full of love, Natalie, did you know that? You overflowed with it, and you never noticed or cared that we didn't return it."

"I noticed," she said, her voice trembling. "I cared."

"I saw us turning into a bad play on an old fairy tale," Fiona said. "You as Snow White and me as the Wicked Queen. But instead of having some huntsman lose you in the woods, I got Anthony to send you away until he needed you again."

"Needed me? For what?"

She smiled and it felt like the curve of a headsman's axe blade on her lips. "That's why he didn't mind so much that you ran away from Sorrows. It saved him the trouble of having to come up with a reason to fetch you home in time to play your part in his big important plans."

The doors opened again on a tile-lined corridor leading to a security booth. Beyond the booth's bulletproof glass windows, where an attendant sat reading a magazine, was the concrete tomb of the underground parking garage and the echoing rumble of traffic.

Fiona saw her own flashy little sports car and wished she was in it, music on, rolling away from this depressing place and the deathwatch upstairs.

"Go home, Natalie," she said. "There's nothing for you here."

"What about … ?" Though the girl had stayed stronger than Fiona would have expected through a conversation that had ranged from spite to venom, her voice wavered and she couldn't bring herself to say Karen's name.

"She's dying," Fiona said. Natalie stepped out, and Fiona pushed the button to return to the 5th floor.

"What does he need me for?" the girl asked as the doors once more began to close. "What's this really all about?"

"Ask him. It's quite the ambitious endeavor." She smiled coldly. "And if you decide you don't like it, why, you could always walk through the park on your way home some night … "

Chapter 23

"They're moving in this afternoon," Magdalena said. "Make sure none of your helpers are wandering around, would you?"

"I haven't any at the moment," Lazarus said. "No need for them. Unless you have a specific use in mind?"

"They're no good at housecleaning."

"Rubbish," the dead man said. "Of course they are. They can sweep and scrub with the best of them. Although they do drop bits of themselves and leave smears of unidentifiable bodily fluids, don't they?"

"Not to mention the stench," Magdalena said.

"You don't breathe."

"I can when I need to, and we can hardly bring living people into this house and expect them not to notice that the place reeks of rotting flesh."

"Our predecessor in this charming locale never had any such troubles with his neighbors and dinner guests," Lazarus said, a low chuckle bubbling in his throat. "It's a shame that the state electrocuted him. I fancy he would have made a top-notch vampire. He had the right sadistic streak, the right bloodlust."

"You could always seek out where he was interred."

He shrugged, the motion causing one of his shoulders to pop out of the socket and the skin of his neck to split in a seeping line. "I looked it up. They cremated him."

With the windows tightly shuttered and shaded, Magdalena only knew it was mid-morning by instinct, by the waning of her powers, as the sun grew stronger in the sky. Below, in the cellar, her blood-children had retired to their coffins to hide from the day.

When night came, they would arise and slip from the house like shadows, making their way to the park that they liked to haunt. She wondered if it was because the wooded park reminded the oldest of them, in some dim way, of the forest lair that had been their home before. The newer ones simply followed the lead of the older, and Magdalena was content to give them free rein as long as they were cautious.

Some of them were not so cautious. After that brutal Christmas slaughter fifteen years ago, they had been fairly well-behaved, but there were always a few troublemakers. They were the ones that didn't restrict themselves to the out-of-the-way places, and risked being seen.

"What are we supposed to do while your pet mortals are here?" Lazarus asked. "You may be able to fool this Sevrin for a while, but the man is reputed to be a genius. In time, even he is bound to notice some of your peculiarities. Let alone mine!"

"He must not see you, then," she said. "As for myself, if I must, I will fog his mind. I'd rather not. As you say, he is a genius."

"I said he was reputed to be a genius," Lazarus corrected dryly. "Whether he is or not, I'll judge for myself."

"If he can do what he claims he can do, I care nothing for the rest of it. I want nothing to interfere with this. It will be an inconvenience to us, having Sevrin and his Natalie under our roof, but in the end it will be worthwhile."

"So long as you keep your fangs out of that succulent girl-child," he said, leering.

"In the interest of our greater goal, I think I can control myself," she said.

The house had been cleaned top to bottom – well, not quite *bottom* – by a hired agency. Some of them were familiar with its unsavory history, quickly whispering it to the others in ghoulish glee – "Don't you know who used to *live* here?" But the legacy had deterred the maids from lingering or poking about in odd corners. Now the second floor bedrooms and baths were all sparkling, as were the rooms on the first floor.

As an added bonus, the serial killer had been a retired physician with a small in-home office; this would be the new workroom of Anthony Sevrin. Much of the equipment from his own secret lab had already been installed in the former examination room.

She was beginning to regret having finished off her captive Centurion. Michael would have come in handy once there were other mortals staying here, could have kept an eye on them, seen to the stocking of the larders and other such concerns. Magdalena did have to rest sometimes, and would find it harder as spring turned into summer and the days lengthened.

If all else failed, she could corrupt Sevrin as well, could give him to drink of her cold blood and bring him even more utterly under her control than the brief mesmerism afforded by eye contact. Doing so at regular intervals, she could keep such a devoted servant for as long as she desired... or until time wore them down like the springs of old clocks.

"So, it will take less than a year," Lazarus said, in a tone of both eager anticipation and satisfaction. "You're sure of this?"

"No," she said. "It is science. But when the ancient lore fails, we may be forced to accept that the world has moved on. Reason over ritual. Method over magic."

"You sound as though our time has passed," he said. "I don't know if I like that."

"The very reason we're doing this is so that our time will come again," Magdalena said. "If we can use the tools of this modern age to our advantage, so be it. When logical minds reject even the possibility of beings such as ourselves, and lose the ability to counteract us, so much the better."

"What am I to do while your scientist has the run of the house?" asked Lazarus. "Keep hidden, I suppose? For a full year?"

"Is it so great a sacrifice, given what else we've been through and how long we've waited?"

He grudgingly saw the wisdom of that, and by the time the moving truck arrived that afternoon, a great diesel-snorting beast crowding into the driveway, Lazarus had absented himself to the cellar. Magdalena greeted Anthony Sevrin.

"Where is your lovely Natalie?" she asked, lingering in the shade of the house to keep from casting no shadow on the steps.

"School." He yawned. His eyes were nearly as red as any vampire's. "Neither of us got much sleep last night. Too much excitement. But she will be here. We're both very glad to be here."

"You're both very welcome." She ushered him inside.

"I can't thank you enough for inviting us to stay while I complete my work," he said.

"There is no need. If there's anything you require, please, let me know. We're in this together, Doctor."

"Call me Anthony," he said. "I no longer feel deserving of any lofty titles."

Something in his manner seemed off to her, but she was no great judge of the living. Once, perhaps. In a former life two thousand years gone. Still, even to her, he gave off an aura of twitchy fatigue. His smile was too fleeting, too distracted. His gaze flicked aimlessly over the house before settling again on Magdalena.

"Well, then," she said, remembering to draw regular breaths. "I am Madeline."

As the movers went about their duties, Magdalena ushered Anthony into the house. She noticed the flare of his nostrils and a faint frown that he quickly masked. She wondered if the cleaning had not been as thorough as it should have been, and if she was inured to the lingering odors that might permeate the old house. But Anthony said nothing, and once they reached his office and lab, he waxed ebullient with praise and delight.

"When do you plan to begin?" she asked, after allowing him ample time to poke into cabinets and rearrange furniture.

"The sooner the better," he said. "You'll provide the sample, as we discussed?"

"Tonight, if you wish."

"Excellent!"

Magdalena had been worried about mealtimes, but Anthony was too immersed in organizing his scientific equipment, and Natalie emerged from her room only long enough to make a sandwich before vanishing again.

Night came, bringing with it the sense of activity in the bowels of the house. Magdalena visited her blood-children and they flocked around her like devoted pets eager for attention. She impressed her will upon them again, her decree that they stay out of the upper stories, and *not* hunt the living who were under her protection.

In fact, she ordered, they were not to pass the threshold of their crypt without her express permission, did they understand?

Their cowed shufflings told her that they did.

And would they obey?

Craven postures and hanged heads assured her that they would.

With that out of the way, she went to her secret sanctum and found Lazarus prowling with the demeanor of a caged animal.

"I don't like it," he said. "Already, I don't like it."

"Nor do I, but we must tolerate it if we hope to see our goals reached."

"Spare me the lecture. It's nothing I don't already know."

"Then spare me the complaining, because that, too, is nothing I don't already know."

"Have you always been this bitchy, Magdalena, or is it just in the last couple of centuries?"

She picked up the heavy wooden coffer with its seal of hammered silver. "Even we can change, Lazarus."

Music issued from the closed door to Natalie's room. Magdalena stood at the bottom of the stairs, listening long enough to shake her head. Some of the newer vampires liked that discordant modern clangor and screeching, and they were welcome to it.

Anthony, she found on hands and knees under the desk, fiddling with the various cords that led from the guts of his computers.

She took a step into the room and stopped short at the sight of a large cross resting atop a pile of papers. The cross, plated with mother-of-pearl, stank of the death of one of her kind.

The box made a thump when she set it down. Anthony's head made another as it struck the underside of the desk. He backed hurriedly out, and flushed when he saw her.

"You startled me," he said.

She stared at the cross. The ancient hate churned in her–bad enough to see them other places, but here, mockingly, in her very lair!–and she hesitated in reaching out for it. Her fingers trembled.

"An heirloom," he said, picking it up and holding it out to her.

Mother-of-pearl, not silver. It would not physically harm her to touch it. She took it and fought an urge to bring it down like a hatchet into his face.

The smudge of blood on the back was dried to a crust and nearly invisible against the stained wood. She surreptitiously scraped it with her thumbnail before returning the cross to Anthony. He admired it before setting it aside.

"I know I really should get some sleep," he said. "Had none last night, but the excitement is such that all I'd do in bed is toss and turn. Here, at least, I can get things ready. Do you have the item?"

"In the coffer." She licked her thumbnail. Yes, one of her kind. Not one that she knew, not one of her own blood-children. A male. A stranger.

"Ah," sighed Anthony, looking at the box. "What a piece of workmanship. Obviously antique, but it's been well cared for. Look at this silver. I'd swear it started as a Roman coin before being beaten into this shape."

"You'd be right." She spoke through clenched teeth.

Judas, the betrayer, had been rewarded with thirty such coins. By some alchemy that even Joseph of Arimathea hadn't understood, from then on none of the disciples or their blood-children could touch the hateful metal without blackening, blistering, and pain.

"May I?" Anthony paused with his fingers on the clasp.

She inclined her head, and he lifted the coffer's lid. Within, the length of the stake hummed with the power of the blood, power that only she could feel.

A soft breath of wonder escaped Anthony as he peered inside. "The Holy Lance."

"The one and only," she said, still with jaws locked tight.

"It isn't as I pictured it. Hardly resembles a spear, at all. I would have expected the point to be made of iron or bronze. Then again, legend and time turned the humble Grail into a chalice of purest gold."

Magdalena smiled thinly.

He didn't even notice, still gazing with awe into the coffer. "May I ask how you came by this?"

She countered with, "May I ask how you came by that so-called Shroud?"

"Ahem, well ... " Anthony cleared his throat.

"Shall we leave both at that?"

"For the best, I think." He used sturdy metal forceps to pick up the stake, and placed it in a stainless steel pan lined with white paper. "I'll begin by extracting a small sample of the substance—on first look, it certainly seems to be blood, but whether human or not is for the computer analysis to decide."

Amid all of the gleaming chrome and tile, washed in that brilliant white light, she felt too conscious of her lack of a shadow, and her lack of even a distorted image cast in the many polished and reflected surfaces where a dozen carnival freak show duplicates of Anthony Sevrin capered and contorted.

"I'll leave you to it," she said.

Already intent on his work, picking at the stained end with a thin metal probe like a dentist's tool, he muttered and nodded.

Restless, she roamed the house, nibbling dried blood from under her thumbnail. Whose was it? Fairly fresh, a vigorous man's. Not undead for long. Someone had been careless in creating him. Had it been one of hers who slipped?

Magdalena went to the windows, parting drapes and opening shutters to gaze out at the velvet-black night.

The taste of the blood, unpleasantly male though it was, nonetheless wakened her appetite. She did not *need* to drink, could go for months or years without it. Still …

She dared not leave Anthony on his own so soon, not when she was still wary of him. Whether he could, in fact, do what he promised. Whether she could trust him, as far as she trusted any living being. What he might do if he realized the truth.

Clearly, he'd had some sort of a run-in with one of her kind. He couldn't have made the connection, or he would never have been so open with her. He would hardly leave Natalie alone and undefended in the enemy's camp. Not Natalie, so vital to his plans if he insisted on doing everything by the book. Or by the Book, as it were.

Natalie. Alone and undefended.

The thought, the temptation, tolled in her like a deep bell. The girl would be asleep by now. Innocent and vulnerable in her bed.

Her bedroom door was shut. The music still played but the lights had been doused. Magdalena heard the gentle, steady breathing of the girl on the other side.

Young and untouched, so sweet…

Anthony didn't really require this particular girl, after all. Any healthy young woman would do for his plan. Only his superstitions made him think that it had to be Natalie.

And how easy to diffuse and slip beneath the door, a wraith of mist… to feel the slumbering heat of Natalie's body, pulsing with the slow and rhythmic tide in her veins.

A sip, only. Not enough to kill. Not even enough to harm. A sip. A taste. Foregoing the neck and the fine wrists, biting where it wouldn't show. The sole of the foot, the back of the knee, two little pinpricks and a taste, enough to satisfy the craving but not a drop more.

And she hadn't had a tender young virgin in months… not since Sarah.

She caught herself at the last instant.

Whether Anthony needed Natalie or not was beside the point. She needed his good will, his skill and expertise. If anything happened to the girl, it would affect his work whether his suspicions fell on Magdalena or not.

What was more, she would soon have *him* again. And his blood, richer than wine, was worth passing up any hundred succulent schoolgirls.

CHAPTER 24

Natalie looked up at the building, chewing her lower lip. Her backpack, loaded with Latin, math, and biology, dragged at her shoulders.

In one hand, she held a grocery bag full of fried chicken, potato wedges, coleslaw, and lime gelatin parfait salad. The battered-and-deep-fried greasy aroma was already drawing a crowd of stray cats, the slat-thin mangy things meowing their queries and demands from the corners of garbage bins. A raggedy-looking homeless man eyed her from a stoop, openly salivating into the tangles of his beard.

Right. She'd better get moving before she was mobbed.

She stepped through and around the obstacle course of cans, bottles, newspapers, and boxes between her and the door. The day was unseasonably hot, and the stink baking out of the stifling apartments overpowered the smell of chicken.

The inside proved just as grubby and depressing as she remembered, but her spirits lifted with familiarity as she climbed to Seth's floor. His door stood open. The boards had been pried from the windows, leaving gaping square-edged holes through which a listless breeze blew.

"Seth?" she called before she got more than halfway down the hall. Knowing him, at the first hint of a strange footstep, he'd spring out and karate-chop her, or something. Never mind that it was broad daylight. "Seth, it's Natalie. Remember?"

He stepped into the doorway, and her heart skittered a little. Khaki shorts and a dark red tee shirt. Great legs. Great arms. Slightly scruffy. Dark blue eyes lighting up with pleasure and recognition at the sight of her.

"Natalie, hi." There was a pause as he took in her school uniform. She wasn't sure if he was admiring it – guys had a thing for schoolgirls, she'd been told – or assessing its churchgoing affiliation. "What are you doing here?"

"I brought dinner. I had to talk to you."

"Sure. Come in."

"I didn't know if you'd still be here," she said. "It's been a while."

"Yeah, but where else was I going to go?" He took the bag, peered inside. "Looks better than what I was going to have."

"More of those gross energy bars?"

He made a face, then brightened as he dug through the contents. "Hey, they even gave you paper plates. And these spork things."

His apartment hadn't changed much since her previous visit. She found it hard to believe that over a month had gone by since then. Sometimes it seemed to Natalie like it had only been a few hours, and sometimes it felt like a year.

So much had happened. If she'd foreseen everything, she might never have left Our Lady of Sorrows.

Then again, she never would have met Seth. And she never would have found out about her mother. Karen would have died and been buried without Natalie ever seeing her face.

She and Seth sat down, using an old crate for a table. They dished out the food, and he tore into his with a ravenous appetite. Natalie followed suit. She never felt hungry in Madeline Margos' house, but now she was starved.

"So, I killed a vampire last week," she said five minutes later, peeling crispy skin from a chicken breast.

Seth almost spat coleslaw. "You *what*?"

The horror of it swept over her again, and this time she surrendered to the shakes that she'd been suppressing ever since that night. Falteringly, she told him about the man called Philips, what she'd seen, and what she'd done.

"I have to know if we got rid of him right," she finished. "I can hardly sleep for thinking that he'll come back. Dig himself out of the garden and find us somehow, track us down."

As she related the tale, Seth's pace of eating slowed. Now he dropped a few potato wedges onto his plate and wiped his fingers. "You beheaded the body when it didn't turn to dust?"

"Yes, Anthony did. With a shovel."

"Should be okay, then."

"Really?"

"As far as I know."

"What about the new people, the ones who bought the house?"

His grin was tight and lacking humor. "Better hope that they don't decide to re-landscape the yard. If they turned up a body back there, they'd probably call the police."

"A body with no head and a stake through its chest. What would they think?"

"Don't worry about that part. It'd get covered up."

"What, the body or the story?"

"The story. They always cover up stuff like this."

"But if people knew that there really were vampires, they'd know how to protect themselves."

"For one," he said, picking up the wedges again, "people don't want to know. For two, the vampires aren't that serious a threat, mostly."

She goggled at him. "They're murderous monsters!"

"You don't have to convince *me*. But regular, everyday folks kill each other a lot more often than the vampires kill anyone. Besides, if people did know, they'd want to know the rest of it… and they wouldn't like to hear that part. I saw how you reacted when I told you. Not wanting to believe that everybody's been fooled for this long."

"It's awful, though," she said. "I can't stop thinking about it. Anthony's religious, you know. We always went to church, and had a chapel in the house. He sent me to Sorrows, and now to St. Andrew's. I've got pictures on my bedroom walls of the Madonna, and the Ascension. And now … "

"Now you know better."

"I don't want to know better! How do you think it feels, going to a Catholic school, nuns in the halls, plaster saints in every classroom, morning prayers, and knowing it's all a big fat lie? I hate it, Seth. But there's nobody I can talk to about it, except you. And –"

"And you're still not convinced I'm not crazy."

"The vampires *are* real," she said. "If that part is true, what about the rest of it? I don't know anymore. I don't know what to do. My whole life is turned inside out. I'm not even who I thought I was."

"Huh?"

"If I tell you, you'll think *I'm* crazy."

"That's fair," he said, with a smile warm and agreeable enough to draw one from her despite her distress.

"My mother died the other day," she said, fixing her attention on the chicken meat she was methodically shredding from the bone. "I didn't even know she was still alive until a couple weeks ago. I couldn't even go to her funeral. My grandparents were there. I didn't know I had grandparents, either, and I can't ever meet them."

He listened as she told him about Karen Cross, perfect angel Karen in her eighteen-year coma. About Anthony, the brilliant scientist who thought that cloning a comatose woman was somehow God's will. About Fiona, whose resentment and hatred were finally out in the open. About what would happen to Natalie if anyone found out who she really was. The missing baby, miraculously returned. So many questions, interrogations. What the blood tests would reveal.

"Anthony would go to jail, and probably Fiona would too," she finished. "I... it's mean, but I don't really care so much about that. It's not like they were ever a loving family to me. Now I know why. Maybe Anthony thought he was doing a good thing, but it was still wrong."

"So why not tell someone?" Seth asked. "Your mother may be gone, but what about your grandparents? Wouldn't they want to know?"

"The shock might be too much," she said, with a bitter chuckle. "My grandfather's been sick for a long time, and my grandmother works herself half to death taking care of him. If I showed up, all of a sudden, there'd be reporters and a whole big mess."

"Uh-huh."

"Okay, okay. What I'm really scared of is… is that people, scientists, would take me away someplace and study me."

He considered, and did a half-shrug, half-nod. "You're probably right."

"With all that, and these vampires, and everything else, I just don't know what to do anymore. Sometimes I think I should run away, but where would I go with no job, no money?"

"Take it from me, it's not impossible," Seth said.

"Oh, come on!" She waved around at the room. "You can't tell me that this is how you want to live for the rest of your life!"

"What life? I know what it's like out here. If the other Centurions don't catch up with me, there's always the vampires. And if *they* don't get me, hell, there's plenty of strung-out street people willing to do the job. Face it, Natalie. I don't have a future. Neither will you, if you think about running away. Yours would be shorter and worse than mine."

"I realized that as soon as I got off the bus," she said, grimacing. "But what should I do?"

He ripped most of the meat off a chicken leg in one ferocious chomp. "What's so bad about staying where you are? Okay, so maybe this Anthony guy is nobody's father-of-the-year, but he looks out for you."

"I'm his prize experiment! He thinks I've got this big important destiny, that I'm going to save the world or something. I don't want a destiny. I want to be like everybody else."

"Join the club."

"You're a lot of help." She poked her plastic spork into a mound of gelatin parfait.

"Hey, I'm trying to be realistic, here. My own mother lied in order to cut me off from everything that matters to me. Sounds like you've got it pretty good."

"For a lab rat."

"Yeah, so? For a lab rat."

"Fiona said I should ask him about this big important destiny thing. She made it sound really sinister."

"Why don't you?"

Natalie stirred the green goo. "I don't know what to say. Ever since we moved in with that Margos lady, too, he's been so busy that I hardly see him anymore. That house is just spooky. Quiet. Library quiet. Claire, a girl at school? She told me that it used to belong to a mad serial killer cannibal."

"Oh, that's nice," Seth said, setting down his fourth piece of chicken.

"It smells weird. Like maybe when they cleaned the place out, they didn't find all the body parts hidden under the floorboards."

"Why'd you move there?"

"Some project of Anthony's. He started off trying to unload a bunch of his old books on that Margos woman, but she ended up hiring him. I don't know what for. He wouldn't tell me. Just said it was complicated, scientific. He tried to make it sound boring but I could tell he's really excited."

"You're sure not."

"I don't like that house!" she said, surprising herself with the volume. "I don't like that woman, either. The way she always looks at me... I feel all slimy."

"What's wrong with her?"

"She acts nice enough, she's pretty, she must have plenty of money, but there's just something weird about her. Living in that house... none of it feels real. It's like one of those furniture showrooms."

The conversation dried up as they sank into their own brooding thoughts. Natalie couldn't get Madeline Margos out of her mind. Those smoky eyes. The way she was so silent, gliding when she walked, hardly even seeming to breathe.

Sometimes, she woke in the dead of night thinking that there was someone in the room, that she could smell the dark-spice of the woman's perfume.

She collected empty food wrappers and paper plates, putting them in a trash bag. "Do you want to keep the rest of this? There's a lot of chicken left."

"No refrigerator," he said. "It'd go bad too fast in this heat."

"Well, I hate to throw it out. Can we give it to that man out back?"

"Viking?"

"Is that his name?"

"It's what people call him," Seth said. "The beard, and the way he sometimes shakes his fists and yells about Odin and Thor and Eric the Red. Once, he was in the middle of the street daring Thor to strike him down with a lightning bolt. Everybody cleared out of the way. You know, just in case."

They packed up the leftover chicken and coleslaw in a cardboard box, and carried it downstairs.

The cats had dispersed, but Viking was still where Natalie had seen him. He'd fallen asleep, leaning against a wall with a bulging duffel bag for a pillow. A large brown bottle rested in his lap.

Seth crept up, navigating the obstacle course of litter with a stealth and grace that Natalie envied. He placed the box near Viking's boot, which had been mended with duct tape.

"Mission accomplished," he said when he rejoined Natalie.

"I guess I should go. I've got homework to do."

"Are you okay alone? It'll be dark soon."

"Yeah, fine," she said. "I know the buses now, and if Anthony saw me with a boy, he'd hit the roof."

"He… doesn't let you go out?"

"On dates, you mean?" She snickered. "He wanted me to become a nun, remember?"

"Right. Never mind."

"Were you going to ask me on one?"

He scuffed his foot, took a deep breath, laughed a little, and she thought he looked incredibly cute. "I've got no car, no money, and whenever I'm outside at night I'm on the lookout for vampires. Some date, huh?"

"We could meet after school," she said. "For pizza, maybe? My treat."

"Okay," Seth said. "But I can pay half. I'm not totally broke." He named a pizza place, not too far away. "Friday, maybe? What time do you get out of class?"

"I'll meet you there at four," she said, thinking that it would give her time to change clothes before the date.

The date! It made her giddy.

"See you then," he said.

Chapter 25

He hardly dared say so, for fear that it would turn out to be untrue. But the proof was there, right there, in front of him.

"I think I have it," he whispered.

Saying it didn't undo it. The words did not act as some evil curse, ruining his work and leaving him with dashed hopes and useless dreams.

No one else heard him. He was alone in the lab, possibly even alone in the house.

Anthony cautioned himself to stay calm. Cool head, steady nerves. Now was not the time to let excitement interfere. Never mind that he wanted to shout, cavort, and go wild in his victory.

"My moment of triumph," he said, and wished someone was there to share it with him.

How he would have relished the opportunity to gloat to his old professors! They'd lectured so sternly about ethics, and done their best to shoot down the aspirations of class after class of budding young scientists.

Madeline would appreciate the news, but he didn't know where she'd gotten.

Even Fiona, though she'd never understood his work and had hardly spoken to him in days. She'd nearly blistered his ears during their last few phone calls, expressing her opinions on Natalie finding out the truth about Karen.

As if he'd had anything to do with that. He'd only admitted to his part in things once the girl had already uncovered most of it.

What harm was there in it, really? He hadn't told Natalie *everything*. He hadn't told her what would happen next.

He left the lab before he could surrender to the temptation to keep fiddling with his successful result. The last thing he'd want to do would be to mess it up now.

The house was wrapped in silence. Natalie had said something about staying late after school, diligent good student that she was.

When to do it? The sooner the better… and not only because he was so eager to see his project reach fruition.

There was scant time to waste. The world was in dire straits and getting worse. Matters were out of control. If ever there had been a need for a new era of peace, love, brotherhood, and renewal, this was surely it.

In the kitchen, he heated some pastries and then decided he was too keyed up to eat.

He paced instead, snapping his fingers in intricate medleys. His feet hardly seemed to touch the floor. He felt glowing, sparking, crackling and alive with the thrill of his success.

What this occasion needed was a bottle of champagne to celebrate. Yes, a celebration… he and Madeline could toast to their endeavor. Then, tonight, implement the next step. Maybe she had some in the pantry. He could have everything ready by the time she got back from wherever it was that she'd spent her day.

The shelves were stocked with cans of juice, cases of soda, and gallons of bottled water. No beer, no wine, no alcohol except for cooking sherry. He made an exasperated noise, not wanting to have to go out in search of a liquor store.

A house like this must have its own wine cellar. Under the circumstances, Madeline would forgive him a bit of trespassing if it meant surprising her with a champagne toast to their triumph.

A cool draft sighed past him when he opened the basement door at the rear of the pantry. Musty-smelling darkness lay beyond. He groped for a switch, or a pull-cord, and found nothing.

The unsavory history of the house occurred to him. The serial killer. The butchered bodies.

But Anthony Sevrin was a man of science, not superstition. Even his devout faith didn't lend itself to believing in hauntings by vengeful or tormented spirits.

The dead went on to a better place, or a worse one, depending on how well their lives had been lived in the glory and purpose of God. Spirits didn't linger. Surely, the killer himself roasted in the deepest fiery manure pits of Hell, while his victims had been elevated, transported into angelic splendor.

Nonetheless, Anthony got a chill as he peered down the shadowy flight of stairs. He fancied he heard rustlings – mice, he thought, and told himself not to be a ninny.

No flashlights or candles presented themselves, so he made his descent in the dark. Slow and careful. One foot at a time, testing each tread. He kept one hand on the rail, the other waving the air in front of him in deliberate passes, hoping to contact a chain attached to a light fixture.

He found one, batted it away by accident, and caught it again as it swung. The old and grimy bulb cast a limp urine-yellow glow.

The stairs led down not to a tidy wine cellar but into a basement of dank brick and cracked concrete and derelict appliances, the shelves thick with greasy dust, the floor marked with silty stains where water had seeped up.

Anthony noticed a cleaner path of sorts, worn into the grime, leading to a doorway hung with a heavy curtain. The metal rings and rod looked scraped clean from fresh use.

Beside the doorway was a niche that held a candlestick – brass, in the shape of a female angel with wings raked back – and a box of matches. He crossed to it, struck a match, and lit the white taper that rose between the angel's wings.

He moved the edge of the curtain and looked through.

The leaping flame-flicker illuminated a long room with a low, arched, vaulted ceiling... here was the wine cellar he'd sought, lined with wine racks and huge oaken casks, and scrupulously clean by contrast with the outer basement.

It struck him as odd. And the smell, not of soured wine but something... earthy, rotten... spoiled his thirst for champagne.

A queasiness in his stomach likewise quashed any celebratory feelings, replacing them with indigestion.

He inched past a massive marble-topped table, also scrupulously clean and disturbingly altar-like, to peer through a side archway.

His first impression was that it must be some sort of family crypt. Or that one of the house's previous owners, before the serial killer, perhaps, had been an undertaker and this was a surplus showroom or storage area.

Why else have so many coffins and caskets, from the plainest pine boxes to the most ornate models, displayed on stone biers jutting out from the walls?

Then it occurred to him to think of vampires.

Even in his horror, he was able to be chagrined at himself for not having immediately leaped to that conclusion. Anthony Sevrin, smart as he was... genius that he was ...

He turned, and the candlelight fell full on the grinning, leprous face of a corpse.

"Good afternoon, Doctor Sevrin," it said in a harsh voice like the rattle of dry leaves on brittle branches.

The light stuttered as the candle shook in Anthony's grasp.

The dead man seized his wrist, steadying it in a bony but relentless grip. The fingers were cold, and stiff, but strong. A blackened fingernail snagged on Anthony's sleeve and peeled off. The flesh beneath was the color and texture of beef jerky, something desiccated to a husk in an arid desert climate. A thin sand-colored worm wriggled out and dropped onto Anthony's arm.

"Poking into things, are we?" It cackled. Dry flecks of skin sloughed and sifted. The breath that blew into Anthony's face was tepid, rank.

"Dear God," Anthony said strengthlessly.

"Lazarus, let him go."

With a rusty creak of tendons, the man turned his head. The robe hanging from his knobby shoulders looked older and more timeworn than even the false Shroud of Turin had been. "I wasn't about to hurt him."

Madeline Margos, in a plain blue robe that lent luster to her black hair and fell over her lush form in a way that would have made other men almost forget about living corpses, stepped up to them in her smoothly gliding way. At a signal from her, the dead man released Anthony.

Immediately, Anthony dropped the candlestick. The taper sputtered but did not go out. He flicked away the creeping worm, holding back a revolted cry. He scrubbed his hand on his pants.

"Anthony."

Not looking at her, still frantically trying to rub away the memory of the feel of the man's flesh, Anthony said, "Oh, my God, what is this? What's happening here?"

She touched his shoulder. "Anthony. Look at me."

He recoiled and stared at her with the stark, terrified gaze of a cornered animal.

Somehow, her plum-dark eyes calmed him, and made him able to think rationally.

"What are you doing down here?" she asked.

Though her tone was mild, he sensed her forbidding displeasure, and quailed. He wanted to avert his eyes. He felt low, and unworthy. After everything she'd done for him, he had shown himself to be a most ungrateful guest. Yet he couldn't look away from the kind, sad beauty of her face.

"I… I was looking for champagne," he said. "To celebrate."

"Celebrate? You mean … ?"

"I've done it," he said, emboldened by the hopeful apprehension in her voice.

His own shock and fear at these subterranean horrors – coffins, vampires, walking dead men – seemed far removed then from the joys of success and discovery. The longer he looked into her eyes, the less anything else seemed to matter.

"Show me," Madeline commanded.

He headed back the way he had come, with her at his side and the dead man bringing up the rear.

From the corner of his eye, Anthony caught another glimpse of the long room full of coffins. Something was different in there. The one nearest to the archway stood open, its lid raised, its interior empty.

But, for some reason, that didn't seem to matter either. Nor did his questions or concerns. He was aware of the dead man – Lazarus – following them, wreathed in his sour yellow stink... but it wasn't important. Not with Madeline beside him.

Back through the basement, up the stairs, into the pantry.

"Lazarus, stay below, in case the girl returns."

"Fine," the dead man said peevishly. "I'll just do that, shall I?"

Guiding Anthony by the elbow, Madeline took him to the suite of rooms that had been converted into his tidy office and workroom. It registered on him that her touch was also deathly cold, but he forgot all about it as they came to the lab.

"Here," he said. "Here it is. As you know, I took blood samples from the object you provided. I revitalized the blood with a chemical solution of my own design, which rendered the DNA suitable for cloning. Once I had extracted the genetic material, I merged it with this ovum."

"Where did you get --?"

He smiled, so very pleased with himself. "I obtained them from a fertility clinic. Donor eggs. It's a thriving business, and you would be amazed at the scams that do go on. Clients think that they're paying extra for eggs or sperm from attractive, intelligent, talented people. Most of the time, what they're getting come from prisoners, mental patients, or other undesirables."

"Is that what you have there?" Madeline's frown worried him. "An undesirable?"

"No, oh, goodness, no! Well, originally, but it won't have any effect on the end result. I took the healthiest ovum I could find and... washed it, essentially. Removed the individual genetic markers so that it was a blank slate. It's the cell structure and the nutrients that we want. Then, I wove the DNA strand into the cell. And, *voila!*"

"Already? You're done?"

"With this stage, yes. The next bit is where it becomes slightly more complicated. The embryo must be implanted, and given time to grow naturally. That part cannot be rushed. Why is there a dead man in the basement?"

The last question popped out on its own, and Anthony was startled to hear it. Dead man? Yes, there had been a man…

Madeline rested her fingertips on the sides of his face, touching his temples. Her dark gaze held him captivated. "Forget about what you saw down there, Anthony."

"Down where?" he asked, honestly baffled.

Her thumbs caressed his cheekbones. "That's right," she murmured. "Hear me, and let it go."

"I hear you." He felt as though he was sinking into a pleasant daydream.

What an incredible woman. Beautiful enough to stir even his heart, though his emotions toward her were not of any sort of carnal nature. No, he loved and admired her much as he had loved and admired Karen Cross.

She released him, and he blinked.

"When can we begin the next stage?" she asked.

"The next stage? Ah. Yes. I think there's no reason why we couldn't do it this very night. Tonight, Madeline. How will that be?"

Such a radiant smile… he saw only the briefest glimmer of her teeth before she demurely covered her mouth with a hand.

"Tonight, then," she said. "Tonight it is."

Chapter 26

Natalie went straight to her room upon her return to the house each day. She blamed it on schoolwork, letting Anthony think the late hours she'd been spending at the hospital or visiting Seth were due to extra-curricular activities. Choir practice. An independent Bible study group. Things that met his approval.

Friday, after her first official date with Seth, she hurried upstairs as soon as she got back. If Anthony happened to catch a glimpse of her, she might not be able to pretend she'd been up to something as innocent as choir practice.

Which wasn't to say that she'd been up to anything *bad*. Only having pizza. Not kissing, not even holding hands.

Which was too bad... Natalie would have liked to kiss Seth. She'd heard how the best kissers were the serious, intense guys, and that was Seth, all right. Serious and intense.

She tried to do homework, finding it difficult because Seth kept intruding on her thoughts. They had a matinee movie date for next Saturday, a theater that showed old movies, two dollars for a double feature. She hadn't been to an actual movie in a theater in ages.

The house was as quiet as ever when she ventured downstairs later to rummage for a snack. Gorgeous periwinkle twilight filled the few unobstructed windows. The evening star twinkled above the horizon, and, like a child, Natalie silently wished on it that Seth might lean over during the movie and kiss her. Silly, but wouldn't it be nice if it came true?

She sliced an apple, spooned a blob of peanut butter onto the plate, poured a glass of milk and was about to look for cookies when Madeline spoke her name.

"Natalie."

A gasp tore at her throat. She jumped backward and bumped into the counter, knocking the glass to the floor so that it broke.

"Natalie, I'm sorry," Madeline said. "I frightened you."

"No, really, just… well, a little." She crouched to pick up the pieces and jabbed her thumb. "I'll clean up this mess."

"It's all right. No crying over spilt … " Madeline trailed off. A dry click came from her throat as she swallowed. "Oh. You've hurt yourself."

"I'm okay," Natalie said, though it did sting and there was a welling red droplet.

"Here. Let me see." But the woman looked suddenly ashen, and was almost swaying on her feet, like someone who couldn't stand the sight of blood.

"I'm fine, really." Natalie wadded a paper towel around the cut. "Is… um… Anthony here?"

"He's in his lab. He had something of a breakthrough this afternoon." Madeline tore her gaze away, with effort, from Natalie's hand. "You're sure you're all right?"

She peeked under, then removed the red-spotted paper towel and waggled her thumb. The pressure had done the trick, the bleeding stopped. "Yes, looks like it. Sorry about the glass."

"Think nothing of it."

"Um, sure, if you say so." She took her snack to her room, finished her algebra, and got into bed with a book until sleep stole up on her

She dreamed of Seth walking with her on a beach, endless waves rolling foam-capped sapphire under a golden sun, their shadows trailing them along the sand.

She dreamed of combing her hair in front of a mirror, and seeing Fiona appear over her shoulder, a witchlike Fiona with envious green eyes, holding out an apple. *The* apple, Snow White's poisoned apple.

But, spinning away from the dream-mirror, she found Madeline behind her, and Madeline's hand closing on her arm, long fingernails digging in with a sharp silvery pain.

And heard Anthony's voice, echoing in the slow roll of the waves as she found herself back on the sunny dream-beach with

Seth. Anthony's voice saying, "There, that should do it. Give her a few minutes."

And the waves, indigo now, no longer sapphire. Indigo night-waves surging up the beach. She called out to Seth as the water churned and foamed around her knees, as the tricky sand slipped liquidly away beneath her feet and she felt herself sinking, sinking.

The next image was bright, a painful white brilliance that made her eyes water. She couldn't close them, could only stare unblinkingly up at florescent tubes in frosted fixtures. A sharp hospital smell hung in the air. She couldn't feel her limbs, couldn't move.

Karen. She was Karen, her mother-twin-self, trapped, helpless, unable to communicate, unable to respond.

A shadow fell over her, eclipsing the harsh white light. A man's head and shoulders. A surgical mask obscuring his nose and mouth, plastic goggles over his eyes. Anthony Sevrin.

Was this what Karen had gone through? Karen's memory?

Had she heard him mumbling about destiny, about saving the world, even as he swabbed her abdomen with something cold and wet on a cotton ball? Like he was doing now? As his gloved fingers palpated, and he raised the longest needle she had ever seen?

Like he was doing now?

Natalie, in the throes of the dream, tried to wrest herself back to wakefulness.

Her mind was as unresponsive as the rest of her. She watched the tip of the needle descend, felt the pinprick of it and a thin icicle pain as it pierced deep.

Then, somehow, she was past that and back at Our Lady of Sorrows, surrounded by other girls, kneeling for evening prayers, some of them somber and devout, some giggling and whispering whenever the watchful Sisters were looking the other way.

And above them, on the chapel wall, loomed the cross. But the figure upon it was not the same one that Natalie remembered. This was no holy and suffering Christ.

A vulpine man-shaped thing gnashed and snapped at the air with curved fangs. It yanked at the spikes transfixing wrists and feet until the wounds ripped wide and ran with dark blood.

She stood in the crowd, Natalie but not-Natalie, watching the vampire king writhe in agony. Seth was there, too, his face set as he readied a stake, a hammer. And Madeline Margos, robed and veiled, turning her back on a red-haired stranger with a horrible blackened burn mark covering the side of his neck.

Natalie woke, soaked with sweat, to the twitter of birds in the peaceful morning outside of her bedroom window.

She sat up, heaving for breath, in a bed that was a disastrous tangle of sheets and blankets, pillow on the floor, nightgown twisted, hair matted and clumped. Ugh.

Groaning, she rolled out of bed and stretched. Every part of her ached like she was coming down with the flu. Despite the fact that her clock showed it to be two hours later than the time she usually got up, she felt as though she had hardly slept a wink.

A hot shower revived her. As she toweled, she recalled the dreams, and shivered even in the steamy air. The needle. It had been so vivid, so real.

Anthony was in the kitchen when she went downstairs, sound asleep at the table with his head on his folded arms and a half-empty cup of cold coffee by his elbow.

She tiptoed around him and got orange juice and a bagel, though she didn't feel particularly hungry.

He didn't stir. If he hadn't been breathing in snuffling snores, she might have thought he'd had a heart attack or something.

The needle.

It sent shivers down her spine. She poked at her stomach and imagined she felt a tender spot where the silvery spike had pierced her. But, by lunchtime, the details had receded the way nightmares often did, and she put the rest of it out of her mind to concentrate on a history paper.

The week passed at an agonizing pace leading up to her movie date with Seth. Most days, it was as if she lived alone in the house, Madeline Margos off doing whatever, Anthony clattering away on his computer or buried in his research.

Saturday, she woke early and eager six hours in advance of the time they'd agreed to meet.

She put on breezy white slacks, a pearly pink shell top, and open-toed pink sandals. She brushed her blonde hair shiny and tied it back from her face with a scarf that matched her top. A bit of lip-gloss, a dusting of eye shadow, and she was ready to go.

"Ah, Natalie," Anthony said as she reached the bottom of the stairs. He looked more alert and cheerful than she'd seen him in a while, though in need of a shave. "Going out?"

"To a movie," she said.

"How are you feeling?" He studied her intently. The way his eyes bored into her made her feel like she was on a microscope slide. "Been sleeping well?"

"I'm fine."

"You're sure?"

"Yes. Why wouldn't I be?"

"No reason. A movie, you say. I haven't been to a movie in years… want company?"

Uh-oh, thin ice. "I'm meeting a friend."

"One of your girlfriends from school?"

She smiled, figuring that a smile wasn't a nod, so it wasn't exactly a lie. "We might go for ice cream after, but I'll be back before dark."

"Good," he said. "Good, see that you are. I would hate to have anything happen to you."

"I'll watch out for myself," she said. She got her purse from the hook in the hall and went out into a day almost too nice to waste by staying cooped up in a dark theater.

Seth met her under the marquee, dressed in new jeans and a plain white button-down shirt with the sleeves rolled up. He grinned.

"I got a job."

"That's great! Where? Doing what?"

"You won't believe it. Remember that coffee shop where we met? I went back there this morning. Passing by, you know, to see what had happened to the place. If it had closed, or what. But it was open, and there was a help-wanted sign in the window."

"What about Pamela? Is she all right?"

"Yeah. She even recognized me from that night, though I don't think she remembers much else. The shock, you know… it messed her up. She thinks the vampire was just an ordinary person."

"Ordinary?"

"Scratch that. A drugged-out crazy. Psychotic. Anyway, she wanted to thank me and said she understood about me not wanting to get involved with the police."

"Was she hurt?"

"Not bad. Spent a night in the hospital, and the coffee shop was closed for more than a week while the cops went through it. You'd never know what went on in there. Everything's as good as new."

"And she hired you, I'm so glad!"

"Nights," he said with a wry twist of his mouth. "Ten to six, Fridays through Mondays. Thirty-two hours, but it's better than minimum wage and I get all the coffee I can drink."

She kissed him on the cheek, an impulsive move that felt so right. "Congratulations!"

Seth turned red. "Thanks."

"I'd come and see you at work, but –"

"Don't. I mean, I'd like you to, but it's so near the park … "

"Sometimes I think I'll never be allowed outside at night again," she said. "They can't be everywhere, can they?"

His only answer to that was a world-weary shrug.

He bought the tickets and the popcorn, insisting on it because he was now gainfully employed. The theater was an old-fashioned one, not a shopping-mall multiplex but a cathedral with soaring ceiling, gigantic chandelier, threadbare faux-velvet seats, chipped gold paint on pseudo-baroque walls, and miles of thick curtains that rose in gathering folds away from a vast off-white screen.

Midway through the first movie, she and Seth somehow ended up holding hands. She wasn't sure whether she'd taken the initiative, or he had, or it had been a mutual thing that had just happened when they both went for the popcorn.

As the credits rolled, she turned to ask him a question and he had already turned to say something to her. She forgot what she'd been wanting to ask, conscious only that their faces were just a few inches apart. He hesitated, and Natalie, not about to let the moment pass by, leaned up and pressed her lips to his.

At first, he didn't move and she thought she must have shocked him. But then his hand slipped around to cradle the back of her neck and he kissed her, until the rushing in her ears totally drowned out the soundtrack.

She fell back from him, exhilarated and scared and tingling and overcome, and knew that if they did that again, she'd want to climb right into his lap and neck all the way through the second movie. As Seth sat back and reached for his soda, she was certain she read similar thoughts in his eyes.

PART FIVE – THE CENTURION
June

CHAPTER 27

Three weeks passed, and Seth still hadn't seen or heard from Natalie. He went from moderately concerned to seriously worried.

At first, when she didn't show up for their next scheduled date the weekend after the double feature, he'd assumed – to his dismay – that she didn't want to go out with him anymore.

He must have come on too strong, kissing her like that. Scared her off.

But further reflection made him jettison that notion. Natalie wasn't like that. She had initiated that kiss as much as he had. More, even.

Maybe *that* was it. Maybe she felt embarrassed by it, and was afraid he'd think she was easy.

That idea, too, didn't hold up. Somehow, it didn't seem like Natalie. If something were wrong, she would have said so.

Had she gotten in trouble with her guardian and been grounded? He tried to look up their new place in the phone book, but was stumped before he began because he couldn't remember that Anthony guy's last name… and the Margos woman wasn't listed… and when he even searched online at the library, had no luck there either.

He tried waiting outside her school next, drawing glares from boys who must have thought he was here to poach on their female classmates, not to mention some sidelong glances from girls who didn't look like they'd mind being poached on. He also got a forbidding glower from a nun in an old-fashioned black and white habit.

When the flow of students had ended and Natalie still wasn't among them, Seth steeled his spine and went inside to ask at the office.

The school was old, weighty, stark and solid, and loaded with religious imagery that might have been meant to be comforting or instructing. Worst of all was a towering crucifix with a greater-than-life-size Christ figure mounted on it.

They always got it wrong. The slash mark in the chest was too low, too off-center, to the side and grazing the ribs. It should have punctured the heart.

He didn't know how anyone could possibly buy into this faith, take comfort from it. Even the believers should find nightmares, not salvation, in the torture and guilt of that dying figure on the cross.

At the office, he was confronted not only by nuns but a priest in collar and black cassock. The nuns eyeballed Seth with suspicion—not just a boy but an outsider boy!—but the priest smiled and greeted him pleasantly enough.

It didn't last long. As soon as Seth said he was looking for Natalie, the priest's smile fell off his face like a brick and his formerly warm eyes went frosty.

"She is no longer a student at this school," the priest said.

"Did she transfer? Did she move?"

"I really couldn't say."

"It's important that I talk to her."

"Oh, is it?" asked the priest, eyebrows raised. Behind him, a bevy of nuns muttered and cast disapproving looks.

His instincts told him to forget it and leave before he dug himself any deeper into their bad graces, but he gave it another try.

"I'm a friend of hers," he said. "Please, could you tell me where she lives? Or give me a phone number?"

"Young man, I think you've had far too much to do with Natalie already," the priest said. "And I suggest that you keep your distance from this school."

"Is something wrong?" Seth asked.

The priest's mouth tucked into a tight seam. When he spoke, he hardly moved his lips at all. "I don't believe you have any more business here. Please show yourself out."

Seth did, before the tangible hostility he felt in the air became an actual physical force. Could they *know* he was a Centurion? The Legion had faced opposition from priests before.

Or had someone seen him with Natalie, reported back, and gotten her in trouble with the school? If that had happened, if she'd been expelled because of him, what would Anthony have done?

He really had to find her now. She'd said something about the house where the Margos woman lived. The house had belonged to a mass murderer, wasn't that it? But how was he supposed to find out where it was?

As he walked away from the campus, he spotted a boy and a girl watching him from a bench. The girl was short and curvy, with brown curls and a dimpled smile. Her boyfriend was tall and gangly, with a shock of carrot-colored hair and a facial war going on between acne and freckles. They both wore the school uniforms and had backpacks resting at their feet. Seth saw the girl give the boy a nudge, and nod toward him.

The boy got up, unbending with a stork like awkwardness that said his growth spurt had come on him suddenly. He moved toward Seth. The girl followed, prodding him when he slowed. Seth read, "Go on!" on her lips.

"Can I help you?" he asked when they got close.

"Um… you're Seth, right?" asked the red-haired boy. "I'm Danny, and this is Claire."

"Okay. Have we met?"

Claire shoved Danny aside and took over. "You're a friend of Natalie's, aren't you? We saw you at the movies. I asked Natalie about you later and she told me your name."

"So you go to school with Natalie?"

"Well, we *did*," Claire said, and her expression turned foxysly. She even winked. "She's not going to school anymore. Hasn't been for a month, almost."

"I know that."

Danny snorted. "Bet you do."

"Look," Seth said, "if there's something going on, I wish you'd tell me. I asked at the school and got nothing. I'm worried about her."

"Oh, boy," Claire stage-whispered to Danny. "I bet he doesn't know. I bet he really doesn't."

"Tell me." Seth looked back and forth between them. "Is she sick? Did she move? What?"

"I don't know if I should say," Claire said. Her hazel eyes glittered and she seemed about to burst with her secret anyway. "If you don't already know, I mean."

He held onto his temper with both hands. "I'd really appreciate it."

"Well, I don't know anything for sure, but it doesn't take a genius to guess what's going on. When a girl's family pulls her out of school with no explanation, we all get the picture."

"What are you talking about?" Seth asked.

"Natalie," Danny said. "They sent her to, you know, visit relatives."

"She doesn't have any relatives."

Claire scoffed like he was hopeless. "She's *pregnant*! Duh!"

He gaped at her. Words formulated in his brain but fell apart before they could reach his mouth. Finally, he said, "That's impossible."

"Hey, pal, accidents happen," Danny said. "My brother, him and his girlfriend were super careful, used condoms and everything, but still they had to get married."

"It wasn't... you must be wrong," Seth said. "There's got to be a mistake here somewhere. She can't be."

"That's what my brother said." Danny bobbed his head sagely. "But now I'm an uncle."

Claire's eyes widened. "If it was me, and my dad found out, he'd send in the Marines!"

"Wait," Seth said. "Wait a minute, here. Look, Natalie can't be… she can't be pregnant."

"Uh-huh … " Claire, smug, crossed her arms and grinned.

"Whatever you say." Danny winked at him.

"Can you at least tell me where she lives?"

They swapped a glance, and then Claire shrugged. "Sure. She lives in the house where Gutman Greaver killed all those people."

"*Gut*-man?"

"They called him that because of what he did with their –" Danny began.

"I get the picture," Seth said.

"Anyway," Claire went on, "it's on Bellaflora Avenue. 5419 or 5491, I can't remember exactly. Big white house with columns."

"Thanks."

He hurried down the street, glad to get away from them and their school. What they'd told him couldn't possibly be true… not Natalie… certainly not *him* and Natalie… but if that was what people thought, well, no wonder he'd been met with that kind of a reception!

Bellaflora Avenue curved off into the hills on a long, sinuous course. Its neighborhoods consisted of increasingly expensive homes on increasingly large lots. An abundance of old trees and high hedges made everything shady and cool, like a premonition of the night to come even in the middle of the afternoon. No people were out and about, no kids playing, no gardeners at work. Seth felt conspicuous, the only moving thing in sight.

Fifty-four nineteen turned out to be a garish pink-and-yellow Victorian that looked like a birthday cake, but he tried the doorbell anyway. A tiny lady with white hair answered, cradling the world's most spoiled-looking Persian cat, and said that, no, she didn't know anyone named Margos. The cat seemed to sneer and gave an arrogant flick of its tail.

Seth went on, and the house numbers continued to climb. Eventually, he came to a cross street, this one cutting a ruler-straight line downhill toward a more commercial district of businesses and apartment buildings. He paused at the corner to regain his bearings, which had gotten jumbled with all the meandering twists and turns.

To his unease, the sign read "Landover Street." When he looked along it, he saw the unmistakable white form of the hospital... the ominous dark green of Landover Park... Bellaflora's scenic route through the hills had brought him most of the way around to downtown.

Fifty-four ninety-one turned out to be white with columns, like something out of the Old South, just as Claire had told him. Despite the pleasant spring day, the shutters were closed. The driveway, guarded by stone posts but not gated, had no car in it.

He risked a quick peek into the mailbox and found it full of bills, letters, and medical supply company catalogs... addressed to Anthony Sevrin.

Sevrin. Mental note. That was the man's last name.

If he'd needed to steel his spine before approaching the priest at the school, he needed to titanium it before going up onto the porch and knocking. He had no clue what he'd say, but neither did he want to have hiked all this way for nothing, only to turn around and leave.

No one came to the door. The house gave off a sense of stillness and vacancy, as if it was not just empty but completely abandoned.

Seth knocked again anyway, with the same result. He backed up onto the lawn to survey the windows, seeing only shutters and drapes.

A peek into the mailbox was one thing. Breaking into someone's home was another. Just because he couldn't see any neighbors watching didn't mean the reverse wasn't true. A phone call, a burglar alarm, and next thing he'd know the police would be there.

He tried a third knocking. As he waited, listening intently to the silence, a prickle shivered down the nape of his neck and he knew he was really pushing his luck.

At the next corner, he turned right on Drayton to head downhill, the road cutting through a steep section of hillside woodlot between the backyards of the Bellaflora houses and the smaller yards of much less fancier suburban type tract homes. Another right at a closed family-run daycare brought him onto a street called Fortuna. He saw a lot of 'For Sale' signs, a lot of lawns that were knee-high and turning brown, and a general impression of run-down despair. He did see more people than he had before – some kids playing on a swing set, a guy washing his car, a lady out for a jog – but none of them looked very happy, or very friendly.

A glance up the hill showed him the back fences and hedges behind the Bellaflora Avenue houses, rising like medieval battlements. He wondered if it might be possible to get a better look at 5491 from another angle, and decided to give it a try.

The woodlot separating the neighborhoods was dense, weedy, trash-strewn, and overgrown with scrub brush and wildflowers. Party debris – beer cans, broken bottles, condoms – suggested he wasn't the first teenager to tromp around out here.

His attention divided, he almost stepped on the body before he saw it.

Seth stopped short, at the same time shocked and somehow unsurprised.

A body, here in the weeds. Dismembered. Bones, really. Bones and scraps of flesh, torn clothes, a tangle of hair.

Blonde hair. Like Natalie's

CHAPTER 28

Seth crouched, careful even in his horror to touch nothing.

Here was an explanation that Claire and Danny hadn't dreamed of.

"No," Seth said, with a feeling like blunt rusty claws digging into his gut.

How long since he had seen Natalie? Three weeks? Three and a half? How long had these poor, sad remains lain on this weed-choked hillside? He was no forensics expert, able to determine time of death by the age of the ants crawling around the scene.

His mind threw together a scenario. Natalie returns from their last movie date and is found out. In a fit of rage, maybe even by accident, her guardian kills her. Panics. Dumps the body behind the house. Conjures up some story to placate the school.

He straightened up, scuffing away his footprints more on instinct than coherent thought. All at once, the wooded hill above the dying Fortuna neighborhood felt as open and exposed as the fifty-yard line of the Rose Bowl.

"Natalie?" he whispered.

Maybe it wasn't her.

Maybe it was some other blonde girl, dead in the dirt just a few dozen yards from where Natalie was staying.

Judas, no.

He'd saved her from the vampire, sure... only to let her be hurt by someone else? After she'd told him how safe he made her feel? How protected? What a bitter joke that turned out to be!

Fifty-four ninety-one, above him, had no visible gate in the wall enclosing the rear of the property. He headed that way all the same, doing his best to leave as little a trail through the brush as possible.

Not that he needed to bother. It seemed there already was something of a track beaten through here. He followed it, senses on full alert.

His stomach knotted when he saw more bones... dry and picked clean, arm bones, the pale twigs of fingers. A gold-tone watchband still encircled the wrist. The cheap crystal was cracked, the hands stopped at 11:40.

Did Natalie wear a watch like that?

Seth couldn't remember ever having seen her wear a watch at all. At first, this sparked hope in him, but the hope didn't last long. Just because he'd never seen her wear one didn't mean she never did.

Or this belonged to a second body...

Hadn't Natalie told him a serial killer used to own the house? But surely the police would have scoured the area at the time, found anything there was to find. These had to be more recent.

Twenty feet further along, he saw a drain culvert set into the hillside. For rain runoff, flood control, he figured... except that this one had no water-eroded gully spreading from it.

He shined his keychain penlight into the pipe. It was maybe three feet in diameter and only ran a short distance before a metal grate blocked him.

Seth looked up. He was almost right under the back wall of 5491. If the house had a basement...

It was crazy, what he was thinking.

He stuck his head in the pipe to get a better look. The air was close, dank, thick with scents that made his nose wrinkle.

In that moment, he missed and wished for his father more fiercely than ever. He missed and wished for the training he'd been cheated out of, for the weapons and equipment he didn't have.

Crazy. There could be a killer in here, a human monster or something even worse.

Crazy, but he went in anyway.

The metal sides scraped at his shoulders, the ribbed surface dug painfully into his palms and knees. What waning afternoon sunshine reached into the pipe got blotted out by his own shadow.

He reached the grate and aimed the penlight through at a small room like a root cellar, with earthen walls shored up by planks. It was empty except for rags and old newspapers in the corners. The door on the far side was warped but looked sturdy.

When he tested the grate with a tug, it remained solidly in place. But he saw a latch, and hinges, and realized the grate was rigged to swing like a door.

If, that was, he could reach the latch... which was on the inside.

He worked his left hand through one of the gaps, stretching and straining, twisting until he touched the catch with his fingertips. It was balky, the angle awkward, and he ground his teeth with frustration as he struggled.

It gave.

Though he'd been expecting it, he hadn't been braced for it. He'd been leaning against the grate, and now his weight pushed it inward. The hinges squalled. His arm bent at angles it didn't like to go and for a bad moment, he was sure his wrist would snap.

Seth extricated his hand without breaking any bones. It hurt, though. The bars had left deep marks in his forearm and wrist. The flesh already felt swollen and sore.

Crazy. Crazy and stupid. Here he hadn't gotten past this one obstacle uninjured, and outside, the daylight was turning a brassy gold. Soon the gold would become burnt copper. Then the copper would become lead, and the lead would become black anthracite.

Night. Night falling and here he was... far from the scant safety of his own place... close to Landover Park...

Natalie.

If she was alive, he had to find her. If she was dead, he had to avenge her.

And if it cost him his own life in the process, well, he should have died with the rest that night in the Cohort, shouldn't he? This was all borrowed time.

The door from the root cellar was locked. But it was also old, warped wood, and ill-fitting. A few good blows or kicks would take it down. Not subtle or stealthy, but effective.

One kick and the door shuddered in its frame.

A second kick and wood cracked.

At the third, the door groaned open. Its splintered bottom grated over stone. The penlight's beam danced thinly off into a large dark space.

Seth paused and listened. If anyone had heard his entry, they were keeping quiet.

He stepped forward and saw rows of coffins on raised stone biers protruding from the walls. One's lid stood open. The rest were closed.

A look over his shoulder showed him the culvert opening, seeming very far away. It was a reddish copper coin, a rusty glow fading even as he watched.

Sunset.

Then he heard the slow creak as a coffin lid lifted.

Chapter 29

Vampires.

Natalie's guardian had moved them into a house above a nest of vampires.

It made no sense. Hadn't she told him Anthony Sevrin *knew* about them?

Sense didn't matter right now.

There were vampires. And he, fully trained or not, armed or not, injured or not, he was a Centurion and he knew his duty.

He spun to the wooden door, kicking at it again, kicking irregular slivers and pointed chunks from it. He heard more coffins open. Heard movement, and stirring.

The bloody light was almost gone from the culvert. Darkness would rule. They would have him. Even if he ran, they'd follow, they'd chase and catch, this was their territory, they'd have him.

Seth dragged together as many rags and newspapers as he could, struck a match from his pocket, and ignited the pile. The flames flared and guttered with sickly orange light.

Behind him, he heard an inquisitive sniffing, followed by a hiss of eagerness. He snatched up one of the sturdiest wooden slivers and whirled to meet the oncoming vampire.

It was a female, wearing a ragged and stained waitressing uniform. The fire's sullen glow reflected in her red eyes, and on her gold earrings and eager, spit-shiny fangs.

He let her get within two steps of him, avoiding her dangerous gaze. His right hand curled around the sliver, this makeshift stake held low against his thigh. As the vampire reached him, Seth brought it up in a hard, fast undercut.

The splintery tip punched into her torso, just beneath her left breast. Dark fluid, cold and gritty, gushed out over Seth's hand. The waitress keened and staggered back. Seth rammed her into the wall, pinning her body with his as he forced the stake scraping past ribs toward the dead black heart.

Her nails raked his brow, splitting the skin. She snapped at his nose and only a reflexive jerk of his head saved it from being bitten off.

Seth pushed with all his might. A frantic slash of her filthy nails left three parallel scores down the side of his neck, jawline to collarbone, a hot triple-sizzle of pain, shallow but stinging, oozing blood that the rest of them would detect.

He felt her body lose cohesion and collapse in on itself. The earrings tumbled from her earlobes. The waitress uniform crumpled, caving in. Dust fell in a spattering avalanche onto Seth's shoes.

The smoldering heap of clothes and newspaper spewed out greasy black billows of smoke that collected in the upper reaches and made his eyes water. He swiped at them, squinting through the gloom, the splintered length of wood still in his hand.

He saw more coffins opening, more vampires clambering out. Seth threw himself on one lid, his weight slamming it shut on the half-in, half-out vampire like the bar of a rattrap. The vampire, a portly middle-aged man in a business suit, thrashed. Their combined struggles sent the coffin sliding off the bier. It toppled in a crash, pile driving the trapped vampire headfirst into the stone floor.

Seth rolled, banging his hurt wrist but managing to hold onto the stake. He recovered as the businessman vampire fought to flail free of the wreckage, planted a knee in the small of the thing's back, and staked him from behind. The businessman's body curved into a stiff bow, feet drumming on the floor. A huge glut of used blood ejected from his gaping mouth. He sagged toward the wet, fleshy decay of the gluttonous newly made.

Scrambling away, Seth snatched up another likely length of pointed wood. He sensed quick movement and whirled to see a kid in a Spider-Man costume perched atop a coffin. The kid sprang. Seth met the leap point-first with the stake, not a heart shot but impaling into the soft belly. Spidey screamed and began to cry. It sounded so genuine, so real... but Seth remembered all too well the little girl who'd tried to trick him, and wasn't fooled. He held the kid down with his foot, yanked the stake from his stomach, and corkscrewed it into his chest. It made a gruesome crunching sound. The wood split, leaving part lodged in Spider-Man and part clenched in Seth's fist.

More of them closed in. A gorgeous woman in an off-the-shoulder evening gown was nearest... a stocky man in the blue of a police officer behind her... others converged... a grandfatherly old man, a disheveled bum, a nurse in stained scrubs...

"Darling," said the evening-gowned woman in a voice like velvet. She wore enough diamonds to be attending an awards show, but her feet were bare except for scarlet nail polish, and shreds of stockings hung off her legs like molting snakeskin. "Look at me, darling."

He averted his gaze, thinking sourly that at least that Greek hero had been able to use a mirror to some effect against Medusa. She reached out and touched his arm, a gentle lover's caress. Faint scents of perfume and champagne lingered under a stale slaughterhouse waft of blood.

"Oh, darling," she sighed.

Seth thrust the uneven point into her chest. Her sigh became a screech. She reeled away from him, hands clasped over the rough end where it jutted out. She pawed at it, clawed at it. Found purchase. Started to pull.

He went after her, seized her arm, whirled her like a dance partner, and flung her. The woman collided with a bier, knocking the still-unopened coffin from it. The impact drove the stake the rest of the way home.

The coffin slid, teetered, tipped, went over, and unceremoniously dumped a youngish androgynous Goth in black mesh and shiny vinyl. The evening-gowned woman jittered on tiptoe, smoky wisps rising from her skin.

Fangs sank into Seth's shoulder. The pain was immediate, white-hot and frost silver. He felt a hideous suction, heard the greedy slurping. He shouted, battering at the vampire's face and head, wrenching himself away with another burst of gouging pain. He clapped his palm over the bite, blood flowing down his arm, soaking his sleeve.

It was the police officer, Seth saw by the sputtering, feeble light from his dying fire. And he'd lost his stake, such as it was. That was that.

He set his back to the wall. He'd given them a good fight, destroyed four before they got the better of him, and he supposed that was some kind of consolation.

His keychain penlight, in a bizarre miracle, hadn't been dropped in the battle. Seth switched it on and directed the fine beam around the room.

They had him and they knew it. Their prey. Cornered, surrounded, overwhelmed. Wounded, the rich promise of his blood stirring their hunger. Vampire faces leered moon-pale, ash-grey. Eyes gleamed crimson. Teeth gleamed ivory. Some, wary by his kill-tally, hesitated or hung back. Others looked to be biding their time, savoring the moment.

The police officer, Seth's blood smeared over his mouth and cheeks and chin, advanced. The Goth crouched, all dark eyeliner and chalky complexion, to dabble fingertips in spilled drops and lick them, sampling the taste.

A naked teenage girl shoved her way to the front. Seth's first thought–Natalie?–turned to relief when he saw it wasn't her, and then he surged with renewed horror when he realized he did know this girl after all.

"Sarah?"

If Sarah was here …

Ice sheathed his spine.

If these were the ones …

The Cohort… Michael… Jason and Deborah… the Centurions… his father…

His light also showed him an arched doorway at the opposite end of the room from where he'd come in. He couldn't see what lay through it, but the vampires were between him and the only other exit and Seth figured it was worth a shot.

Seth fished a chain from his pocket, nothing fancy, just a loop of the linked tiny steel balls sometimes used to secure pens to countertops. The cross dangling from it was nothing fancy either, by no means the large and elaborate one that had been his father's – that one was tucked safely away in his case, right when he most needed it – but a cheap silver-plated thing set with fake garnets.

Still, the sight of it, swinging and flashing in the penlight's beam, made the vampires hesitate again, cringing from the hated symbol. He held it out at them. Most recoiled. Sarah's lips peeled back and she hissed.

It held them, but for how long? With the temptation of his bleeding shoulder, their greater numbers, his helplessness? How long before ravenous rage overcame caution?

He edged forward anyway, the cross raised, the penlight centered on it... or, as centered as he could manage, the way his arm trembled. The beam stuttered and strobed. Dust motes danced in the dank air.

The vampires parted and fell back, but Seth wasn't stupid enough to move into their midst. He gave the cross a sudden whirl on its beaded chain and flung it at them. They scattered. Before they could recover, Seth dove over a coffin and bier. He somersaulted onto the floor–felt like someone set off a cherry bomb in his hurt shoulder–lunged to his feet and ran for the archway.

Sarah snarled and leaped after him. The others spent a disorganized second or two scrambling around before following. They gave chase. A new, wild urgency seized them. Sarah's fingers hooked into Seth's collar. She yanked, nearly throttling him.

He hurled himself through the opening, tripped, and went sprawling face down on a stone-slab floor. His penlight spun skittering away. The edges of his vision caught fleeing impressions of casks, bottles, a wine cellar.

Then Sarah landed on him. Her weight was a cold, corpselike, loathsome nakedness filled with furious wiry strength. She grabbed him by the hair and craned his head up.

"No!" Seth got her hair, which felt both dry and greasy. He managed some kind of half-assed judo throw that flipped her body off his.

She tumbled and came up in the kind of weird-jointed unnatural spidery crouch familiar to him from horror movies. But instead of pouncing, she froze. Her eyes widened. A very human expression of guilt and fear contorted her face.

The rest had stopped short at the threshold. They crowded there, gnashing and grimacing. Seth, breath heaving, blinked in bewilderment. But, a reprieve was a reprieve and whatever lucky break this was, he wasn't about to argue.

Uttering a shrill, desperate whine, Sarah fled to the door. Her fellow vampires didn't make way. She slapped, clawed, and fought until she was past, gone from his view.

Seth rose, holding his bleeding shoulder again. He stared at them. They stared at him. But not one of them ventured to put so much as a toe across into this room.

Never taking his gaze from them, Seth backed away, hunkered down, groped for and found his penlight. It did seem to be a wine cellar, clean, but not obviously used for that purpose. A heavy curtain blocked another archway. He made for it, cautious.

They didn't follow.

The next room was a more proper basement, square, musty, full of packed shelves, old furniture, broken appliances, bundled magazines. A perfectly normal-looking yellow bulb hung from the ceiling. A perfectly normal-looking flight of steps ascended to a perfectly normal-looking interior door.

Which, in turn, led to a perfectly normal-looking, very well-stocked pantry. Someone had done a supply run to one of the big box stores... bottled juice and water, canned goods, dry goods, spices, cereal, the works.

It occurred to him that this awful chapter of his life had started in a pantry, in the Cohort pantry when Deborah had sent him looking for paper towels. Now here he was in another.

Quietly as he could, he shut the door he'd come through, slid the bolt, and moved a carton in front of it. This barricade wouldn't keep out any determined vampire, he knew, but it might buy him a little time, and give him a little warning.

The outer kitchen was unoccupied, lit only by the light in the range hood. Everything was quiet.

Seth sank onto another carton, exhausted. Thirsty, too, though not with their terrible thirst. He found a plastic jug of apple juice and chugged it, the room-temperature liquid more reviving and refreshing than anything he'd ever tasted in his life. Then he took personal inventory – sprained wrist, bitten shoulder, assorted scratches and scrapes and bruises.

This pantry also contained paper towels, and bottled water, which Seth put to use cleaning himself up. He stripped off his shirt, and examined his shoulder as best as he could.

Ugly. Two gored holes, dark punctures surrounded by raw red mangled meat. It throbbed with spikes of pain that seemed in time with his heartbeat. He had to cleanse it, but the pantry shelves held no peroxide, not even any cooking alcohol.

He knew what he had to do and knew it was going to hurt like a son of a bitch.

The canister of salt was large, new, and unopened. Seth peeled off the sticker, pried up the little metal spout, poured a granular white stream of it into a partly empty water bottle, sloshed until it was cloudy, and then sluiced it over his wound before he could chicken out.

The only reason he didn't shriek was because he couldn't. His throat locked too tight for any sound. His fists clenched, tears gushed from his eyes, his feet rattle-bounced helplessly against the pantry floor, and he bumped the back of his head several times against the shelf behind him.

He did it again.

And again.

It felt like he was on fire from ear to elbow.

Finally, he rinsed with a fresh bottle, until the searing salty agony subsided to a minor stinging burn. His whole arm was weak and shaky, spasming. He folded it against his chest, held it with the other arm, leaned his head on the shelf again, and waited for his rapid, whimpering breathing to slow.

Vampires. The one time he hadn't been expecting them, hadn't been armed and ready... and he blundered straight into the lair of a whole pack.

The culvert was how they got out, and from there made their way through the wooded hills and back alleys, hunting yards and parking lots. The slowly dying neighborhood down on Fortuna Street owed its decline to them, no doubt... all those homes with 'For Sale' signs... probably on the market because their owners had vanished, or lost loved ones and decided to sell and move rather than live with daily tragic reminders of painful memories.

Vampires, the ones who stalked Landover Park. The one who'd attacked at the coffee shop might have come from here, too.

And they were the ones responsible for the massacre at the Cohort. For his father's death, and his own exile.

He recalled what Natalie had said about the woman who owned the house. Margos, her name was. And how she gave Natalie the creeps.

An Elder One? *The* Elder One, the female whose voice he'd heard the night the Cohort burned?

No sooner had he thought it than he heard that same voice again.

"… knows what he's doing," she said. "We have to trust in that, just as we've trusted in him from the very beginning."

"I don't like trusting in him," a man answered. "Whether you have him controlled or not, I think it's a mistake."

Yes, Seth recognized them both. They were the two he'd heard speaking as he cowered in his hiding place after Jason's death. The ones who'd stolen the Reliquary, the mysterious contents of which his mother had refused to reveal.

"What would you have me do?" the woman asked after a pause to draw breath. "Get rid of him?"

"Why not? We don't need him anymore, do we? Not if we have the girl."

"Someone must look after her," the woman said. "He's the best qualified."

At the mention of a 'girl,' Seth felt a flicker of hope. Maybe the decomposing body on the hillside hadn't been Natalie…

"I suppose you're right," admitted the man with the dry, rasping voice.

"Once we no longer have need of him, I promise that he'll die. Once we're sure, Lazarus."

The name burned in Seth's mind.

He'd thought that somehow they must both be Elder Ones, ancient vampires from the earliest time of their race. The ones bitten by the king himself, the ones who'd drunk his unholy blood.

But that power and curse given to his disciples was not the only mark that the vampire king had left. Once, famously, or infamously, he'd raised a man from the grave. That man became the master of the undead, the temporary and decaying animated corpses known as lazarenes.

Such as the ones his mother had told him of, the ones who had crossed the running river… and their leader, who'd killed the innocent sister Seth had never known.

This was that same being, that same undead master, that same man. Lazarus.

"At any rate," Lazarus said, "thank you for so graciously allowing me to return to the upper reaches of the house. I've never cared for crypts, as you know. Besides, your blood-children are objectionable roommates. They're careless, too, trying to bring their dinners home. It's only a matter of time before someone finds the leftovers strewn all over that hillside."

Seth did not move, tried not to make a sound, useless though he knew it was. They would smell him, if nothing else. Smell the blood, and his sweat, and his very life.

Through the half-open pantry door, he saw the woman moving across the kitchen.

She was shorter than he'd expected, petite, no more than five feet tall. Beautiful. Long dark hair fell to the middle of her back, framing a striking face with olive skin, full lips, and eyes like pools of midnight. A simple blue robe draped her shapely figure.

Opening the shutters of the window above the sink, she gazed out for what seemed an eternity. Night had fallen, leaving the sky dark but for the ambient glimmer of the city and a smudge of deep amethyst to the west.

"What will you do if he does grant your wish?" she asked.

"That depends on how he grants it," Lazarus said. "Do you think he'd turn me mortal again, and let me live out my allotted life span? Or would the temerity of asking to have this mixed blessing removed offend him, and lead him to strike me fully dead?"

"You could become like us … "

He scoffed. "All things being equal, I'd rather not."

"You prefer the existence of a deathless, lifeless corpse?"

"Potato, po-tah-to," he said. "I may not have your strengths, but I make do. You have so much more to fear, and so many more needs. That terrible thirst is something I could do without. No, I'm content only having to worry about an excess of sodium in my diet."

"You don't eat."

"Figure of speech."

Their casual conversation astonished Seth. If he'd stopped to think about it before, he realized he would have guessed they'd still use old languages, archaic idioms. Not contemporary English, not modern slang.

Lazarus stepped into view. Unlike a vampire, he did cast a shadow, and even the single bulb of the range light showed Seth more than he cared to see.

By rights, the dead man should have rotted away long since, but whatever strange force kept him going also provided a continual if imperfect regeneration of tissue, replacing the skin that sloughed off or the flesh that dropped from the bones. His yellowed, dirty, tattered burial wrappings flapped around his legs.

Why, Seth wondered, if he had adopted current language, did Lazarus still wear the same moldering cerements instead of taking on modern dress? Then he quirked his lips. Even in an Armani suit, a creature like Lazarus would stand no chance of mingling with mortals.

Did they know he was here? Did they sense him?

Maybe they were playing some game. Pretending to be unaware of his presence, waiting to see what he would do. Toying with him in the cruel way cats toyed with mice before the final, fatal pounce.

"I'm going out," the woman said. "That terrible thirst you mention is heavy upon me tonight."

"It's the girl, isn't it? You can't get her out of your mind. Ever since I caught you chewing on that bit of paper from the trash, the one she'd blotted her boo-boo on."

"I was to let it go to waste?"

"Go on, then. You'll be better company once you're sated. Just don't bring it home with you."

"I won't be long," she said, heading for the door that gave onto the back yard.

A trick. Seth knew it. At the last minute, she'd change course and burst into the pantry and attack.

But she opened the door, a breeze swirling the hem of her loose garment around her shins and stirring errant strands of her hair. She stood poised there for a few seconds, eyes shut, chin raised, lips parted as if tasting the night.

Seth inched his hand along the nearest shelf, never averting his eyes from the scene in the kitchen. Not even when the door had closed behind the dusky woman did he relax. They had to be on to him, and he wouldn't let himself think otherwise. He wouldn't be lulled or fooled into a false sense of security.

His groping hand found again the stout cylindrical canister.

In the kitchen, Lazarus shook his head and started to mutter to himself, then coughed and worked his mouth and spat some lumps of spongy-looking brown meat into his palm. Eyeing these pieces of himself with evident disgust, he turned toward the trashcan.

The trashcan, which stood right beside the pantry door.

Lazarus shuffled two steps and stopped. His murky eyes narrowed. His head tilted to one side, neck bones creaking.

He hadn't seen Seth yet, but …

Seth threw his weight against the pantry door. It swung open in a swift arc and smacked into the dead man.

Like the woman, Lazarus was short, and he was also scrawny, bony, like a scarecrow. The impact knocked him backward. He collided with a kitchen chair and fell over it with a crash.

Seth took a long stride and swept the salt canister in a wide arc. The stream of fine white crystals glittered in the range light like the world's tiniest diamonds.

Salt.

Cleansing salt. Searing, purifying salt.

Excess sodium, he'd said.

Black, bubbling craters formed, seethed, spread. Ate their way through leathery flesh toward the bone like drops of acid.

Lazarus screeched. He flailed and rolled. The chair, still tangled with him, banged clattering on the table leg, against the floor.

The narrow spout wasn't fast enough. Seth pulled it out, dug his fingers into the hole in the lid, and tore it open. He threw a gritty white cloud over Lazarus.

Screeching again, the dead man tried to shield his face, but the corrosive substance flayed his fingers to bare bones. One eye popped and dribbled thickly from the socket. The other glared at Seth.

"Centurion!" He spat the word, spitting out two teeth and part of his lower lip with it.

Seth didn't know how he had guessed, and didn't care. He took another step and upended the canister over Lazarus' head.

Lazarus screeched again, but he'd no sooner gotten started than the screech turned into a reedy whistle. The salt eroded the soft tissues of his tongue, his throat, his larynx. The naked jawbone wagged mutely. The other eye dissolved into mush. Blister-edged pits stippled Lazarus' cheeks and forehead. More of the salt settled onto his chest, eating away the flesh to expose collarbones and ribs.

Tendrils of yellow-grey smoke rose from the wounds. The stink was astringent, weirdly oceanic, low tide and decaying fish and ammonia. Seth's eyes watered. He sneezed, then sneezed again.

The chair went over with a clatter. So did the table. Lazarus lurched upright. He tried to paw the salt from his face, his skeletal hands smoking, loops of shriveling skin hanging from his forearms like tattery sleeves.

He seized Seth by the neck, choking him. They reeled in a grappling, staggering waltz across the kitchen, bumping into cabinets and the refrigerator. Their faces were less than a foot apart. Seth saw into the gaping eye sockets and nasal cavity, where a greyish, wrinkled mass wobbled inside the skull.

Lazarus, blind but strong, slammed Seth against the counter. Cupboard doors opened. Dishes rained out, smashing on Seth's head and shoulders. Drawer pulls jabbed into the small of his back.

His lungs begged for air. His neck felt cinched in iron bands. He kicked, connected, felt Lazarus' kneecap give way. The dead man's weight canted to the right, pulling Seth with him. They landed on the salt-strewn tiles.

Seth quit trying to wrench Lazarus' grip loose from his neck and swept up a fistful of salt instead. He punched Lazarus in the face. The facial bones, already weakened, cracked apart like eggshells. His arm plunged wrist-deep.

The strangling grip on his neck tightened. The room went dim and fuzzy around the edges. Starved for oxygen, Seth realized he was blacking out.

His fist uncurled, fingers relaxing. Salt spilled. The world wheeled and rotated. Consciousness was a mirage, teasing, not quite there.

Then he could breathe again, gasping great gulps of air through a throat that felt swollen and sore. He sat up, shedding a litter of sticks and rags.

A rough, hollow, gourd-shaped thing covered his hand. He shook it off with a revolted cry. What was left of Lazarus' skull fractured like a clay jar when it hit the floor.

Nothing was left of the dead man but bones and wrappings. Salt lay everywhere, salt in snowdrifts and sand dunes, some still pristine white, some nasty and discolored. It caked his various scrapes, stinging like a hundred angry wasps.

Seth rested his forehead against his knees, waiting for reality to settle back into something steady.

For the first time, he thought that maybe his mother *had* had a point in not wanting him to become a Centurion. Not if it was like this.

But this was probably extreme even by Legion standards. Alone, injured, and unarmed in the very lair of the enemy... not good odds. Not good odds against ordinary vampires, never mind an Elder One and the ancient lord of the undead himself.

Groaning, he got up and brushed off.

He needed a weapon. He also needed to get his butt out of here, but he couldn't do that until he'd found the girl they'd mentioned. Maybe Natalie; it seemed a lot to hope for but what good was life without hope?

A quick search of the kitchen drawers didn't turn up much. Sure, someone had left salt in the pantry, but whoever had bought the utensils didn't choose wooden spoons or rolling pins that could be sharpened into a stake. He couldn't even settle for wrenching a leg off a chair, because the chairs were stylish metal and leather.

He moved further into the house, alert for any other signs of movement or activity. If anyone had heard the struggle in the kitchen – Lazarus screeching, the thumps and crashes, the shattering dishes – they hadn't come to investigate.

Natalie had mentioned how the place felt more for show, a façade, a set. She was right. Nothing about it felt homey or lived-in. There were no personal touches, certainly no family photographs.

Upstairs, he found a study, and guessed by the medical and scientific contents of the bookshelves that this was the domain of Natalie's guardian, Anthony Sevrin.

A second door led from the study into a room as well-lit and white and clean as any doctor's office. But before Seth could take a closer look, something on the desk snared his attention.

A box... *the* box... heavy wood and carved sides, a clasp made from hammered silver. *The* box, the coffer, the Reliquary.

This was what the Margos woman had taken from the Cohort. This was what his father had been assigned to guard, what his mother hated, what had cost his sister her life.

Seth went to it. His hand faltered as he reached for the clasp. He hadn't been initiated. He wasn't a full Centurion, never would be. He had no right ...

Did he?

Wouldn't his father would want him to do this? Take back what belonged to the Legion?

His mother would –

Never mind what his mother would want. Hadn't she done enough?

The clasp was cool under the pad of his thumb. Silver. *The* silver, one of *the* coins, the sacred thirty pieces given to Judas for leading the first Centurions to the lair of the vampire king.

A shiver went through him. Here was the very touching of history, the touching of the beginnings of the Legion.

He lifted the lid.

Empty.

Something had been inside; there was an impression in the cloth where something had lain. Something long and straight.

Troubled, not fully understanding why... feeling as if he should know or already knew the answer somewhere inside himself but couldn't bring it to the front of his mind... Seth closed the coffer. He turned from it, frowning, and took a quick look into the doctor's-office room.

No, not a doctor's office. A lab, small but extensively equipped, full of computers and assorted equipment Seth couldn't begin to identify.

And, in the middle of it, incongruous against that stark white background, was a length of old, weathered wood in a stainless steel tray under a clear plastic cover.

Seth knew at once what he was seeing.

His breath whooshed out. He moved like a sleepwalker, into the lab, to set aside the cover and stare down at the ancient wood, dark with rusty stains.

Blood. Not just any blood, not even just any vampire's blood, but the vampire king's own blood. *His* blood.

He picked up the stake.

As he did so, he jolted as if electrified. A sensation of power and strangeness surged up his arm.

The room around him vanished.

He stood upon a barren hill. He stood beneath a scorching desert sun, gazing in sick terror at the cross rising in stark outlines against a fuming orange sky.

Chapter 31

Insubstantial, mist-form, a wraith in the night, Magdalena floated over the rear wall and descended to the weed-grown hillside below the house. She resumed her solid form, relishing the feel of cool wind in her hair, and looked around.

Lazarus had been right, though the mess wasn't as bad as she had anticipated. Ravaged corpses didn't litter the hill. There were only a few.

Still, her blood-children should have known better. They weren't supposed to hunt so near to the lair. They certainly weren't supposed to leave the remains out where somebody's pet dog or adventuresome brat might stumble across them.

Discipline, however, could wait. She hungered, eager for another visit to Ashleigh.

Seventeen and virginal, Ashleigh fancied herself a daughter of darkness. She dressed all in black, affected worldly disdain for the happiness in life, and spent her time writing reams of poetry about death, abandonment, and suicide.

Magdalena had sampled her kind before. They played at being vampires themselves, and when they met a real one, they often didn't realize the danger until the fangs were already embedded and the rich blood flowing.

Ashleigh made for easy, succulent prey. This was Magdalena's fourth visit, via the bedroom window willingly opened for her. She'd cloud the girl's memory afterward, leaving it dreamlike. Should Ashleigh prove pale and listless, well, who would know the difference?

The trouble with that ilk was, if transformed, they tended to make poor actual blood-children. Too much of their moods carried over. They lacked the savagery necessary to survive in the night world. They wanted only to die... not to kill. To be the bitten, not to bite.

So, though the girl begged her nocturnal lover to grant her the eternal gift, Magdalena had no intention of taking that step. Ashleigh's eventual death would take the guise of only a bathtub wrist-slitting to account for the lack of blood.

Satisfied – or as close as could be, what with this mere substitute for the promise of Natalie – Magdalena made to enter the cellars by way of the culvert that led beneath her house.

As she reached the opening, she sensed something amiss... something wrong, very wrong. That faint smell in the air was one she knew all too well. It was the dust of her kind's destruction.

Moments later, she stood aghast at what she found. Her lair, invaded! Several of her blood-children dispatched, and the rest in a milling confusion, crazed with kill-lust but bound by her strict orders not to pass the threshold.

And oh, the stink of a Centurion! Youth and vigor, sweat, vitality... a healthy male... only one, which struck her peculiar, as she'd never known Centurions to hunt alone... but...

Of all the times for her blood-children to diligently obey her... they hadn't been able to follow. They had been forced to let him go.

She found signs in the pantry that he'd stopped there to rest, to tend his wounds. Had he been there even while she and Lazarus spoke in the kitchen? Was she so distracted by thoughts of Natalie and Ashleigh that she had failed to detect his presence even then?

It had been a long time since she'd feared for her own physical safety, knowing herself to be more than a match for any normal man. This one, though... this Centurion... could not be so normal. He should never have gotten through the cellar.

In the kitchen, a strange salty-smoky-meaty acrid odor overpowered the scent of blood. She stood aghast again, more aghast than ever, more than she'd been in two thousand years.

"Lazarus ... " She had forgotten to take a breath first, the word was as silent as her lack of heartbeat, mouthed only on her lips.

He had been so caustic and irritating that she might have thought she'd be glad to see him like this. But instead, a pang of loss shot through her. Caustic or not, irritating or not, he had been her only real companion for these many long and lonely centuries.

A new and sudden terror rocked her. She had lost Lazarus, but that loss would still be bearable if, as planned and yearned for, she soon had her king restored to her. But if she lost him as well...

Heedless of caution, she raced to Anthony Sevrin's study, nearly flew through it toward the lab, and halted at the sight of a grim, injured, determined young man blocking her way.

His haggard eyes made him look three times his age, his face that of someone who'd been through the darkest of wars and staggered out the other side with his soul bent by the experience.

She should have sensed him, should have smelled the blood, but in her hurry and her terror, she hadn't been paying attention. Again!

His dark blue eyes were filled with pain, but also with purpose. She had not seen eyes quite like that in... in two thousand years.

The eyes of a Centurion. Not just any Centurion.

The Centurion.

He stared at Magdalena. "You," he said. His voice was hoarse. He trembled with emotion. "My father, the Cohort, Jason, Deborah. All dead because of you. Dead and burned to ashes."

Understanding came, and with it, restored confidence. This was not some punishment out of past eons, not some immortal hunter who had been stalking her all these centuries. Just this boy, a survivor who'd escaped the attack somehow, and sought her out in hopes of exacting vengeance.

She settled her mesmerizing will upon him. "It's all right," she said, her tone soothing. "It's done now. It's over."

He had bested her blood-children, even bested Lazarus, but he was no match for her. She held him enthralled as she took a step closer. Another step.

"What's your name?" Magdalena asked.

The word seemed to jerk out of him. "Seth."

"Seth," she said. She took another step toward him. Two more, and she'd be close enough to open his throat. She smiled. He blanched at the sight of her fangs but did not move. "Seth," she said again, and took yet another step. She could see the heady pulse throbbing in his neck.

The Centurion's arm, which had been down at his side, shot up and around, lifting a curled fist high above his head. Magdalena's gaze followed it. Now she was the one held enthralled... motionless, speechless.

The stained length of wood swept down in a brutal arc.

At the last instant, she tried to scramble out of its path, but she was too late. The rough-hewn point ripped through her robe and sank into the fullness of her breast.

Magdalena screamed and staggered backward. She clutched at the spike.

Through the shearing pain, she felt the brilliant inner fire of *his* blood, the blood of her king still staining the wooden stake, mingling with her own.

Seth threw himself against her and bore her to the floor. He landed on his knees, straddling her waist.

She swiped at him, four long gouges cutting diagonally across his chest.

With her other hand, she tugged at the stake, it grinding against a rib with a sensation that vibrated through her bones. She was keenly aware of her lifeless but vulnerable heart, that still, dark bird in its ivory cage, mere inches beneath that violating tip.

Every second of the millennia that made up her long life condensed to this moment, when she was closer to the true and final death than she had ever been, her very essence leaking out around the embedded shaft.

Magdalena heaved with all her inhuman might and dislodged him, sending him thudding to the carpet. She wrapped both hands around the stake. She pulled. In torturous sucking increments, it slid out of her flesh. The oozing flow thickened to a gush.

She almost had it out when Seth, panting and wild, snatched up the heavy wooden coffer from the table. He raised it over her, arms wavering from the strain.

"No," Magdalena said.

"Yes," he said.

He brought the coffer down.

It should not have found its mark, and even if it had it should have been too feeble a strike – he was at the flagging end of his endurance – to matter at all.

But, as if some other and far stronger arm guided his, the Reliquary met the Relic in a sure, solid blow.

The stake shattered Magdalena's ribs into slivers and punctured her heart in a violent slashing agony. A red-black torrent of blood erupted out. Her nails slashed at Seth, slashed at him.

She felt it begin while she still raved and fought. A gritty heat like the wind of that long-ago fiery desert blew through her, parching her with a thirst that dried her from the inside out. Her limbs stiffened but at the same time went loose, skin and flesh like banks of sand eroding and sliding like crumbling dunes.

And then she was gone.

CHAPTER 32

Seth backed slowly from the spill of dust in the flattened, blood-sodden blue robe.

Tremors shook him.

He knew now the extent of what he'd done. A vampire, yes. An Elder One.

Mary Magdalene herself.

He looked at the stake – no mere stake, either, but the Holy Lance, the spear of a true Centurion – which had fallen on its side as her body decayed apart around it.

Breath rasped in and out of Seth's sore throat. He swallowed. It hurt. Everything hurt.

The idea that he had survived, that he had won, made a gradual impression on him.

He gently retrieved the stake, cradling it in both hands, and returned it to its resting place within the Reliquary. He shut the lid, and secured the silver clasp.

The bright lights and reflective surfaces in the lab showed him far more than he wanted to see of himself. He looked like he'd been dragged by the heels through a meat grinder.

He staggered to a stainless steel sink. Shedding the rest of his ruined clothes, he splashed water over himself as hot as he could stand it. He heard himself sobbing and didn't care.

The peroxide came next, found in its dark brown plastic bottle on a shelf with other chemicals and solvents. It foamed and frothed and sizzled. He followed it with sluicings and dousings of whatever else he could find… rubbing alcohol, antiseptic. As bad as the pain was, he welcomed it, wanting to be cleaned, needing to be cleansed and made whole. Seth writhed with agony and exultation, though it was mostly agony.

At last he went back to the sink, rinsing with cold, drying off with a couple of thin cotton hospital-style gowns from a drawer, patching himself up with first-aid supplies, and tugging on a set of pale green surgical scrubs from the same drawer.

He studied himself in a shiny metal cabinet almost as good as any mirror. His eyes looked wild, total crazy-eyes… red, but red from fumes, red from watering, not red from vampiric hunger.

The reflection of a wall-clock caught his gaze next, and Seth started. Sure, he'd dispatched Lazarus and Mary Magdalene, but what would happen when Anthony Sevrin got home? What would – what *could* – he do against Natalie's guardian? The normal laws might not apply to the undead, but they did apply to regular people. If Sevrin found him here …

Lugging the heavy, bulky coffer, he returned to the desk and made a quick rummage through the drawers in hopes of finding a weapon or something useful.

He struck partial pay dirt on the very first drawer. No weapon, but, something useful… a ring of keys, with an ornate ivory crucifix as a keychain.

That seemed strange, the crucifix. Either Anthony Sevrin had no idea about the true nature of his hosts, or they hadn't minded this blatant offense. But, Seth decided, he didn't care which. He dropped the key ring into a pocket of the scrubs, hoisted the coffer into his arms again, and went to search the rest of the house.

One of the bedroom doors was fitted with what looked like a recently installed exterior lock. Seth set the coffer at his feet and pressed his ear to it, listening.

Silence.

He tapped, and called quietly, "Hello?"

Why he was tapping and calling quietly, after the screeches, commotion and assorted crashing around…

So he knocked louder. "Hello!"

There was a rustle, and a groggy mumble in response. A girl's voice, and even in groggy-mumble mode he knew it.

"Natalie?"

"Hunh?"

"Natalie!"

He hardly sounded like himself, so he wasn't surprised when she asked with a wary, half-awake tone, "Who's there?"

"It's me. Seth."

"Seth?" That got a spark of energy, a ray of light through the fog. If an incredulous, unsure one, not quite daring to hope. "Seth, is it really you?"

"Yes." He leaned against the door, resting his forehead on the wood. "I'm here. Are you all right?"

"I … " she broke off with a watery sob. "They locked me in… they've been keeping me locked in for days and days… weeks… what day is it?"

"Hang on. I've got some keys." He tried them until one worked, undid the lock, and opened the door.

The bedroom was luxurious enough for a prison cell, he supposed. It had decent amenities: attached bathroom, a modest entertainment center with collection of music and movies, a generous bookshelf, and a mini-fridge. No phone and no internet, but still, better than the place he'd been living by a longshot. Except for the bars on the inside of the windows and shutters on the outside. And that lock.

And the religious art on the walls, which seemed even more out of place than the crucifix keychain. Reproductions of famous paintings… photographs of famous sculptures… New Testament stuff, the lies, the spin…

Natalie, sitting up amid a tangle of bedclothes, blinked at him. Even in the mild rose-amber glow of a nightstand lamp, she looked awful. Face pale and eyes puffy, hair a sleep-mess, like she had the flu.

"What's wrong?" he asked. "What did they do?"

"I don't feel very good. I think they've been… drugging me or something… I just feel so tired, so pukey and gross. But, Seth, what are you doing here?"

"Long story." He hurried over to her, tipping up her chin to examine her throat. Her skin felt warm but clammy. Her neck was unmarked. Seth held up the ivory cross to her. She peered at it, blond brows knit. Then she touched it like a good luck charm, and he relaxed. "Let's get out of here first."

She nodded. "I have to get dressed."

"Then do it." He turned his back.

As she gathered clothes and went into the bathroom to change, he told her the condensed version of his afternoon. She sputtered with indignation that her friend Claire, and apparently the whole school as well, thought she was being kept home because she was pregnant... and squeaked with blushing outrage that they'd think Seth responsible.

Then he told her the rest. Natalie stared at him, so much color draining from her face that she'd looked healthy by comparison when he came in. She'd put on leggings and a roomy oversize fleecy sweatshirt, pulled her hair through a scrunchie, and washed her face.

"Vampires?" she whispered. "I knew there was something wrong with this place, I knew it, but ... "

He told her about Lazarus, and the coffer, and the confrontation in the study. As he spoke, Natalie hugged herself, shivering. By the time he got to the part about Madeline Margos, or Mary Magdalene, she'd turned green, and rushed back to the bathroom to throw up.

"So, I staked her," he said when Natalie emerged again, toothbrushed and mouthwashed. "Destroyed her."

"With... with the ... "

"Yeah."

Natalie donned shoes and socks, crammed some essentials into her bag, and faced him. She still looked queasy, but determined. "I'm ready."

"I'm so glad I found you. Glad you're all right. When I saw that body out back ... "

"Don't. Just... just don't." She hugged him, mindful of his injuries, not wanting to hurt him. "Oh, Seth. Thank you. I'm so glad you found me, too."

It hurt anyway, but he wasn't about to say so. The pain was worth it. He leaned against her, not wanting to ever let her out of his sight again.

"Let's go," he said, reluctantly unwrapping his arms.

Natalie nodded. "I never want to see this place again!"

They went into the hall. Seth picked up the Reliquary coffer. Then they hurried toward the stairs, only to be brought up short by a stern voice.

"And where," inquired a man from the bottom of the stairs, "do you think you're going, young lady?"

CHAPTER 33

"Away!" Natalie said, the word bursting from her in a shrill cry. She felt Seth move, as if to interpose himself between her and Anthony, but pushed past him. "You can't keep me here! You don't own me!"

"Can't I?' Don't I?" Anthony, at the bottom of the steps, tipped his head and smiled a you-silly-girl kind of smile that made her want to slap him.

"You're not my father. Not my legal guardian or my legal anything! You don't own me! I'm not your property!"

He looked to have just come in from wherever, his coat on the hook, the day's mail piled on a little table in the entryway.

"If cloning were legal, I could have patented the process," Anthony said. He put his foot on the bottom riser. "Then you *would* be my property. But that doesn't matter, Natalie. Like it or not, you are mine. We are bound together by the will of God."

"Stay away from her," Seth said.

"And you… this is what you've been keeping secret from me, Natalie? This friend of yours? This boy? Ah, well, but I suppose even he has his part to play in all this, doesn't he?"

"Stop it!" Natalie started down, intending to shove right past him if he wouldn't get out of her way. "We're going."

"Natalie, please. You don't understand."

"You're right. I don't. I don't and I don't want to!"

"If you'll only let me explain it to you, then we wouldn't have to argue. You'll see for yourself how important this is. How important *you* are. I had planned to tell you soon, anyway."

"There's nothing you can say that I want to hear. After what you did? After you kept me prisoner, let the school and all my friends think that I was pregnant–"

"But you are."

"Not to mention that you've been working with va—... what did you say?"

"That's a lie!" said Seth, furious. "We never-"

"Oh, I know, I know."

"You're crazy!" Natalie cried.

"Am I? You know about your mother. Dear, perfect Karen. You know how she came to conceive."

Her insides felt scooped hollow and refilled with quivering jelly. She remembered her nightmares, the long silvery needle, the stark bright lights, the chill, the helpless paralysis.

"What's he talking about?" asked Seth. "What's he saying?"

"You... you cloned me? Her? Like... wait ... " Natalie's head spun. She pressed the heels of her hands to her temples, not sure if she was going to throw up again.

"No, oh, no," Anthony said. "The embryo implanted in you was cloned from another source." He regarded her with cloying sympathy. "The term 'morning sickness' is a misnomer, you know --"

"What did you do to her, you sick son of a bitch?" Seth demanded.

"Joseph, please. This is a glorious gift --"

"My name is Seth!"

"It should have been Joseph. As hers should have been Mary. I considered it at the time, obvious though it was. Then I heard one of the hospital staff remark how Natalie made a nice name for a baby born on Christmas, and I thought that would do nicely."

"Mary... Joseph... what?" Natalie's knees unhinged. She plopped to her butt on the carpeted stairs. "You can't mean that you think *I*... "

"Born untouched by carnal sin," Anthony said. "Born pure. A hallowed, holy vessel. It's a common mistake, you see... the Immaculate Conception was that of Mary herself. What better subject to begin with than angelic Karen?"

"I'm not... I... this isn't ... " She was shaking too badly to continue.

"I was chosen, you see." He managed to sound both humbled and arrogant at the same time. "This is the age of science. Who better for this glorious task than a man of science *and* a man of God?"

"You said, 'cloned from another source'... *what* other source?" Seth's voice was tight, his eyes dark and narrowed.

Anthony shot him a look of mingled pity and scorn. "Do you not even know what it is you hold in your hands? What priceless treasure that coffer held?"

"Oh Judas, no. No, you didn't."

"I tried, first, to obtain a sample from the Shroud of Turin," Anthony went on, conversationally. "God was testing me. I nearly failed that test, because when the Shroud turned out to be false, I came close to giving up. My faith wavered. I admit it freely. I sank into despair. Then, God sent me Madeline Margos."

Natalie recoiled, beginning to cry. "It's not true!"

"She brought me the Holy Lance, the spear that pierced the side of Our Lord as He suffered upon the cross," said Anthony, his eyes feverishly alight. "*His* blood. The sacred blood of Christ. From that blood, I achieved a miracle. The very miracle that now grows and thrives within you."

The needle... the dreams...

The nausea, the tiredness, how she felt ...

What he'd done to Karen... what he'd done now to her ...

The dark truths that Seth had revealed ...

Anthony ascended another few steps. "This is a blessing beyond belief, Natalie. You carry the salvation for which the world's been waiting... been needing, desperately needing... this wretched, sinful world... for two thousand years."

He sank to his knees before her, reaching out as if in supplication. His expression was beatific, reverent, adoring.

And Seth smashed him square in the face with the heavy wooden coffer.

There was an awful crunch, a wet spatter, and a grunted bleat of pain. Anthony pitched backwards down the stairs, rolling and thumping. He came to rest on the entryway floor in a loose ragdoll sprawl. His chest heaved. He groaned. His nose and mouth were a busted red ruin. He tried to sit up, then flopped over.

"Let's get out of here," Seth said.

"Yeah," said Natalie. "Yeah, let's."

But before they did, as Seth eased the door open to check the street, some urge she couldn't quite identify made Natalie bend over her unconscious guardian.

She dipped her fingertips in the thick scarlet, and brought them to her lips to sniff... and then sample... the rich sweetness of his blood.

ABOUT THE AUTHOR

Christine Morgan works the overnight shift in a psychiatric facility and divides her writing time among many genres. A lifelong reader, she also writes, reviews, beta-reads, occasionally edits and dabbles in self-publishing. She has over a dozen novels in print and more due out soon. Her stories have appeared in several anthologies, been nominated for Origins Awards, and given Honorable Mention in two volumes of Year's Best Fantasy and Horror.

She's a wife, mom, and possible future crazy-cat-lady whose other interests include gaming, history, superheroes, crafts, and cheesy disaster movies.

http://christine-morgan.net/

www.ingramcontent.com/pod-product-compliance
Lightning Source LLC
Chambersburg PA
CBHW020340180626
46812CB00001B/279